Francesca Clementis was born in 1958. Following a degree in Philosophy from Sussex University, she spent ten years in advertising before becoming a full-time writer. She lives in London with her husband and daughter.

Francesca is the author of *Big Girls Don't Cry, Mad About the Girls, Would I Lie To You?* and *Strictly Business*, also published by Piatkus. She is the recipient of an Arts Council of England Writers' Award and her novels have been translated into ten languages.

# Can't Buy Me Love

*Francesca Clementis*

PIATKUS

Copyright © Francesca Clementis 2003

First published in Great Britain in 2003 by
Judy Piatkus (Publishers) Ltd of
5 Windmill Street, London W1T 2JA
email: info©piatkus.co.uk

**The moral right of the author has been asserted**

*A catalogue record for this book is available from the British Library*

ISBN 0 7499 3415 8

Set in Times by
Phoenix Phototypesetting, Chatham, Kent
Printed and bound in Great Britain by
Mackays of Chatham Ltd, Chatham, Kent

For my new goddaughter, Natasha Bingle-Williams, wonderful miracle.

For Chris Fouty, craziest and sanest friend, immigrant and, now, emigrant.

For Elspeth, Ian, Iona and Kirsty Donaldson, good friends to me, Steve and Freya.

And with thanks to Gillian Green at Piatkus for pushing me into making this book better – and gently encouraging me to rewrite the ending!

# 1

This is my life, Tess thought wryly. This dinner party defines it. Not *me*, of course, that's something quite different, but my life. Here it all is, neatly summarising my choices and preferences, my achievements, my subplots. It says it all, sums up my past and lays down the foundations for my future.

The food isn't *just* organic, it doesn't *just* come from shops that don't put barcodes on the packaging, it *isn't* just unrecognisable and vaguely unpalatable, but it is *actually* constructed according to recipes handwritten by barely literate Tuscan mammas encountered on that holiday to that place which doesn't appear in brochures.

The wine isn't *just* ominously cloudy, it doesn't *just* have a label that tells you everything about the vineyard and its owners apart from their astrological influences, it isn't *just* vile, but it *actually* came from an eco-commune on a Greek island that doesn't appear in atlases and to which access is only granted if you are willing to forego deodorant and depilatory cream.

The guests aren't *just* conspicuously wealthy, they aren't *just* successful in both their professional and personal lives, they aren't *just* bewilderingly fertile with their four kids per couple, they aren't *just* the teensiest bit smug, but they're loyal, funny and they've all been firm friends for over ten years.

This is my life. Wow. Tess inhaled slowly, breathing in the richness of her world, filtering out her uncomfortable awareness of its glib superficiality. My life. My dinner party.

She wasn't enjoying herself as much as she was supposed to, as much as she always had done in the past. Not that she was much of a party-lover. She hated them. But she loved her friends, small gatherings of her small number of friends. She could apply the part of herself that she was happy to let go; these people only knew as much about her as she'd been willing to show them. They wouldn't push or pull her or shake her to see what else might be there.

So this would normally be an easy evening for her. But something felt not quite right.

For several months now, something intrusive had been tapping away at her sense of complacency, whispering words that she couldn't quite hear. It unnerved her.

She'd decided to invite everyone round at the last minute, hoping to induce a much-needed sense of normality, an illusion of routine. It was a strategy that was failing.

'Red or white, sweetheart?'

Tess blinked, realising that she'd drifted off. She looked up at Max, who was bent over her in an exaggerated Mine Host pose, trying to shave a few inches from his six-feet-five elevation, hunching inwards to narrow his hefty bulk.

Even in their wedding photos, he'd employed his full repertoire of 'comic' stances to avoid towering over Tess who was five feet two and tiny in build. He would slouch forward, his hands pressed hard into his trouser pockets, as he'd seen Frank Sinatra do in one of his films. Or he'd lean back, arms outstretched, knees bent, one leg kicked forward in classic schoolboy fashion. And there were dozens of photos with him down on one knee, gazing ironically into his new bride's eyes.

Tess liked these pictures best because she knew that she was the only one who perceived the insecurity behind his outwardly confident displays of showmanship. When he ran his fingers through his hair, it was not to mask his stress but to try and tame his unruly hair that had no natural parting, no crown, no resting style into which it settled after washing. It also kinked erratically if not tamed with discreet applications of gel. Once he'd undergone a severe crop in an attempt to tidy himself up, make himself worthy of his beautiful wife. He'd even hoped it would have a knock-on effect on the rest of his life, adding order, permanently severing his emotional split ends.

All that had happened was that he was regularly stopped by the police who wanted to know how an escaped terrorist could come to be driving a BMW.

So he finally accepted that he was a permanently unruly-looking person, too big and messy, fated to stick out in every respect. It didn't matter that Tess had spent 18 years trying to persuade him that she loved his size, found it comforting, reassuring, safe. He would always loathe his height and would seize any opportunity to diminish himself, become less visible.

He didn't understand that Tess needed his size to hide behind, needed his bulk to deflect attention from herself.

Sometimes, he'd watch Tess getting dressed for a big night out. He never got bored of seeing the transformation from the lovely fresh-faced girl (she would always be a girl to him, it was that size thing again) to a girl who'd been messing about with her mother's make-up.

'Why do you insist on wearing all that stuff when you don't even like it yourself?' he asked her occasionally, still waiting for an excuse that made sense.

Tess looked without interest at her reflection, fully aware that she looked better without it. Her face was unlined, the gift of good genes rather than any commitment to skincare. Her hair, being thick and straight, always fell into shape for months after a good cut. Dark hair and blue eyes, pretty and petite, both combinations that resisted age most efficiently. She always dressed neatly, everything closely fitting, and she coordinated her colours with instinctive good taste.

'You have to,' she replied. 'It's what grown-ups do.'

She never expanded on these oblique references to adulthood, because she hadn't yet worked out the significance for herself yet. But she knew that the great unsolved mystery of her life was the exact point at which she grew up. She needed to identify the moment it happened so she could scroll forwards from then and make sense of the rest of her life.

Because she couldn't shake off the scary feeling that she'd missed something between the ages of 13 and 39.

'Red or white?' Max repeated, an irritable edge making itself heard as Tess yanked herself back to Battersea again.

'Sorry! White, please.'

Max filled her glass. Tess smiled at him. Or rather, she tried but he seemed to be avoiding eye contact.

I must be imagining it, she thought. But even while she deluded herself, she knew that something was up. And she knew that it was bad because Max didn't have that twitchy eye thing he did which hinted at a good surprise that he was having difficulty keeping secret. And she knew that it was very, very bad because she didn't have a clue what it could be and that meant that he'd buried the clues very, very deeply.

'Why are you frowning, Tess?'

Tess quickly reassembled her face into a sociable smile. Damn. The downside of having such close friends was that they tended to be too sensitively attuned to each other's moods, spotting the slightest downturn in tones of voice, the barest hint of resignation in a marital exchange, the merest droop of the mouth.

'Sorry Fi!' Tess said, overcompensating for her unforgivable lapse of jollity by laughing pointlessly.

Fiona was her best friend inasmuch as they were the founder members of this circle. They'd met at their local Clapham Active Birth classes when they found they were the only two to collapse in hysterics when the teacher pulled a knitted cervix from a Marks and Spencer carrier bag. After being tutted and glared at by their female comrades, who saw nothing remotely humorous in woollen gynaecological parts, they crept to the back row from where they proceeded to bitch cheerfully about their unevolved sisters.

After just one session, Tess and Fiona both reached the same conclusion that this was not for them.

'I could be wrong,' Fiona suggested, 'but it seems to me that these bizarre women actually *want* as much pain as possible from the moment of conception right up to breastfeeding their children for at least five years per child.'

Tess giggled into her coffee ('Double espresso,' Fiona had ordered for her stubbornly, 'with extra caffeine, if that's available,' she added, wanting to offend the other pregnant women, from whom she now chose to disassociate herself). 'Did you watch them all signing up for antenatal yoga?' she asked, dunking a chocolate biscotti aggressively.

Fiona nodded. 'Well, they're the type, aren't they? Probably gave up wheat and dairy years ago.'

Tess entered the swing of this enjoyable generalisation. 'And their partners will all have beards and alpaca jumpers ...'

'... who will support "Mummy" through childbirth with no pain relief apart from an eagle feather gyrated above their abdomens ...'

4

'... while they chant ...'

They'd continued in this way for two hours, pausing only to check that they were both of the same mind that the epidural was the only reasonable birth choice for the sane woman.

Tess was thrilled to meet someone who not only thought like her but was brave enough to give voice to her thoughts. Fiona did not appear to be governed by the conventional rules of social interaction. She spoke first, considered the consequences later, if at all.

Tess, on the other hand, considered consequences every second of her waking day (and often during uncomfortable dreams at night), always having feared becoming either the victim or the instigator of any dramatic ones during her life.

The two women eased into a comfortable fit as Tess moderated some of Fiona's wilder excesses of tactlessness while Fiona encouraged Tess to prise open some of her jammed emotional doors.

Their friendship sped up, swept along by pregnancy and childbirth, second and third children following quickly for Fiona – not for Tess – dragging their husbands into each other's company, teaming up with Millie, another like-minded mum from playgroups, working their way through every child-friendly open and closed space in London, sending their children to the same schools until they became ... the people who have dinner parties like this.

This was a new era for them all. Their last children were now at primary school, their families complete, the last baby paraphernalia finally dispatched to the charity shop, mornings reclaimed, a degree of freedom clawed back. There were fewer evenings cancelled with last-minute illnesses; children could even occasionally be trusted to join the grown-ups without fear of throwing up over the table (or the guests). Dinner parties became more regular. The group of friends talked and worried about different things but, generally, life was becoming easier. Or maybe they were just sleeping better.

Except for Tess and Max who were not sleeping well at all.

'The wine's not that bad,' Fiona whispered conspiratorially as Tess's smile faded for the fifteenth time since the retsina had been opened.

Tess grimaced. 'Yes it is. I don't know what possessed Max to buy so much of it. It was foul enough when we drank it in Greece but somehow the sun and the sea made it—'

'I know,' Fiona interrupted. And she did. The great reward of real friendship is the shorthand that pares conversation down to affectionate exchanges of shared assumptions and references. This allowed more time for the big conversations. Like the one that Fiona was now trying to start but Tess was determined to avoid.

She was saved from any awkward questions by gasps of admiration (at least she hoped they were admiring) as her guests took their first tastes of the sort of risotto made from quinoa instead of rice. Immediately, everyone began speaking at the same time.

Tess watched Max sit down finally. And for the first time in weeks, she caught him before he'd had the chance to organise his face into the sociably inscrutable mask that he'd been wearing for too long.

He's worried, she realised. And not just the usual worried about Lara's grommets and reading and braces and the pointing on the roof and the foxes chewing up the electrical cables in the garden. He's wearing that fear-of-nuclear-holocaust expression that he first developed after their precious only child was born.

Max had always been a worrier. Tess had found this endearing rather than annoying. As someone born to nurture, she appreciated a manageable weakness in a partner, something to distract from her own endless list of unmanageable weaknesses. She made it her job in this marriage to reassure him. His job was to let her think she was succeeding. But recently she'd failed. And for the good reason that she didn't know what she was supposed to be reassuring him about.

Max summoned up an amiable half-smile and began eating mechanically. Tess could almost hear him counting the number of times he chewed each mouthful before he swallowed.

What she really wanted to do was take Max upstairs, sit him in his favourite comfy chair, the only possession he had brought from his bachelor flat, and refuse to let him go until he told her what was wrong.

But she couldn't. There were two more courses, coffee and more coffee before everyone left and, by then, she and Max would both be too tired to talk about anything more meaningful than who

6

was doing Lara's packed lunch and who was taking the school run the next day.

'We've got an announcement!' Fiona suddenly exclaimed.

Everyone became quiet. For the first five years of their friendship, on what seemed like a monthly basis, this had generally meant that another baby was on the way.

'Er no, not that type of announcement,' Fiona added quickly. (Too quickly, Tess thought. What was that about?)

Fiona went on. 'Well, I *am* announcing a new arrival, but it's not exactly a baby.'

Her husband, Graham, muttered something that Tess guessed was probably not supportive. Fiona glared at him and he compliantly shut up.

'My mother's coming to live with us.'

The imminent arrival of quadruplets would have been greeted with less surprise. And horror.

This was a generational first. While, between them, they had nine children and, between them, had probably encountered every common parenting problem identified in the Western world, the problems of the elderly parent had so far politely waited offstage.

'That's nice,' Tess said feebly.

Fiona grimaced. 'Don't be so ridiculous, Tess! It's not remotely nice. You know what she's like.'

Tess did know. She struggled to find something positive to say about the woman. Nope. Couldn't think of a single thing. Until now, the best thing that could be said about Fiona's mother was that she lived 100 miles away.

'Well, that put a dampener on the evening!' Graham said to Fiona.

Fiona stuck her tongue out.

'I'm sure it will all be fine,' Tess said firmly. And since Graham wasn't married to her, he didn't argue with her. That was the rule. He speared a piece of chicken ferociously. Probably pretending it's his mother-in-law, Tess thought, fully sympathetic to his misery.

'Is there a reason?' she asked Fiona.

'Of course there's a reason,' Graham answered. 'It's to torture us. The old witch is not content with buying me an acrylic cardigan every Christmas and insisting I wear it when we go out. Now she's going to spend the rest of her life with us, punishing me for marrying her daughter when I wasn't a doctor, dentist or solicitor.'

'What's she got against accountants?' Max asked.

'She's convinced I'll know a thousand cunning schemes to defraud her of her life savings.'

'Reasonable assumption,' Fiona agreed. 'To answer your question, Tess, she's sold her house. She says the stairs are too much for her.'

'Can't you get her one of those stairlifts?' Tess suggested.

'That's what I said!' Graham shouted. 'But she refused, said it was undignified! I explained to her, if I'd suggested hiring a school leaver or illegal immigrant to schlep her up and down stairs in a fireman's lift, *that* would be undignified. But a stairlift? It was good enough for Thora Hird and she was a national institution! And speaking of institutions—'

'Thank you, Graham!' Fiona interrupted firmly. She turned to the others. 'He's so tactful. When we went to visit last time, he took a whole load of brochures for old people's homes.'

'They're not called old people's homes any more,' Graham pointed out. 'Old people's homes smelled of cabbage and the poor devils who lived there wore pyjamas with the trousers pulled up to their chins and were herded into yellow-painted rooms to play compulsory bingo and have their hair forcibly dyed magenta. Now they're called things like Bella Vista and The Grosvenor and the inmates are called guests and they play bridge and eat fettuccine and wear tracksuits.'

Millie's husband, Tim, wisely refilled Graham's glass which upset the timing of his rant and stemmed the flow. They were all taken aback but not wholly surprised by his outburst. Being married to Fiona, a talker of world-class volume and volubility, Graham had never had the opportunity to be particularly vocal.

He was essentially a reserved person in every way; even his hair was repressed and had started to recede from view when he was only 19. Fortunately he lacked physical vanity so he accepted the premature signs of middle age with equilibrium. When his waist expanded, he bought new trousers rather than join a gym. When faced with reactionary viewpoints, he hid behind his copy of the *Independent*. He left all the extremes to Fiona.

But the one subject guaranteed to coax him from his cocoon of silent passivity was his mother-in-law. The slightest mention of this demon in his life caused every opinion he'd stifled during his quiet periods to come spewing out, red-hot, deadly and utterly focused.

Since the people round the table had met the formidable Daphne, they were all extremely sympathetic.

'What Graham is so eloquently trying to say is that my mother refuses to go into sheltered accommodation. She thinks it's a waste of money when we have such a big house.'

Graham downed most of the glass of wine in one frustrated swig, muttering as he swallowed. Tess tried to imagine her own mother moving in with them. The scary thought distracted her and, frankly, even the scariest of distractions was welcome with a very real problem rapping urgently at her subconscious.

The evening seemed to move in slow motion for Tess as she counted the minutes until she could finally get the truth from Max. She spent most of the time drifting away from her guests, preparing hypothetical dialogues to meet every possible situation.

'Tess, Millie is talking to you,' Max said irritably.

Tess jumped back from imaginary situation no. 32 where she was reassuring Max that the lump he'd found on his knee was a boil and not cancer.

'I'm so sorry! I was miles away. I don't know what's the matter with me today. Just tired, I think.'

Everyone nodded understandingly. They all loved these evenings. Only other parents of young families could truly understand the general fatigue that fell at the end of every day. Even with au pairs and schools, the pervading worry of having responsibility for other people's lives was exhausting. In the company of such friends, they could all relax. There was no pressure to be entertaining or clever. They knew each other too well for that. They went on holiday together once a year, a chaotic bonding experience that they just about survived, all feeling they knew the others a little better – maybe too much so.

'Sorry, what were you saying?' Tess guiltily gave her full attention to Millie who, she now realised, had been particularly quiet this evening. This wasn't like her.

They'd met Millie at a twee little playgroup run by a woman in dungarees who insisted on being addressed as Miss Smileybun.

Tess and Fiona had looked at each other in mock horror. It was the knitted cervix all over again. As they expertly swallowed their laughter, another mum walked past them. 'Resistance is futile,' she whispered, extending her hand. 'I'm Millie. Welcome to hell.'

And while Fiona and Tess had enjoyed the exclusivity of their friendship, Millie somehow completed them. She punctuated their streams of consciousness, joined the dots between their occasionally diverging paths, filled their silences and she always had home-made cake in her kitchen – the perfect friend. She had that chameleon-like quality of being exactly the sort of person required on every occasion.

If you had a problem, she'd empathise; if you were bored, she'd entertain; if you hated your kids, she'd take them off your hands; if life suddenly terrified you, she'd laugh with you or cry with you, whatever you needed to help you through; she could get a party going or sit in silence and eat chocolate and listen to old Neil Diamond albums with you on those days when that was the only thing to do. She seemed to be able to reinvent herself daily. If she had an identity that existed independently from other people's expectations, nobody had found it yet.

One day, we'll get the measure of Millie, Fiona and Tess used to say.

But whoever Millie truly was, tonight she wasn't herself. She blushed as everyone waited for her to say something important or interesting.

'It's nothing, really.'

Tess looked awkward. Everyone else looked embarrassed. Millie had clearly wanted to say something in confidence to Tess and had missed the chance. Tess resolved to encourage Millie to help her bring dessert through. They could talk privately then.

But Tess forgot.

The conversational rhythm began. To a silent accompanying beat, they sang the litany of middle-class stay-at-home mothers and work-obsessed fathers. Reassured by the familiar backdrop of old comfortable sofas, modern art and cosmopolitan accessories, they could all talk as freely as if they were in their own homes. In fact, they might just as well have been in their own homes, the similarities in decor were so noticeable. Tess found herself listening selectively, editing out the padding, concentrating only on the facts needed to be able to respond if challenged.

'So I said to Walburga, I don't mind you having men round (although I think your mother might be a little alarmed at some of your choices) but when you leave beer cans out and the children find them ...'

'So I said to Richie, our share has been a static 14.6 per cent for three years, all I'm asking is that we shift three per cent of the total marketing spend ...'

'... and then he refused to eat any of it, so I told him, then there'll be no computer for a week ...'

'... and then he refused to listen, I mean, nobody liked the man but then nobody expected him to up and leave a week before the budget proposals ...'

'... first Carly was sick, then Nathan, and that woke Lucy up ...'

'... I felt physically sick, I mean I worked for three months on that research and then to be told that I wouldn't be giving the presentation ...'

Max was also indulging in some carefully edited listening. He had an advantage over Tess. He knew exactly what was wrong and exactly how serious it was. It was from this superior position that he processed the fragments of conversation that drifted his way.

'... well, you know what a pain an au pair can be ...' (£120 a week, Max thought)

'... so we ordered a case of the Sancerre and a case of the Chablis ...' (about £250)

'... and we thought we'd go back to Venice for our wedding anniversary ...' (£2,000) '... and, of course, we'll leave the kids with Mum and Dad, maybe treat them to a few days at that great camp in France ...' (£500)

'... Millie said she'd divorce me if she didn't get a new kitchen ...' (£5,000)

'... now, don't exaggerate, what I said was that if you're getting a new car ...'

'... not you as well! Graham insists we need a new car too!'

'... well, if we're all going to drive over to Provence next summer, we'll need ...'

Max had stopped calculating, stopped listening altogether, at this point. The sums of money were too big, unmanageable, almost incomprehensible. He had been depressed enough when he found the grocery receipts on the kitchen table earlier.

'Twenty-three pounds for a chicken?' he'd whispered, unable to speak the numbers any louder. 'That's forty-six pounds for two chickens.'

Tess had carried on unpacking the shopping, not registering the accusing tone. 'Not just any old chickens, two corn-fed, free-range chickens. That's what they cost.'

Max had continued to stare at the receipt. 'I'd expect them to cook themselves in a good Burgundy for that price, then serve themselves up while singing 'Lady in Red'. Did you know that you can get a chicken for three ninety-nine in Tesco? Is there really nineteen pounds difference in flavour? I mean, would anyone really notice the difference? You're going to smother the thing with herbs anyway so why not just start with a nice, plain, simple chicken?'

Tess stopped and looked at Max curiously. 'What's this about, Max? Since when have you been checking on chicken prices in supermarkets?'

Max spotted the concern growing on his wife's face and back-tracked quickly. He screwed the receipt into a tiny ball and flipped it expertly into the bin. 'Ignore me. I suppose it just makes me laugh when I know these people. They're just like us, after all. They all finish up their kids' fish fingers and chicken nuggets, and steal their sweets after bedtime and they were all students like we were once. They used to be happy with spaghetti bolognese and a litre of Bulgarian wine. People don't really change. I can't help thinking that they'd be equally happy with beans on toast!'

Tess relaxed slightly. 'Fine, then next holiday, you can make everyone beans on toast when it's your turn to make lunch. Speaking of which, Fiona's getting details of this amazing gîte! It has a huge swimming pool. We're going to take a look at all the bumf tomorrow. Apparently we'll have to commit this week if we want it next summer.'

Max turned away so that Tess wouldn't see how pale he'd become.

'Sounds terrific,' he said flatly.

Tess patted him absent-mindedly as she squeezed past him on her way to the fridge. 'Anyway, you can start fine-tuning your beans on toast recipes another day. But for tonight ...'

Max had forced himself to smile indulgently and he'd worked hard at maintaining this calm, cheerful, tolerant facade all evening. But now he was struggling.

Across the table, he watched Tess's eyes glazing over. This used to amuse him in the past. He would tease her about it in bed afterwards and she would always deny it tetchily, insisting that she thoroughly enjoyed every moment of the evening and heard every word that was spoken.

But they both knew that a part of Tess always resisted being pulled completely into anybody else's world. In fact, Max even felt that she'd held something of herself back from their marriage, from him. He usually respected this, even loved it, but occasionally he resented it.

Right now, he hoped that this quality was going to save them.

Almost over. It was 10.45, late enough for a Wednesday. Besides, they all had babysitters to consider. At least we didn't have to pay for babysitters, Max thought grumpily. Although for the price of two corn-fed free-range chickens and assorted vegetables which were no doubt flown in by private jet from the rainforest, I could have probably hired a *Blue Peter* presenter to entertain Lara for the night.

It was time for the kissing and effusive thank-yous and promises to return the pleasure and swappings of recipes and outgrown childrens' clothes. It was only as she kissed Millie that she noticed that she wasn't looking very well. Damn, she thought, I forgot I'd meant to talk to her. She made a mental note to call her the next day. And when Millie's husband, Tim, kissed her goodbye, she realised that he had hardly spoken through the meal. Of course, he had never been very adept at talking to women, even his own wife, and he always seemed overwhelmed when Tess, Fiona and Millie were together monopolising the conversation, but normally he would talk to Graham and Max. Tonight, he'd appeared distracted, absent,

Tess dismissed the thought, more concerned about Millie. Unless Tim's reticence was linked to Millie's? Oh well, it was too late to explore this tonight. She had other, more pressing questions that needed answers.

Finally they all left.

On autopilot, Tess and Max piled up the plates and carried them through to the kitchen, Tess scraping the plates into the waste disposal unit while Max loaded the dishwasher.

He tried not to watch the leftover food being tossed out,

mentally stopped himself from working out how much money was being so casually and literally flushed away.

Without asking, Tess put a jug of milk in the microwave and made mugs of hot chocolate for them both. She placed them on the kitchen table, sat down, grabbed Max's hand and gently guided him into the other chair.

'OK, Max. No more. What's wrong?'

They'd been together for 18 years, married for 15, and Tess didn't need to indulge in any dramatic outbursts to convince her husband of her determination to hear the truth tonight. Max knew from her expression that she would not be put off.

Besides, if he didn't tell her now, he would have to in the next few days. It had reached that point.

'We're broke, Tess,' he said quietly.

Tess raised her eyebrows. 'I think I'd already worked out that we had money problems. All that fuss about the chickens! You don't have to worry. We'll cut back. We've done it before.'

Tess had expected him to hug her in relief but, instead, Max said nothing. She correctly interpreted the silence as evidence that cutting back on chicken quality and switching to own-brand baked beans was not going to solve their problems. 'Is it that bad?' she asked, half-jokingly. 'Am I going to have to pull out my sausage casserole recipes?'

Max said nothing. Tess swallowed nervously. 'Oh no! Back to colouring my own hair and cutting yours? Peeling and slicing vegetables instead of buying them pre-prepared? Playing Scrabble instead of going to the theatre? We'll survive!'

Max decided to interrupt before she began eulogising the joys of chain-store clothes, library books and shepherd's pie that lasted three days.

'It's a bit more than that, Tess. We're really broke. We're going to lose the house, the business, all our money, Lara's school, everything.' Once he started, the words just spilled out.

'The shop has been losing money for months now and I've been paying out all the expenses on credit cards and I had to extend our business loan just to cover the interest payments and we haven't paid the mortgage for three months and the school fees cheque is going to bounce and the house is in negative equity ...'

Tess placed her finger gently on his lips. She couldn't take in the full implications of what he'd just said and certainly didn't want him to say any more. Alarmingly, his list seemed to be building up to some kind of financial climax. It was already worse than she could ever have imagined and it sounded as if he hadn't yet got halfway through the catalogue of their disasters.

In her head, she quickly rewound the film of the last few months of their lives, immediately spotting the clues that were now so glaringly obvious: Max suggesting she try and avoid using the bank account and put everything on her personal credit card, because he was moving money around between their personal, business and tax accounts to minimise their tax liability, or something like that; Max suggesting that he take care of all their credit card bills each month while he was doing the company books and free her to look at new developments for the shop; Max suggesting that they take in a lodger or three since their large house was too big for one small family, saying they could use the rent to expand the business. She was to recall many further examples in future days.

What an idiot! she screamed to herself. Anyone with a gram of intelligence would have picked up on at least one of these warning signs! But not me, I was too busy ... With what? Agonising over the respective merits of camomile versus aloe vera soap for the guest bathroom or rag-rolling pine chests picked up in Oxfordshire antique shops.

But she wasn't ready to take any responsibility for this particular disaster, not yet. Something prevented her from slinging the hot chocolate over his head and screaming abuse at him. He was fragile and she was strong. At this particular moment. This dynamic would change. The time for drink slinging and verbal abuse would no doubt come later. In marriages, it generally did.

But for now, she had to get Max through to tomorrow. That was her only aim, all she could cope with.

He rested his face in his hands, exhausted from the confession.

They sat in silence for what seemed like hours but was actually no more than ten minutes. Then Tess crouched in front of Max and waited until he finally looked down at her.

'Sorry,' he said.

Tess laughed softly. 'What for? It's only money. We managed without it before, we'll manage again. We've still got each other,

Lara, our health, our friends. All the things that matter, they won't change.'

And as they held each other tightly, they both pretended that they believed this.

As if.

# 2

Tess sat in Organique, sipping a camomile tea, not even registering its unique flavour that only came from flowers grown in a Sicilian valley she and Max had discovered a couple of years ago.

She couldn't bring herself to visit the kitchen which she normally did each morning. Max was going to have to let the cook go today along with Ros who helped in the shop. Neither of the women needed the money and probably regarded their jobs as extensions of their social lives but they would still be upset when they heard the news. She knew that Max felt terrible about letting them down, particularly since he was unable to give them any pay in lieu of notice.

Tess looked around at the four tables in the small café area they'd set up in the front of their shop. This is a failed business, she said to herself in amazement, trying to evaluate the place in the light of this knowledge.

Well, four tables, she spotted instantly, one of which is almost always occupied by me or one of my friends. And of course, we'd never expect friends to pay. That left three tables, monopolised by women nursing a medicinal infusion or decaffeinated (i.e. flavourless) coffee and the occasional slice of gluten-free cake. A chunk of expensive sales space taking in less than £5 an hour.

Her newly enlightened eyes moved to the rest of the shop. How could I not have noticed before? she thought. There's nothing here, not enough at least. She remembered discussing the decor with Fiona and Millie. They'd all agreed that it should be uncluttered. 'Think of the feng shui,' Fiona had advised.

So they'd left seemingly vast expanses of profitable floor and counter-space empty except for a strategically placed

17

aromatherapy candle and a single dried bamboo stick in a massive terracotta urn. One large shelf contained nothing but sugar-free lollipops selling for 35p, of which they sold two or three a day. Antique mahogany bookshelves displayed jars and boxes of unimaginable delicacies: preservative- and colouring-free glacé fruits at £9 a box, most of which would soon be out of date and have to be dumped; pasta shapes flavoured with cuttlefish ink that, when cooked, resembled slugs; things with Arabic labels that, even in translation, defied definition.

Why did I never notice this before? Tess cursed herself. More to the point, why didn't Max? He's the one here all day, surely he must have seen how unrealistic we were being in our approach.

Tess shifted her thoughts away from Max, trying hard not to add more accusations against him to the pile that already filled her head. She concentrated instead on the other customers. There were seven of them, all women like herself. She sat up a little straighter. They truly are like me, she realised for the first time. How can I never have noticed this before?

They were dressed like her in their tight cotton trousers and cotton jumpers, their thick shoulder-length hair cut and shaped immaculately to look as natural as if a hairdresser had never touched it, their shabby but classically expensive bags and shoes, their calm, confident expressions that quietly announced 'I know where I belong, where I am going and the sort of people I'm going there with.'

Of course, there was no indication of who these people actually *were*, but maybe that didn't matter to them. Maybe that was the question they were trying to escape in their relentless pursuit of conformity. Since Tess asked herself the question continuously, she didn't think she could use that excuse.

It's a uniform, Tess thought. I belong to this club and I'm wearing the uniform. But I don't remember joining. Perhaps someone else filled in the form for me, forged my signature, sneaked the clothes into my wardrobe when I was sleeping. I wasn't always this person, I'm sure of it.

Then she remembered that she wasn't going to be this person for much longer. Despite her reassuring words to Max that nothing of importance would change, she was wise enough to understand that everything was going to change, they were going to become different people. They'd have to be.

18

'Of course, I'd have to say that the best camomile flowers are grown in Tibet, watered, drop by drop, with Himalayan water brought down mountains by year-old llamas, each petal picked and blessed by a Buddhist monk before being dried on cashmere sheets in the sunshine...'

'Hi, Fiona!' Tess found herself laughing. What a relief, she thought. I was wondering if I might ever be able to laugh again.

She scrutinised Fiona, looking for similarities to herself and, therefore, to the rest of these women. Nothing like me, she concluded. Fiona's face was a little longer, her hair shorter, with blonde streaks ferociously highlighted on her mid-brown hair, her features sharper, less pretty. After four children, her figure had softened and no amount of abdominal crunches could return her stomach to its previous concave shape. Her strategy was to distract the observer's eye from her flaws by applying the reddest, most vibrant lipstick available without a prescription. Fiona's lips shone like a beacon against the backdrop of the other customers with their barely noticeable make-up. She also rejected the Boden catalogue, so loved by Tess and her compatriots, in favour of combat trousers and hooded sweatshirts. She believed that they served a dual purpose of loosely draping over her stomach and showing her to be a woman with attitude. Fiona was simply cut from a different pattern to the rest of them, Tess included.

Tess bristled at the idea that she shared a pattern with anybody. But she recognised that now was not a good time to get precious about her identity.

Fiona sat down opposite her and grimaced as she gulped the murky brown tea that she'd only bought to show solidarity with her friend.

'I'm sorry, Tess, I know that this is your place, but I don't know how you can drink this stuff.'

'It looks like you're not the only one,' Tess said grimly.

Fiona put the cup down and looked at her friend. 'What's up?' she asked.

Tess looked around the shop and café. 'This place.'

'Well, the tea stinks,' Fiona said bluntly, 'but otherwise it's great, everyone knows that.'

Not everyone apparently, Tess thought. She took a deep breath, about to tell her friend what had happened, when she was stopped by a piece of paper being slammed on the table in front of her.

'What do you think?' Fiona asked.

Tess picked up the sheet and looked at the grainy photo of a beautiful house, obviously French, obviously expensive.

'It's not the best quality picture, I had to download it from the internet,' Fiona said, apologetically. 'But it's such a bargain!'

Tess didn't dare read the description of all the fabulous facilities. It didn't matter how much of a bargain it was. There was no way she and Max would be joining the others on holiday this year. If ever again.

'Most important of all, there's an annexe. We can put Millie and Tim there with all their lot plus the new baby if it arrives early.'

Tess looked up. 'What new baby?' she asked blankly.

Fiona clamped her hand over her mouth. 'She hasn't told you?'

'Millie's pregnant?' Tess asked, genuinely shocked.

Fiona nodded. 'And before you ask, no it wasn't planned and she's not very happy about it. But Tim's pleased, or so Millie says.' She mulled this over. 'But who knows what goes on in any marriage?'

They both absorbed this disturbing truth for a couple of seconds. Fiona rotated her head a couple of times to loosen the neck muscles that had suddenly tightened.

'I wonder why she didn't tell me,' Tess said, before it hit her – it was obvious.

She'd kept her voice level for just long enough to tell Fiona that she had to get something out of her eye. She rushed to the ladies' room which her now-experienced eyes observed was big enough to house three frozen food units.

It had been some time since she'd had to deal with the flood of acidic feelings that burned her so deep within that no amount of self-therapy could ease the pain. She just had to ride the pain out. It passed quite quickly, more quickly than in those early years. After an efficient application of foundation and powder, she was ready to face Fiona again.

'You know, you could have just cried here rather than waste valuable recycled, chlorine-free toilet paper,' Fiona said archly. 'I'm used to it. I could have covered up for you, chucked a few gynaecological terms into the conversation just to bore or embarrass eavesdroppers and drive them away.'

Tess smiled despite herself but her eyes began to feel scratchy before she could stop herself.

Fiona took Tess's hand firmly. 'Don't start all that again.'

Tess employed some superhuman self-control to prevent tears from forming. It was one of her great talents, one that she seemed to be putting into use a great deal recently.

'I just wish she didn't feel she had to hide it from me. And it's not as if I wasn't going to find out eventually.'

She spent a few seconds replaying at top speed all the old regrets and pain that had not tormented her for a long time. All the miscarriages, the tests, the inconclusive diagnoses, the final acceptance that they would probably only have one child when everyone around them seemed to be able to plan their families like an unimaginative chef writing the day's menu:

APERITIF: Girl

STARTER (16 months later): Boy

MAIN COURSE (16-18 months later – let's not be too picky): Boy

DESSERT (16 months later – know my ovulation cycle like an old friend): Boy or girl – it hardly matters at this point, but a girl would provide an attractive symmetry to my family.

Tess couldn't believe the way all these other women seemed to get pregnant so easily. She hated the way they took it for granted. Even more, she hated the way they didn't appreciate it. They obviously loved their babies, or at least she assumed they did, but where was their joy? They handed the baby to a nanny or au pair within weeks and they were off down the tennis club to resume their social lives a minute later. Even Fiona and Millie, whom she loved, were happy to be away from their kids whereas Tess (and Max, while she was on the subject) couldn't get enough of Lara.

It was as if these women loved the idea of children, babies, but were constantly surprised and disappointed by the reality.

The secret thought, the one Tess knew she must never speak, was that she deserved more children than all these other women. But it didn't matter that she never uttered this truth; Fiona and Millie both knew how she felt and worked hard to protect her from her sense of injustice.

Fiona decided to prick the bubble forming around Tess before it grew too big. They'd said everything there was to say on this subject and it wouldn't help Tess to drag it up again. She assumed her best girls'-boarding-school bossy tone.

'Anyway, I think she must be crazy. We've all put that behind us. I don't know how she can face going through it all again. Besides, it'll play havoc with our social life. We'll all end up helping out with babysitting. And bang go Sunday lunches when we can eat in peace with the kids playing in the garden unsupervised. Not that you could ever leave Millie's children unsupervised. What do you think this one will be like?' she asked wickedly.

She was referring to the fact that Millie and Tim had the four most appallingly behaved children in South London and there was some pretty stiff competition among the liberal classes who believed that discipline stifled creativity.

Tess giggled at the prospect of them coping with another human neutron bomb in their lovely home.

Fiona was encouraged by Tess's apparently lifted spirits. 'It's bad enough having my mum moving in,' she said. 'Whoops! Was that selfish of me?'

But Tess hadn't noticed any selfishness on Fiona's part. She was too ashamed of her own. Putting aside her pang of envy at Millie's news, she'd finally worked out that the three of them were going through a rarely advertised phase of women's life that inevitably strikes after 30 and before menopause: the cosmic joke. This is a cataclysmic event whereby something unnecessarily cruel or horribly unexpected is downloaded onto a woman for no other reason than that the particular woman's life is apparently going too smoothly.

It was clear that they were all being dumped on from above to a greater or lesser extent. But Tess felt strongly that her extent was definitely greater than the others'. Definitely. And right now she wanted Millie's extent. Or even Fiona's. Or that woman's in the corner bleating about her broken Aga. Or Madonna's.

'No, that wasn't selfish of you,' she assured Fiona. 'Well, no more selfish than usual,' she added wickedly.

Fiona almost spat her tea out in laughter. 'You're starting to sound like me! So what do you think about it? Millie having a baby, that is, not the epic tale of my lifelong selfishness – I've got the next twenty years of my mother telling that story to me each blessed day.'

Tess shrugged. 'I won't lie. I'm as jealous as hell. But if you're asking me how I think it will affect Millie ... who knows? Millie does seem to be the one person who can cope with anything. Nothing seems to floor her. Although I think even she would be a little challenged by my own little ... bombshell, shall we say.'

'What bombshell?' Fiona asked, giving up on the tea and sucking on a rock-hard, brown sugar lump in an attempt to take the taste of the tea away.

Tess inhaled then exhaled with a dramatic whoosh. 'We've gone broke.' There. I've said it.

Fiona looked puzzled. 'What exactly do you mean? Sausage casserole broke? Home hair colour broke?'

Tess shook her head sadly. 'Much, much worse.'

Fiona's eyes widened. 'Moving into a coal bunker with a dozen asylum seekers? Sitting in underground stations with tin cups? Tying your child to your back and walking two thousand miles through the Russian steppes, living on grass and yak's milk?'

*That* finally made Tess laugh. 'All right! You win. Not that bad. But bad enough.' She sobered up and gestured around her. 'We're going to have to close the shop. And we'll have to move.'

Fiona was stunned. She tried to process the information but wasn't finding it easy. 'But you can't! I mean, how? Surely you're exaggerating! Move? You can't move, you know you can't. You only planted that wisteria last year and it'll be five years before it flowers.'

Tess had forgotten the wisteria. The thought of this brought her closer to breaking point than any of the other poignant reminders that kept popping into her head. Planting the wisteria had been an act of commitment, a sign that her family and this house had a long-term future. She wished she'd stuck to busy lizzies now.

Her voice dropped as she explained to Fiona just how serious their situation was. 'We'll have to rent the house out as soon as possible. We can't sell it because we've overextended the mortgage and we'd end up with nothing. So if we can just get a good rental on it for a few ... years or so, we might just be able to recoup some of our losses.'

'But where will you go?' Fiona asked, becoming desperate as she saw yet another strand of her own future beginning to fray.

Tess looked exhausted. 'We haven't worked out the details yet. But we'll have to move away from here. Find somewhere to rent.

A flat or maybe a small house or something. In an area we can afford.'

Fiona wanted to know all the details. She wanted to know what Tess was going to do about Lara's school and what would happen to the complicated rota of school runs and homework nights their kids shared. She wanted to talk about holidays and dinner parties and lunches and girls' nights out and health clubs and all the other things that made Fiona's life bearable. But she couldn't mention any of them because they all cost money and Tess no longer had any. She didn't know what to say, for the first time in all their years of friendship.

Tess took pity on her. 'Don't feel too sorry for me. At least when we move, my mother won't be coming with me.'

But Fiona had lost her sense of humour. 'I don't get it. How did this happen? This place must be raking it in. I mean, look at it. Every table's occupied. There are three people queuing at the till in the shop and look what's in their baskets! They must each have about twenty quid's worth of vegetables. This has got to be a gold-mine.'

Tess shook her head sadly. 'That's what I thought. But our rent was put up a year ago. And it seems that to make a profit with that kind of rent, those lovely people would have to be putting organic BMWs in their shopping baskets.'

Neither said what they were both thinking. That Fiona's husband Graham had warned Tess and Max about this possibility three years ago. That everything he'd predicted would happen had now happened. And more.

'This small section of Clapham is one of the most expensive residential areas in London,' he'd said gently. 'But don't forget that we've had booms like this before. And surely you remember the last recession?'

Tess and Max had closed their ears to his warnings as he went on. 'You have to understand that there are patterns, inevitable tides, and just as property prices rocket astronomically high, rental prices will inevitably follow.'

He'd explained that they would be unable to raise their own prices to compensate for such large rent increases, with organic food already priced at a premium, and that customers would simply shop elsewhere. He also observed that supermarkets were now selling organic products and that a privately run small shop could not possibly compete with massive retail chains.

The friendly advice was punctuated with uncompromising terms like 'repossession' and 'bankruptcy', words that found no frame of reference in Tess and Max's cloistered, affluent mindset.

They listened politely then discounted everything he'd said. They remortgaged the house to the limit of its market value with an independent financial company, since none of the major banks or building societies would lend to them.

At the time, Tess had been stunned by Max's willingness to take such a risk. Until then, he'd been the sort of man who paid all bills the day they arrived, terrified of the prospect of the red ones that would otherwise follow.

'Are you sure about this?' Tess had asked him, time and time again before they signed the papers.

'Absolutely,' he'd said firmly. 'Definitely. Categorically. Without any doubt whatsoever.'

Except this was a lie. He was eaten up with doubts. He could barely sleep and he felt permanently sick. But he had to do it, he knew. After all these years of Tess pandering to his obsessive tendency to worry, not pushing him when he trod water for years in a nice safe career that bored him, he had to take this one risk for her. Just to show her that he could.

'It'll be an adventure for us,' he'd said with forced enthusiasm. 'A new future, something we can do together.'

'Yes, but what about all the things Graham said?' Tess pressed, anxious that he understood all the implications of the decision.

'Well, we both know what Graham's like,' he'd said. And then Tess relaxed. She knew exactly what he meant.

For while Graham had a magnificent grasp of finance, he had no imagination. That was Tess and Max's cruel assessment. In fact, neither of them quite understood his marriage to Fiona. They seemed absolutely mismatched, Fiona so colourful and Graham so dull.

'He's the only person I know who's looked and acted fifty ever since he turned thirty,' Tess joked unkindly, looking for reasons to discount his warnings.

He doesn't understand the uniqueness of this area, even though he lives here, they agreed between themselves. He may understand the abstracts of business, they reasoned, but he wasn't taking into account the potential of this particular location. To him, it's a comfortable place to live, surrounded comfortingly with People Like Himself. But a more creative mind would see beyond the geography to the sociology. Even the media had latched on and given it a snappy and singularly appropriate epithet: Nappy Valley.

'I hate that name!' Fiona said. 'I hate being lumped together with everyone else just because we share a postcode!'

'It's a bit more than that, Fi. I mean, look down the street! Have you ever seen so many small children in one place outside a theme park?'

'Yeah, but the houses are all big family houses, you'd expect them to be filled with big families,' Fiona pointed out, forgetting for a moment Tess's one-child family. 'There must be areas like this all over Britain. Your average council estate must be awash with kids.'

'True,' Tess agreed, 'but the media isn't interested in that. The difference here is property prices.'

And that's what Tess and Max had banked on. They were living in a neighbourhood that, within a few years, had gone from being an average suburb of Victorian and Edwardian semis and terraced houses to a speculator's paradise. Prices increased 100 per cent, 200 per cent until a brand new social group had emerged: previously average families, moderately comfortable, husbands earning enough to allow their wives to give up work when the children arrived, who were suddenly sitting on modest houses worth £500,000 plus.

They didn't consider themselves rich but, by almost any reasonable standard, they were. With their relatively small mortgages and massive equity in their homes, these fortunate families found themselves with more money than they knew how to spend.

Tess and Max belonged to this elite. They found themselves being carried along up this escalator to a whole new social class – the New Affluents, not millionaires, not upper class, but suddenly and unexpectedly wealthy in assets and disposable income.

And if this philosophy had to be summed up in one word, that word would be ORGANIC.

Like the other mums in the area, Tess bought into the organic cult. She read up on the subject, believing the experts who persuaded her that the decision would make her a conspicuously better mother, ignoring the scoffers who insisted that it was a con.

'Admit it,' Max had challenged her one day, as he peeled a misshapen potato, vainly searching for a cube of vegetable that was not black or soft.

'Admit what?' Tess was examining the apples, hoping to find one without suspicious holes. Lara had stubbornly refused to eat anything that was 'broken' and was demanding a return to proper round apple-shaped apples. Basically, if it hadn't been collected by an impoverished farmworker enslaved by brutal conditions within a totalitarian regime, Lara didn't want to know. If he was honest, Max was sympathetic to this viewpoint because he liked his carrots to be perfectly straight and evenly tapered and his fruit to be, well, maggot-free.

Max continued peeling desperately. 'The only reason you buy this stuff is because it's so expensive. If it was cheaper than regular ...'

'Poisonous,' Tess corrected.

'... *traditionally farmed* produce,' Max went on. 'If it was cheaper, you'd never buy it. I mean look at this stuff. How much did this lot cost?'

'About thirty pounds,' Tess replied, looking him straight in the eye, daring him to display shock.

To his credit, he didn't react outwardly (although inwardly, his scriptwriters were penning diatribes of the most vicious nature to spring on Tess at a more appropriate moment). Instead he cleared his throat weakly.

'Right. Thirty pounds. For two bags of fruit and veg that will barely feed this family for a day once you've removed the bruises, scabs, mould and predators.'

He lifted a protesting slug from a lettuce and held it at arm's length towards a horrified Tess.

He continued. 'But if they tried to offload this in a trolley near the tills in the supermarket, with a 'reduced' sticker and the bargain price of two pounds fifty, you wouldn't touch it.'

Tess refused to be swayed by the argument even though Max was obviously correct. 'Maybe, maybe not. But the fact is that I *feel* like a better mother when I buy this stuff.'

And it was this unshakeable truth, coupled with the sheer

numbers of similar-thinking parents in the immediate neighbour-hood, that led them to formulate the idea for their business. Max overcame his initial distrust for misshapen vegetables, his vision being diverted by the prospect of making a profit from an honourable business. Surely that was the perfect incentive for taking the first risk of his life.

'We can't lose, Tess!' Max had said excitedly. 'Think about it. A shop selling every kind of organic product, plus a small café as well, maybe getting Millie to do all the baking. You could work there when you wanted, pick your hours, then we'd hire someone else the rest of the time. At decent wages, of course.'

And Tess was persuaded because she wanted to be. Because they needed something at that time. They'd hit a stagnant patch in their lives. Lara was at school. Max had been recently made redundant and was finding it alarmingly difficult to find another job in advertising. Tess was ready to work again but wanted to do something that didn't involve a full-time commitment.

Their marriage had become a little stagnant too. The blissful distraction of Lara, who'd arrived after six traumatic years of trying, had occupied every moment of their existence, dominating every conversation, every decision. Tess and Max had forgotten how to be a couple and had begun to find each other rather annoying.

In the rare moments of introspection that Tess tried to avoid, she wondered if the marriage had ever had any staying power. At the very moment when they'd run out of things to say, they'd begun trying for a baby and had talked about little else until Lara arrived. After that they talked about Lara. They'd stopped being a couple years ago, Tess realised sadly, and were now little more than cohabiting parents. But they were determined to keep their marriage going and that meant taking action.

There were two choices: a personal change, i.e. going back on the treadmill in the painful attempt to have another baby (which they sensibly realised would bring problems of its own) or a radical professional change.

Years later they were to ask themselves why they didn't consider a third choice, of addressing the issue of the cracks in their marriage before moving on. They were to torture themselves with the agonies of 'what ifs' and 'if onlys' for a long long time.

But maybe their marriage was too precarious an area to probe so they shut their eyes to the underlying problems, silently praying that the cracks would heal by themselves. They clamped the blinkers firmly to their eyes and decided to go into business together.

All their friends thought it was a great idea. Or rather, the women thought it was a great idea. 'It sounds perfect!' Millie had said. 'Of course I'll make all the cakes. I'll do all my shopping there as well!'

'Me too!' said Fiona. 'Not the baking bit. I don't do baking as you know. But I'm very good at shopping and spending money and I will certainly bring that gift to this enterprise. I'm also the rudest, most difficult person you will ever meet so, if this place can please me, it can please anyone.'

So they went for it, ignoring the bank manager's advice, ignoring the advice of anybody who recommended any kind of caution and definitely ignoring the inner warning whispers faintly audible to them both when night fell and each was alone in thought.

In retrospect, Tess wondered if the most compelling motivation to go ahead was that both Max's parents and her mother thought it was a terribly risky idea and strongly advised against it.

'Your mother has never thought much of me,' Max had complained. 'When I was made redundant, I know that she believed that it was somehow my fault. And my parents know nothing about risk. They have that classic Civil Service mentality. Do you know my dad has been putting five per cent of his salary into a Post Office account since the day he started work forty-five years ago? He's never touched it, refuses to transfer it to a more profitable account. Says he doesn't want to change a habit that suits him, that he believes his money is safe and he likes to know that whatever emergency may befall him, he's financially prepared for it. That's the kind of man he is.'

Years later, Tess was to wish that Max had been that kind of man himself.

They'd needed money, more than Max's redundancy payment could cover. So they remortgaged the house to its limit. Of course they did. This was Nappy Valley, the place where every family wanted to live. Houses were worth a fortune and the values seemed to be rising daily. All that equity in their home just sitting there! So they released it.

And now it had brought them down.

'You're looking tired, Millie,' Fiona said kindly.

Millie grimaced. 'Thank you.' But she already knew. She was a woman brutally aware of her own limitations. She was of average height, a little overweight, with skin that had never recovered from adolescence and long thin hair that needed daily washing to look all right. She knew and accepted that, if she spent an hour attending to herself, applying careful make-up and contact lenses, she would look presentable, no more than that. On a day like today when she hadn't showered or even looked in the mirror and was wearing unflattering glasses, she looked like the 'before' picture from a dramatic makeover story. But her appearance was currently the least important thing on her mind.

Fiona filled Millie in on Tess's grim situation. 'It was awful, Millie,' she said. 'And I was a complete cow! All I could go on about was much this was going to affect me, how much I was going to miss her. Fat lot of good I was.'

Millie smiled sympathetically. 'She was probably grateful. If you'd gone all weepy and touchy-feely, she'd have been really worried. After all, I'm the nice, conciliatory one, you're the bitch. Don't confuse everyone by changing roles.'

Fiona slapped her friend's hand affectionately. 'I love you too!'

'How do you think Tess would feel if I offered her some money?' Millie said tentatively. 'I'd say it was a loan so she wouldn't be so embarrassed.'

Fiona shook her head miserably. 'I've just been talking to Graham about this on the phone. He thinks that Tess might go for it but that Max would never forgive us for even offering. He said that he would feel exactly the same.'

'But that's silly! Surely we all know each other well enough by now?'

Fiona looked doubtful. 'I think that we have to help them as much as we can, go as far as we can, without actually mentioning money.'

They slumped back into silence, each summoning up their underused imaginations to come up with some non-financial plasters to apply to festering financial wounds.

Then Fiona began rubbing her forehead in distress.

'What's wrong?' Millie asked.

'I know you're going to think I'm terrible for saying this ...' Fiona began.

Millie raised an eyebrow in amusement.

Fiona scowled before continuing. 'It's just that, before she told me her news, we were talking about the summer.'

She took out the details of the gîte in Provence. Both women stared at the paper that now represented the end of a comfortably regulated life and the beginning of an unpredictable existence.

'Do we go without them or not go at all?' Fiona asked. Millie didn't answer.

Tim sat in his office, staring at his desk diary, filled with gloom as he looked at the crammed pages. Looking for solace in his personal organiser, he found his family time equally stuffed to overflowing. He turned page after page, searching for a blissful white space that he could look forward to. He longed for empty time, a vacuum in which he could float aimlessly, just occupying space, moving neither forwards nor sideways, just ... sitting.

How did I end up like this? he'd been asking himself with increasing frequency recently. How did my life end up so busy? I was a quiet person. What am I thinking? I *am* a quiet person. All I ever wanted was a quiet family life, a moderately successful career with minimal risk, some gentle peaks of happiness, nothing excessive that could generate equally excessive troughs.

So I married Millie, a nice girl who seemed to be just like me, quiet, modest in her ambitions, happy to abandon her career as soon as children came along. But then, it crept up on me, the noise the clutter, all the other people, Millie's friends who were expected to be my friends too. And we weren't a tight nuclear family, cosy and self-contained; we became a commune, our doors and lives permanently open.

The sheer busyness of their lives had robbed Tim of essential reflecting time and it had taken years for him to work out where he had gone wrong.

It was Millie's fault, he'd concluded. She'd deceived him into thinking she was just like him, when all the time, she'd been acting, pretending to be the person he wanted her to be. And she was good at it, he had to concede. A real pro, in fact.

It was only when he'd seen her develop her friendships with Tess and Fiona that he saw how she operated, reflecting the expectations of each person in turn, shifting gently, seamlessly, from one persona to another.

And while he admired her professionalism and amazing dedication at maintaining such a pretence, year after year, he had never expected his own wife to be performing such a delicate balancing act in their own marriage.

Now he was floundering. He no longer knew this woman. The news about the baby had left him reeling. He had no idea whether she'd become pregnant on purpose, when they'd both agreed to stop after Nathan. She said that it was an accident, but she'd said a lot of things since he'd known her and he no longer knew what was true and what was a skilfully delivered line.

The one thing he did know was that he didn't like his life and he needed to talk to someone about it, someone who really understood him. Only one name immediately sprang to mind but he dismissed it as preposterous, totally inappropriate.

But who else is there? he asked himself before he took a step that would rob him of the last empty white space in his diary and his life.

Tess and Max followed the rental agent around the house like puppies, lapping up his mms and aahs, trying to work out the undoubtedly disparaging descriptions he was whispering into his state-of-the-art dictating machine.

They appreciated, perhaps for the first time in years, the sheer amount of time it took to travel through their property. There were three floors and the steep, open staircases gave them a reassuring sense of substance. This was a proper house.

The ground floor was where they lived, a sprawl of four rooms consisting of a kitchen, dining room, living room and playroom. The distressed wooden floors were their last major outlay and represented their final break from parental influence. Both sets of parents had frowned at the absence of wall-to-wall carpet that, in their worlds, symbolised respectable affluence.

Tess and Max both experienced the familiar pang of discomfort as the estate agent walked in and out of the six bedrooms, four of them so clearly underused yet still extravagantly decorated.

WE THOUGHT WE'D HAVE MORE CHILDREN! they both

wanted to shout. We didn't buy a place of this size just so that we could compete with the average small country hotel in our spare room availability.

Max stood close to the agent whenever he could, hoping that the man would be commenting appreciatively on the furnishings that told the story of a marriage and family. Surely he would be impressed by the solid furniture that weighted the house to its foundations; surely he'd spot that no MDF had sullied any of these rooms; surely he'd gasp at the awesome pieces of modern art and sculpture that were so bizarrely abstract they they simply had to be expensive; surely he'd realise that the corner-fitting sofa had been handmade to detailed specifications that had preoccupied Tess and Max during one of many difficult weeks in their marriage; surely he'd know that the curtain fabric had come from Hong Kong and the rugs from China.

But it all seemed to be irrelevant, insignificant, to this stranger who was quantifying their lives. They were disconcerted by his apparent disregard for their lovingly planned decor, as he strode from room to room, almost psychotically fixated on his electronic measuring device.

At least it's clean, Tess thought, surely that must matter.

Fiona and Millie had come round the day before straight after dropping the kids off at school. They'd spent all day helping Tess clean the house from top to bottom. Millie had worked harder than anyone else. Tess hugged her in gratitude, not just for her help, but because she recognised that Millie was trying to compensate for her irrational sense of guilt at conceiving so easily.

All nine kids joined in the compulsory activity after school (after all the parents had agreed to write that their offspring were ill in their homework diaries) and even Walburga, Fiona's sluttish au pair, was press-ganged into service. In the evening, when Graham and Tim got home from work, and Max returned from a grim meeting at the bank, they too joined the cleaning party. Tim ordered (and paid for) pizza to be delivered for them all. Graham popped home and fetched some good wine. This display of cheerful loyalty made Tess weep.

It was to be the last jolly gathering of this kind for a long time.

After they'd all left, Tess and Max collapsed onto the sofa in exhaustion. They already felt slightly distanced from the house, which hadn't looked this clean and tidy since they'd moved in.

'I can't believe it's only been forty-eight hours,' Tess said. 'Only two days ago, everything was normal, our lives stretched out before us in an unbroken line from now to then, and suddenly I can't see beyond tomorrow.'

Max wanted to take her hand but he was too overwhelmed with guilt. He believed himself to be totally responsible for this situation and felt that an offer of comfort might be justifiably rebuffed.

Tess took his hand, knowing exactly how Max felt, wanting to comfort him back even though she had to agree that he was largely responsible for the mess. She decided that now was the time to ask the one question she'd held back.

'Why didn't you tell me?' She tried to keep the tone even, without a hint of recrimination. This was not easy since part of her wanted to put her hair in curlers, grab a rolling pin, pull on a floral nylon housecoat and shriek at him like a cartoon fishwife.

Max had been dreading answering this question as much as Tess had dreaded asking it.

'I thought everything would work out. I had some ideas. I just thought that if I could weather a few tricky months, I'd be able to pay back the money I'd borrowed and get us back on course.'

Tess felt the anger rise against all her efforts to force it back.

'I? What's with all the "I"? What happened to the "we"? Did it not occur to you that I might have ideas? And what about the fact that it was my future on the line as well . . .'

She stopped abruptly, something inside warning her that certain words must never be spoken if they were going to get through this, certain accusations must never be made because they would trigger off certain defences that could deepen the cracks in the foundations shakily underpinning their marriage.

It didn't matter. Max knew what she wanted to say. He shrank slightly, that instinctive movement towards self-diminishment that always stabbed Tess.

'I knew all that. I just wanted to protect you.'

There, he'd said it. Only when the words escaped his mouth did he realise that they were true. Up until that moment, he had no idea why he'd kept this all to himself. After years of feeling that he was the protected one in the marriage, the one whose feelings mattered, he wanted to be the protector. And he'd failed badly.

'You as well?' Tess said furiously. 'First Millie and now you.'

'What's Millie protecting you from?' Max asked.

Tess cursed silently. 'Nothing.'

Max stared at her.

Tess sighed. 'She's pregnant.'

Max considered this for a few moments. 'How long have you known about this?'

'Fiona told me a couple of days ago.'

Max nodded carefully. 'So why didn't you tell me before?'

'Because I wanted to protect you.'

They both smiled weakly at her admission.

'What a pair we are,' Tess said.

One of their marital cracks moved a fraction closer towards healing. They enjoyed the moment of silent harmony.

'I thought you'd got over all that,' Max said.

Tess narrowed her mouth. 'I just knew that you didn't like talking about it, so I stopped.'

Max jumped up. 'That's a terrible thing to say. Now I feel a complete failure as a husband, that my own wife can't talk about her feelings to me because she's afraid of upsetting me.'

Tess hurried to pacify him. 'I didn't mean it like that. It was just that I didn't need to upset you. I could talk to Fiona and Millie and leave you to deal with your feelings your own way.'

Max stared at her. 'And what would my own way be? Worrying, panicking, obsessing? Bringing them all to you to deal with?'

Tess shuddered. The crack opened up again, a little wider than it had been before. Not that the crack had ever completely closed up.

Max had wanted a large family as badly as she had. Tess looked back with amazement on how they'd taken the idea of children for granted in those early days.

'When do you think we should start trying?' Max had asked after their first heady year of marriage.

Tess had tilted her head to one side as she did the calculations.

'I think I'd like the first one just before I'm thirty,' she had said. 'That way, I'll have got myself established in my career and will be able to go back to it later. Then I think I'd like to have the others quite closely together, get the baby stage out of the way and let the kids grow up together, become friends.'

Max had agreed. He and Tess were both only children and were determined not to pass the same pressure on to their own children.

'What do you reckon on four?' he'd asked. 'I've done the sums and I think four is as high as we can go, assuming interest rates stay steady and we send them all to private school.'

Tess loved him for taking it so seriously. A reflective person by nature, the thought of children turned her into a woman of wild impetuosity. She relied on Max to keep her grounded.

'Not sure,' Tess had said. 'I think three is enough. In the beginning at least. Maybe we'll get to three and then have another think.'

They both wept to recall their ludicrously naive expectations. It had simply never occurred to them that they wouldn't be able to have babies whenever they wanted. And when they found themselves living in an area where fertility seemed to be included in the facilities provided by the council tax, they felt confident that their expectations were absolutely reasonable.

Their marriage had only just survived the years of trying for a baby before Lara arrived. When they'd decided to get married, neither had considered the possibility that children might not necessarily form part of the equation. Had they known this in advance, would they have got married? Whoa! Neither of them dared ask themselves that, let alone ask the other person. Too, too dangerous.

But Lara arrived, miraculously and in the nick of time. They never spoke about it but Tess and Max had both been contemplating divorce in the months before Tess became pregnant.

Then it started all over again. The expectations, the plans for the big family, then the miscarriages. They stopped before they destroyed each other. They had Lara and she was all they could have hoped for.

But Max's reaction to Millie's news reminded them both that the issue was still there.

Tess didn't say any of the things she wanted to say. Instead, she wisely decided to change tack. She scrambled around for any safe subject and then it struck her: from now on, there weren't going to be any safe subjects. Their life was changing – it was unlikely to be for the better – and they were going to have to deal with every problem head on. They would no longer be able to go out and buy a piece of antique garden statuary or book a weekend break or join a wine appreciation course to bypass a rocky patch in their relationship. They wouldn't have any money and, besides, the practical challenges they would be facing would be so great that they would have to be dealt with just to keep afloat.

What do I say now? Tess wondered. How about something big to get Max off the unmentionable subject of babies?

So she went for the biggie. 'Have you had any thoughts about where we're going to live?' she asked, very very carefully.

Max pulled himself back from the other place and tried to focus on this not-insignificant question.

'As long as you're not going to jump down my throat for thinking about this without consulting you ...'

Tess pulled a face which almost, *almost*, brought a smile to Max's lips.

'... I've worked out our money, phoned around a few places and been on the Internet and it looks like if we don't want to move too far from here, the best we can afford would be a flat.'

Tess opened her mouth to protest. Max lifted his hand to stop her.

'Not in a tower block or anything like that, a converted flat, in a house.'

Tess was momentarily appeased. 'That doesn't sound too bad. So whereabouts?'

Max went on. 'Then we have to consider schools.'

Tess felt sick when she thought about taking Lara out of the private school she loved so much, with all her friends, with Fiona's and Millie's kids.

'So I pinpointed the decent state schools in the borough and worked out the catchment areas; obviously we're not committed to anything but there weren't that many options...'

'Just tell me where!' Tess snapped.

Max mumbled something.

'Pardon? I didn't hear what you said,' Tess said irritably. Everything he said and did irritated her at the moment.

'I said, it would have to be in Heaverbury.'

Tess wrinkled her eyebrows. 'Heaverbury? *The* Heaverbury?'

Max sat forward, ready to go into the hard sell. 'It's not as bad as you think. It had a bad reputation in the seventies but then loads of the tenants bought their homes and did them up—'

Tess interrupted. 'And they closed down most of the crack dens and served eviction notices on most of the cockroaches and towed away most of the petrol-bombed cars ...'

Max gently placed a finger on her lips in a spectacular demonstration of patience that Tess didn't know he possessed.

'You're mistaking reality for *The Bill*, sweetheart. Heaverbury was never that bad. The houses are all of a decent size.'

'That's because they were built for pregnant teenagers who they were expecting to have twenty-five children by twenty-five different fathers,' Tess interjected.

Max looked at his wife in amusement. 'I have this theory that everyone turns into a Conservative Party leadership candidate when their status quo is under threat.'

Tess tried unsuccessfully not to laugh. 'Maybe that was a little reactionary of me,' she conceded.

'A little?' he asked teasingly.

Tess groaned. 'OK, I admit it. But you'll never convince me that anyone would *choose* to move to Heaverbury.'

Max scratched his head, searching for an easy way of putting it. 'The thing is, Tess, we *have* no choice. I promise you, I've explored every option. Unless you want to move out of London, it's Heaverbury or nothing.'

Tess sighed. 'Have you heard what they call it?'

Max shook his head. 'No. Surprise me.'

'You'll find this amusing,' she said, without a shred of amusement in her voice. 'You know they call this area Nappy Valley?'

'Of course I do,' Max said. He was finding Tess irritating too.

'Well, in Nappy Valley circles, Heaverbury is "laughingly" called Crappy Valley. You're moving us to Crappy Valley. Thank you so much.'

And with that, she got up, marched into the garden and sobbed over the tiny wisteria plants that she'd never see flower.

# 3

Tess sat in the tiny empty kitchen.

'What do you think?' Max asked hopefully.

'It's fine.' It was the only thing she could say. This was the only flat available in this area at short notice which was within their price range. And it was fine. Small but fine. Two bedrooms, a living room, a kitchen and a small overgrown garden.

'What will we do with all our stuff?' Tess thought out loud. 'It's not going to fit in here. I suppose we'll have to sell it?' Her voice cracked at the prospect of such irrevocable action.

Max was encouraged by this tacit acceptance of the flat. 'We can put it in storage; it's not too expensive, I've looked into it. Don't forget this doesn't necessarily have to be permanent. We still own the old house. We just need to make some money, pay off our debts, and then we can go back.'

Going back? Tess thought. I have to concentrate on going forward. Moving would be the easy bit, if any of it was easy. The making-money bit that Max was mentioning so casually, that wasn't going to be such a breeze.

'We'll sell all the fittings in the shop and café,' Max said. 'And there's a fair bit of stock.'

Ah yes, Tess thought, the stock. The stock that moved at the speed of approximately one jar of Tuscan olives per hour. That'll help.

Max was oblivious to Tess's look of scepticism. 'Anyway, the proceeds will cover our rent for the first two months and a down payment to all of our creditors. It's not in their interest to make us bankrupt, not when there's an outside possibility that we might pay them back everything we owe. Right now, they're all satisfied that we're taking radical action to address our debts. So if we can find work in the next few weeks, we'll be able to go to them with a full repayment plan.'

'Just like that? Find work in the next few weeks?' Tess argued. 'Do you ever read any of the papers apart from the sports and financial pages? There are people who haven't been able to find work for years.'

'I know that, but we're both professional people.'

Tess made that whooshy noise that was normally saved for Lara when she insisted on picking every tiny piece of herb from a sauce that her mother would dare to place before her. She'd been on a school trip to a local farm and the farmer's wife had proudly showed the children her herb garden. Halfway through a sing-song description of how the lovely rain makes the lovely herbs grow to be so lush and tasty, the farmer's dog trotted up and proceeded to cock its leg over the plants – just to make them that little bit lusher and tastier. All the kids had gagged in delighted horror. It was the highlight of their day. But it had left Lara (and most of the class, it transpired) with an unswerving aversion to the concept of herbs or any other unidentifiable speck that graced their food. It drove Tess nuts, the way that only an ten year old can do, but now Max was beginning to have the same effect on her.

'When you say we're professional people, are you aware that this renders us virtually unemployable? Look at us both. You spent fifteen years in advertising then three years running a shop. You were made redundant from one and failed at the other.'

Max flinched and Tess felt an ache of guilt but she knew it was vital that she keep Max grounded in reality. Since taking responsibility for their current circumstances, he seemed to have undergone a complete personality change. All sense of caution had been tossed aside and he was blundering ahead with no thought for consequences. If he was at all worried about anything, Tess couldn't tell.

And that worried her.

She spoke more gently. 'All I'm saying is that it could take ages to get back into advertising or something similar, months. I heard you on the phone this morning, calling all your old contacts. They weren't begging you to come back, by the sound of it.'

'I was putting out feelers, that's all,' Max said defensively.

Tess sighed. 'I know. But even if something comes of the

feelers, it's not going to happen quickly. I really think we need to be looking at something in the short term.'

Max's face hardened. 'And what about you? You haven't worked since before Lara was born, apart from helping in the shop.' He wanted to hurt her back and didn't care if he sounded spiteful.

Tess was exasperated. 'That's what I'm saying! It doesn't matter that we've got university degrees, that we've both earned massive salaries in the past. Right now we're desperate and we have to lower our expectations for a while.'

Max couldn't prevent himself from sinking into a major sulk. 'Right then, I'll go and apply for a road-sweeping job straight away.'

Tess laughed. 'We're not that desperate,' she said, crossing her fingers behind her back. She kissed the top of his head, which was still lowered in a sulk. This cheered him despite his best efforts to maintain his mood.

'So what about you?' he asked. 'What will you do?'

Tess had already considered this. 'Well, I can't work full-time because we've always agreed that I should be here when Lara gets home from school and, besides, there are the school holidays to think of. Anything I did earn would have to go on childcare. And everyone knows that employers aren't sympathetic about women taking time off to look after their kids when they're sick.'

'All right, all right! You've made your point. It's all down to me.'

'That wasn't what I meant,' Tess objected. Except that it was.

'So what does that leave?' Max asked, sinking again.

Tess ruffled his hair, the way she used to in their early days together. She'd always loved its unruliness as much as he hated it. 'I'll think of something. I always do. I'm a mother, I'm used to a challenge. Give me a shoebox, a toilet roll centre, some cotton wool and some conkers and I can make a dialysis machine. Something will come up and I'll just leap in. You know me.'

She and Max exchanged one of their old glances, the look that said: We know each other, we're alike, we want the same things, we have a history, we can read between each other's lines.

A flicker of hope suddenly brightened their horizons. This optimism encouraged Tess to broach a delicate subject.

'I had to phone Mum and let her know that we were moving.'

41

Max tensed up visibly. 'What exactly did you tell her?'

'I couldn't lie.' Tess sounded defensive. 'I told her that the business had hit some difficulties and that we had to move to pay off the debts.'

'That's terrific,' Max hissed, so that Lara wouldn't hear. 'So now all her suspicions have been confirmed and she can tell the world that I have finally proved myself to be the failure she always knew I was.'

'Don't be ridiculous,' Tess argued weakly. 'She was worried about us—'

'About you and Lara, you mean,' Max interrupted.

'About us all and wants to help us out.' There, I've said it. She stopped breathing, waiting for Max to explode.

He exploded. 'NO. Absolutely not. Not under any circumstances. Not even if we were homeless and starving. I will never, ever take money from your mother.'

Tess opened her mouth to protest but Max hadn't finished. 'And before you ask, I won't be taking handouts from my parents either. This is *my* mess, *my* family and I will get us out if it.'

Tess began to seethe; she could even feel her fists clenching at her husband's obstinacy.

'Mum, this is brilliant!' Lara ran into the kitchen and dragged her tense parents out onto the patio. She had been given the day off school to come and see the new flat and to take a look round some potential new schools. 'Look!' she said delightedly.

Tess and Max tried to find something brilliant in the pocket-sized wilderness. Lara ran over to the back wall which was covered in ivy and brambles and who-knows-what-other climbing greenery. Then she slipped behind the foliage as if it were a curtain. Seconds later, she jumped out, eyes shining with excitement.

'It's a den! I've always wanted a den!'

She rushed up to her parents and hugged them. And Tess and Max hugged her back. The familiar contact temporarily restored them.

Once Lara had picked her bedroom (the one with the view over the greyhound stadium – now *that's* urban chic, Fiona was to observe), Max suggested they take a walk around the area, their new neighbourhood.

'Good idea,' Tess agreed, taking one last look at their soon-to-be new home before locking the ominous number of locks and venturing out with her family into the New Land.

Tess checked she had her can of hairspray in her handbag ('The middle-class woman's equivalent of mace,' Fiona had advised. 'Spray first, think later').

Max checked he had his old football referee's whistle in his pocket ('The middle-class man's version of a gun,' Graham had advised. 'Blow it in the little thug's face, then run like the wind!')

Both felt slightly stupid but unexpectedly brave and adventurous as they stepped out. Both wished they could just go home, to their old home, and pretend that none of this was happening.

Fiona sat in Millie's kitchen, toying with a piece of fruit cake. She watched Millie moving slowly, obviously trying to control her morning sickness.

Neither of them had been pregnant for five years and Fiona was shocked at the brutal effect it was having. Millie looked worn out and, frankly, old. Her flat hair hung loosely around a pale exhausted face and a pair of thick, unflattering glasses completed the picture of the downtrodden housewife of the 1930s.

'Why aren't you wearing your contacts?' Fiona asked.

'I'm throwing up all day at the moment and my eyes are getting sore from it all,' Millie replied gloomily.

Fiona wanted to tell her friend that this was no excuse for not washing her hair and putting on clean clothes. But Tess was the one who was good at saying that sort of thing. If Fiona said it, she knew she'd just sound like a bitch.

'I feel disloyal sitting here without Tess,' she said finally. 'And I know that's a ridiculous thing to say but I can't help myself.'

Millie was pulling a tray of brownies from the oven and putting a fresh batch in. 'I feel the same. I mean, while I'm still baking for the café, I feel she's still part of ... us, but when that stops and she's moved ...'

Fiona folded her arms stubbornly. 'I don't care what happens. I'm not going to let her drift away. I need her. Our circumstances will change but that doesn't mean that *we* will. We can't.'

Millie felt the same way.

Their conversation was stilted. Although the three of them hadn't been surgically grafted together and they'd frequently paired off to do certain things that one of them didn't enjoy, this was different. It was a gloomy foretaste of how their lives could be in the near future. Just two of them.

They were a threesome, that's how they were supposed to be. They each knew their place within that threesome. They liked having that definition in their lives. They got their bearings from each other. With one of them leaving, they felt everything falter beneath them.

Tess was leaving them not just by moving, because Heaverbury wasn't that far away, but by extracting herself from their shared lifestyle. She wouldn't be able to afford to do the things they'd always done together. And when they thought about what these were, then took out everything that cost money, there wasn't much left. This realisation had made them all feel slightly uneasy and more than a little shallow.

'We'll still meet up for coffee all the time,' Fiona had said desperately when Tess had started crying the night before. They'd found tenants for the house and would have to move out in two weeks' time.

'In each other's houses,' Millie had added, worried that Tess wouldn't even be able to afford to buy coffee. She was right to be worried. Tess and Max's financial situation was grimmer than their friends could ever imagine.

Tess laughed despite her tears. 'You mean, you'll take the wagon train over to Crappy Valley?'

Fiona pretended to consider this. 'Well, obviously we'll have to get our jabs done ...'

Millie joined in. '... and buy bullet-proof vests ...'

'... and change our currency ...'

'... and pay a local juvenile villain to stand guard over our hubcaps ...'

'... mind you, we'll be able to place bulk orders for crack ...'

'... it could replace the after-dinner mint as the essential dinner party accompaniment ...'

Tess held up her hands in surrender. 'I think you're mistaking reality for *The Bill*,' she intoned, mimicking Max's voice wickedly. 'It's not that bad actually.'

'You're kidding!' Fiona held her hand to her forehead in mock-despair. 'But we were looking forward to you going native. It would have been so cool, like guest-starring in a Guy Ritchie film.'

Millie tutted. 'And now you're telling us that it's not that bad. What kind of sales pitch is that? "Heaverbury – It's Not That Bad Actually!" '

Tess didn't answer. Because it wasn't that good either. Or at least it hadn't seemed so at first. And even the good things brought complications with them.

Tess and Max loosened their grip on their ridiculous weapons after a few minutes. Once they realised that this was not the post-apocalyptic wasteland they'd envisaged, they relaxed and began to see the possibilities for them as a family. As always, it took a child to see beyond the superficial flaws to find the values that were really important.

'Look,' said Lara, 'an adventure playground! Fantastic!'

Tess noticed that it was run down and looked like a minefield of potential accidents. Then she realised that this was half the appeal to Lara. This was a child who had been given every material luxury a girl of her age could desire but who'd been cosseted and protected to such a degree that danger was the last remaining item on her wish list – free but forbidden.

Tess swallowed her apprehensions. At least we're only five minutes from the nearest casualty department, she reminded herself. She made a mental note to take a couple of practice drives to the hospital before Lara submitted her hitherto unscarred body to the onslaught of this death trap.

'Did you see any needles in there?' Max whispered, as Lara ran on, occasionally gazing back in wonder at the playground. Since Tess's apparent acceptance of this new situation, Max had dropped his enthusiastic sales pitch with relief.

Exhausted from all his exertions, he wanted Tess to take over the role of team leader, Mr Motivator, happy bunny. Most of all, he wanted to be able to sit in a quiet room by himself and worry away happily while Tess brought him glasses of red wine and found solutions to all his problems.

'Don't be so paranoid!' Tess snapped. But no, there weren't any. She'd looked at the ground very carefully as they passed but she didn't want Max to know that she shared his worries.

She wasn't sure why this was important but she'd decided that, at all times, one of them must be taking the positive line. She just hoped it wouldn't always have to be her. It was tiring being positive.

'Look Mum!' Lara had found something else that was magical.

'It looks like a large public toilet block,' Max observed under his breath. Tess hit him on the arm with her hairspray, which she'd taken hold of again when some teenagers walked by. They hadn't mugged her, hadn't even been interested in her. They'd just smiled at Lara and walked on.

'It's a community centre!' Lara read from the tatty board outside the main door. 'Wow, we didn't have a community centre before.'

That was true, Tess conceded. In Clapham we had alternative health centres, organic cafés and large kitchens in friends' houses. That met our needs before.

Lara was thrilled. 'Look at all the stuff they do here!'

Indeed it was an impressive list, including Brownies and Guides, keep-fit, dog-training, karate, salsa, it went on.

'Can't see carjacking for beginners,' Max muttered.

Tess hit him again.

Without hesitation, Lara pushed through the unlocked double doors and ran inside. Tess and Max hurried to catch up with her, both worried that she might stumble upon the local chapter of the Petrol-bomb Making and Riot Society.

When they got inside, the hall was spacious and spotlessly clean. Lara was talking to a woman about Tess's age. She had a striking face with deep brown eyes and a wide thin mouth. She was also completely free of make-up. The natural look was completed by her long shining blonde hair falling untidily over her shoulders. She was tall and angular, wearing tracksuit bottoms and a massive sweatshirt that looked as if it belonged to a heavy-weight boxer. Her complete disregard for grooming appealed to something in Tess that she'd forgotten had once existed. She'd become so used to looking and dressing and even acting in a certain style that she'd lost touch with the carefree, careless girl and young woman who'd been more interested in pursuing her dreams than co-ordinating her separates and deep-conditioning her hair.

Tess felt tiny and fragile next to this imposing woman. Since Fiona and Millie were both fairly short, like her, she'd got used to the notion of women as being fundamentally small. She shook her head in an attempt to shake out this and other preconceptions that Nappy Valley had engraved on her critical faculties.

46

The stranger turned and stretched out her hand to Tess and Max.

'Hi there! Your lovely daughter tells me you're new to the area. Welcome! I'm Heather Rigg.'

'Tess Keane. And this is my husband Max. And you've met Lara.'

They all shook hands and Tess felt instantly comfortable with this friendly woman.

'Can't stop and chat right now,' Heather said briskly. 'Got a meeting with the council. We're trying to get more funds for the centre. But why don't we meet up for coffee?'

Tess was too stunned to come up with an excuse to say 'no'. She wanted to say: 'I'm sorry, but I don't know anything about you and my life is so complicated right now that I can only handle being with people I know well.' But she didn't. 'Erm, well, yes, that would be nice.'

'Great,' Heather said with enthusiasm. 'If you're free on Friday, why not pop round here at about eleven?'

Tess found herself agreeing even though she'd originally had no plans to come back here until the day she moved. She hadn't wanted to spend a single moment longer in this place than was absolutely necessary but suddenly she was looking forward to seeing this woman again.

She was immediately transported back to the day she'd first met Fiona and had experienced that wonderful buzz of sensing that she'd made a new special friend.

Children always think that this feeling is unique to them, that it stops when you grow up, that adult friendships lack the thrill and magic of those early connections. But Tess was 39 and she still marvelled at the impact a friend could make on the quality of her life.

Then, just as quickly and completely irrationally, Tess felt that she was somehow being unfaithful to Fiona and Millie by taking a step towards making a new friend.

But it was all too much to think of at this time. She'd agonise over it later although she didn't know who she'd be able to share it with. Max would think she was being ridiculous and she couldn't tell Fiona and Millie in case they *didn't* think she was being ridiculous and were genuinely offended by her swift and easy desertion of them. Her imagination took a leap forward in time to that fraught possibility of having to live a double life, with

47

two sets of friends who must never meet because they'd never get on.

She shuddered at the thought. Friendships are supposed to ease one's life not muddy it. Her life was already becoming tangled in ways she'd never considered.

Heather bustled around them, gathering papers from a small side office before encouraging them out of the main door and locking it behind them.

'Right, well, see you Friday. Good to meet you,' she said hurriedly and strode off. After a few paces, she turned and walked back.

'I know this will sound a crazy question,' she said, 'but I'd kick myself for not asking and then finding out that you could help.'

'Ask ahead,' Tess asked, amused.

'Well, we run yoga classes here but our teacher left suddenly last week. And no,' she said, looking pointedly at Max, 'before you ask, she wasn't the victim of a drive-by shooting or kidnapped by Yardies.'

Max flushed furiously. It was bad enough having a wife who could read his mind; he didn't need it from a complete stranger.

Tess coughed to stop a treacherous giggle from escaping. Heather went on.

'She found out she was pregnant. Don't ask. Anyway, we're looking for a new teacher. We've had a notice up for a while but nobody's come forward. So we're all asking everyone we know on the off-chance they might have a contact. It's not brilliant pay, but it's regular and it's cash-in-hand.'

'I could do it,' Tess said.

She looked around to see who'd spoken. Oh, I did, she realised. Max was staring at her in disbelief.

'Could you?' he said carefully. 'Shouldn't you think about it? I don't want you to ... overextend yourself.'

'Of course I could.' She turned towards Heather so she wouldn't have to face Max. 'In fact, we were just talking about me getting a part-time job.'

One that you could actually *do*, Max was communicating to her silently.

'That's absolutely amazing!' Heather exclaimed. 'I had a feeling you'd be a good person to ask!'

Tess smiled weakly. 'Amazing,' she agreed.

'We'll discuss it on Friday then. Bye!' And she was gone.

'Mum, what's yoga?' Lara asked innocently.

Max just stood there shaking his head like a dog in the back of a cheap car. 'Have you gone completely mad? You've never even done yoga, let alone taught it!'

Tess became defensive. 'I've done loads of other exercise. Yoga's just like slow aerobics. Anyway, I can get a book out on it and buy a video. I'm fit. I'm intelligent. I'm a fast learner. It's a job and I need a job. How hard can it be?'

Max didn't answer. He didn't dare. He'd just worry about it when he had a private moment.

Tess met up with Fiona and Millie later that afternoon. She told them all about the area, leaving out the first meeting with Heather. And the business of the yoga job. She now regretted her impulsive gesture in grabbing the job and didn't feel like dissecting her folly at this time.

Now I have secrets from my closest friends, she thought miserably. Great. It's even worse since they're both proving themselves to be true friends and not hiding behind the curtains, screening my calls and avoiding me as if debt was contagious. Unlike everyone else we know.

'So no pawnbrokers? No transport caffs with gangsters setting up contracts on rival gangleaders while talking about how much they love their mums?' Fiona was disappointed by the initial description of Tess's new homeland. Where were the tales of local colour they'd been banking on to entertain them, since they wouldn't be sharing costly trips to the cinema every week from now on?

Tess looked apologetic. 'I bought a local paper and looked in the classified section for dens of iniquity, but there were none listed.'

'I suppose if you can't find any dens of iniquity, you could always start your own,' Fiona suggested.

Tess considered this. 'You mean like a literary salon but instead of local writers and wits, I'd have fences and narks ...'

'What exactly is a nark?' Millie asked Fiona, who seemed to be very clued up on the London underworld all of a sudden.

'No idea,' Fiona replied, 'but if Tess is starting a den of iniquity, she should definitely have at least one of them.'

Tess had quickly forgotten about Heather and her earlier twinge of optimism. These were her friends. These were all she needed. She and Fiona and Millie had eased back into their old rapport, the comfortable banter, each knowing their place, their cues. She was afraid of leaving again. She wanted everything to stay just like this forever.

'What does one wear to a den of iniquity?' Millie asked.

'Anything but Gap, I would guess,' Fiona opined.

And so they'd gone on, terrified of having to talk seriously of their future. But the demands of being relentlessly upbeat had exhausted them. Later that evening, Fiona had phoned Millie and they'd agreed to meet the next morning.

'So how do you think she's coping?' Fiona asked.

Millie shrugged. 'I don't think the scale of what's happening has hit her yet. She's doing her best to treat the whole disaster like a big adventure for Lara's sake, and also for her and Max. I don't know about you but I can't think of a single positive thing about all this.'

Fiona agreed. They sat miserably, hating the awkwardness that had almost overnight replaced the glorious ease the three women had shared for so long.

'On a lighter note, when does your mother arrive?' Millie asked wickedly.

'Thank you for reminding me of that,' Fiona said gloomily. 'She flies in on her broomstick next week. But first of all, we've got to move all the bedrooms around. She'll need to be right next door to a bathroom, so Nathan will have to give up his bedroom and move into the spare room.'

'How do the kids feel about their gran moving in?'

'They can't wait! She gives them money all the time. And sweets. And she lets them eat whatever they want. She even cooks them all separate meals!'

'Poor you,' Millie said sympathetically. 'Here, have another brownie.'

'Aren't these supposed to be for the café?'

Millie thought about this. She picked up the brownie, dropped it on the floor, then picked it up and put it back on the plate in front of Fiona.

'There you go. The café couldn't use it now it's been on the floor. Besides, it closes down at the end of the week and it was never able to sell everything I produced.'

Fiona took a bite from the still-warm cake. 'You are truly shameless. Do you realise we'd scream at our kids if they ate food off the floor?'

Millie stole a corner of brownie from Fiona's plate. 'That's why we became parents, Fi. So we could wreak injustice on our children the way our parents did to us and their parents did to them.'

'Good point,' Fiona spluttered with her mouth full.

She felt better. The brownie helped, as did Millie's company. But Fiona had a nagging feeling that this would be not enough to support her when her mother finally landed. Her life stretched before her like a prison sentence with her mother playing the part of warder. She knew that this was melodramatic but, then, she knew what her mother was like.

She had relied on having Tess to help her through this. While Millie's nurturing presence was a comfort and while she had a gift for adapting her persona to reflect and meet Fiona's needs, Tess was a constant. Fiona had grown dependent on Tess's calm reserve. She'd perceived, quite early on in their friendship, that Tess had completed a stage of her development that in most women is still evolving. That she had decided how much of herself was available for public consumption and how much was to be locked away. Fiona found this inflexibility inspiring. She wanted to be like Tess and, with the imminent arrival of her mother, she needed lessons in self-protection on an ongoing basis.

She had to believe that the essence of their friendship would survive the external onslaught.

'I don't think I'm going to survive this,' Graham said grimly as Fiona massaged his aching back. He'd obediently moved all the furniture around as his wife barked out her orders. He wasn't the most physical of men and this activity had strained all those muscles that were not exercised during his completely sedentary working day.

Fiona loved the soft compliance of his body. It was a vulnerability that she didn't permit herself. She had exercised rigorously from the day she stopped breastfeeding each of her children. While she'd never managed to tame her stomach, which she became expert at camouflaging, she insisted that the rest of her body remain hard, with no tell-tale 'give'. It was the closest thing she'd ever discovered to a suit of armour and easier to maintain than any kind of emotional barrier.

Graham wasn't ashamed of his slightly flabby body or his thinning hairline that he did nothing to disguise, and she loved this too. The reality of Graham was that he cared more about her than he did himself. She hugged him suddenly.

'Don't be silly!' she said, fully aware that there was nothing silly about his concerns.

The furniture-shifting was the easy part. The shift in their lifestyles would be far more penetrating. Having any elderly parent move in would have a far-reaching impact on any young family's life. Having Daphne Guinn, a woman whose sole hobby seemed to be annoying relatives, move into an already crowded house (where her most hated son-in-law lived), was certain to bring disaster.

Fiona and Graham had spent many unpleasant evenings arguing about Daphne.

'Why can't we just burn her at the stake like other evil witches?' Graham asked reasonably. Actually, he didn't ask this. But he thought it a lot and gained a great deal of comfort from indulging his more vicious flights of fantasy at his mother-in-law's expense. It kept him sane to think these things while his civilising impulses, sorely challenged by this woman, forced him to debate the subject lovingly and logically with his wife.

'Why does she have to live with us?' Graham asked in an even voice. 'Your brother has a much bigger house than us.'

Fiona sighed, adopting the same tone used when trying to persuade her sons that eating a sandwich with one hand in their trousers is not socially desirable. 'I've told you, she thinks she can help with the kids. Her other grandchildren are all grown up. If she's going to live with one of us, she wants to make herself useful.'

Graham spent a pleasant hour thinking of ways his mother-in-law might make herself useful, none of which were fit for sharing with his wife but all of which served to suppress his resentment in the short term.

Later that night, he noticed that Fiona was uncharacteristically subdued. This happened so rarely that he was immediately concerned.

'Oh just ignore me,' Fiona said, trying, and failing, to appear casual. 'It's just Mum.'

Just Mum. Two words when Fiona would usually use a thousand. Graham cursed himself for all the abuse he'd heaped upon Fiona during recent weeks when he should have known that Fiona must have been feeling much much worse.

He pulled her close and held her tight. She relaxed for the first time in an age. He didn't need to say anything. She knew what he was thinking.

I know what your mother does to you with her judgemental silences, he said without speaking; I see how she favours your brothers, praising their wives' bland cooking, their colourless children, their magnolia homes while subtly putting you down at every opportunity; no, you're not paranoid, she does very slightly turn her mouth down at Tess and Millie; yes, she does enjoy watching you try so hard.

That's the main reason why I love this man, Fiona thought, as if I need any more, simply because he knows and loves me. And because he's kind.

'Sorry I've been such a pain,' Graham said softly. 'Of course your mum can come and live here.'

He knew why this was so important to Fiona. All she wanted was to win her mother's approval, as a daughter, mother and woman. And this was her chance.

Graham summoned up all his resolve that had run for hiding at the mention of the dreaded Daphne. Whatever it takes, I'm going to help Fiona do whatever she has to do, be whatever she has to be, to break the stranglehold her mother has over her.

And if that means our home turns into a battlefield, then so be it.

Max and Tess weren't speaking to each other although they were holding hands to reassure Lara that they were OK. A year earlier, the parents of one of her schoolfriends had got divorced and Lara had been terribly affected. She'd started having nightmares and had become obsessed with her own parents splitting up.

Tess and Max only had to argue about the TV remote control for Lara to burst into tears and panic about having to choose which parent she wanted to live with. She refused to be pacified and, in desperation, her parents had agreed that they would always present a picture of comforting solidarity even when they wished to tear each other's heart out.

Tess broke the silence. That was her role in this marriage.

'I don't see why you're getting in such a state about this. It's my problem not yours.'

'I suppose I was just surprised at the way you lied so easily. It wasn't like you. We've been married a long time and I thought I knew you. It makes me wonder what else you're capable of.'

'For heaven's sake, Max, it's just a little yoga class in a community centre, I'm not pretending to be a qualified heart surgeon!'

Max bristled at her sarcasm. 'It's more than that and you know it. I'm as nervous as you are about starting up again here. I just really need to rely on some kind of constancy. And right now, the only constancy is you and me, us, our marriage. And now, all of a sudden, you've reinvented yourself as a liar and a yoga teacher!'

Now it was Tess's turn to bristle. She longed to yank her hand out of his but Lara's needs always took precedence over any of her own.

'I think you're just annoyed that I got a job before you.'

Lara stopped walking to look round at her parents. They responded by beaming insanely at her and each other but succeeded only in looking like snarling bull terriers. Lara turned away and walked on, strangely reassured.

Tess and Max allowed their alarming grins to drop in relief. Continuing in silence for a while along the main shopping road, they saw Lara stop again outside another building that looked vaguely municipal.

'Oh goody,' Max said drily. 'Perhaps you could get a job here as well. Maybe as a nuclear physicist? Or maybe a Latin-American formation dancing team leader? How do you feel about that for a career move?'

Tess dug her nails into his hand to make her feelings clear, before remembering that she'd bitten them all to the quick a few days earlier. I'm regressing, she'd thought. Just at the time when I'm supposed to be taking great strides forward, I take up old habits again. If I don't keep a tight grip on myself, I'm going to end up plucking all my eyebrows out, which was another favoured method of self-mutilation when faced with problems in adolescence.

'What is this place?' she wondered out loud.

'I think it's called a *library*,' Lara replied, her annoying little fingers framing annoying little quotation marks around the word. 'You can tell because it says "HEAVERBURY LIBRARY" on the sign.'

Max and Tess were united once more in common hatred of their smart-aleck daughter. They grimaced, swallowed the abuse they wanted to hurl at her and concentrated on this new cultural nugget they'd stumbled upon.

'Hey look, Tess, a noticeboard,' Max called. 'Why not see if there's something here for you!' He smiled teasingly, a smile that stopped a few millimetres short of a withering glare.

They skimmed over the notices to pass the time while Lara proceeded to climb up an abstract sculpture of . . .

'What is she climbing over, Tess?'

Tess squinted to look for some form in the metal structure. 'I could be wrong but I think it's a naked man and a woman.'

Max squinted and then saw the same as Tess. 'Can you see what she's standing on?'

Tess saw, then closed her eyes quickly and turned away. 'It's best not knowing,' she said.

But Max wasn't listening. He was studying an ad on the noticeboard. Tess waited for him to make yet another dig at her about her new job but he was engrossed in a small card at the top of the board.

'What are you looking at?'

Max pointed to a yellow notice. Tess read it, sure that he must be pointing at the wrong card. MINICAB DRIVERS NEEDED. CHOOSE YOUR OWN HOURS. GOOD RATES OF PAY. MUST OWN CAR.

Tess was confused. 'Why are you looking at that?'

Max became animated. 'That would be perfect.'

Tess looked again, wondering what he was talking about.

Max prodded the minicab ad with an eager finger. 'This! Think about it. I can carry on looking for the sort of job I want but then do some taxi work to make some money. It will be completely flexible and you can make good money doing it.'

'Now you're the one who's mad!' Tess exclaimed. 'You're not a minicab driver. They're called Mickey and Terry and drive rusted Vauxhall Astras with their radios tuned to local soul music stations.' She tried to keep her voice light but she was actually concerned at Max's impulsive attitude. He was jumping in and out of character with such frequency that she was losing her grip on who he was.

Of one thing she was certain – she preferred the old Max. She knew where she was in relation to that husband. If he was going to insist on changing personality by the hour, she was going to have to do the same. Unless she just broke away and free-fell.

No. I can't do that.

Max shot a cold glance her way. 'If you can become a yoga teacher, then I can become a minicab driver. There, you said we both needed to get jobs quickly and now we have!'

Yes, but this wasn't quite what I'd had in mind, Tess thought. Just how many more surprises are we going to have to deal with?

# 4

'Oh dear, you have been in the wars, haven't you?'

Miss Blowers, the headmistress, tutted sympathetically as she read all the forms Tess and Max had provided which told the whole sad story of their enforced move and Lara having to leave her private school.

Because this was the middle of term and Heaverbury C of E Primary School was officially full, they had been forced to take extra measures to try and persuade Miss Blowers to admit Lara.

Max wanted to get up and leave immediately on the grounds that any grown woman who spoke to other adults using phrases like 'been in the wars' was not fit to be responsible for preparing young minds for the harsh world ahead of them.

Lara had been taken on a tour of the school and was to be interviewed by the deputy head. It wasn't an academic interview but she was being assessed for suitability for attending a church school.

Tess and Max had argued about this for hours.

'It's the best state school in the area,' Tess had insisted. 'It gets the best results, it has a good disciplinary record, what more do you need to know?'

Max was dubious. 'I just don't feel comfortable about sending her to a church school when we're not "churchy" people.'

'Do you think all the other families there are?' Tess asked in exasperation. 'They send their kids there because it's a good school. If that means they have to go to church for a few months to get them in then so be it.'

'But we don't go to church!' Max had exclaimed. 'And you have to go *before* your child is accepted.'

'Then we'll have to find a way around it,' Tess said firmly.

'No way.' Max put his foot down, only to have Tess prise it from the floor a few days later.

'Heather told me of this incredible vicar she knows. She gave him a call and told him all about us. He says that if we go and see him, he'll put a word in for us with the school.'

Max groaned. 'Oh no, please. Anything but incredible vicars! Do you have any idea what churches are like nowadays? The vicars are all called things like Jimbo and Baz and they all wear stripy jumpers and back-to-front baseball caps.'

Tess laughed. 'You saw that in a film on Channel Four!'

Max retreated to the sulk where he was spending ever greater periods of time lately. 'I know what it's like. They don't sing hymns any more, you know. They have drummers and everyone claps and people come up to you and say "Peace be with you" and things like that.'

'There should be a law against it,' Tess said drily.

Max glared at her. 'If a complete stranger comes anywhere near me with his hand outstretched and mentions the word "peace", I'll deck him.'

And so, when Tess phoned Heather's Incredible Vicar she asked, in the most diplomatic terms, if he could keep his hands and his peace to himself when he met her husband. He laughed and agreed. Because of the urgency of their situation, he agreed to speak to the school governors immediately so that they could get their application started without delay.

'So I'll look forward to seeing you in church on Sunday, then Tess?' he said finally, 'you and Max and Lara?'

'Of course,' Tess agreed, thinking that even divine intervention would not be able to persuade her husband to set foot in a church.


'My husband was exactly the same,' Heather had said when Tess mentioned her reservations.

'So how did you get round him?' Tess had asked, always open to new initiatives in husband-manipulation. She felt that she had exhausted Fiona and Millie's repertoire of techniques and ploys and this new challenging life was going to require some serious strategic planning. Heather was prevented from answering the question by the phone ringing. Tess was impressed by Heather's smooth handling of a complicated request about t'ai chi classes for the deaf.

At the end of the call, Heather handed Tess a chipped mug filled almost to overflowing with stomach-eroding tea. It was so dark that Tess wondered if Heather had actually added milk or merely introduced it to the picture of a cow. But she was getting used to Heather's tea. More to the point, she was getting used to Heather.

Settling into a new friendship is no different to any other new relationship. There is that early awkwardness when you share cautiously edited autobiographies and try to make yourself seem more interesting and individual than you really are. Then, if you're lucky, comes the elation when you start to recognise something of yourself in the other person. It's a bit like falling in love, that intoxicating feeling that you might have a slightly different future than you'd imagined because you'd be accompanied on the journey by a different tour guide.

The only thing missing from the experience was the opportunity to share the excitement with your old friends. Tess didn't tell Fiona and Millie about Heather, wisely sensing that they might be less than thrilled to hear they'd been replaced so quickly.

Too, too strange, Tess had thought recently, as she held a silent debate with herself, arguing the definition of betrayal.

That first coffee (which had turned out to be Tess's first experience of Heather's tea) had been a far cry from leisurely mornings frittered away at Organique.

Instead of collapsing into comfy armchairs covered in chintz, Tess and Heather had to rummage around the community centre chairs until they found two with clean (ish) seats.

Instead of a latte made from organic milk and coffee beans picked by someone in Brazil paid a fair wage (Tess and Max imagined that his name was Juan and he sang revolutionary songs to his Juanita), they had tea made with tea bags stuffed with a grey powdery debris.

Instead of a harmonious background hum of chatter, guffaw and the occasional whine of a toddler demanding an organic satsuma, Heather and Tess struggled to make themselves heard over the fearsome background thunder of road drills, daytime television at top volume and some ripe language emanating from the adjoining primary school playground.

And instead of discussing reading systems, respective merits of the two local violin schools and property prices in the Dordogne, Tess was relieved to finally have someone who was not only happy to discuss money worries and husbands who refused to go to church, but actually shared the problems and had practical tips for overcoming them.

'You'll think I'm terrible,' Tess began cautiously.

Heather waved her hand dismissively. 'Unlikely. Go on, try and shock me.'

Tess looked embarrassed. 'It's just that I think I'm more scared of the lack of money than anything else. My parents were quite well off and Max and I have always been fairly comfortable. And although I know you can't buy happiness or buy your way out of trouble, I've become used to options where money is not a consideration. When you're broke, well, I'm simply not sure I have the resources ...'

Heather almost spat her tea out, she was laughing so much. 'You've got to be kidding! Broke? Tell me. In your allegedly tiny flat, will you be bringing a TV? Video? DVD player? Furniture that was not assembled from a flatpack? Breadmaker?'

Tess nodded sheepishly at each question. Heather continued.

'Computer?'

'Obviously,' Tess said. 'But that's a necessity, not a luxury.' She spotted Heather's amusement and felt obliged to expand on her generalised statement. 'We used to have three.'

Now Heather laughed out loud. Tess smiled, embarrassed at her own self-destructive words. 'In our defence, we *needed* three, or it seemed as if we needed three. Lara had one for all her school work, then we had one for the business and one for family use in the living room so that Lara could only use the Internet under our supervision.'

Heather raised one eyebrow. 'So you are struggling to get by with one computer. And you call this being broke?' Her kind eyes softened the bluntness of her accusation.

'I said you'd think I was terrible!' Tess said. 'I mean, I'm not stupid. I know that we're not really poor, we won't be requesting soup runs from the Salvation Army in the immediate future, but ...'

'... but you've got used to having things easy, never knowing exactly how much money is in your bank account but always knowing that there'll be enough, buying the best, getting used to the best, until you actually believe you *need* the best.' Heather finished Tess's excuse smoothly.

'I'm not that bad. I don't think I've ever wasted money. But you're right about not having to think about it. It's a worry and I've spent all my married life telling my husband about the pointlessness of worrying.'

'In time you'll learn that they do sell food in shops apart from Marks and Spencer,' Heather said, teasing her.

'Now you think I'm shallow,' Tess said miserably. 'Next, you're going to remind me of the starving millions.' She punished herself by taking a deep swig from the grim tea. 'When I think how many times I've given that speech to Lara and finally I learn for myself how powerless we are to acquire any sense of perspective in our own situations.'

Heather was watching with a suppressed smile while Tess tried to mask her shudders as she swallowed the tea.

'You're not shallow. Well, no more than the rest of us. I've been there.'

Tess looked surprised. 'You?'

Heather nodded. 'I used to run my own PR consultancy. We had it all – the big house, kids at private school and, don't tell anyone, but we had four computers!'

Tess became aware that her look of astonishment could be interpreted as insulting so she quickly settled it into a bland listening expression. Heather snorted as she read Tess's motives behind this failed attempt at tact.

'Don't worry, I know what you're thinking and I'm not offended. Let me guess how your reasoning goes: she's not wearing a floaty Monsoon dress so she can't be an earth mother who's choosing to slum it for bizarre political reasons; her clothes are cheap which means that she's got no money; she's not working but it can't be because she doesn't need the money so that means she's probably not qualified to do anything lucrative; she's at home in a community centre so she's used to socialising with people who can't afford health clubs or West End theatres. Conclusion: she is a soap-opera working-class heroine struggling to exist in a cruel world which offers her no prospects for escape or improvement.'

Tess's rising colour confirmed that this was pretty much her take on Heather. She was even more embarrassed that she'd judged Heather so quickly and so inaccurately on their first meeting. She hadn't heard Heather's pleasant, educated voice, she'd simply taken in her scruffy clothes and unstyled hair and placed her in the mental compartment which she had prepared in advance for Heaverbury types. Before she could deny this in any convincing manner, Heather touched her hand gently. 'Don't worry. As I said, the reason I know what you're thinking is that I've been in your position.'

'So what happened to you?' Tess asked, ashamed at her almost desperate hope that Heather's story would be more appalling than her own. If this well-adjusted, likeable woman could survive a devastating change of circumstances then maybe Tess could too.

Heather took Tess's cup and washed up quickly, before switching off the lights and striding towards the door in an almost seamless flow of activity. Tess found herself following this dervish, exhausted by Heather's purposeful drive.

As Heather locked the doors with keys from an enormous bunch, she answered Tess's question. 'The same as you. Overextended loans, husband losing job, me being out of the job market for too long, house repossessed, debts that may never be paid off.'

Her cheerful smile made Tess feel humble and more than a little uncomfortable. She decided to return to safer waters. 'You mentioned that you had trouble persuading your husband to go to church to get your kids into the right school?' she said, hopefully. 'How did you manage it?'

Heather turned to look at her. 'Didn't I mention it?' she said. 'I never did manage it. Alan refused to accept that things had changed, that we were going to have to make sacrifices where before we'd bought our way into and out of every situation. He didn't even want to move here. He thought we should find some way of borrowing more money and renting a shoebox somewhere in our old neighbourhood. He was possessed with a need to avoid change.'

Tess understood this need but didn't say anything.

Heather went on. 'He refused to think about state schools for the kids. He said we'd have to get a loan somehow to keep them in their private schools. While I was going round looking at other schools and houses, Alan was answering these really dodgy ads in the *Sun* which claimed to lend money to anyone!'

Now Tess was shocked. 'So how did you bring him round finally?'

'I didn't,' Heather replied. 'He refused to face reality. He seemed determined to drag us even further into debt, although obviously he didn't see it like that. Alan always believed that, any minute now, his fortunes would change for the better.'

'So?' Tess asked, unable to see how this couple could have resolved the gulf between them.

'So,' Heather answered simply. 'I left him.'

Tess found herself clinging to Max a little more closely whenever she thought of Heather's marriage which collapsed so quickly under similar pressures. Until now, her focus had been on sorting out their immediate practical problems. But she'd become painfully aware that a greater threat was hanging over them. If they didn't unite *before* they began this difficult stage in their married life, they might not have the chance once the tough new reality descended and engulfed them.

Their first challenge was the school interview. It was nothing like the interview for Leonard Hall, where Lara's current head-teacher seemed to have been assessing parents according to their potential for providing valuable or original donations for the school's famous annual auction.

They had been advised by other parents that this was the secret of getting their child into this, the best private school in the area. At the time, Max had been handling the advertising for an airline account and he'd casually mentioned the possibility of obtaining long-haul tickets.

Needless to say, Lara was admitted.

This current interview at a shabby but cheerfully run state primary school was another country and neither Tess nor Max knew the language.

Miss Blowers seemed to be genuinely concerned about how Lara was being affected by the family's recent problems and suggested a strategy for encouraging a particularly sensitive teacher to be designated to Lara. It would be an ongoing mentoring relationship that would pick up any problems Lara might be experiencing and deal with them before they became insurmountable.

'Do you have auctions?' Max asked cynically, refusing to be

swayed by all this well-meaning kindness after months of harsh treatment at the hands of creditors.

Miss Blowers looked confused and Tess had to explain what Max was referring to.

'Oh! No, we don't do anything like that, but of course we have a summer fair and we do like parents to help out.'

Max looked sideways at Tess smugly.

Miss Blowers continued. 'By which I mean helping out on stalls. If Lara joins us, she'll be in Year Five, and her year is in charge of the Throw Wet Sponges At The Grown-up stall. So obviously, if you could be generous enough to volunteer your time and your face, we'd be terribly grateful!'

Tess returned Max's smug glance, already looking forward to throwing the first sponge.


Millie took a small bite of her brownie then dashed out of the room. Animal noises drifted down the hallway from the bathroom until she returned looking pale and miserable.

'Is it as bad as the others?' Fiona asked, remembering how seriously Millie had suffered from morning sickness before.

Millie nodded feebly. 'Worse, actually. I resent it more this time because I didn't plan this. With the others, I'd prepared myself for all the misery. Also, the kids were so little, I could just dump them on the au pair and go to bed. Now they're older, it's more complicated. There's a lot to think about, reading, homework, outings, that sort of thing. And you have to stay on the ball or they'll all turn into juvenile delinquents when you're not looking.'

Fiona understood. Once the kids started school, even the most selective private school, they slipped out of their parents' control to a large degree. Within days, they were coming home with words that they'd definitely not learned at Miss Smileybun's playgroup.

'You'll be fine in a few weeks,' she said, trying to sound comforting. 'The sickness will pass and then it'll all come back to you. It'll be like greeting an old friend! You've done this before, after all.'

Millie glared at her. 'If you even think about saying it'll be like shelling a pea after my last four, I'll have to shoot you.' She meant it as a joke but neither of them laughed.

Fiona held her hands up. 'Wouldn't dream of it.'

Millie was sorry for snapping but too preoccupied to apologise. Nothing about this pregnancy was right and it seemed to have triggered off a whole string of disasters. Rationally she knew it wasn't her fault that Tess was having to move, but she still took it personally.

She'd been relying on having the support of her two friends through this difficult time. Tim was claiming to be pleased about this 'happy accident' but she knew him too well to be fooled. He had pulled away from her slightly since the discovery. He'd been working later, phoning less often, kissing her more perfunctorily. She realised that she should talk to him about his feelings but she wanted to sort her own out first. And for that she needed her two friends.

The phone rang. Fiona was surprised to find herself feeling relieved at the interruption. In the past, they'd always been annoyed when someone called while they were chatting. But the silences were becoming more frequent and were no longer so companionable.

She squished tiny crumbs of brownie between her fingers and listened as Millie resumed a row that she and Tim had obviously started that morning. She amused herself by guessing what Tim was saying from Millie's side of the conversation.

'I left everything out, all you had to do was make their sandwiches ...' (But I missed my train and that made me late for the meeting)

'You should have got up earlier ...' (I would have done if I'd known you were going to dump all the kids' packed lunches on me)

'Well, it wasn't my fault if I was sick ...' (Are you trying to say that this was all MY fault?)

'Well, it wasn't an immaculate conception ...' (Excuse me if I'm not completely up-to-date with the vagaries of your ovulation peaks ...) Actually, Fiona was getting a bit carried away with her imaginings at this point, she realised. Tim was not the sort of man who talked about ovulation, but she chuckled at the thought.

'Sorry, Tim, can you hold on a second?' Millie put her hand over the mouthpiece. 'What are you laughing at, Fiona?'

Fiona stopped laughing. She sat up straight like a naughty schoolgirl caught cheating at a maths test. 'Nothing,' she said, blushing furiously.

Millie went back to her call. Fiona gave up her original game and tried flicking bits of brownie at the ceiling instead.

'Look I've got to go, Tim, Fiona's here.'

Fiona didn't like the long silence that followed. It was far too long for the perfectly adequate and polite 'That's nice, dear,' which would have been the appropriate response to Millie's announcement of Fiona's presence. It sounded ominously as if Tim was running through a list of expletives. Millie was still listening. Fiona was aghast. What is that man saying? There was even enough room in there for a 'Never let that trollop darken our door again.'

What's the matter with me? Fiona asked herself. I must be going mad. I'm imagining conversations I can't hear, I'm even insulting myself on behalf of my friend's husband, a man who probably doesn't find me interesting enough to insult.

Millie replaced the receiver just as a piece of brownie shot past her towards the ceiling.

'What exactly are you doing, Fiona?' she asked, genuinely curious.

Fiona stopped mid-flick. 'Trying to get bits of brownie to stick to the ceiling.'

'Of course you are.'

'So how's Tim?' Fiona gave Millie an opportunity to repeat all his insults. Or not.

'He was in a bit of a mood. Bad morning. But he cheered up towards the end. He's going out to lunch with an old schoolfriend.'

'Well, that should do the trick. Graham always cheers up after a lads' lunch. They can bore each other about cricket and go "phwoar" discussing beach volleyball and have belching competitions.'

'I don't think it's going to be that sort of lunch,' Millie said quietly.

'What other kind is there?'

'It's a female schoolfriend.'

Fiona raised an eyebrow. 'Oh, well then, it'll be an hour of reminiscences then they'll run out of things to say to each other, lie about keeping in touch and leave swiftly. I've done it myself.'

Millie got up to remove another tray from the oven. 'I think this will be a bit different. This is his childhood sweetheart.'

*

'Now,' said Miss Blowers efficiently. 'Church.'

Max tensed visibly. He and Tess had discussed this before they got there. Once he'd been convinced that this was the only suitable (free) school in the area, Max grudgingly conceded that they were at least going to have to keep up a pretence of being moderately churchy people until Lara was settled.

The hypocrisy didn't bother either of them. Well, it would have done a month earlier. But now they were desperate. They no longer had the money for principles. Principles were like organic food, obviously the correct choice but only if you could afford them.

They'd agreed that Tess would do all the talking, since Max couldn't talk about church without getting carried off on a tirade about how *Songs of Praise* had dumbed down and was now full of *Big Brother* rejects babbling on about how 'All Things Bright and Beautiful' had been their favourite hymn in school and how they loved daffodils.

So Tess smoothly fielded the questions, referring to John, the Incredible Vicar, as if he were their very own personal spiritual guide, or at the very least as if they'd met him.

But Miss Blowers was no fool. She played along but it was obvious that she didn't believe a word.

'The key thing we're looking for is your *future* commitment rather than your past,' she said pointedly, focusing particularly on Max, who had the grace to blush.

'Of course,' Max said guiltily.

'Good,' Miss Blowers seemed satisfied with the responses. 'Then I'll look forward to seeing you in church every Sunday!'

Tess and Max looked puzzled. They'd thought they could amble along for a few weeks then drift away without being noticed.

Miss Blowers smiled. 'Didn't John tell you? I go to that church myself.'

'Who?' Graham asked.

'Tim Parsons,' his secretary replied.

Graham looked puzzled, then it clicked. 'Oh, Tim! Yes, of course, can you put him through? Hello? Tim? What's up? Is it Millie? Is she OK? The kids?'

They were the obvious questions. While they'd socialised with their wives and families for ten years, they'd never become friends as such. They'd had the occasional lunch or dinner when Tim needed financial advice or Graham needed computer advice; they went to see the sort of violent, brainless films that their wives loathed but that was as far as it went. Phone calls at work were almost unheard of.

Tim was anxious to put his mind at ease. 'Nothing to panic about! All are well apart from Millie throwing up all day every day. Still, I'll have to get used to that, won't I?'

Graham detected a hint of resentment and wondered if Fiona was right in her belief that Tim was pleased about this new baby. 'I'm glad everything's all right. So what can I do for you?'

Tim cleared his throat. In fact he cleared his throat continually throughout the conversation. Graham was not the most intuitive man in the world but even he could work out that Tim was suffering from nerves rather than a lazy epiglottis.

'This is a bit awkward,' Tim said finally.

Graham waited for him to go on then realised that he was going to have to coax it out. Unfortunately he wasn't experienced in this area.

He'd been married for 12 years to Fiona, a woman who told him every little thing that passed through her mind, whether he wanted to hear it or not. Living with Fiona was like having a radio on 24 hours a day. He'd developed a technique whereby he could tune in and out at will, instinctively turning up the volume when something of (relative) importance was being mentioned.

As their marriage settled in, he grew to realise that this verbal barrage was one of the positive reasons he'd married her rather than an unexpected downside. It liberated him from having to make small talk, something at which he was hopelessly inept having sadly been born with no intuitive sense of tact or diplomacy.

'It's like a disability,' he confessed to Fiona after he'd offended all of her friends and most of her family (especially her mother) within four weeks of meeting her. 'It's best for everyone if I don't say anything or if I only respond to clear, unambiguous questions requiring factual answers.'

Once he'd made this resolution, he realised that everybody would find him dull but knew that boring was preferable to offensive: less entertaining but more conducive to keeping marriage and friendships intact.

Fortunately Fiona had found this an endearing quality and had not regarded it as an impediment to marrying him. In fact, just as Graham had grown to see her volubility as a desirable attribute, so she had learned to regard his enforced reserve as the perfect foil. She was smart enough to realise that she couldn't possibly have married someone as talkative as herself. Apart from anything else, they'd never have been invited anywhere.

He only ever relaxed totally when he was with Fiona. She knew him and, even knowing him, loved him.

But the disadvantage of this long and happy marriage with his verbal opposite was that he'd never had the opportunity to develop his conversational skills beyond those of the average monosyllabic teenager. Unless his mother-in-law was the subject, of course, in which case a magic switch was flipped on turning him into a ghetto-raised rap singer spewing out his resentment with uncontrolled venom.

Unfortunately he didn't think Tim had phoned to discuss Graham's mother-in-law so he was at a complete loss. He was also praying the man wasn't about to ask him any questions requiring an input that wasn't strictly factual or analytical.

Unable to think of an original gambit to keep this torture flowing, he repeated his earlier opening. 'So, Tim, what can I do for you?'

He cringed at his feeble effort but it seemed to do the trick. In fact, he couldn't shut Tim up after this.

'Probably nothing but I didn't know who else to ask. I mean obviously I couldn't ask Millie, I spoke to her about it, or rather I mentioned it to her, but then that tone came into her voice, you know the sort of tone, so I didn't go any further but then when I put the phone down, I realised that I had to speak to someone but there was no one else. That's the thing about being married and having lots of kids, you lose all your old friends, well women don't lose them, they even make a whole load more ...'

He rambled on along this track while Graham slipped into his marital listening mode, editing the sounds with real talent, waiting for something, anything, meaningful to be said. Eventually, his sensors zoomed in on the point of this call.

'Excuse me for interrupting, Tim, what did you just say?'

'That I'm having lunch with an old schoolfriend. More than that, if I'm being honest, she was my first girlfriend. We went out together in the sixth form and then we split up when I went to university. We promised to stay in touch, of course, but you know what it's like when you go away to college.'

Graham knew. The mention of first girlfriends had stripped off an emotional plaster that he'd applied to his heart 20 years ago, a plaster that had been peeling off painfully in recent weeks. He closed his mind to that image.

'So she contacted me via that website, you know the one where you can track down all your old schoolfriends ... what am I saying? Of course you know! You were the one who put me onto it in the first place.'

'I just thought it would be interesting to see what became of old schoolfriends,' Graham said defensively. 'I only recommended reading the potted biographies. I didn't say anything about contacting anyone.'

'I know, I know. But it seemed harmless to add my name to the site.' He hesitated before continuing. 'In the beginning we just e-mailed each other, catching up on everything we'd done, that sort of thing. Then she gave me her phone number so I felt obliged to give her mine, just my work number. And to cut a long story short ...'

Graham raised his eyebrows at this patent misrepresentation of the last 20 minutes of their lives.

'... she phoned me this morning and I agreed to meet her for lunch. Today. But I feel strange about this as if I'm being disloyal to Millie, although I swear it's just curiosity. I think if I just see Alison once then ... well, you know.'

Graham knew. He'd replayed a similar scenario a thousand times himself. But he hadn't even gone as far as sending an e-mail. Too dangerous, something warned him. And not fair on Fiona who he sensed would feel betrayed by such an action. But if Tim was going to do it, maybe he could watch, see how it went and if it wasn't too disastrous, then, maybe ...

He was interrupted by the one question he hadn't wanted to answer.

'So the question is, Graham, do you think I should go or should I cancel and never contact her again?'

This was easy. Of course Tim should cancel. He was opening a door that he might never be able to close. He could end up with a foot, even just a toe, wedged in his doorway. Then he'd have to

70

open up a bit further. That was the thing with doors. Unless you sawed out a foot-shaped hole and closed the door that way. But then you ended up with a broken door. And what use was that?

Besides, what was the point in stirring up feelings, whether they were good or bad, if there was never any intention of carrying the process forwards? Of course Graham should tell Tim not to go. As one married man to another, whose wives were close friends, he should unequivocally advise him against this action.

'I think you should go,' he said.

'Well I think I can speak for both my husband and myself when I say that I'm very grateful for you agreeing to accept Lara mid-term like this and we would be delighted to take the place if it's offered to us.'

Max said nothing, still shocked at the thought that he was going to have to attend church every Sunday. Tess kicked him and he beamed reflexively. Years of under-table dinner-party kicks had trained him well.

Miss Blowers proffered her hand and they all shook enthusiastically.

As they all got up to leave, the headteacher suddenly seemed to remember something. Tess groaned inwardly. No more difficulties. Please.

Max was tensed, ready to pounce on this woman if she made one more demand of him. But it was Tess she was interested in this time.

'Heather Rigg was speaking to me about you last week.'

Max shook his head in amazement. It was like *Deliverance* here, everyone seemed to know each other, they were probably all related and played banjos every night in the bloody community centre. And Heather was turning out to be some kind of all-knowing, all-seeing goddess. Her presence was everywhere. Max hadn't met her since that first encounter but already he didn't like her.

Miss Blowers warmed to her topic. 'I must say I was very excited when she told me about you. It was the answer to a prayer!'

Now Tess was becoming uneasy. 'In what way?' she asked, cautiously.

'Well, we're very progressive here, you know. We're always

71

looking to expand our curriculum so when we lost one of our teachers a few weeks back, we were left with quite a problem.'

Now Tess was moving from uneasy to queasy. She had an ominous feeling she knew where this was heading.

'A problem?' Her voice was shaking.

'Not any longer!' Miss Blowers announced breezily. 'Heather said she was quite sure you'd be prepared to teach yoga to our children as well as in the community centre!'

Tess glared sideways at Max, silently willing him not to laugh.


Later she was to wish she'd allowed him that one moment of pleasure, even if it was sadistically motivated. Because this was turning into the worst, the absolute worst day of both their lives. Twenty-four hours before their move, they were packing their possessions, many of which they might not see again for years, if ever, into boxes. They'd measured the new flat carefully and calculated exactly how many of their things they'd be able to take with them and how many would have to go into storage.

When did we accumulate so much *stuff*? Tess asked herself in wonder. How can two people have so many possessions? She could account for all of them, or most of them. In the early years of their marriage, they'd spent their weekends in pursuit of conspicuous acquisition, filling their empty home and unwritten life story with purchases and anecdotes.

She let her eyes wander over all the stressed pine, the saggy, mismatched sofas and armchairs, the wall-to-floor shelf units stuffed with hundreds of books, most never to be picked up again; every surface lovingly filled with more stuff, antique pots filled with pot pourri or incense cones, windows and furniture draped with heavy, sensuous fabrics.

The effect was genteel but modern shabbiness, this particular effect only obtained at enormous expense and with considerable commitment. You'd have to dedicate a hefty chunk of your life to the exercise, to the exclusion of anything else of significance, before you could reach this pinnacle of class-ascending consumer achievement.

Tess sighed as she began the filtering process. It was like taking an inventory of their marriage. Worse than that, it was a competition. It was human, real-life *Pop Idol*, voting for your favourite anniversary present, your most precious pictures, the chairs, souvenirs, novelty stocking-fillers. If it was bigger than a paperback book, it had to be judged. In or out.

It was bloody, vicious and bloody.

'Which chair do you want to take?' Tess asked, pointing to two: his comfy bachelor chair or a big, deep armchair that they both snuggled up in to watch TV. There was only room for one.

Max was confident he knew the right answer to this one. 'The big one, of course.'

Tess stared at him. 'Then you're going to make me feel guilty for not letting you take your favourite chair,' she said accusingly. 'You'll resent me every time you sit in it. How do you think that will make me feel?'

'Then I'll take my favourite chair.'

'That was very clever, manipulating me into making the decision for you!' Tess cried.

'This isn't fair,' Max said quietly.

Well, whose fault is that? Tess didn't say it but she wanted to. That would come in time but her theory was that the longer she held back from unleashing it, the less raw the pain would be, the less collateral damage might ensue. She might even have forgiven him.

Ha ha.

Tess sighed. 'Take your chair. The other one is too big for the flat anyway.'

'That's great,' Max snapped, 'subtly implying that the new flat is tiny which, as you remind me continually, is my fault.'

And so it went on.

'Why are you putting that in the "no" box? That's a picture of the house we stayed in on our first holiday with Lara,' Tess whispered emotionally.

'I know, but we've already chosen all the pictures we're taking. We've no more wall space left.'

Tess started rummaging frantically in the "yes" box. 'Then we'll have to take something out. What about this one?'

'That's the place where we spent our honeymoon,' Max said. 'Are you saying that's less important than the other one? That our life had no meaning, no substance until Lara was born?'

And still it went on. Until their house, and 15 years of marriage, had been divided into 'yes' and 'no' boxes.

It was two o'clock in the morning by the time they'd finished.

They sat exhausted, physically and emotionally. There was nothing left that had not been boxed or tagged.

Except for two things, the first and only two things they'd needed and bought for their new life: a yoga video and an *A-Z* of Greater London and the surrounding counties.

Because in 48 hours' time, Tess would be leading her first lesson and Max was taking a family of four to Stansted Airport.

The only problem being, Tess had learned that yoga was nothing like aerobics and Max had learned that the car was being repossessed tomorrow.

# 5

Tess wished it could be raining or that black clouds would cast gloomy shadows over the green wisteria shoots and red comforting bricks. She wanted this goodbye to be easy, or at least easier than this. But the scene was shimmering in sunlight like a clichéd film set.

Tess adjusted her sense of perspective, looking at the road through the eyes of an interested observer rather than a smug resident. While it could be any residential street in any English town, with its mix of Victorian and Edwardian semis and terraced houses, there was something safe and affluent about this particular one.

Maybe it was the reassuring presence of state-of-the-art alarms on every front wall; or the well-established climbing plants smothering the brickwork, promising that there was nothing transient about the population; or the absence of graffiti and litter, all swiftly removed within hours of appearing by a community-proud resident (or his underpaid cleaner); or the big shiny people carriers parked bumper-to-bumper, the Renault Espaces and the Ford Galaxies stuffed with child seats and Bob the Builder wellington boots, the Land Rovers with roof racks specially adapted for skis, all confirming that the drivers, the house owners, were people like Tess and Max, or rather how they used to be.

Fiona and Millie were standing on the front pavement biting back tears while their husbands looked embarrassed and their kids looked bored. It was eight o'clock on Sunday morning and the street was silent (although Tess felt certain that somewhere an orchestra must be hammering out some Wagner to accompany this tragic drama).

There was no removals lorry, no team of men in overalls dropping boxes of priceless crystal on top of each other, just a battered white van with FRANK'S ECONOMY VANS — CHEAPEST IN SOUTH LONDON splashed across the sides. Max had rented it for a day and would be shunting back and forth until all their possessions had been redistributed either in the storage depository or their new flat.

To save the humiliation of big men in suits and sunglasses coming to repossess the car in front of their friends, Max had driven it to an agreed garage at six o'clock that morning where he surrendered it to a bleary-eyed teenager with a clipboard who might not have understood what he was signing, since he didn't speak during the entire transaction.

Tim and Graham were going to help with the loading and unloading once Max had dropped Tess and Lara off at the flat to begin the tricky process of turning it into a home.

Tess hugged her two friends bravely and they all smiled with lips pressed tightly together to stop scary words from spilling out. They'd all promised each other that they wouldn't treat today as if it were some kind of final farewell. But the memory of the promise was crumbling as Max staggered past them carrying a box labelled TESS AND MAX'S STUFF.

They'd allowed Lara to keep as many of her things as possible, wanting to protect her from deprivation at this level at least. But this left less space available for themselves. They'd reduced their 'stuff' to one box after a lot of agonising, and this small tatty box seemed to symbolise the fragile and impoverished state of their lives.

Millie and Fiona found themselves wondering whether they'd be capable of reducing and compartmentalising their own marriages into such small boxes. Finding the prospect too disturbing, they concentrated on Tess's misery.

'God, Tess, I know we said we weren't going to blubber but this is horrible,' Fiona said suddenly, clutching Tess as if she would never see her again.

Millie immediately adopted her usual role as moderator, pulling her two friends back from their emotional extremes into a more bearable zone.

'Come on now, stop this,' she said briskly. 'We're all meeting at Tess's for coffee on Tuesday. That's forty-eight hours away.

We've gone longer than that without seeing each other before. It's not exactly going cold turkey.'

They all pretended that they believed this and pulled themselves together. They chatted more calmly while Max tried to remember Frank's complicated instructions for closing the van's warped rusty doors involving a fist, a sharp kick and any swear word that came to mind.

Tim meanwhile was standing by the gate, ostensibly to prevent any of the nine children from throwing themselves beneath a car (or a milk float, which was the only vehicle about at this time). But actually he wanted to separate himself from all these people to think. Thinking was impossible at home with four children and a pregnant wife who was becoming increasingly irritable and demanding. Ironically, it was only in a more crowded situation like this that he was able to slip aside and escape attention.

He had a lot to think about. Or rather he had one thing to think about but with many, many implications. Lunch with Alison.

They'd recognised each other immediately and that surprised them both. They hugged without a trace of awkwardness before being shown to their table and immediately sinking into a fog of nostalgia that was both exhilarating and terribly sad.

'You don't look any different!' they'd both said at the same time before laughing awkwardly at the synchronicity.

'I know it sounds corny, but it's true,' Alison said simply.

Tim nodded in agreement. 'I suppose I always think I must have changed physically because every other part of me has changed.'

Alison leant forward. 'I feel exactly the same way. I mean, when you look at all the things we've both done over the last twenty years ...'

They both sat back and mentally ran through the life stories they'd shared by e-mail in recent weeks. Tim had found it difficult to embellish his and was embarrassed by the thinness of his adult achievements when his potential at 18 had seemed (to him and Alison, at least) unlimited.

Decent degree in Maths from a decent redbrick university, couple of years gaining computing experience while attached to large corporation with conservative reputation, steady rise to directorship, marriage at 28 to Millie (who he described in his 'e-biography' as interesting and complex), four kids in five years. That was it.

He found himself editing out the minor detail of a new baby on the way and refused to analyse his reasons for the omission.

He knew he ought to add some personal information to show Alison he was still a person of substance. But without lying he didn't know what to say. He played golf but was reluctant to mention this in case he sounded middle-aged. Which he knew he was. He was a member of the Friends of Covent Garden and attended the opera and ballet there regularly but didn't want to sound middle class. Which he was. He received contemporary literature from a book club and New World wines from a wine club but didn't want to sound middlebrow. Which he was.

If he was being honest, her comment that he looked the same was a relief. He'd worked hard, consciously, to keep his appearance constant. It seemed to be the last element of his life over which he had any control. The best, although complicated, time of his life was when he was 18. So by having his hair cut with the same sharp centre parting and wispy fringe for 20 years, by maintaining a lanky, untoned body, he could fool himself into thinking he could go back to those days, any time he chose. He even insisted on wearing the same style of glasses, despite the fact that the round John Lennon shape hadn't suited him as a teenager and looked faintly ridiculous now.

As it was lunchtime on a working day, he was wearing a suit, but Alison might be surprised to learn that, at weekends, Tim dressed the way he'd done all those years ago, in ill-fitting jeans, baggy shirts hanging over the waistband, white T-shirts peeping out over the collar. And the reason he dressed like this was because Alison had told him that he looked nice when she'd first spoken to him. Since no one else had subsequently paid him such a compliment when he was experimenting with other styles, he'd regressed to the look that had once worked for him.

'I was surprised when you answered my e-mail,' Alison said, breaking the silence.

'Why?'

Alison stared at a spot somewhere in the distance. 'A few years back, I wouldn't have got in touch myself. From what I'd heard, the only people who actually make contact over these websites are the ones who are ...' She hesitated.

'Are what?' Tim asked defensively.

Alison struggled to find an appropriate word. 'Dissatisfied,' she settled on finally. She waited nervously to see if she'd caused offence.

Tim was more surprised than offended. Until she'd said the word, he hadn't considered the possibility that he was dissatisfied. This was probably because dissatisfaction had dictated his mindset for so long that he'd forgotten any other state of being was even possible.

But loyalty to Millie, along with a refusal to admit that his life was anything other than glittering, forced him to deny the accusation.

'I can't honestly say I thought about it. I'm certainly not dissatisfied with anything,' (Tell her you have a new baby on the way, something screamed at him, tell her how ecstatic you are about your continually expanding family and continually evolving wife.) 'I was just pleased to hear from you and thought it would be nice to get in touch.'

He knew it sounded weak. So what? I'm a weak man, he reasoned. 'What about you? I mean, you made the first contact. Were you acting out of disappointment?'

'Yes,' Alison replied simply.

Tim was taken aback by her bluntness until he remembered that this was exactly what he'd always loved about her all those years ago.

'You're smiling,' Alison said.

Tim stopped smiling immediately.

'That's more like it,' Alison teased. And 20 years dissolved away.

Boy; 18; A-level year; bad (improving) skin and bad (deteriorating) eyesight; shy, studious, waiting for something exciting to happen without having to take any chances; living in the hope that tomorrow must have more possibilities than today.

meets:

Girl; nearly 18; perfect skin and eyesight; plain features, beautiful energy; outgoing, hardworking, grabbing every excitement today in the fear that tomorrow all the possibilities will disappear.

Tim couldn't believe his luck when Alison began pursuing him. At first he thought she was doing it for a dare or a bet so he avoided her, not needing any more humiliation in his life than his acne and glasses already brought him.

'Why are you avoiding me?' she'd finally asked him.

'Why are you following me?' he'd asked in an unexpected (to him) show of courage.

'Because you play the saxophone,' she'd answered.

Tim was baffled by this. He didn't even bother mentioning his musical skills when describing himself, so unaware was he of the saxophone's sexual potency to women. He only played the saxophone because his dad taught it and he and all his siblings had been forced to learn it. And while he enjoyed the physical exertions of playing, he wasn't moved by the music.

'But I'm not that good at it,' he protested. 'Gary Chisholm's won awards for his violin-playing and have you heard Keith Wilson's piano?'

Alison shook her head pityingly. 'You don't get it, do you?'

Tim didn't.

Alison enlightened him. 'Nothing compares to the saxophone, nothing. It's so deep, so dark, so meaningful, so profound, so ...'

So terribly adolescent, Alison recalled, cringing. She covered her eyes in mock shame as she recalled her teenage self.

'I can't believe I spoke like that!'.

'I couldn't even believe it then,' Tim pointed out. 'I didn't have a clue what you were talking about.'

'And you're not just talking about the saxophone, are you?' Alison teased.

Now it was Tim's turn to cover his eyes. 'You were like an alien creature to me,' he admitted. 'All of my friends were like me, proper teenagers, complete social misfits, pretending to be into Genesis when we secretly preferred The Carpenters, spending all our Saturday job money on Clearasil. None of us had a clue about anything that wasn't laid down in the A-level syllabus.'

'I was the same,' Alison confessed. 'I was just good at acting as if I was different.'

Tim looked at the 17-year-old girl through his 38-year-old eyes and recognised the gulf between them to be as wide as ever. Twenty years on, and he still hadn't learned how to act as if he was different. He was the same as everybody else even though something deep inside told him that he was not born to conform, no one was that fully formed.

'You were very good at it,' he conceded. 'Everything about you was different. You seemed so certain about everything that confused the rest of us.'

'Just acting,' Alison repeated.

But Tim knew this wasn't the case. Nobody could sustain that kind of act for a lifetime. And Alison had been remarkably consistent, judging by her life story.

Three years spent backpacking around the world, picking up half a dozen languages, a recurrent gastric complaint and a Brazilian doctor. Returned to England and went to medical school. Travelled some more. Became a GP and bought into a small village practice with the Brazilian who was now her husband. Wrote bestselling self-help books for women and climbed Everest on her thirty-fifth birthday. A rocketing ascent that made Tim dizzy with its heights.

He noticed the absence of children in the account but didn't mention it. And neither did she.

'So what made you contact me when you did?' he asked again.

'I left my husband.'

'I'm sorry, Ali.' And Tim took her hand. That was the first tentative step of his life outside his emotional safety buffer. And into the danger zone.

YOU ARE NOW ENTERING A DRUG-FREE ZONE the jolly sign announced as the van turned into their new street. The cutesy illustrations of Say-No Squirrel did little to alleviate the gloom that descended on Tess and Max as they officially joined the population of Crappy Valley.

'Was that sign there the last time we came?' Tess asked.

Max's fingers tightened around the wheel. 'Don't ask me. You're the one who's practically been living here with your new best friend.'

Tess had become slightly more positive about the move since growing closer to Heather. Maybe positive was a bit of an overstatement. But the coming of the end of the world had receded to a distant glow rather than a dazzling spotlight on a big arrow pointing at Tess's head.

Max was perversely irritated by his wife's complaisance. After countless hours of enduring her accusations, both spoken and suggested, that he'd ruined all their lives, her conclusion that the move might not be so bad after all infuriated him.

He took this shift as an indication that she was taking some of the responsibility on herself, a move he embraced willingly. He hoped they would quickly move back to their original balance of power, both of them pretending that he possessed the power, both of them knowing that this was not true.

'We've never driven this way before,' Tess observed, trying to avert a row, in particular a row that would be all her fault as most things were recently.

'That's because we used to drive a car with suspension that could handle speed bumps. Now we're driving a van which has an exhaust held on with a Crystal Palace scarf.'

And that's my fault too? Tess thought bitterly.

Eventually they had no choice but to approach their flat by some treacherous humped road surfaces. They just about held onto their breakfast and the van just about held onto its exhaust, although there were some ominous scraping sounds as the vehicle inched over the bumps. Tess and Max pretended to ignore the sound but Lara, who had no concept of the fear of losing one's deposit to Friendly Frank, Economy Van King of South London, enjoyed every rattle and shake.

'This van is so cool! Can we keep it now that we haven't got the Range Rover any more?'

Tess smiled and, finally, Max did too. It was such rare and brief shared moments of unity that allowed them to continue with the fantasy that they were as solid as ever, that nothing could fracture this family unit.

This particular moment was more short-lived than most. As they turned into their street, they caught sight of something that, from a distance, looked like a carnival float. Unfortunately it was their house, or rather their flat which occupied the ground floor of the house, with balloons stuck to the front door, the windows and the sad dying tree on the pavement outside.

'Look Mum, they're having a party at our house! Fantastic!' Lara still hadn't fully understood that they only lived in part of a house. There was a lot she didn't understand, Tess thought, hoping that her daughter's innocence would not be too cruelly shattered when the full extent of their reduced circumstances made itself known.

As they pulled up at the kerb, they saw the banner draped across the top of their door. It was torn from an old yellowing sheet and gloss paint had been scrawled across it to read HEAVERBURY WOMENS' YOGA GROUP WELCOMES TESS AND FAMILY!

'That's nice, isn't it?' Tess said dubiously.

'Nice for you, maybe.' Max sounded grumpy. 'They're welcoming you. Lara and I are just "AND FAMILY". It's not as if your friend Heather hasn't met us all and doesn't know our names as well.'

Tess wisely ignored this barb and quickly jumped out of the van, followed by Lara. She was a little concerned by the evidence that the Heaverbury Women's Yoga Group was organised enough to assemble in one place at short notice with decorating materials and create this (admittedly shabby) banner.

She had been banking on the assumption that local women popped into the yoga class on a casual basis, that they contorted and chanted or whatever before rushing off to pick up children or get back to work. She hadn't anticipated that they might actually talk to each other. This made it much more difficult to pull off her deception.

Tess herself had often dropped in on a new exercise class and found herself completely unable to keep up with the skinny model masquerading (badly) as the teacher. Of course she never complained in case she found out that everyone else was perfectly happy with the teacher and any problems Tess was experiencing must be down to her own ineptitude.

This was the principle that she was hoping to exploit as she tried to persuade the women of Heaverbury that she was a qualified yoga teacher or, at the very least, a woman who could touch her toes.

But now she realised that these were women who communicated with each other and, having met Heather, she wondered why she was so surprised.

Change of plan urgently needed, she thought. First lesson is tomorrow. I know, I'll throw myself down the stairs and break a leg or ankle.

And she might have considered this more seriously if she didn't have such a low pain threshold. Also, that would render her completely unable to take the job and she had no better ideas for finding immediate part-time work that didn't involve cards in telephone boxes.

But it did give her an idea. She didn't have to actually break a limb. She could pretend. It didn't have to be a dramatic injury. She could just put an elasticated bandage on her foot and limp bravely. It was a brilliant idea, she concluded.

'That's a terrible idea,' Graham said to Tim as they struggled to manoeuvre the massive sofa out of the door.

'But why?' Tim asked. 'I'm not doing anything wrong. It's no different to meeting up with an old male schoolfriend. We had lunch but that was rushed because Alison had to catch a train back to the country. This is the same, except we'll be eating outdoors.'

Graham shook his head, both at Tim's folly and the impossibility of ever getting this huge piece of furniture out of the house.

'You know perfectly well that this is completely different. If this was two men, sure, you might have arranged to meet up again, but it wouldn't have been for a picnic and you would tell Millie.'

He almost spat out the word 'picnic', an emphasis which was immediately picked up by Tim.

'I know how it sounds and that's precisely why I don't think it's sensible to tell Millie. Not the way she is now. I mean, if *you* think there's something automatically suspicious about a picnic, imagine what Millie would think, when she's so jumpy about everything. I think it's the word "picnic" that's putting you off. How about thinking "pork pie" instead? Because if Alison's anything like she used to be, she'll be a pork-pie woman rather than a smoked-salmon-followed-by-strawberries-dipped-in-cream-spooned-into-our-navels type. Does that kill the suggestion of anything untoward?'

Graham felt queasy at the thought of anyone eating out of his navel and was once more grateful that he'd married Fiona and nobody too strange.

They suspended this debate while they both studied the dimensions of the sofa and the dimensions of the door, neither wanting to be the one to admit that the former could not physically pass through the latter. In a less than companionable show of machismo, they resumed the attempt, this time using brute force. They seemed to be working on the principle that the laws of physics themselves would crumble under the irresistible force of two such powerful men.

Fiona and Millie watched them in amusement. Fiona turned to her friend and said: 'Which one of us should tell them that there's more chance of getting that through by saying "abracadabra" than by all the pushing and shoving?'

Millie raised her eyebrows. 'Oh, please don't spoil my fun. Tim's out of the house so often nowadays that I haven't been able to enjoy the pleasure of watching him suffer for ages.'

She quickly added a smile as a full stop. But her timing was off and Fiona found herself shocked by the unexpected venom.

'How did his lunch go?' she asked quietly.

'I don't know,' Millie replied. 'I didn't ask him.'

'Why not? Aren't you desperate to know? I would be.' Fiona was amazed at Millie's self-control.

'Of course I want to know. But I want him to tell me without my having to ask him.'

Fiona shook her head. 'Sounds too complicated to me. I mean, you obviously know Tim better than me, but he always strikes me as a man who needs to be . . . drawn out.'

Millie looked as if she were about to cry. 'He's not good at lying. I don't want to ask him in case he lies. Or he might tell me the truth and I won't like it. No, it's best for him to tell me when he's ready.'

Fiona was grateful that she wasn't clever enough to play such games with Graham. It sounded a dangerous way to manage a marriage.

Millie continued. 'But I'm watching him very carefully. Very carefully.'

Graham continued his half-hearted attempt to show Tim the moral dubiousness of his behaviour. Also, he was more than a little jealous of Tim having listened to his ecstatic account of lunch with the saintly and youthful Alison. Graham didn't want to find out that this was a positive, life-enhancing experience since it was one that he would never be able to explore for himself. He wouldn't dare.

'It sounds to me that she's just using you to get over the split from her husband,' he said, dredging up some platitudes that he'd absorbed from being forced to listen to some of Fiona's inter-minable conversations with her female friends. 'This is a diver-sion for her, one in which she has nothing to lose whereas you have everything.'

He inclined his head in the direction of Millie, who was

unfortunately not looking like such a great asset at this particular moment. She was glaring at both Graham and Tim as if she knew they were talking about her.

Graham felt guilty and tripped over his own foot in embarrassment. He banged his elbow on the doorframe and dropped his end of the sofa in pain.

'Careful, Graham!' Tim yelled.

Graham looked at him closely. 'That's just what I was going to say to you, Tim,' he said.

Daphne Guinn watched disapprovingly as the young men packed her things into crates.

'Be careful with those, they're antiques,' she shouted.

Young Man number one whose badge read: *My name's Macca, Can I Help You?* swore under his breath.

'I heard that! Don't be so rude or I'll report you to your superiors. And my oldest son's a lawyer, so don't think you can steal things or break them and get away with it.'

Macca turned to Young Man number two (*My name's Trev, Move With Me*) and sent him an anxious glance that asked deep philosophical questions about the meaning of life and whether a person's individual purpose might ever be revealed while packing limited edition decorative miniature teapots into cardboard boxes for grumpy old women.

'And you can take that look off your face,' Daphne continued. 'Service with a smile, that's what they said to me when I phoned. Cheerful and reliable. Well I'm not seeing much of either at the moment. You were five minutes late and you've done nothing but stomp around, complaining about this and that, and scowling like spoilt teenagers who don't get their way.'

The tirade served to speed up Macca and Trev, who became highly motivated to complete this job in record-breaking time so that they could escape from this woman. In fact, so downtrodden were they by Daphne's non-stop harangue that they both resigned the next day and set up their own moving business, dealing only with young people, absolutely nobody over the age of 50.

Daphne sat back carefully in her last good chair. She wanted to apologise to the boys. She didn't mean to go on like that, it was just that her back and legs hurt so much, all the time. The only way to control the pain was to take a level of painkiller that sedated her, preventing her from getting on with her life.

I'm not ready to take to my bed, not yet, she told herself as she breathed her way through one of the regular waves of agony that twanged up her spine like a sequence of electric shocks. I'll be fine at Fiona's. I'll be able to help out in the house with the kids and I won't need to go out so much.

I'll be useful. This is my last chance to be useful and my last chance to make my daughter forgive me.

'Hard-faced old cow,' Macca muttered to Trev as he watched Daphne trying, through an act of pure will, to breathe through her pain, both physical and emotional.

'So why exactly does it have to be a picnic?' Graham asked.

He and Tim were now attempting to get the sofa out through the downstairs window. Graham was inside the house, Tim out.

Tim groaned. 'I'm beginning to wish I'd never told you about it now. What's the big deal? Alison works in Kent, I work in the City. I can hardly take a day off and the weekends are out of the question what with ...' He gestured defeatedly towards all the children, half of which were his.

He continued. 'But we can both squeeze a couple of hours in the middle of the day so it made sense to meet halfway. And a picnic is more practical than going to a pub or a restaurant. It'll be quicker, more efficient.'

More romantic, Graham thought grimly.

More romantic, Tim thought hopefully.

'What are you doing?'

They both stopped pushing and pulling. Max had just come back with the van and was watching them with interest.

Graham and Tim stared at him. 'What does it look like?' Graham asked.

'You won't get that out of the window like that,' Max said.

'Well, we've already tried to get it out through the door and that was definitely impossible,' Tim said.

'Like that it is,' Max agreed. 'You need to flip the switch on the bottom to fold the whole base in half. Then it's simple.'

Graham and Tim looked underneath the sofa and found the switch along with a large label explaining exactly how easy it was to fold the base in half for easy removal. Without saying a word, they left the sofa in the window frame, walked into the now sparsely furnished kitchen and grabbed the open bottle of burgundy that was chilling in the fridge. Dividing the bottle into two large glasses, they toasted each other's phenomenal patience in not smashing the sofa through the window and dropping it on Max's head.

Fortified by substantial quantities of wine on empty Sunday-morning stomachs, they quickly became mellow.

'To your picnic,' Graham said quietly, strangely, raising his glass.

Tim didn't reply. In his mind he was already there. Anywhere but here.

'So here we are,' Tess said to Max much later that evening. They were drinking hot chocolate using up the last crumbs of their expensive tin of pure chocolate shavings from Belgium.

'Here we are,' Max replied.

The flat was warm even though it was the coldest night of the year. Tess had switched on all the heating the day before so that it would be cosy when they arrived. Only later was she to think about the costs involved in keeping heating on all day and all night.

That's another thing I've never had to consider before, she thought.

She looked around the flat, unable to stop herself from comparing it to the family home she'd just left. Even if she stared out of the window in an attempt to avoid facing the reality of her new home, the sense of displacement was just as powerful.

Strangely, the set-up of Victorian and Edwardian houses was not too dissimilar to the street they'd just left. So why does it all look so depressing? she asked herself, hoping that some glib answers might just suggest strategies for improvement.

But the problems were so pervasive as to seem insurmountable. The individual defects were not enormous: the peeling paintwork of the doors, the dusty windows framed with half-hung curtains, the stripped cars with council warnings attached to the wipers, a stained bathroom suite abandoned in a neighbouring front garden.

Tess spotted the odd house which had clearly been bought by a middle-class family hoping that gentrification would reach Heaverbury in their (young) lifetime. The skip overladen with building materials, the occasional people carrier, even a loft conversion in progress. She was touched with optimism that people like her, or the old her, had actually staked their future happiness (and quality of life) on this place, apparently through choice.

But when her gaze shifted inside, her mood sank. The tiny living room was stuffed to overflowing with their oversized furniture. The extravagance of the furnishings clashed horribly with the wallpaper that had surely been left over from an old-fashioned Indian restaurant. The effect was of a grotesque parody of their old life, taunting them, reminding them of how things used to be. She now acknowledged to herself that they would have been wiser to put all their things into storage and buy some cheap second-hand furniture for this flat. The transition would have been more drastic but it would have been cleaner.

'What are you thinking about?' Max asked.

Be careful, Tess advised herself. He doesn't really want to know what I'm thinking, he wants me to reassure him. Stick to positive things.

'I was just thinking how kind it was of Fiona and Graham to lend us a car.'

Unfortunately Max did not see this as a positive. 'Well, it was no great sacrifice, was it? They have three, after all, four if you count Fiona's mother's car that they'll soon have as well. If we're lucky, the next thing they lend us might be Fiona's mother herself. She'd fit in well here with her ready wit and easygoing charms.'

Tess considered handing Max her large yoga book and asking him to beat her to death with it, rather than kill her with sarcasm. Whatever Max believed, she was moved by Fiona's offer which was unconditional and open-ended.

'Take it,' Fiona had insisted. 'What am I going to do with it? It just takes up garage space and we'll probably need the garage for Mum's car when she arrives. I don't think she'll be driving for much longer but she's refusing to get rid of her car.'

Tess marvelled at the astonishing timing that had seemed to be operating in her chaotic life since everything started going wrong. Just when a situation appeared insurmountable, just when a final missed deadline threatened to leave its fatal impact, at the very last minute a miracle would occur.

These miracles all consisted of spontaneous acts of generosity on the parts of their friends, both old and new. Not only had Fiona lent them a car which Max was going to need for his new minicab job, not only had Millie written off the debts owed her from her small personal investment in Organique, but Heather had opened her home to Tess, inviting her to wander in at will, helping herself to anything she needed.

Tess had been thrilled to learn that Heather only lived a street away. She fully intended not to take advantage of Heather's kindness but was certain that she would be making at least daily visits for morale-boosting if not for sponging essential supplies.

'As long as you haven't told her that our house is also as open to her,' Max said, when she tried to win him over to Heather.

'When did you become so mean?' Tess had asked him.

'When generosity ceased to be a viable option,' he'd replied.

But tonight, they had declared a ceasefire, one they both hoped to sustain for longer than the few hours they'd been managing up until now.

'It's good to see Lara settling in so quickly,' Tess said, resorting to the failsafe subject of their daughter.

Max relaxed. 'Kids are amazing. But then, we've managed to protect her from most of the bad stuff.'

You mean *I've* managed to protect her, Tess thought. That's all I seem to do. The one and only time you consciously set out to protect me during this marriage, we ended up in this state.

Max watched her, wondering if he was imagining that her lips were moving slightly. I bet I know what's going through your mind, he thought, but I wish you'd say it out loud.

He'd thought about their marriage a lot lately. While he'd become used to Tess holding back a certain part of herself from him, from everybody, she had retreated even further. Max believed that there was a minimum level of constructive communication necessary to maintain before the load-bearing walls of a relationship started to crumble from neglect. Tess's contributions were dipping precariously low and Max was seriously concerned that she might never be able to scrape that last lost foothold back. And that would leave him stranded and unreachable.

But he didn't say anything. Like Tess, he'd made an unconscious decision to avoid any controversial subjects until the immediate crisis had passed. Unfortunately that left them with very little to talk about and, with the immediate crisis in no danger of passing in the near future, a long time not to talk about it.

'So what time is your pick-up tomorrow?' Tess asked, hoping she sounded upbeat and positive.

'Why do you have to sound so negative about everything I do?'

Tess made a mental note to cross yet one more subject off her list of safe topics. The list was diminishing rapidly to the point where soon there would be only Lara, the weather and their shared hatred of any film starring Kevin Costner.

'I'm sorry if I sound negative,' Tess said carefully. 'I don't mean to. I'm genuinely interested. Apart from anything else, I need to work out my own timing tomorrow so it would help if I knew when you were going to be in or out.'

Max was appeased. Just about. 'I'm picking the family up at ten-thirty in the morning. I'm allowing an hour and a half to get to Stansted, just in case there's a problem with traffic. If they miss their flight, I don't get paid.'

'I'm sure it'll be fine,' Tess said with a smile that she hoped was more encouraging than her voice had obviously been.

'Of course it will,' Max echoed. After this successful exchange, he ventured the same approach with Tess. 'And what time is your class?'

'Eleven o'clock. For an hour and a half,' she added weakly.

Max smiled at her wickedly. 'I would say you'll be fine but I can't imagine how that will be possible.'

Tess threw a cushion at him. 'Actually I've had an idea about that.'

Max looked surprised. 'Really? What did you have in mind?'

But Tess realised she couldn't tell him. She was ashamed of resorting to the deception of an injured foot and couldn't face Max losing even more respect for her.

She improvised quickly. 'I thought I'd tell them I needed to start with some absolute basics so I could see what level they were all at, then I'd structure the class to suit their needs as a group. I can stick to really easy movements that even I can handle.'

Max was impressed. So was Tess. Why didn't I think of that before?

'Do you want to try some of your ideas out on me?' Max offered.

'You're joking!'

91

Max held his hands up. 'Think about it. If I can follow your teaching, me, a totally uncoordinated ten-foot-tall dimwit, then you'll sail through with your double-jointed ladies tomorrow.'

Tess shuddered at the thought that any of the women might be double-jointed or even moderately agile. But she accepted Max's challenge.

'OK. First of all, I want you to stand up, feet hip distance apart, arms down by your side and very, very slowly, bend your head forwards. Slowly, slowly, slowly.'

Max showed astonishing grace and self-control as he followed Tess's instructions closely.

'Now let your chin drop to your chest. Slowly, slowly, slowly ...'

This is a doddle, she thought, I can drag this out for at least ten minutes. But she was forced to revise this estimate when Max, misunderstanding the bit about the chin on the chest, thrust his head forward, overbalanced and fell straight ahead, landing on the coffee table which smashed under his considerable weight.

As he sat up, slowly, slowly, slowly, rubbing his chin which was now bleeding, he looked at Tess in amusement. 'If you can just stick to bending the head, slowly, slowly, slowly, for ninety minutes, you should be OK,' he said.

# 6

Today is the First Day of the Rest of Your Life!

Tess suppressed a smile at the clumsily written words painstakingly inscribed in glitter across the card.

'Oh Lara, it's a lovely card! Thank you.'

'Isn't it fantastic! I read it in a book. I'm never going to forget those words!'

Max peered at the card through tired eyes. He'd slept badly. 'It's really great. That was very thoughtful of you, sweetie.'

They'd given Lara a cautiously-edited account of the reasons for their new circumstances. Tess was careful not to attribute the blame to Max and Max worked hard to protect his daughter from some of the harsher implications of the unfamiliar poverty. So far, her cheerfulness suggested that they'd done a good job.

As Lara bounded off to put on her new school uniform (or at least the best-quality second-hand set that her parents had been able to afford), Max turned to Tess. 'Although if she was looking for an appropriate cliché, she might have done better with; "You Don't Have to be Mad to Work Here but it Helps".'

Tess slapped him playfully, relieved that Max's voice had lost that undertone of self-pity. She cuddled up to him for a few seconds before their new morning routine engulfed them both.

'The bizarre thing about clichés is that they really are true.'

Max pulled away from her and examined Tess as if she were an exotic species. 'Do I know you? What happened to my wife who despised unoriginality? Are you suddenly going to start talking in birthday card sentiments?'

Tess pulled a face. 'I was just thinking that when it comes to the really big things ...'

And they both knew that this was a very big thing indeed.

'... we're not equipped to deal with them. We haven't got any experience, we don't know the words. I can come up with twenty different ways of saying: "I'm sorry your au pair ruined your Baccarat crystal which had sentimental value in the dishwasher" but I don't know what to say to you before you do your first minicab run. And I don't know what to say to myself when all my instincts tell me to curl up under the duvet and not come out until everything's back the way it used to be.'

Max held her tight. 'Maybe if we put the radio on, a totally apt song will come on that will make us both smile wistfully and represent a positive sign that we will be able to get through this. It always happens in films.'

Tess was dubious but didn't want to sound a bell of discouragement at this optimistic suggestion. She switched on the bedside radio which was permanently tuned to Radio 2, in keeping with their status: too old for Radio 1, too uncultured for Radio 3 and now no longer posh enough for Radio 4.

A famous atmospheric instrumental was playing, but neither of them could recall the title.

'It's by Fleetwood Mac, I know that much,' Max suggested.

Tess was screwing up her eyes, trying to wring the title from her memory. But it wasn't until the end when Terry Wogan announced the record that they both clicked their fingers in recognition. Then they instantly sank into an introspective fog as they pondered the significance of the song.

'Albatross'.

Millie didn't care that it was Monday. It made no difference to her state of mind. Every day seemed as bad as the one before and had done since she found out that she was pregnant.

'But it's not just the pregnancy,' she said. 'Although that doesn't help. It's that on top of this woman turning up out of the blue, at the worst possible time. The way I feel right now, I can't deal with my own hair, let alone a husband who's behaving strangely.'

'Has he said anything about this old girlfriend yet?' Fiona asked, having given up asking Millie to broach the subject herself.

Millie shook her head. 'I'm really worried. If it was just that lunch, I don't think I'd be so worried, but there's been a long build-up to this. Things haven't been wonderful for months, maybe years, I don't know.'

She cut a huge chunk of carrot cake and presented it to Fiona. Organique had closed the week before but Millie still had a freezer full of cakes and cookies. Since she'd lost her sweet tooth recently, she was plying guests with massive portions, whether they wanted them or not.

Fiona immediately lost her appetite as Millie's depression wafted over her.

'Millie, it's just your hormones, you must know that even if you hate me saying it. They make everything seem black.'

Millie shook her head. 'No it's more than that. The trouble with having four kids is that you never get a chance to think any more.'

Fiona forked a large mouthful of cake into her mouth at this jolly reminder.

'So although I had this nagging suspicion that Tim was unhappy,' Millie continued, 'it always got pushed to the bottom of the endless lists I found myself making. You know the ones that start with "remember to feed your children" and pass through the reminders for swimming bags, money for school trips, presents for parties, picking up dry-cleaning and so on. Unfortunately, the list is so long that I never reach the item marked "ask husband if he's happy with his life". Tell me you're the same.'

Fiona wanted to agree just to make Millie feel better but she felt this would be unhelpfully misleading and might prevent Millie from taking some action to remedy the situation.

'I know what you mean about the lists. Graham ends up at the bottom of my list most of the time. But if something is wrong, I always shunt him straight to the top.'

'But how do you know when something is wrong?' Millie asked. 'I'm so tired, it's all I can do to cope with the kids' demands. I'd always anticipated that, once the children got a bit older, I could get things back on track with Tim. I thought he understood that this was just a temporary chaos.'

'Maybe he did and he's just a bit shell-shocked about another baby. After all, it extends your "temporary chaos" by at least another five years. I don't think Graham would take it too well either.'

Millie looked dubious. 'So you think I might be imagining that this has been going on for longer?'

Fiona wasn't sure about this. She'd noticed that Tim had become quieter in recent months. Of course, it was hard to tell because he was not the most outgoing of men to begin with. But he'd developed a sense of distance that made Fiona feel slightly uncomfortable about starting a conversation with him. It was as if she'd be interrupting him talking to someone else even though he was actually just lost in himself. She phrased her words to Millie carefully.

'I don't think there's any point in speculating. The fact is, you're going to have a baby and Tim is unhappy. Tim is not going to get any happier when the baby arrives, he may even feel worse, so I would suggest you try and sort things out with him now while things are relatively calm.'

Millie considered this. 'I was wondering about leaving it until the holiday. It's only a few months away. We always get some time to ourselves when we're away and Tim's always more relaxed when he's away from London.'

'What holiday?' Fiona asked, confused.

'The gîte in Provence,' Millie replied. 'I thought it was all decided.'

'It was,' Fiona agreed, 'until Tess and Max had to pull out. I thought we said it wouldn't be right to go without them.'

Millie looked as if she was about to burst into tears. 'When did we say that? Surely Tess wouldn't begrudge us the holiday. We're doing everything possible to support her but I'm sure she doesn't expect us to scupper all our plans just so that we can all be miserable together.'

'If I were Tess, that's exactly what I'd expect!' Fiona said, lightly.

'Yes, but Tess isn't like you,' Millie said without thinking.

Ouch, Fiona thought. ' Maybe you're right but I still think she'd be hurt and I don't think it would do any harm to wait, maybe leave it till October half-term.'

Millie's face collapsed. 'But I was banking on it. Nothing's going to change while we're stuck here and if we wait until October, the baby will have arrived and then things will be even more difficult. It's got to be July!'

Fiona was alarmed by the colour rising on Millie's face. 'Well, maybe just our two families could take a short break before the summer, a long weekend or something?'

Millie leapt on the suggestion with enthusiasm. 'That's a fantastic idea! And I'm sure Tess couldn't mind that.'

Fiona wasn't sure about anything any more. She reached down for another chunk of cake until she noticed that it had all gone. In her stress, she'd finished the lot. Terrific, I'm turning into a comfort eater.

Millie immediately dropped another large slice onto her plate. Fiona immediately started eating it. Her stress melted away. At least now I understand the appeal of comfort eating, she thought. That makes me a more well-rounded woman and able to participate more fully in daytime television phone-ins which, if not about adultery with one's sister's husband, tended to be about eating disorders.

Millie watched her eating, which killed Fiona's appetite in an instant. She took a deep breath, not that easy when very few of her internal body workings were not jammed with carrot cake. 'I'll tell you what, I'll have a word with Tess, test the waters, get a feel for how she stands on this. If she's not too bothered, then maybe we can still go.'

Millie brightened up.

Fiona held up a warning finger. 'But I wouldn't leave talking to Tim until July. If things are bad now, there's no way of knowing what can happen between now and then. I'd do something if I were you.'

Do something? Like what? The way things are at the moment, if I get out of the front door in matching shoes I feel I've achieved something. But maybe Fiona's right. Maybe doing something will be more effective than talking. Chances are that Tim would just say everything was fine if I asked him.

Maybe I could hire a private detective. Then if anything is going on with that woman, I can arrange to have her killed by a painful bloodthirsty method. Perhaps Tess could help out there, she's bound to have met some contract killers in her neighbourhood by now.

She made herself a sanity-restoring cup of tea before she ended up thinking about phoning Quentin Tarantino for advice.

Suitably sensible once more, she tried to sum up her concerns in terms she could grasp in her addled state of mind. It seemed to boil down to one overwhelming problem: she was being driven crazy with jealousy because Tim was seeing an old girlfriend.

Once she looked at it like this, the solution leaped out at her, breathtaking in its simplicity: I must do the same to him, so that he realises how hurtful his behaviour is.

Now all I have to do is find an old boyfriend. Tricky because I never had a boyfriend before Tim.

Tim felt happier than he had done for months. It was an illusion, he knew. But suddenly his reality had become bearable now that it formed no more than a reference point to a picnic with the woman he first loved. It was a fantasy, he was aware of that, but his life had been short on fantasy since ... well, since Alison.

'Come with me!' she'd said 20 years earlier.

'I can't,' Tim had replied. 'I've got a place at Southampton in October.'

'You can defer it for a year, then if you want to come back you can.'

'I haven't got any money,' Tim had argued.

'We'll get jobs as we travel,' Alison had argued back.

For every excuse he put forward, Alison had an answer. He was even citing his tendency to throat infections as a reason not to stray too far from home. He could hear how feeble he sounded but couldn't stop himself.

Finally Alison stopped arguing and just stared at him. 'Is it me or the world?' she asked.

'What?'

'Me or the world you're afraid of?'

He hadn't been able to answer her because he didn't know. It was a question, an eventuality, that he hadn't planned for. He'd foolishly hoped that he and Alison would go to university together, study together, live together, get married (to each other, obviously), and then, well, that didn't matter.

In Alison, he'd found the part of him that he'd been unable to develop in himself. She was his confidence, his imagination, his courage, his certainty. As a self-absorbed teenager with non-existent self-esteem, he believed that none of those qualities were present in him. He needed to acquire them, like the right brand of jeans, and in Alison he'd found the perfect fit.

But he had never anticipated that Alison would have higher ambitions than simply providing the missing 40 per cent of an angst-ridden spotty adolescent's personality.

And he couldn't just change all his plans and follow Alison around the world, because, deep down, he never truly believed she could love someone who was only 60 per cent of a person. Years later Millie told him that he might not have everything, but he had all the bits that mattered. Then at last he began to appreciate that he was no more flawed than anyone else, that everyone had different levels and areas of inadequacy.

This self-knowledge differentiated him now from the boy he was then. It enabled him to approach Alison afresh, as someone she didn't know. He was different this time and that allowed him to wonder, even if just frivolously, if maybe the outcome of the renewed relationship would also be different this time.

He rearranged his morning, shifting as many appointments forward from the afternoon so that he wouldn't have to rush back from lunch. His colleagues were bemused by this rush of activity. He was normally a beacon of calm, quiet efficiency, an oddball conformist in the informal environment of this computer systems design company. The office joke was that you could set your watch by Tim's lunch hour. It always lasted exactly an hour, even if he was squeezing in a trip to the dentist.

But everything he did today was out of character, as if he was trying to prove that his evolution was not yet complete, that he could still develop a few more survival aids.

'Not sure what time I'll be back,' he said quietly to the receptionist as he left at 12.15. 'But my mobile will be switched on.'

Everybody watched in astonishment as he left.

'Got to be an interview,' was the agreed rumour that spread around the office.

'It's obviously not another woman!' they all laughed. 'Not the type,' was the consensus.

But Tim was unconsciously reinventing his type and he could have no idea yet what type he was going to be.

Max had reverted to type. He was worried, very worried. This was not what he was supposed to be doing, ferrying strangers to airports, talking to strangers about their holiday. It was not even his car. He felt displaced sitting in the driving seat of Fiona's Renault Clio, a woman's car, in his opinion. And beholden. Two alien feelings for which there was no room in his emotional repository, already stuffed to overflowing with anxiety.

He'd spent an hour in the minicab office discussing routes with his new workmates ('colleagues' seemed an overstatement in this smoky cubbyhole).

He felt out of place in his jeans with a neat ironed crease and T-shirt that actually fit. But that was how he always dressed. While his body was continually betraying him with its awkward size and protruding hair and limbs, he made sure that his clothes were immaculate. It was one of the few obsessions that he shared with Tess. They each believed fervently in maintaining a tight control over the elements of one's life that could be controlled. While his life was taking a drastic turn for the unfamiliar and he was churning up inside with apprehension, it had seemed even more important that his outward appearance remain constant.

He'd been surprised at the variety of men who were congregating in the office. While some of them did live up to the urban stereotype of the minicab driver, incomprehensible accent, shifty eyes, worrying stains on their car seats, others were just like him: men doing a casual, not badly paid job while waiting for their fortunes to change for the better.

His boss was called Archie, someone who could have been anywhere between 50 and 70, with a face lined either by smoking, drinking, hard living or just age. It was impossible to tell whether he was an essentially happy or gloomy man; there were too many creases surrounding his mouth and eyes to know in which direction his face had been most stretched.

His expanse of thick dark hair, with only a smattering of grey, suggested to Max that Archie was not as old as he might appear. But the clothes ...

He was wearing brown corduroy jeans straining under a gently protruding stomach topped with a check lumberjack shirt and a black waistcoat. The only thing missing was a guitar, some cowboy boots and a Nashville bar full of line dancers shouting 'Yee-haw!'

Max managed to suppress a smile at the image.

Once Archie had hammered out the rules of his establishment to Max, he turned out to be quite friendly. Or, at least, friendly according to Max's original expectations of being threatened with a gun if he ever dared get stuck on the M25.

'Leave plenty of time, don't speed, don't wind the customers up and you'll be fine,' Archie said.

'Erm, what do I do if the customers give me any trouble?' Max asked tentatively.

The other drivers laughed at his innocence.

'You have to be able to spot a troublemaker before he gets in your car. Otherwise, you're on your own. That won't happen too often though, not if you look like you're a man who can handle yourself.'

After receiving this advice, Max had decided to scruff his hair up, not shave for 24 hours and practise not smiling.

'Your biggest problem is drunks chucking up in your car,' one of the other drivers told him.

Max thought of Fiona's car and sent up a quick prayer: I can take the drug dealers, the axe-murderers, the fare-dodgers, but please don't let anyone vomit over Fiona's upholstery. He considered adding an 'amen' to his plea, but felt that was too silly. Nonetheless he was quite proud of resorting to a prayer, however unconventional it was. It made him feel a little less hypocritical about agreeing to go to church with Tess and Lara the following Sunday.

After much argument, he was persuaded to take the M11 to Stansted Airport, not having the confidence or, indeed, the sense of direction to follow the complicated directions down the B-roads suggested by some of the others.

Picking up his first fares went smoothly. They were a family of four going to Disneyworld. The two sons were hyperactive to the point where Max feared for the radio aerial. It also brought back ominous memories of Lara being sick with excitement the first time they went to Florida.

Should I do the prayer thing again? he asked himself. How does this work? I'll have to ask Heather's Incredible Vicar when I see him. He silently repeated his plea for a vomit-free journey, just to be on the safe side. No one got chucked out of heaven for praying too much, that was his uneducated theory.

'Don't worry,' the kids' father said, as if reading Max's mind. 'They've been given travel sickness pills and they'll fall asleep soon.'

Wow, Max thought. Impressive. I'll draw up a list of things to ask for as soon as I get home.

The children didn't fall asleep, they were too wound up for that, but they did calm down and they didn't throw up. Max felt odd driving a family that wasn't his own. He kept wanting to ask the woman for a Polo mint. At one point, one of the boys complained that his brother was stupid.

'We don't say "stupid",' Max found himself saying without thinking. He blushed and apologised quickly.

'Don't worry,' the boys' mother said. 'It's nice to hear someone else tell them off for a change. They might take more notice of you.'

Max felt rather proud that, even in this lowly job, a man of honour could make a difference. Until he'd dropped the family off at the airport and found a lump of chewing gum stuck to the passenger door handle with STUPID carved into it with a fingernail.

But even that could not take away the glow of receiving the £45 in cash for a couple of hours' work. Even knowing that he would have to pass a commission on to Archie, he hadn't felt this kind of thrill since his first pay packet as a paper boy when he was 13. He did some quick calculations. A couple of these a day, some night-time airport runs that paid even more and he'd still have some useful hours available to look for a more permanent career move.

His optimism took him to his new local off-licence, which had shutters that looked bulletproof, where he treated Tess and himself to a half-decent bottle of Australian Pinot Noir. Looking around the shop as the assistant went into the back to get his change, Max acknowledged that he would probably not be invited to attend tastings of new vintages from the New World as he had been in his last regular haunt.

Instead of posters, recommending precise temperatures at which specific wines should be served, this shop's walls were covered in handwritten notices screaming: STEAL FROM US AND WE'LL HUNT YOU DOWN LIKE DOGS! and ONLY LOOSE CHANGE KEPT IN TILL — NOTES KEPT IN BACK ALONG WITH BASEBALL BAT AND HUNGRY PIT BULL TERRIER!

Max crossed this shop off his list of places to rob if he ever took up a life of crime.

The Asian licensee returned with his change and a big smile. This was probably the most expensive bottle of wine he'd sold for some time, Max thought.

'Do you like good wine?' he asked eagerly.

'I do, but I have to watch the pennies,' Max said apologetically.

'My name is Rav,' the man said, extending his hand, which Max shook. He was not a tall man, at a few inches over five feet, but his proud stature made him appear taller. He was incongruously dressed in formal, sharply pressed trousers and a thick cotton sweater with the picture of a golfer knitted on the front. Yet he had a sense of joy about him, that was the only word Max could find to describe the sense of wellbeing that the man seemed to inspire in him.

I like this man, Max found himself thinking. This slight shift towards positive thinking went some distance towards chipping an edge off the bitterness that engulfed him.

Rav grinned warmly. 'You come by here again and I'll let you taste my specials.'

Max laughed inwardly at his own snobbery that had led him to misjudge this humble shop which still had lofty pretensions. 'I'd love to,' he said gratefully. 'What sort of things do you specialise in?'

'They're wines made by my family and this is the only shop in Britain that sells them.' His pride was clear.

Max looked confused. 'Your family? Do you mean ...?'

Rav nodded. 'Bombay! You didn't know they made wine in Bombay, did you?'

Max knew for a fact that they didn't but he wasn't going to argue with a man who had a baseball bat and a pit bull terrier.

'I know what you're thinking,' Rav went on. 'But I'll surprise you. Next time. You'll see.'

Max left, strangely looking forward to meeting Rav again and tasting Indian wine.

During the course of this first day of the rest of his life, he was starting to feel quite cosmopolitan. His social and professional circle was expanding way beyond its previous tightly defined radius. He was coping with people and experiences of a type that he'd never encountered before. And he was surviving all by himself, without Tess needing to tell him on an hourly basis that everything would be fine.

This isn't going to be so bad after all, he thought proudly.

This is worse than I thought. Tess's lungs were hurting and every muscle in her body had been stretched beyond endurance. That would have been fine if she hadn't been forced to hide her strain in front of her class. To be fair, all the women looked as if they were close to death. But then they were supposed to. The teacher is supposed to look as if the whole routine is effortless, being so basic for a woman of her experience.

Heather had greeted her warmly, standing up before the class to introduce her.

'Ladies, I know you'll all be as thrilled as I am to meet our new yoga teacher. She's not only stepping in at short notice to help out here, but she's also agreed to teach our kids too. Tess Keane!'

All the ladies clapped and smiled. Their warmth was so genuine and powerful that Tess wasn't sure how to respond. This didn't happen in Clapham. At exercise classes there, women spoke quietly to their friends, or concentrated on keeping their hair in place, or showed off their elasticity by stretching pointlessly. The teacher was just a member of the health club staff. You didn't expect to become her friend.

But these women looked nothing like the people she'd generally encountered at private clubs. They all looked different, for one thing, not conforming to the amorphous huddle of generally slim, well-toned women who normally presented themselves for public display claiming, unconvincingly, to be in dire need of self-improvement. Their attendance at a gym seemed to be little more than an excuse to show how shapely their bodies looked in Reebok bodysuits.

No, these Heaverbury women really did appear to want improvement. Whether they needed it or not was difficult to assess since their bodies were all shrouded in oversized T-shirts and baggy tracksuit bottoms. Certainly there were some large women there but some of the smaller ones looked even less fit, dragged down by the exhaustion written on their faces. They represented ages from the early 20s all the way to that indeterminate stage once called middle age but now lasting as long as a woman wants it to.

She resolved that she would not let these women down. This might just be a money-making stunt for her but the job was important to these people. She just wished she'd made this resolution a few days earlier so that she might have been better prepared.

'Let's start with a warm-up,' she announced shakily before clearing her throat and repeating it, more forcefully this time.

The women followed her instructions for the head movement, slowly, slowly, slowly and no one fell over.

Result!

But this only took 90 seconds and Tess knew that she was going to have to be more adventurous than she'd planned. She made a quick decision. Instead of keeping it simple and risk making the women restless or suspicious, she would go to the other extreme. She would have them performing moves so advanced that they wouldn't notice how inept the teacher was, they'd be concentrating so hard on achieving impossible positions for themselves.

Yep. That'll work.

'Right everybody, lie on the floor and close your eyes.' As they all complied and Tess murmured calm encouragements to breathe and relax, she reached into her gym bag for her *Yoga For Dummies* book that she'd smuggled in for just such an emergency.

She turned towards the end of the book for some real corkers then roused her pupils with renewed purpose.

'OK. Now I'm new to this class and I was going to put you through some simple moves to see what level you're all at but I thought that would be very boring!'

The ripple of agreement reassured her that she'd made the right decision. She continued.

'So I'm going to gently guide you into some more advanced moves and see how far we all get. Now I don't want anyone to hurt themselves so there'll be nothing that you are not physically capable of at least attempting.'

That's what it said on the jacket of the book. She had to believe that it was true. When Heather had asked her about Public Liability insurance, Tess had grinned inanely and said that, of course she had insurance and would get the paperwork to the community centre committee as soon as she'd unpacked all her boxes and found it. She'd given the same excuse to Miss Blowers at the school who was asking to see Tess's teaching certificates.

And she'd get round to sorting all this out once she'd overcome the challenge of this first class. In the meantime, she had to make sure no one broke anything either in the community centre or any part of their bodies.

She'd propped her book behind her bag where no one apart from herself could see it.

'OK. So let's all get down on our knees facing the window and stretch out our arms along the floor as far as they can reach. Now stretch out your left leg ... '

As the women groaned and puffed, she jumped up and began

walking round the room, as if checking they were all following her instructions properly. Just when she anticipated that they were going to give up and ask her to show them how it was done, she spotted that Heather's pose was an almost perfect copy of the photo in her book. In astonishment she clapped her hands.

'Everybody! Look at Heather. You see, it can be done.'

And for the rest of the class, she assumed the role of puppet-master, bringing Heather to the front of the hall and manipulating her body into the impossible positions she'd picked out. It hadn't been planned, but it worked out more effectively than if she'd actually demonstrated the moves herself. Anyway that was what she believed.

It was still physically tiring for Tess, who couldn't avoid joining in with some of the movements. She felt obliged to go that bit further, try that bit harder, than the others and her body was resisting. But she got through and was still just about able to walk if she concentrated very hard and breathed through the pain.

At the end of the class, she made them all lie on the floor for more breathing and relaxation. This was one exercise she did join in with, having developed a stress headache from maintaining the facade for over an hour.

She proved to have a true gift for relaxation and meditation, lulling herself to sleep in sixty seconds. Fortunately she woke up before the end of the class and she was convinced that nobody had noticed.

As she gently led the class to their feet to avoid dizziness (that had been written in capitals in the book, so she assumed it was important), she was exhilarated by the enthusiastic applause of the exhausted women.

'That was fantastic,' one of them said. 'The last teacher wouldn't let us do any of that stuff, she said it was too dangerous.'

Tess felt uneasy at this but hid her awkwardness as she had done for the last hour and a half.

Heather hugged her warmly. 'See! That wasn't so bad, was it?'

Tess returned the embrace gratefully. 'It's always a bit nerve-racking the first time with a new group. But we'll get used to each other.'

'Of course we will,' Heather agreed. 'Now, are you joining us for lunch?'

Tess hesitated. Her first thought nowadays before doing

anything was about money. Heather read her mind. 'Don't worry. It's dead cheap. That's the good thing about living around here.'

The women all cajoled Tess until she caved in and said that she'd go with them.

This isn't so different to my old life, she thought happily.

Tess had never been inside a place like this in her life. She didn't know what to call it. It was too big to be a café and too shabby to be a restaurant. The sign outside said CARTER's. The menu was the longest she had ever seen, 12 pages of every combination of meat and vegetable that the English diner could desire.

'There aren't any prices,' Tess whispered to Heather.

'That's because it's a set lunch for one ninety-nine. Any main course and pudding and a cup of tea.'

Tess was horrified, completely certain that anything that cheap had to be dreadful. And it definitely wouldn't be organic. She scoured the menu, looking for the safest option.

'Have the spaghetti bolognese,' one of the women suggested. 'It's always good.'

Tess was concerned that a bolognese sauce could hide any kind of abomination masquerading as meat. Once more, Heather seemed to read Tess's mind. 'It's all prime beef,' she said. 'You see Carol over there?' She pointed at a large, cheerful woman at the end of the table. 'Her husband's a butcher and he gets all Carter's meat for him at a discount. No horsemeat, I promise!'

Tess had the grace to blush and ordered the spaghetti from Carter who was about 150 years old, had immaculately Brylcreemed hair and wore a black evening suit that was shiny with age. Tess had become immensely sensitive to the new people she met in the light of the rejection she was experiencing from her old acquaintances, apart from Fiona and Millie of course. Carter had the slightly bowed shoulders of a man who had known great sadness or had worked hard, maybe both. But his face showed acceptance of all that life had heaped over him and his warm eyes hinted that a sense of humour had been his most valuable weapon. When he spoke, Tess noticed that his dentures were fractionally too big for his mouth. This gave him a smile of extraordinary breadth and charm. Tess loved him.

'How do you always know what I'm thinking?' she asked Heather. 'Is it some kind of gift?'

107

Heather snorted. 'Nothing so spiritual, I'm afraid. I told you, I've been where you are. Everything seems strange and suspicious because it's new. When I moved here, I met someone who helped me to settle in. I was so grateful that it's really a privilege now to be able to return the favour for someone else.'

Tess felt tears forming but, this time, they weren't of self-pity. They were of simple gratitude for unsolicited kindness from a relative stranger.

'Thank you,' she said simply.

When the food arrived, Tess was stunned by the gargantuan portion. 'I'll never be able to finish it!'

'You have to, or you'll offend Carter,' she was warned.

Tess tasted her pasta squeamishly. 'This is ... absolutely incredible!' she said. She couldn't honestly say that it was the best she'd ever tasted, not after all the holidays in Italy she'd enjoyed, but it certainly tasted like the best home-made food she'd had for a long time. The tea was like Heather's tea, gravy-brown and pungent. But Tess was beginning to like it.

She cleared her plate with ease and sat back, undoing the button at the top of her jeans.

'How does he make a profit at these prices?' she asked Heather.

'He charges more in the evenings, quite a bit more, but he still gets a good crowd in.'

Tess was disappointed. 'That's a shame. I'd like to have brought Max here, but if it's expensive ...'

'Did you get a local paper through your door last night?' Heather asked.

'Yes,' Tess said. 'But I haven't had a chance to look at it yet.'

'Well, when you do, you'll find loads of coupons, different money-off vouchers for eating here in the evenings. You only find them in our paper, it's Carter's way of thanking the community for the lunchtime custom and all the favours he's done by the local traders.'

'Puddings, ladies?' Carter asked, with a flourish of yet another menu which offered two pages of puddings served with cream, ice cream, custard or any combination of the three.

Tess had no room for pudding but managed to force down a treacle roly poly with custard.

'Now that *was* the best I've ever tasted!' she announced.

Heather beamed with pleasure that Tess was as won over by the delights of Carter's as she herself had been that first time. It all suggested that Tess was going to fit in just fine.

Tess meanwhile was thinking of her old friends. Perhaps we could all come here one night. If I love it, then I'm sure Fiona and Millie will love it too.

Fiona walked home after eating too much cake in Millie's kitchen. She was dismayed to see a small lorry outside her house and a couple of disgruntled young men, unloading the boxes with little consideration for the contents.

Oh no! she thought. She ran up the street and through her open front door where her au pair, Walburga, was cowering in the kitchen being lectured on the correct way to make tea by Fiona's mother.

'You always warm the pot, otherwise the tea leaves are shocked and their flavour gets locked in.'

Walburga was translating and concluded that this woman was insane talking about surprised tea leaves. But she nodded appreciatively, vowing never to set foot in the kitchen if this mad woman were there.

'Come on then, girl!'

Walburga realised that she was expected to make the tea and jumped up. She wasn't sure if she had to take orders from her employer's mother but she was not brave enough to refuse. She picked up the teapot and put it in the Aga.

'What are you doing?' Daphne yelled.

'Warming the teapot,' Walburga replied nervously. 'As you told me.'

'Stupid, stupid girl. You put boiling water in it and swill it round to warm it.'

Walburga burst into tears. Fiona had explained to her that her children were never to be called 'stupid' because it was such a pernicious little word. The girl had come to regard the word as a dreadful insult, one which must only be used on the most criminally idiotic lowlife. And now she was being called stupid when she was just doing what she was told! She ran out of the kitchen and pushed past Fiona.

I'm sorry, Daphne wanted to cry out. But she couldn't. She'd never been one for saying sorry, not in her marriage and not to her children, so certainly not to strangers. She'd always believed that people should just know when you're sorry and not expect to be told. Of course she didn't mean to upset the au pair; surely the girl realised. It was just that she really wanted a cup of tea; she'd been looking forward to it for hours since her kettle had been packed away this morning. And she wanted it to be just right. That was all.

'What did you say to her, Mum?' Fiona said accusingly.

'Nothing at all. I was just explaining to her how we make tea in England. I thought you said that au pairs are here to learn our language *and* our culture. And I knew you wouldn't be teaching her that, what with your obsession with tea bags.'

'It's hardly an obsession. Most people use tea bags nowadays because they're more convenient. Would you say they're all obsessed?'

'Perhaps they weren't all brought up like you, to do things properly'.

Fiona bit her tongue, her lip, the inside of her cheek, anything to stop herself from inflaming Daphne any further. The woman's been here five minutes and look what she's done to us already, she thought.

'Whatever you say, Mum.'

'And you don't have to patronise me either. I'm not senile.'

Fiona stood still for a few seconds to centre herself. Then she concentrated all her attention on making tea the way her mum liked it done. If Daphne had been in the other room, she'd just have used a tea bag and lied, saying it was made in a pot. She'd done that before and Daphne had never noticed. But while her mum was watching her, scrutinising every detail, she had to do it 'properly'.

'I thought you weren't coming till this afternoon,' Fiona said, careful to eliminate every trace of accusation from her voice.

'So you think I should have sat on the floor in an unheated house with no curtains just so that your schedule isn't disturbed?' Daphne said. Why am I saying all these things? she asked herself in despair. Why can't I just tell my daughter that I'm in agony but that I can't take any more painkillers for two hours and I just need to be doing something otherwise I'll weep. Why don't I just say, Ignore me, it's just the pain talking?

But she didn't want Fiona to treat her like a crippled old lady. She didn't really know how she wanted Fiona to treat her. She wished she could turn back the clock and rebuild their relationship

110

from scratch. This time, she would talk to Fiona and listen to her. She wouldn't criticise her all the time for doing her own thing because she'd know that it made no difference – Fiona would still do what she wanted, however, with her mother's blessing, their lives would be so much more peaceful.

But she couldn't change the direction of time. She had to start from here, from now, on jagged, rotting foundations. And she couldn't even think of anything remotely positive until her back stopped throbbing.

'Are you all right, Mum?' Fiona said in concern. 'Is your back hurting again?' Ever since Fiona had been called by the hospital and told that her mother had been admitted with terrible back pain, she'd been infuriated by her mother's determination to deny that she had a problem.

Unfortunately Daphne's campaign of denial had been successful and Fiona believed that her mum had the pain under control. If only they'd been more open with each other, Fiona would have understood Daphne's constant irritability and been less ready to attack her.

'Stop making such a fuss! There's absolutely nothing wrong with my back that a decent cup of tea won't cure,' Daphne snapped.

'Fine,' Fiona said.

After she'd made her mother the tea, which was grudgingly assessed as acceptable, Fiona helped her up to her room. Daphne gingerly lowered herself to the bed where she lay down and slowly stretched out.

'I'll take a nap now,' she said abruptly. And, after Fiona had left, Daphne cried.

When Fiona got downstairs, she phoned Graham at work.

'She's arrived,' she said tersely.

Graham said nothing for a moment. 'Do you want me to come home?'

Fiona blessed him in her heart, knowing that he would come home if she asked him and knowing that he would much rather sit in a pub, hoping that a hitman might offer his services, the way they seem to do to Sunday newspaper journalists. But she was going to have to deal with this herself so she might as well get used to it.

'That's OK. But thanks for offering. I just wanted to hear your voice.' She told him about the incident with Walburga and the tea. Graham made all the right sympathetic noises. Fiona hated herself for scrutinising his voice, searching for signs that he was being *too* sympathetic. It's my mum's fault, she thought, making me doubt myself, doubt Graham.

'I'm on your side, Fi,' Graham said finally, meaning it but not managing to convince his wife.

He hadn't been able to throw himself fully into his role of supportive husband although he really wanted to. He just had other worries. As he began preparing himself mentally for the ordeal waiting for him at home, he thought about the e-mail he'd just received. It was the fifth in a month and he didn't know what to do about it.

I could really do with someone on *my* side right now, he thought sadly.

# 7

'So how was the picnic?' Graham asked.

'If you're planning to give me another lecture, then forget it,' Tim said aggressively. 'I'm glad I went and I don't feel a bit guilty.'

'No, no, that's not why I called. I'm genuinely interested. I feel responsible in a way. After all, I'm the one that first told you about the website.' Graham hoped he sounded casual.

Tim bristled. 'But it's not as if I hadn't heard about it. You were just the first person I knew who'd actually tried it.' He didn't like the idea that Graham was stealing all the credit for the first spontaneous act of courage in Tim's adult life, entire life actually.

'Well anyway, how did it go?'

Tim took a deep breath, inhaling the memories that had been following him around since yesterday. 'It was incredible,' he said. 'Amazing.'

Graham groaned inwardly. This wasn't what he'd wanted to hear. He wanted specifics, an analytic breakdown of the encounter, all the emotions experienced and, most importantly, the lasting impact on Tim.

But Tim had turned into a teenage schoolboy, pouring out adjectives into his first love letter. 'She was so beautiful—'

'Sorry to interrupt,' Graham interrupted. He didn't like having this kind of conversation at any time, but while he was at the office, surrounded by other men working in silence, he wanted to keep the call as short and factual as possible. He'd even worn his least interesting tie, the one with a discreet logo for a mobile phone company that he'd won in a tombola, to avoid attention when he knew he'd be making this call. But now his colleagues were looking through his office door at him.

'What actually happened?' he asked.

What happened? Tim thought of little else.

Alison had picked him up at the station and driven him to a country park five minutes away.

'That's my house,' she'd said casually, as they drove past a tiny cottage. Tim craned his neck round but only glimpsed the back of it as they sped past. That had been Alison's intention, to tease him with possibilities.

Tim enjoyed the journey, taking the time to look at Alison's face while she concentrated on her driving. After their first lunch, he'd been amused to realise that he hadn't paid any attention to her appearance. He still imagined her as she'd been as a teenager.

But on closer inspection, he noticed that she had aged slightly more than he believed he had himself. Lines of discontent, frown lines, were well-established around her mouth and eyes. Her eyes, which he once believed to be the colour of plain chocolate, now appeared to be muted by the dramatic application of black eyeliner and brown eye-shadow that distracted the onlooker's eye from her weak mouth. Of course, even as Tim acknowledged her physical flaws, he was still moved by his perception of her beauty.

She was wearing a long red corduroy dress that perfectly matched her hair. Her hair! It was only then that Tim noticed that she'd dyed it. It was a harsh red demonstrating an over-enthusiasm for henna. The henna had also had a drying effect on Alison's hair causing it to wisp out. Like an old lady's hair, Tim found himself thinking, disloyally. He didn't like it. Dyeing hair indicated a desire for conscious and permanent change, something which he distrusted.

'What happened to your hair?' he asked in dismay.

Alison shook her head in amusement. 'I can't believe you've only just noticed. You sat opposite me for an hour last week and didn't spot that I was no longer brunette!'

Tim wondered about this himself. 'That's because it was never what you looked like that mattered to me. The fact that you were beautiful was a bonus, of course, but it was all the rest of you that I . . . that made you special.'

Alison frowned playfully. 'I could be insulted by that. Contrary to modern feminist doctrine, most women do like their appearance to be noticed.'

'Oh, I'm sorry.' Tim was mortified. He'd become used to Millie and her friends who seemed to have changed into clones of each other after having that first baby. Apart from the occasional night out, all decisions to do with their appearance seemed to be based on convenience.

Sensible shoes, manageable hairstyles, functional clothes, all expensive, all performing the dual function of making a conformist lifestyle statement and enabling the individual to smother every last vestige of their individuality.

But none of that had bothered Tim, truly it hadn't. If Millie had dressed in yellow ra-ra skirts, it wouldn't have appeased his overwhelming feeling that his marriage was a disappointment.

Alison was the same in every way that was important. She was the same strong, opinionated, courageous, decisive girl she'd been at 18. She was still beautiful. The details didn't count.

'Don't worry,' Alison let her hand gently brush his. 'I remember what you're like. You don't have to explain.'

Tim thought he would explode in relief. He hadn't known until Alison said those words that he had been waiting for someone to say that for years, someone who took away all necessity for explanation.

Of course Millie knew him well. But she always wanted to understand him too. She was constantly asking him questions that he didn't want to answer, always looking for complex motivations when he was essentially simple. It occurred to him that she'd stopped pressing him some time ago. Good, he thought, truculently.

Alison had led them along a path to a small opening with a square of grass surrounded by tall trees. The trees formed barriers that gave the impression of walls.

'It's like being in a room, but outdoors,' Tim said in wonder.

'Come on, sit down,' Alison said. 'I'm starving.'

She unpacked a bag from Tesco where she'd raided the sandwich, salad and cake fridges to provide a feast for at least eight people. No pork pies but no strawberries either. Tim felt he'd be able to face Graham again.

'This is fantastic!' Tim said, laughing.

'What's so funny?'

'None of this is home-cooked or low-fat or organic. You've just bought it. And not even from Marks and Spencer! Millie would feel ashamed to call this a picnic. If there wasn't any suffering involved in either the preparation or the eating, then Millie feels she's failed as a wife, mother and all-round nurturer. I just love how easy this all is.'

Instantly he felt guilty. This was the first time he'd talked about Millie to Alison and he hadn't spoken kindly. He searched for something positive to dredge from this situation. Maybe if I can pinpoint exactly what's wrong with my marriage, Millie and I can work on correcting it, he thought, not believing it for a minute.

'It's OK,' Alison said, this time letting her hand brush his a little more meaningfully. 'You're not betraying your wife just by saying I'm better at picnics!'

But they both knew he was saying far more than that.

'I'm just too busy to waste time on things that other people can do better, like cooking,' she went on. 'It's only food, after all.'

But the food was great and the fact that it was shop-bought saved Tim from having to gush over it or even pay it any attention. This freed him to concentrate on Alison.

A fact that Alison understood very clearly and had exploited when planning the picnic.

'So, don't you find it claustrophobic living in a small village after all that travelling?' Tim asked, lying back on the grass.

Alison stretched back too, inches apart from him. 'It's because I did all that travelling that I was able to settle down at last. I could never have done what you did, go straight from school to university and then right into corporate life, marriage, mortgage, the lot. I mean, don't you ever wonder what's beyond your world?'

Tim felt cornered. 'Of course I wonder. But you can't do everything. No one can.'

'I have. I've done everything I wanted, anyway. And you could have too. You could have travelled with me and still come back. The computer world would have waited. You might even have still met Millie and had all those children. But you would have had those fabulous experiences to look back on, rather than a whole load of what-ifs.'

'Maybe your experiences wouldn't have been so fabulous if I'd come with you.'

Alison raised an eyebrow. 'I don't know how you work that out.

We were best friends. We never argued. We got on. We liked the same things, wanted the same things.'

'I had everything I needed with you. I didn't have to travel the world to find fulfilment. I was clearly not enough for you.'

Alison looked at him. 'It was always either/or with you. With me it was and still is both/and.'

They sat for a while just enjoying the food. Tim ate what he wanted, not feeling obliged to finish everything to avoid giving offence. He enjoyed the peace, not having to keep an eye on children or wipe jammy handprints from his trousers or laugh politely at Millie's friends' jokes. He knew that he was being unfair to Millie even thinking like this but he couldn't stop himself.

His brain felt as if it had short-circuited since meeting Alison again and all of a sudden he was thinking along a new wavelength.

He was rewinding his life to the moment all those years ago when he let Alison go. In the retake, he went with her. And that life was better than this one, much better. The travel not only broadened him, it added brand new bits, not only completing him but fine-tuning him until he had fulfilled all his and everybody's expectations.

He and Alison grew closer and closer as they experienced the world together. She mellowed, learned acceptance from Tim, toned down her ambitions to complement his.

Then, in this idyllic alternative reality they returned to England, got married and had...

'Ali, why didn't you have children?' he asked curiously.

Alison began piling up the rubbish and tipping all the debris of their lunch back into the carrier bag.

'We didn't want them.' She was avoiding eye contact as she spoke. 'Come on then! I've got afternoon surgery and you've got a train to catch.'

'I'm sorry if I upset you,' Tim said, trying to slow her down. 'I shouldn't have asked. I'm sorry.' He took both her hands in his and held them firmly.

He waited until she looked up at him.

'I'm sorry,' he said again.

'Don't be. It's no big deal.'

'You said "we" didn't want them? Was it really a mutual decision?'

Alison considered this even though she had gone over this

question from every angle, over and over again. She wanted to get the answer right for Tim. It was important.

'There's no such thing as a mutual decision in marriage. You must know that. It would be unfeasible to expect each partner to contribute exactly fifty per cent to every decision. In my experience, there is always one partner who tends to hold the casting vote.'

'So it was what's-his-name who didn't want children? And you did?'

'His name's Gabriel. And it wasn't so straightforward. When we met, I told him that I would never want kids. Even when we married I was convinced I wouldn't want a family. We were going to work in England for a few years, save some money, then travel with Médecins Sans Frontières, take our skills to somewhere they're really needed.'

Tim could almost hear the young Alison making plans with her idealistic Brazilian. 'So what changed?'

'I changed,' Alison said. 'I don't know where it came from. Maybe it was all the New Baby clinics or just the old cliché of the biological clock. I hoped that Gabriel would feel the same. But he didn't.'

Tim ached for her. 'So what did you do?' he asked.

Alison sighed. 'We talked about it for months but there was no compromise possible. I wanted a baby, soon, and he didn't, ever. It all got nasty in the end. He left two weeks ago.'

Tim thought back. Two weeks. That was about the time she first tried to contact him. A more perceptive man might have been alerted by the coincidence to the possibility that this was a woman clearly on the rebound. But to Tim, it was simply a logical sequence of events: marriage ends irreparably, move on. That was what he would do. 'So what are your plans now?'

Alison looked at him.

'I don't know. What are yours?'

But it was time for Tim to catch his train back to central London. The question went with him although he omitted it from his account to Graham. Along with every reference to babies. He just forgot that part.

'What are your plans?' Tess asked Max.

Max stretched and yawned. He hadn't got to bed until three a.m. after a run to Gatwick Airport.

'I thought I'd hang around the office. They give first refusal on the best jobs to whoever's there. And I can get to know the other blokes.'

'Blokes?' Tess said in amusement. 'Since when have you said "blokes"?'

Max ignored her. 'What about you? Running a marathon?'

Tess ignored him. She somehow managed to lever herself out of bed but was incapable of straightening her back or her legs. She staggered into the living room where most of their packing boxes were still awaiting attention. She rummaged superficially through the top layers, desperately searching for paracetamol or alcohol or anything that might deaden her pain.

'I thought I was quite fit,' she said to Max who had followed her into the living room, thoroughly enjoying the sight of his wife trying to straighten up or simply walk. 'I must have been a better teacher than I thought; I exercised muscles in myself that I didn't know existed. I mean, did you know you had muscles in your fingertips? Because they hurt as well.'

Max tried to look as if he were taking her seriously. 'If I were being argumentative, I might say that a good teacher wouldn't render her students paralysed twenty-four hours later and would, at the very least, be able to move her own limbs.'

Tess would have thrown something at him, had she not lost the ability to use her hands. At that point, Lara came into the room, already in her school uniform.

Tess and Max were stunned by this apparition. Tess would even have made a dramatic gesture if any dramatic movement were physically possible.

'I can't believe it,' Max said. 'What happened to the girl we used to have to drag out of bed with threats and bribes and the occasional unfair, but cunning, subterfuge?'

Lara rolled her eyes. Damn, Tess thought. I could have done *that* dramatic gesture. She rolled her own eyes just to make sure that they didn't hurt. They didn't.

Lara helped herself to a bowl of cereal. 'I just don't want to be late for school,' she said. 'Some of the girls and I have agreed to meet before register, swap stickers.'

Max and Tess melted with admiration for their daughter's resilience and ease at settling into a new school after such a dramatic upheaval.

119

Lara piled a huge spoonful of Rice Krispies into her mouth. 'And after school, we're all going to Claire's Accessories to buy some glittery tights. Can I have five pounds please?'

Crash! Down to earth fell Tess and Max. They looked at each other in despair. Lara had never been refused anything in her life and, while they'd known that this would have to happen soon, neither wanted to be the first to expose her to their harsh new reality.

'Here you are, Lara.' Max kept his head lowered as he gave her the money. Lara tucked it into her purse with a cursory 'Thanks, Dad.'

Tess glared at Max, barely suppressing her fury. So I've got to be the tough one, have I? She knew that she should snatch the £5 note back from Lara. But she couldn't do it. Later, she thought wearily, I'm too tired to fight right now.

They'd both woken up in an optimistic mood after getting through their first day of poverty with relative ease. Max was exhausted and Tess had lost the use of most of her body but these were new sensations and strangely appropriate when everything else in their life was so new. A hiccup over money like this was inevitable and Tess was determined not to let it ruin the rest of the day.

'I might be seeing you later,' Tess said to her daughter.

'What for?' Lara frowned, resenting her mum's attempts to muscle in on her new territory.

'I'm sure I told you. I'm teaching yoga. Well, it's not exactly yoga, just gentle exercise, breathing techniques, that sort of thing. It's very unusual to find it in a primary school.'

'Is that the same as the thing you're doing with the women? The exercise thing?' Tess nodded. 'Are you sure you can actually do that?' Lara asked dubiously. 'You never did anything like that at my old school.'

'That's because I wasn't asked,' Tess said awkwardly. She and Max had discussed what they should tell Lara about her mother's new job. They couldn't tell her the truth and expect her to keep it to herself. She was ten, she was female, she was born to blab. So they concocted a mildly dishonest story of Tess having taught yoga before Lara was born and only now having the time to take it up again.

Lara, like most children, couldn't believe that either of her parents had any form of meaningful existence before her birth, which made this a convincing cover story dull enough not to warrant further interrogation from an otherwise curious daughter.

'Just promise me one thing, Mum,' Lara asked solemnly.

Tess waited expectantly. 'Go on.'

'Promise me you won't wear those leopard-print leggings or that T-shirt that shows your bra or your stripy tights or any of your things with sequins on. They are so uncool!'

Tess felt unexpectedly hurt by this request. Lara had singled out her mum's favourite clothes, her stay-at-home gear, the things she bought when nobody was with her, that she only wore when she was alone or when they went on holiday without other families. They were her civvies, her inappropriate, unstylish choices deliberately out of keeping with her usual conformist uniform.

Sometimes Tess considered shifting gradually away from her conventional style, one that she couldn't recall ever consciously choosing, into her preferred offbeat clothes. But she knew she couldn't. Too many questions.

She always felt most like herself when she dressed unconventionally, yet her daughter was embarrassed by that mother. That hurt. Tess was being forced back into the cage from where she'd made a few tentative steps towards freedom in recent days.

'Of course I won't,' she said to Lara gently. She wanted her daughter to be proud of her. That was more important to Tess than being proud of herself. 'Perhaps I'll borrow your S-Club crop top,' she added solemnly as she walked past.

'Mum!' Lara shrieked.

'Only joking.' But Tess wished she wasn't. She felt that Heather would cheerfully walk into the school in a see-through body stocking and that she wouldn't give a toss what her children said.

They heard the crash of their letter box and the thud of mail falling to the floor. Lara rushed to get it. She was still young enough to find all post potentially exciting. Even junk mail occasionally had free gifts like stickers or pens. But she knew that this was all boring. All the envelopes were brown. She handed them to Max, who just looked at them.

'We've been living here for forty-eight hours. How can we possibly have bills already?'

'Open them,' Tess said anxiously. 'Maybe they're just information leaflets or something.'

'Let's wait until Lara has gone,' Max whispered.

Tess flinched. Of course they shouldn't do this while Lara was there, but she should have observed that herself, she shouldn't have needed Max to point it out.

'Bye Mum!' Lara called.

Tess looked at the clock. 'Are you going already?'

Lara sighed the age-old sigh of children exasperated by stupid parents. 'I told you, Mum, I want to get in early.'

Max mimicked the sigh. 'She *told* you, Mum.'

Tess glared at him. 'OK, sweetie. Well, have a good day.'

Lara quickly kissed her parents and then she was gone.

Tess turned to Max. 'Can you believe that, up until last week, she hadn't even walked to school by herself, we always took her in the car? Although I suppose the school is only twenty-five yards away now. A car journey would be a bit silly.'

Max sensed that her pride was underwritten with a note of sadness that their daughter was growing up.

'Now she's living in a part of London she doesn't know, in a school where she didn't know anyone and she's as happy as ever.'

Tess smiled. 'We always said it would be nice for her to be able to walk to school.'

'There you go!' Max said cheerfully. 'Sometimes the best decisions are the ones forced upon us.'

'If you say so. Let's see if you're still saying that when you've opened those bills.'

Max sat down and opened each envelope slowly, glanced at each bill (sadly, no information leaflets) then laid the invoices in a neat pile on the table.

'Well?' Tess asked anxiously.

Max took a deep breath. 'We're in big, big trouble.'

Tess closed her eyes. The short-lived holiday romance with poverty was over. It was fun while it lasted. Now they were back home where you could drink the water but you lost your suntan.

What do we do now? Tess asked herself. She knew that she should be saying this to Max but he looked too worried. Later, she thought. She went over to him and rested her hands lightly on his shoulders. She would have rubbed them but her arm muscles had packed up like the rest.

'We'll sort it out,' she said.

'How?' Max was beginning to sound panicked.

'We've both got to work today. Let's talk about it later.'

Max brightened slightly at the mention of work. He'd always liked the idea of practical solutions to practical problems. And he'd always preferred practical problems to the emotional kinds, like the baby kind. He didn't respond well to advice such as: 'take one day at a time', 'think positively' or 'count your blessings'. But he could handle: 'why not drive back and forwards to and from Stansted Airport and see how much money you can make'.

I just want to be with people who don't know anything about me, people who don't expect me to behave a certain way. I want to be able to pretend that nothing's wrong, that I'm a man in full control of his life and that I don't need reassurance from my wife or anyone else.

He remembered how friendly Archie had been at the minicab office when Max had agreed to take the midnight job that nobody else wanted. Archie, the cheeky chappie. He wouldn't try to protect him or ask him how he was ever going to get out of debt.

That's who I want to be with right now. Archie.

He jumped up. 'I'll just have a quick shower then I'll be off. I might be able to pick up a businessman needing a last-minute airport run.'

He brushed Tess's hands away carelessly.

Tess knew that he could take businessmen to the airport every couple of hours for the next month and it would hardly make a dent in their financial problems. She bit back the resentment that she was being left to bear the burden of worrying about their situation.

That's the role I picked in this marriage, she thought. I'll just have to deal with it. But who's going to help me with *my* burdens? Who's going to listen to me and advise me? Max turns to me but who do I turn to?

I want Heather.

'I think we might be in trouble,' Millie said.

Tim bit his lip. He resented every incursion Millie made into his thoughts right now. He was fine if she stuck to the necessities, stuff about the children, what time he'd be home, gossip about her wretched friends, he could switch on autopilot and churn out suitable hmms and haahs and the occasional 'I can imagine' when

123

Millie was clearly expecting a sign of interest. But anything demanding his full attention was an intrusion.

'What?' he said bluntly. He softened when he saw Millie cringe. 'Sorry, I didn't mean to snap, problems at work.'

'You didn't say you had problems,' Millie said, genuinely concerned. 'What's wrong?'

Great, Tim thought. Now I'm going to have make up problems. As if my real ones weren't bad enough. 'Oh nothing much, just a client who's being difficult. I can handle it.'

He forced a smile that made him look alarmingly like Jack Nicholson in *The Shining*. After he'd gone mad and was running round that maze with the knife. One look at that smile was enough to convince Millie that now was not the time to share bad news with her husband. She'd leave it for now, wait until he was less belligerent, then they could really talk. Because, although he couldn't know it, they had something big to talk about.

Tim's jaw was aching from holding the smile. 'So come on, tell me, what's the trouble?'

Millie patted his hand as if he were a baby demanding attention. 'It can wait. You get off to work.' She kissed him on the top of his head then dashed into the bathroom to throw up.

I hate it when she does that, Tim thought, flinching from the cursory kiss. I'm like a fifth child to her. She talks to me and treats me exactly the same as the other kids. I'm sick of it. I want to be a grown-up again. I want to have grown-up conversations with other grown-ups. I want to tell someone *my* big troubles. And more than anything in the world, I want to talk about something, *anything*, that doesn't involve children.

I want Alison.

'Oh by the way!' Millie called from the bathroom.

What now? Tim closed his eyes to concentrate on his dwindling levels of patience. 'Yes, dear?'

Millie took a deep breath. Just do it! she told herself. 'I meant to tell you. You'll need to get back on time tonight. I'm going out.'

'Who with?'

'An old friend,' Millie replied with all the mystery she could muster through her nausea. Tim shrugged to himself and left. Millie heard the door close and hoped the seed had been sown.

She crouched on the bathroom floor. This was the most draining morning sickness she'd ever experienced. She wondered if was made worse by her worries about Tim. She knew that something was wrong and she knew that whatever it was, the news of her pregnancy was not helping.

Well it's not doing me too many favours either, she thought bitterly. I'd been looking forward to being a grown-up again, not just a mother, but a person in my own right. I've forgotten a lot of the skills, how to talk without a squeaky voice and a Mary Poppins smile, how to focus on someone without letting my eyes dart all around, trying to catch sight of one child or another, even how to talk about subjects that are not child-related.

It's hard when I've done nothing *but* be a mother for ten years. But I was going to work at it. I'd already started. I was even making time to read the paper every morning, something I've not been able to do with the kids at home.

But that's finished now. I spend the morning throwing up and the rest of the day trying to catch up with the things I was supposed to be doing in the morning. Later on I'm going to have to pretend to go out to try and make Tim jealous.

I think I'm going mad. I just want someone to talk to. Someone to listen to *my* troubles. Someone who sees beyond the play-doh in my hair. Someone to tell me I'm doing the right thing or, if not, to come up with an alternative.

I want Fiona.


Fiona sat at the kitchen table nursing a lukewarm cup of tea that she'd made with a tea bag. She derived a certain perverse pleasure from that but it wasn't enough to compensate for the previous evening's miseries.

Graham had come home with two bunches of flowers, one for her and one for Daphne. Fiona had looked at him with astonishment. She knew what such a gesture of generosity must have cost him, when he hated her mother, and hugged him warmly trying to silence the nagging voice that asked if he was trying too hard and, if so, why.

'Look Mum! Look what Graham's bought you.'

Graham took the spectacular bunch of lilies over to Daphne who was sitting uncomfortably on an upright chair. He kissed her quickly on the cheek, then presented her with the flowers.

They are so beautiful, Daphne thought. She wanted to cry at his kindness, especially since she knew how much he must loathe having her here. But she couldn't cry. Once she lost her self-control, who knew what she might say or do? So she pursed her lips tightly together and took the flowers.

'Thank you,' she said. 'But I can't have them near me. Lily pollen stains dreadfully. You never get it out. Fiona, arrange these in a vase and put them up out of the way somewhere they can't do any damage.'

It came out more harshly than she'd intended. It always did and she didn't know why. The pain in her body had abated after taking her six o'clock medication and she wanted to make up for her earlier display of weakness by adding a note of feistiness to her voice. I want Fiona to know I've still got all my faculties, she thought, that's all.

But she always ended up sounding plain nasty. She was trying to change but she couldn't. You can't at my age, she wanted to say to her family as they looked at her, resenting her continued existence on this planet. But she said nothing. She'd never spoken to any of her children about things like that and it was too late to start now.

Graham bit back the accusations of ingratitude that were threatening to spill over. You're a wicked woman and a terrible mother, he wanted to say. But he'd prepared himself for this and he wasn't going to let Fiona down.

Fiona however wasn't going to let it pass so easily. 'Why can't you just be nice to Graham for once? Why can't you just say: "They're beautiful. Thank you so much for welcoming me into your home. Thank you for rearranging the entire house to suit me. Thank you for not making me go and live in an old people's home" which is where, incidentally, all your other sons and daughters-in-law wanted to put you.'

Daphne wanted to say all those things but she couldn't, especially not now Fiona had told her she had to say them. Once you start doing and saying what you're told, you've given up your independence. And then you may as well just die.

'I did say thank you,' she said tightly. 'I'm sorry if I was supposed to make a speech. I didn't realise you had to thank your own family for every little thing they do for you. I don't recall you ever thanking me for everything I did for you.'

This was the precursor to a standard argument conducted

between mothers and children everywhere. Fiona knew it by heart. She was tempted to record her lines so that, the next time it came up, she could simply switch on the tape and let it play out without her having to say a word or even be in the same room.

But she was determined that tonight would not be ruined. It was never going to be jolly, but it could at least be civil. On her part. Bring the kids in, she thought. They were guaranteed to keep Daphne under control.

'I thought we'd all eat together as it's your first night,' she said lightly. 'Kids!' she shouted. 'Lay the table please!'

The sound of eight feet hurtling down the stairs distracted them all from the tension in the kitchen. Fiona turned up the heat on the stove to speed the meal along.

Rebecca, their eldest, came into the kitchen. Daphne's face was transformed by a smile. 'Hello, sweetheart. Have you finished your homework?'

'Yes, Granny. Mum, have we got time for a game of cards with Granny before dinner?'

'Of course. You've got ten minutes.'

'Come on, Granny, hurry up.'

Daphne got to her feet as fast as she could and followed her favourite granddaughter into the family room.

'Don't you think it's funny that Rebecca's her favourite and she's the one who looks most like you?' Graham asked, realising this fact for the first time.

'Don't be silly! It's just that Rebecca is the most patient with her and doesn't annoy her. Everyone likes good children. That's why she never liked me. Still doesn't.'

Graham put his arms round her. 'She does. She just doesn't know how to show it or say it. But it's her loss.'

'What has she lost?'

'You,' Graham replied simply.

Fiona closed her eyes, not knowing what to say. Sometimes she found his kindness too much to take. It was an unwelcome legacy from her mother, who was also unable to receive with grace. She had been teaching herself throughout this marriage to simply let Graham love her. But in her mother's presence she found it difficult. It made her question his love. She playfully pushed him away. 'Go and get changed. You'll get lily pollen on that suit and then what will we do?'

Graham pretended to sulk before leaving her alone in the kitchen. The evening hadn't got much better, Fiona recalled. Dinner was fine. Daphne was needlessly tolerant with the children although she constantly undermined Fiona and Graham by countermanding all their orders that the kids finish everything on their plates, close their mouths when eating and generally behave like humans rather than creatures in a David Attenborough documentary.

After dinner, Daphne had read each child a bedtime story in their room. Fiona had listened to her mother's voice echoing through the baby alarms that were still switched on at night. She remembered her mum reading to her and wondered when that had stopped and why.

Daphne too was recalling those nights but she knew when it had stopped. Fiona had come home from school one day when she was eight and announced that she could read herself now and didn't need her mum to do it for her any more.

It was the usual thoughtless cruelty that parents grow to expect from their children but it still hurt. That's why she so cherished the opportunity to restart the tradition with her grandchildren.

Later on, she'd come downstairs to join Graham and Fiona. They were sitting in the living room, chatting about Graham's day. They both stopped talking when Daphne entered the room, making her feel immediately like an outsider. She didn't begrudge them their intimacy. In fact she was happy for Fiona. Her sons had all made fairly dull marriages and she watched them growing old before their time, aware they'd settled for mediocrity but lacking the imagination to do anything about it.

'I'll be going to bed then,' she said abruptly.

'But it's only eight-thirty,' Fiona protested. 'I didn't think you went to bed until eleven or twelve.'

Daphne had already turned round and was painfully making her way up the stairs, one step at a time. 'You don't want me getting in the way. I'll be fine in my room.'

She heard her martyred voice whining and hated herself for it, far more than anyone else could hate it. It wasn't intentional. She was using all her energy to order her disobedient limbs to move in the way she wanted. Her voice just had to take care of itself and if it sounded old and self-pitying, well, she was an old woman who wasn't very happy to be old.

Fiona spent the rest of the evening taking out her frustration on Graham who just absorbed it like the marital sponge he'd been for so long. I wish I hadn't gone on at him like that, she thought the next morning. This is just as hard on him, more so probably because it's not his mother. But he's so good at listening and he's so patient.

She was struck once more by how distant he'd seemed all evening. At the time, she'd decided to put it down to the prospect of living with Daphne, but now she wasn't so sure. Normally, the subject of his mother-in-law would set him off on one of his mini-rants and while he'd expressed a commitment to see this through and support her through the whole ordeal, she'd expected the occasional outburst of rebellion.

There was no point in asking him if something was wrong, he wouldn't tell her anyway. Unless the problem was one which had consequences for Fiona or the children, he felt that it was better to deal with it himself.

And maybe that wasn't such a bad thing if it was just minor, something trivial. Although she'd still rather know about it because, in her opinion, minor troubles could become major if they were not squashed early.

Fiona needed to talk to someone else about it, find out if they thought she was being foolish. Maybe it was just Millie worrying about Tim that had made her paranoid. She needed to run this by someone who knew both her and Graham. I just want to pour it all out, uncensored and unfiltered, without trying to make sense of it all. I want someone who can edit my stream of consciousness into a coherent account of all my current worries. Then I want that someone to tell me what to do.

I want Tess.


Graham accepted that Fiona felt the need to share all the tiny details of her life with him as well as her friends. And the au pair. And her hairdresser. And every total stranger who came into contact with her for more than 30 seconds.

But he was different. She'd always known that about him. He'd never hidden his distaste for endless confession so she shouldn't be surprised if he was now unwilling to share his latest problem with her. Besides, even if he were the type that told his wife every-thing, this would be the one thing he couldn't.

When he'd got to work, there had been another e-mail waiting for him. He opened it, dreading what it might say, but unable to delete it without reading it. Which was what he knew he should do.

*Hi Graham,*

it read.

> *I don't even know if you're getting these messages. I have to send these messages via the website company because they won't pass on your e-mail address.*
>
> *I'll assume you're reading them and don't want to reply. That's fine if you're simply not interested. So just e-mail me back and say so and I'll stop pestering you. And I remember how you always hated me pestering you!*
>
> *But if you're worried about getting in touch, then don't be. I would just love to hear from you, find out what you've done with your life (your biography on the website was a bit sparse!) and if you regret anything. Because I do.*
>
> *I just feel that if we could clear the air over what happened all those years ago, I'd be able to move on. I'm a bit stuck at the moment. Things aren't brilliant and that inevitably makes me want to look back to times when things were better. The best, actually.*
>
> *So, anyway, this is my last try. If I wrote again I'd probably be straying perilously close to stalker territory! So it's down to you now.*

*Love, Christine*

Maybe if things were more settled at home, I'd be able to resist this more easily, he thought. It's not as if I haven't had the chance to stop Daphne from moving in. It was my decision in the end. I did it for Fiona's sake because I love her. Sure, in a different way to Christine, but this is grown-up love. It's more real, more substantial.

But I just wish I had someone I could talk to about all this. Yes, I know I've always said I don't hold with all this talking about your feelings that is considered compulsory with our generation.

But it might be useful to get everything clear in my mind, file each concern in its proper compartment where it belongs so they don't all get muddled up and start cross-contaminating each other.

Obviously I can't talk to Fiona about this. Apart from the fact that she would start panicking about Christine, she might think that this was a new dimension to our relationship and expect me to talk to her all the time, heaven forbid.

I can't talk to Tim because he's so wrapped up in the delights of his own trip to the past that he'll inevitably want to encourage me to do the same.

Max? Well, I like Max. He's a bit like me, keeps himself to himself, lets Tess think she's the boss. But he's the last person who needs somebody else's problems to deal with.

It has to be somebody outside this circle. Someone who knows me but whose influences won't impact on the rest of my life. There's only ever really been one person I've fully opened up to. Of course I paid a price for that, one I was never prepared to pay again. But now I miss that openness.

I miss Christine.

# 8

'How did it go?' Heather asked.

Tess groaned. 'I think teachers of primary school children should all be canonised. Unless they're all on drugs, which is statistically unlikely, they are blessed with supernatural levels of patience. Why they don't beat half those kids senseless, I'll never know.'

'I think because it's against the law,' Heather pointed out. 'They probably fantasise about beating them senseless and exorcise their frustrations by shouting at their spouses like everyone else.'

'Sounds reasonable,' Tess said.

Her first class had been with Year 2, six and seven year olds. Miss Blowers had given her some pointers about what the children could manage.

'Don't expect too much,' the head teacher warned her. 'This is a lively bunch of kids and we're just aiming to calm them down with some gentle exercise, maybe teach them a bit of controlled breathing. Keep it fun and simple and you can't go wrong!'

It sounded great and Tess was confident that this would be a breeze after the demanding women she'd encountered the day before. She greeted the class with her best mummy-voice.

'Now children, my name is Mrs Keane. Would you all like to have a go at saying "Good morning Mrs Keane"?'

'Good morning, Mrs Keane,' the children intoned, bored but compliant, a manageable combination in Tess's opinion.

'Now I want you all to pretend you're trees, so let's all stand up tall and reach up as high as you can. Come on now, reach, reach, reach.'

But when she tried to lift her own arms, the agony forced them straight back down by her sides. She'd forgotten that she was still crippled from her last attempt at teaching. She decided to resort to the trick that had been so effective with the women. She walked around the room, encouraging and correcting until she found her star.

'Now everyone, look at ... what's your name, sweetheart?'

'Davakurunibajeeti,' the girl replied, or that's what it sounded like to Tess.

'What a lovely name!' Tess said, to avoid having to repeat it. Why can't your name be Julie or Mary or Catweazle or anything at all that I can pronounce?

'Everyone look at ... this clever girl.' The class dutifully watched the clever girl reach up while bending rhythmically from the waist.

A boy put his hand up at the end. 'Miss!'

'Yes?' Tess answered, glad to have an opportunity to move away from the girl with the longest name in the world.

'Can you put your legs behind your ears? My mum says the last yoga teacher could do it. And I can do it too. Look.'

He proceeded to sit down, lift up his legs and flick them nonchalantly around his head. Tess felt quite sick. It reminded her how much it hurt her just to move her head.

'You're a very clever boy,' Tess said, hating both this child and the mother that spawned him.

'My mummy went to your lesson yesterday and she said that you're rubbish,' another girl said. 'She said you couldn't do anything yourself so you got other people to do it instead.'

I hate this child and her mother too, Tess thought. Bang goes that idea.

'Sometimes, mummies say things that they don't mean,' she said in her sweetest voice.

The girl looked doubtful. 'My mummy definitely meant it. She said it to my dad and she's always saying "I mean it" when she talks to him.'

Tess felt herself begin to hyperventilate. Then she had an idea. 'I'm going to teach you something your mummies can't do.'

She crossed her fingers and tested Max's theory of the silent prayer that he'd mentioned in passing yesterday.

'Now everyone lie down and close your eyes. All place your hands on your tummies and feel them going up and down as

you breathe in and out. Now I want you to breathe more slowly
…'

Within three minutes the whole class was asleep. She sat on the
floor and pulled out the can of muscle spray that she'd bought on
her way into school. She sprayed herself all over, an act that
caused her more pain than she'd originally been suffering. She
then took some painkillers, the type that said 'fast-acting' on the
box, and sat on the floor waiting for normality to resume in her
broken body.

Minutes before the end of the class, she gently roused the children from their nap.

'Do you all feel rested?' she asked.

They didn't answer, they were too fuzzy-headed with sleep. In
fact, they all looked catatonic. Good, Tess thought, that'll make
their next lesson a bit more peaceful for their poor teacher. In a
trance, they all left the hall to return to their classroom.

As she bent to put her many medications back in her bag, she
felt a click in her back, then a goblin began sticking knives into
her back at rapid intervals, stab, stab, stab. She stood up quickly.
Well, mentally she stood up. Her body stayed resolutely where it
was, bent in classic old-woman stoop, refusing to straighten up.

'Help,' she said quietly to no one in particular.

'Stand still,' came the reply.

I've obviously died and one of those angels has come to get me,
Tess thought, insane with pain. Hopefully I'll be down that tunnel
towards the bright light in a minute then the agony will stop.
Hurry up! I'm ready to die now!

She felt two arms reach round her waist, gently guiding her into
a chair that had miraculously appeared behind her. In relief, she
eased her shoulders against the hard seat's back. Finally she
opened her eyes to face her saviour.

He wasn't an angel (unless French Connection were now
supplying T-shirts at divine level) but he was doing a pretty good
impression. He had one of those faces that are crinkly from
smiling a lot and hair that refuses to behave. A bit like Max, was
Tess's first impression. But she quickly changed her opinion as
she looked at him more closely.

His black hair, while wild, was curly rather than simply
untamed and was actually cleverly cut to look as if it fell naturally
over the tops of his ears. And although his crinkles accurately

reflected an easy tendency to smile, his dark-blue eyes betrayed another, more dangerous tendency – towards risk, taking chances, going too far. That was nothing like Max.

He was only a few inches taller than she was and she was surprised by how comforting the similarity in height was. After years of looking up to Max, she realised that the disparity in their sizes had begun to feel like a symptom of wider, more insidious differences.

'Are you OK?' the stranger asked, kneeling in front of Tess in concern.

Tess gingerly lifted her head and turned it from side to side, then she slowly straightened her spine, managing not to scream. She had decided to defer death for a while but she was still suffering.

'I'm fine,' she whispered. 'I think I just pulled something.'

The man looked towards the door where the last of the comatose children were slouching out. 'Look, that's my class, I'm going to have to go. If I leave them alone for more than a few seconds, they tend to start breaking the tables for firewood.'

Not today they won't, Tess thought proudly. You'll be lucky if they make it back to their classroom without slumping back into unconsciousness.

'You go,' she said. 'I'll be fine in a minute.' Once you've gone, I'll take some more tablets. I have a variety, there's bound to be a combination I can take that won't kill me. And if it does kill me, that's all right too.'

The man looked unwilling to leave but stood up. 'If you're sure. By the way, I'm Jerry Newton. We weren't introduced.'

'Tess Keane, I'd shake hands, but I can't actually lift my arm. You'd have to sit on my lap and then I'd scream because that hurts too.'

'Don't tempt me,' Jerry said. Then he winked and ran off.

Tess watched him leave in astonishment. He ran like a boy, unself-conscious and confident. He turned and smiled at her, not surprised to see her watching him so carefully. That was when Tess noticed that he was stockily built, reassuringly so. Whereas Max had always enveloped her from above, this man could cushion her, wrap himself around her like a papoose.

She shook her head to dislodge the image. It wasn't my fault, she reassured herself. That man was flirting with me. She forgot her pain for a moment. Oooh, I've remembered it again. But as the painkillers kicked in along with a delicious wooziness, she found herself thinking of the man. Then stopping herself for being so ridiculous. And so married. Then thinking about him again.

'I think that was very resourceful of you,' Heather said in admiration.

Tess had given her an abridged version of the catastrophe, one which left out her pain, her ineptitude and a certain mother's savage indictment of Tess's yoga skills that were relayed to her. Oh and the bit about Jerry Newton, she left that out as well.

'I just felt they needed calming down. Once they get used to me, I'll start introducing some proper moves,' Tess added, anxious that she didn't appear completely unprofessional, even though that was exactly what she was.

The little girl's comments were still needling her. She knew she was going to have to confront this if she was going to have the confidence, or the sheer cheek, to continue.

Tess took a deep breath. 'I want you to be completely honest with me. How do you think yesterday went?'

Heather considered this. 'Not great but not bad either. It was your first time, so I think everyone put it down to nerves. I think you mentioned that you hadn't taught since before you were pregnant?'

Tess nodded, trying not to blush as her lie was repeated back to her.

Heather shrugged. 'You're out of practice. It'll take you a few weeks to get back in the swing of things and it'll take the ladies a few weeks to get used to you. The last teacher was like a circus contortionist, she could practically turn her body inside out.'

Tess drooped at the prospect of following such an act. No wonder she seemed so hopeless. But then again, even by a non-contortionist's standard, she was hopeless.

Heather saw Tess's face dropping. 'No, no, don't think like that. We all felt completely inadequate. None of us would ever be able to do the things she was doing. We just weren't built the same way. So it's nicer to have someone we can actually relate to.'

'I don't think all of the women feel that way,' Tess said miserably. Heather's kindness made her feel even worse about her prolonged deception. She wanted to come clean and admit that she was no more a yoga teacher than she was a test pilot.

But then she remembered the pile of bills that had arrived. At this point, her family's need for money was more important than a principle. If she and Max ever made enough money to start having principles again, the first thing she was going to do was pay for an experienced yoga teacher to take over her job. Then she would buy lunch for the whole class. And beg Heather's forgiveness.

But in the meanwhile, there was the problem of money.

'What's the problem?' Heather asked.

Tess was startled by a further display of Heather's mind-reading skills.

'It's written all over your face,' Heather said, smiling,

'I've never had my thoughts written all over my face before,' Tess said. 'I'm sure someone would have mentioned it otherwise.'

Heather shrugged. 'Maybe they weren't paying that much attention to your face. Maybe they were just listening to you, accepting everything you said as an accurate representation of your thoughts.'

Tess was surprised. 'And you don't think that's the case?'

'You have this funny little habit of pausing, ever so slightly, before answering a question, as if you have to get clearance from a higher authority.'

'No I don't,' Tess said defensively. Then she remembered her unconscious decision not to mention her flirtatious brush with the teacher. Do I do that all the time? she wondered, censor myself without thinking.

'Yes you do,' Heather insisted. 'My husband used to do it all the time and he denied it like you. He didn't know he was doing it, it was just a habit as I'm sure it is with you. The only difference is why you both do it. Now my husband did it because he was a fantasist and a liar. That's how we ended up in so much financial trouble. He became so used to filtering his words for anything that might incriminate him, that it became an automatic mechanism. He'd do it even when there was nothing to hide.'

'So why do I do it?' Tess asked, still not convinced that it was true.

'I don't know you well enough to answer that one, although I'm sure it's not for such underhand reasons. You'll have to work that out for yourself.'

137

Great, Tess thought, something else for me to work out.

'Hi, it's me!'

Tim almost dropped the phone. He'd been thinking about Alison and now she'd phoned him. This convinced him that they had some kind of cosmic connection. Of course if he'd considered it logically he'd have realised that he thought about Alison all the time and Alison had said that she would call today so the coincidence was virtually guaranteed.

'I was thinking about you,' he said, lowering his voice so that his workmates wouldn't hear him.

'I could tell.'

Tim's journey into romantic insanity was now complete. 'Really? That's amazing. We used to do this all the time at school, do you remember?'

'Not just then. When I left, sometimes I'd find myself in the most unlikely setting, in a desert or up a mountain, and I'd think of you and imagine you doing the same.'

Now, since Tim continued to obsess over Alison for two years after she left, it will be no surprise to learn that this, too, struck him as evidence of some force of destiny holding them together through time.

'When you've got a minute, Tim!' The voice of his co-director sent the needle scratching along the gramophone record playing the sentimental music which accompanied this scene. Tim returned to normal, if not to full sanity.

'Sorry, Ali, I can't talk for long. Things are a bit hectic around here.'

'That's OK. I've only got a few minutes myself. I was just wondering when we could meet up again.'

The romantic music in his mind had suddenly been replaced with the theme to *Jaws*. Because even if his brain was operating on the level of a teenager, his musical director could see this scene from all angles and knew exactly what was going on.

'I hadn't given it much thought,' he said. This was a lie of epic proportions since he'd thought of little else. But underneath the madman who was treating this whole episode like an amateur dramatics production with himself in the juvenile lead, the other well-adjusted Tim was still there waiting patiently to be released from the locked, soundproofed room.

Which was the real Tim was the question both Tims needed to sort out before making any life-changing decisions.

A picture of Millie suddenly presented itself before Tim's eyes. Even when he closed his eyes the picture was still there. It was an old photo, taken before they had children. Tim barely recognised her. Funnily enough, she looked a bit like Alison. He'd never noticed that before and felt unnerved by the realisation.

I wonder who she's going out with tonight? I know everybody she knows. Normally she'd say: 'I'm going out with Tess and Fiona' or, 'I'm seeing Gill who I used to work with.' Never just 'an old friend'. Strange. Then the thought vanished as quickly as it arose.

Another picture flashed up. It was a family shot, Millie, the four children and himself. There were arms and legs all over the place. It was a mess. There were three hands on him, but none of them were Millie's. They all looked happy. He remembered the photo being taken. They *were* happy. It was taken on holiday and they were all tanned, dishevelled and relaxed.

He put a mental finger over his face in the photo, just to see what the group looked like without him, how *he* felt without *them*. He felt . . . not quite right. But not bad either.

'Are you still there, Tim?' All the pictures disappeared as soon as he heard Alison's voice.

'Sorry, I was just thinking. I'm not sure whether all this is a good idea.'

There was silence on the line.

'Hello?' he said.

'Now I'm the one doing the thinking,' Alison said sadly. 'I can see this is difficult for you. This is all my fault. I'm sorry.' Then she put the phone down.

Tim was horrified. He immediately called her back. 'Please don't hang up! I'm the one who should be sorry. I'm such a ditherer, but then you already know that.' Alison didn't say anything. Tim went on quickly, before she hung up again. 'We're not doing anything wrong, are we? Just talking, catching up on old times. So let's meet up again. Soon. How about tomorrow?'

This time, to make up for his hesitation, Tim said he would try and take the whole afternoon off. To his relief, Alison seemed pleased.

In fact she was more than pleased. After she'd hung up that first time, she'd realised that it was a bit of a gamble. But the gamble had paid off, and Tim had called her back, more eager than ever.

He hasn't changed, she thought, thank goodness. I always could make him do whatever I wanted.

'Hi Tess, it's Fiona. It's ten o'clock. Can you give me a call as soon as you get in. Thanks.'

'Me again. It's now half past eleven. Your mobile's switched off. Are we still meeting up. Call me back, I'm at home.'

'You guessed, me again. One of us has made a mistake, probably me. I thought we were coming over today and you were going to call us to fix a time once you knew what you were doing. Give me a call anyway, I'd really love a chat.'

Damn, damn, damn. My mistake, not yours, Tess thought. She'd completely forgotten about having Fiona and Millie over. She'd lost all sense of time since moving at the weekend. Her routines had been blown away, all the old points of reference had been pulled from her eyeline.

She hadn't realised how dependent she'd become on her morning routines to ground her. Over the years, she and Fiona (and sometimes Millie) had fallen into a set pattern: Monday, coffee at Organique, Tuesday, big grocery shop together, Wednesday, coffee at one of their houses, Thursday, boring stuff at home, Friday, lunch somewhere nice.

It took her a few seconds even to work out that today was Tuesday. Every day was somewhere new right now. She was relying on Heather to help ease her into the new neighbourhood, show her around, tell her where to go, where not to go. But she was relying on Heather for other things as well. Heather was her friend in this place. Fiona was her friend in the other place. It felt easier to separate them. She loved Fiona like a sister but she couldn't share her new problems with her.

If she told her about all the bills which had arrived that morning, Fiona would just want to give her money and that could ruin their friendship. On top of that, the whole yoga thing was too weird and Tess was still embarrassed about it all. And she felt disloyal saying anything negative about Max when the couples knew each other so well.

But that didn't excuse forgetting an arrangement. She picked up the phone straightaway.

'Hello?' Daphne answered the phone, clearly out of breath. Tess had forgotten about Daphne as well.

'Mrs. Guinn! Hello! It's Tess, Fiona's friend. How are you settling in?'

'I know who you are. I wish you wouldn't all treat me as if I'm stupid.'

Now Tess knew why Fiona was so desperate to see her. She was amazed Daphne was still alive. Any other daughter would have throttled this woman by now.

'Is Fiona in?' she asked patiently.

'No, she's gone out.'

'Any idea where she's gone?'

'She doesn't have to tell me where she's going to be twenty-four hours a day. I'm not a prison warder.'

'I'll try her on her mobile. Bye.' Tess put the phone down before she was forced to scream at the woman.

Why was I like that? Daphne asked herself. Why do I have to be so unpleasant? It's not my fault. I could hear it in her voice, the way she spoke to me as if I'm a child. It just makes me so cross. Why can't Fiona's friends just talk to me normally? Ask me what I think of things, what I'm reading, anything. Now she thinks I'm a miserable old bag. And I'm not. Really I'm not.

Miserable old bag, Tess thought, dialling Fiona's mobile. Fiona picked up on the first ring.

'Fi! It's Tess. Look, I'm really sorry about today. Things are really hectic here. I'm not unpacked, Max is never in and I'm looking for work.'

'It's OK,' Fiona said. 'I understand. We can catch up when you've got yourself sorted out.'

Does she sound a little cool or am I imagining it? Tess thought.

'Where are you now?' Tess asked. 'If you're not too far away, perhaps we can meet up?'

'I'm at Millie's. Let's leave it for today. By the time you got here, we'd have to be making a move for the school run. We'll talk later in the week.'

'OK then, bye.' Tess felt flat when she hung up. She also felt left out, thinking of Fiona and Millie, which was a bit rich when Tess had stood Fiona up because she herself was wrapped up with her new friend.

I am never going to have an affair, Tess thought. I couldn't stand all the complications. She stared at the bills on the table which all seemed to bear the words DUE NOW printed in black ink across the large sums.

Mind you, it feels as if affairs are the only complications I don't have in my life at the moment, she thought.

'Do you think Graham might be having an affair?'

Millie burst out laughing then stopped when she saw Fiona's anxious face.

'I can tell you the answer to that without even knowing the facts. Graham is not having an affair. Nor will he ever have one. If I had to pick one man who was not the type, it would have to be Graham.'

'Are you saying that nobody would want Graham? Or that Graham is boring?' Fiona was now indignant on her husband's behalf. She had always suspected that her friends found him dull.

'Of course I'm not,' Millie said, tired of having to be reassuring all the time.

She was finding this exhausting, especially since she was in need of some serious reassurance herself. Why can't Fiona go and offload this on Tess? I don't need this today.

'Sorry, Millie. I didn't mean to snap. I know what you mean. I don't really think he'd do anything like that but he's definitely preoccupied and I can't think of anything that could be bothering him. Unless he's having an affair which, I agree, is not likely.'

Millie stared at her. 'When I told you I was concerned about Tim, you told me to talk to him, spend time with him, you made me feel it was all my fault for not communicating. Now you're in the same position I could say the same thing to you.'

It was hard to know who was the most horrified by Millie's venom. It was the first unpleasant thing Fiona had ever heard Millie say and she resented being the one on the receiving end.

'God, Fiona, I'm so sorry. I should never have said that. I don't mean it.' (Actually she did, but she saw no point in mentioning that.)

Fiona decided to be big and accept the apology. 'So is Tim still being a bit off?' she asked gently.

Millie nodded miserably. 'If anything he's getting worse.' She was about to tell Fiona what she was planning but was feeling too weak to withstand her friend's inevitable opposition.

'Maybe it's just a mid-life crisis?' Fiona suggested. The more she considered this, the more it made sense. 'If you think about it, they're both about the same age, both with four kids, both in the same job for a long time, both having a major domestic upheaval forced upon them. Other men in their position might well go off and have an affair but if that option isn't available what can they do?'

Millie looked stumped. 'Can't they just do what we do? Drink coffee and eat cake until they feel sick?'

'It doesn't work like that with men. Think they're wired differently. No, I think they brood, let it fester. They have no outlet. What they need is all the thrill of the affair without the guilt.'

'I've still got no idea what you're getting at.' Millie was not liking this talk of affairs.

'Us! They can have an affair with us!'

'You mean wife-swapping!' Millie said in horror.

Fiona recoiled. 'Are you mad? Of course not! I'm talking about spicing up our marriages, putting the romance back.'

Millie screwed up her nose. 'You mean, start holding our stomachs in and brushing our hair before we go to bed?'

Fiona despaired at Millie's definition of romance and began to feel a profound sympathy for Tim. 'That's a good start,' she said cautiously.

Millie looked sceptical. She didn't like to say that she'd tried that already and the result was growing inside her. Once she'd got through this pregnancy, she had no intention of spicing up her marriage again until one or the other of them was sterilised. Maybe both to be on the safe side.

Fiona was waiting for her response. Millie settled on something noncommittal.

'I'll leave it till we get to Provence, I think. I know I'll be bigger then but it's easier to do things differently on holiday, less confrontational.'

Fiona thought that Millie would be wiser to start doing things differently right now but she didn't say it.

'Are you still feeling bad?' she asked, changing the subject.

'Pretty bad, but that's not the half of it,' Millie said, grateful for the new topic. She sat down on a stool at the breakfast bar and clasped her hands behind her head in despair.

'What is it?' Fiona asked, quite worried now.

'I went for a scan yesterday.'

Fiona's mouth opened in shock. 'Oh no. Is it the baby? Is it all right? I told you to go and have the scan before. But you wouldn't listen—'

'It's nothing like that,' Millie interrupted. 'But you're right. I should have gone for the scan before now. I just didn't see the point. They can't tell anything in the early weeks anyway. I know my body so well that I would have been able to tell if there was a problem with the pregnancy and if there *was* a problem with the baby, then it probably wouldn't show up until about now.'

'So if the baby's fine, what *is* the problem?'

Millie gazed at the photos of her four children on the kitchen wall.

'The problem is I'm having twins.'


'So what is this place, Archie?' Max asked.

'I told you, it's a club. It's called Carter's. You have to be a member but I can get you membership so don't worry about it.'

Max chuckled to himself at the idea of worrying about being accepted for membership of a club which met in a dingy room above a restaurant. I know I am the King of Worrying, I have been known to worry about the outcome of a table tennis match between two strangers on holiday, but even I will not be losing sleep over this.

'Help yourself to a drink,' Archie said hospitably. He waved an expansive hand towards a rickety table in the corner which held an electric kettle, a jar of instant coffee, a box of tea bags, some powdered milk and sugar. Some chipped and stained mugs completed the spread.

'We're too late for the biscuits,' Archie, apologised. 'Carter puts them out before he opens the restaurant at twelve, but they're usually all gone in the first hour. Come and meet the boys.'

He led Max over to a circle of mismatched threadbare armchairs where a group of men sat discussing last night's football.

'Len, Harry, Mickey, Terry, Rav, Davros, Billy, this is Max, one of my new lads.'

'My old friend!' It took Max a few seconds to recognise the Asian man beaming at him as Rav, the man in the off-licence and world expert in Bombay wines. Today he was wearing a jumper with the New York skyline knitted across it, the twin towers still dominating the scene poignantly and dating the jumper as over two years old. Max wondered if Rav had a wife who liked to knit or whether his jumpers were produced by the innovative family members in Bombay currently creating their unique wine.

'We meet again,' Max said, flattered to be recognised. 'So you're a member too?' he asked.

'Yes.' Rav sounded proud. 'All the local businessmen come here. It's where we do our networking.'

Max stifled a smile. 'Pull up a chair when you've got your drink,' Archie told him.

Max went to make himself a cup of coffee, feeling as if he had been abducted by aliens and was now in a spacecraft heading for a galaxy, far, far away. As he poured boiling water onto the greyish coffee powder, he overheard Archie whispering.

'Yes, he's just joined me. He's keen, a hard worker. Doesn't talk much but I think he's fallen on hard times. Thought we could cheer him up, maybe even help him out once we know his trade. You can tell he's not like the others.'

The mutters of approval made Max choke with emotion. These strangers that he was mocking so readily were more decent than he deserved. He was judging them by the chairs they sat in and the quality of coffee they drank, a habit picked up after years of scrutinising customers in Organique. And look where that got me, he thought cynically.

He went to join the circle, where a chair had already been placed for him. As he sat down, a powerful sense of belonging washed over him, taking him by surprise. I'm not a snob, he said to himself, at least I hope I'm not, but I would never have said that these could be my kind of people. And yet I feel comfortable with them.

'So tell us what you were doing before you came here,' Rav asked.

It took Max some time to realise that they were genuinely interested and, as he found himself telling them the whole story of his collapsed business and current financial crisis, he had the strangest thought: I am among friends.

*

*Dear Christine,*

*Sorry it's taken me so long to answer your e-mails. But you know that I never did anything on impulse. That always used to drive you mad! I expect you want to know why I didn't write sooner and why I finally have now.*

*Obviously you know I'm married and I have four children, that much was on the website. I'm an accountant, you know that too. If this all seems sparse, that's because those are the only things I choose to hold up to scrutiny. They're the elements of my life of which I'm most proud and least confused.*

*So why was I so hesitant about returning your contact? We're both the same age so I suppose we've both gone through the same soul-searching that everyone does when they turn 40. You have a little panic about growing old, putting on a bit of weight, losing a bit of hair (me, not you!) so then you decide to look back instead. Much safer!*

*And looking back for me really only means looking back at you, at us. Frankly, Chris, when I look back, it scares me. I don't like it. And it's pointless. You can't go back in time. Why waste hours or years agonising over whether our lives would have been better with each other?*

*It doesn't matter. This is the life we have. I'm happy with mine. I'm sorry that yours has not worked out so well. Don't forget that the choices were yours.*

*I wish you well.*

*Graham.*

He knew he sounded pompous, even bitter, but he'd planned this message carefully. He didn't want to invite further communication but he did want to draw a line under the past. He'd been tempted to renew contact, like Tim, just so that he could talk to her again. He really wanted to talk to her again. But good sense dissuaded him from that folly.

No, I did the right thing, he told himself. And now I'm going to delete her e-mail address so I won't be tempted to get in touch with her again.

But he wasn't that strong.

Tess walked around the supermarket with a calculator. She'd worked out that she mustn't spend more than £50 a week on groceries but since she didn't know the price of anything, she was having to add everything up as she went along.

She threw things into the trolley and thought she was being very frugal until she checked the running total and found she'd already gone up to £53.49 and she hadn't even got to the cheeses.

'Damn!'

'I occasionally talk to myself. I haven't yet moved on to inanimate objects, I sort of feel that's a madness too far.'

Tess spun round to see the teacher from earlier. She blushed at being caught once more in a humiliating situation by the man.

'Jerry Newton!'

'I'm impressed,' he said. 'I didn't think you were in a fit state to take any notice of my name this morning.'

'I'm just showing off.' Tess wondered how red her face could go before the blood vessels imploded. 'Trying to prove there's a tiny area of my brain still in working order.'

'So what exactly is the problem?' Jerry pointed at the calculator.

Tess was mortified. She couldn't possibly talk about her financial constraints to this man. She'd been brought up to believe that talking about money was common.

'Let me guess,' Jerry said, spotting her embarrassment. 'You're halfway through your list and you've already gone over budget?'

The blush deepened. Nope, Tess thought, clearly still not reached my personal peak of redness. This was either the most intuitive man to exist outside of a Tom Hanks film, or he already knew about her money situation. I must be the talk of the staff room, she thought, flushed with shame.

Jerry was poking curiously around in her trolley. Tess was quite sure that this was not socially correct behaviour but, after her earlier displays, did not feel in a position to criticise.

'How many of you are there?' he asked. 'Five? Six?'

'Er, no, three. Me, my husband and my daughter.' She couldn't believe that she was actually answering this man's prying questions but there was something compelling about his confidence. He was taking command of the situation, *her* situation, and she couldn't stop herself welcoming the intrusion.

Jerry shook his head and tutted. 'All this for three of you! You're new at this sort of thing aren't you?'

Tess stared at him. She was feeling even more awkward but at

147

least she'd stopped blushing. 'Are you in the habit of commenting on the private lives of people you hardly know?' she asked angrily.

'Absolutely. It's one of my character flaws. The only one, now I come to think about it.'

Tess smiled despite herself and shrugged with good humour. This was an unfamiliar state of affairs, as was everything else happening to her on a daily basis, but it felt strangely comforting.

Jerry gently took the trolley away from her, turned it round and started backtracking, depositing half of her shopping back on the shelf. Tess followed obediently, passively, paying attention as he gave her a running commentary on the science of shopping on a budget.

'All this pre-packed fruit and veg can go back. Buy it loose and buy more for your money. You can then use it to bulk up your meat dishes. Now forget chicken breasts, you buy the thighs, add those carrots that are going manky but are half-price, and get two meals by making a pie and a casserole ...'

And so he went on, ordering Tess to keep count on the calculator. It took about 20 minutes and there were a few battles over runny French cheeses and freshly squeezed orange juice. But eventually they reached the checkout with a week's food for £47.20.

'You could get a job doing this,' Tess said in amazement. 'Teaching people how to survive on a shoestring budget.'

'It already *is* my job,' Jerry said drily. 'It's called living on a primary school teacher's salary while paying rent in inner London.'

Tess noticed that he no longer had his own basket. 'What about your own shopping?'

'I'll do it later. I'm exhausted from fighting against your bourgeois extravagant tendencies.'

Tess's head snapped round to make sure he was joking. He looked serious but his eyes were crinkly. She found herself hitting him on the arm the way she did to Max when he teased her. Her instinctive intimacy with this almost-stranger surprised her a bit. And bothered her even more.

'Don't worry about how you're ever going to be able to thank me,' he said. 'You can buy me a coffee and doughnut here. Fifty-eight pence after four-thirty, so you can afford it.'

Before Tess could protest, he had pushed her trolley towards the cafeteria and grabbed a tray. She followed him, nodding vaguely as he pointed at cakes and coffees, then watched him carry the tray in one hand as he expertly steered the trolley towards a table, leaving her to pay the bill.

'Now I'm a kept man,' he said as she sat down opposite him. 'It's a situation I've dreamt of all my life. And you're married as well. Even better!'

Tess interrupted him. 'If you are thinking of next referring to my perhaps being a tiny bit older than you, I wouldn't recommend it!'

He turned down the corners of his mouth in a magnificent frown then immediately stuffed in half of his doughnut. Tess watched him in fascination.

'Are things so bad for teachers that they're forced to supplement their earnings by hijacking trolleys and conning cakes from the unsuspecting woman drivers?'

Jerry considered this. 'I'd never have thought of it before. But now that I've tried it, I shall certainly be adding it to my other extracurricular money-earners like pole-dancing and offering my body for medical research. And what about you? Is your life so empty that you're willing to spend a valuable hour of your time with a relative stranger in a supermarket café?'

Tess was disturbed by his words. They might have been meant as light-hearted banter but they had triggered off some serious questions that she had been avoiding asking herself. Questions about her marriage or, more precisely, the part of her marriage that didn't include Lara. But this wasn't the place.

'I met my husband in a café,' she said wistfully, to herself as much as to Jerry.

'I'll bet it was nothing like this one,' Jerry said in amusement.

'No, it wasn't.' It had been a taverna on Crete. They'd both been holidaying alone, found themselves to be the only English people in a remote village. They'd shared a table, then a long walk in the Cretan mountains, then a tiny sparse room in a converted hayloft, then cramped seats on the charter flight home followed by a swift merging of their separate lives.

'Love at first sight and a holiday romance as well – hardly the ingredients for a successful marriage,' her mother had warned, along with everyone she knew. And maybe she had a point, Tess

149

had conceded during those rocky patches that became more frequent with each passing year.

Like so many couples, they'd made a commitment to each other while still luxuriating on the early heights of infatuation and obsession. By the time, they'd settled down to reality and discovered that the attraction had been fundamentally physical and transient, they were married.

Rather like the decision to go into business in the knowledge that their parents discouraged the idea, they had married quickly, spurred on by parental opposition. Such self-destructive behaviour had united them on one matter at least: they were determined never to be so proscriptive towards Lara that she would feel coerced into rash decisions just to assert her own independence.

'Have you ever tried eating a doughnut without licking your lips?' Jerry asked cheerfully, noticing that her eyes had suddenly become sad.

Tess quickly returned to the present, which was looking more promising than it had done a few hours earlier. She liked this man. She'd never had a male friend before and she wasn't sure whether it was a good or a bad thing. But for now it was good, very good.

# 9

'Well, this was a lovely idea.' In the presence of his old friends, Max had reverted to the jolly host of old. They were all seated round the central table at Carter's, Tess and Max, Fiona and Graham, Millie and Tim. And Daphne.

'This place is totally different in the evening, isn't it?' Tess said to Max.

Max looked around. ' I can't say. I've only been upstairs to the club.'

Tess giggled every time he mentioned the 'club'. Max was indignant. 'Do I mock your ladies for doing PE in a hall and calling it yoga?'

'All the time.'

'Oh yes,' Max conceded. 'So we're even.'

The room was suddenly filled with the deafening sound of Nana Mouskouri singing ... well, no one knew what she was singing. They agreed that everything Nana Mouskouri sang sounded the same.

'Rather like that music your children listen to,' Daphne said accusingly to Fiona. She turned to Millie. 'I happen to think Nana Mouskouri is very good. She had a TV series once, you know?'

Millie nodded politely, wondering who she'd offended to get seated next to this harbinger of misery and vintage TV trivia.

'Now I know what that "Albatross" record was all about,' Max whispered to Tess as they watched Daphne cast a gloomy cloud over not just their table but right across the room.

'Mum, can't you at least make an effort to enjoy yourself?' Fiona hissed.

'I didn't ask to come. I said I'd be quite happy to babysit.'

And she'd meant it. After staying indoors for a few days, her aches and pains had diminished to a tolerable level. She would happily have stayed in for the rest of her life. She'd even been making an effort to sound more cheerful, not complain so much, in the hope that they'd all leave her alone.

But it seemed to have had the opposite effect. She'd overheard Graham and Fiona talking this morning.

'We can't leave her by herself,' Fiona was whispering.

'She won't be by herself, the kids will be here,' Graham reasoned.

'Yes, but in that case, she'll be the babysitter and I don't know if she's up to it.'

'She seems fine to me.' Graham was beginning to suspect that Fiona wanted to think the worst of her mother. Frankly, he'd appreciated the relaxation of tension over the last few days and refused to see a conspiracy theory lurking beneath the calm.

'I think she'd hiding something from us,' Fiona said firmly. 'I think she's sick, I mean really sick, and doesn't want to worry me.'

'Don't be silly. She's just making an effort to fit in.'

God bless you, Graham, Daphne thought.

Fiona was not convinced. 'Don't forget I know her better than you do. The last time she was this amenable was when Dad was leaving us. Even then she couldn't keep it up for long and she made us all feel that it was our fault he'd left.'

That's not true! Daphne thought, clinging to the banister. That's so unfair! I did everything to protect them all. Every day I told them it wasn't their fault. They were the ones who insisted on taking the blame. That's what children do, seeing themselves as the centre of the universe. They *wanted* to blame themselves. Fiona ought to know this now she's a mother herself.

But although Fiona was a mother to four children, she was a child when it came to her own parents and she still saw herself as the centre of their universe. She still believed that everything they had ever done must have been motivated by her or her brothers (but she naturally thought she was the most likely victim, being the only girl and therefore the most special).

Daphne was older and wiser than Fiona and had to accept that her daughter's picture of her childhood and family history was permanently fixed. But she didn't have to like it.

She cleared her throat loudly to alert them to her approach before entering the kitchen.

'Hi Mum,' Fiona said brightly.

Daphne glared at her before walking slowly over to the kettle.

'I'll make you a cup of tea,' Fiona offered, snatching the kettle from her mother. 'You go and sit down.'

Daphne snatched the kettle back. 'I'm quite capable of boiling a kettle, thank you very much.'

Graham telegraphed a silent warning to Fiona, who reluctantly backed down.

'We were just talking about tonight,' Fiona said.

'What about tonight?' Daphne was concentrating on holding the kettle steady as she filled it. She was finding it increasingly difficult to hold any substantial weight in her hands. Damn, she thought, I'm falling apart, bit by bit. It's a shame I *can't* blame it on Fiona since she seems so willing to take everything I do so personally.

'We're going out with friends, you know, Tess and Max and Millie and Tim?'

'Good. Have a lovely time. I can look after the kids, save you getting a babysitter.' There, she used her most pleasant voice. And that's what worried Fiona.

'Well actually, Graham and I thought it would be nice if you came with us. You haven't been out since you got here. A night out might do you the world of good.'

'I'd rather stay in.'

Fiona looked to Graham for support but he was staying out of this one.

'The thing is, we booked the babysitter ages ago and we can't cancel at short notice. We'd still have to pay. Anyway what we're saying, what *I'm* saying, is that I want you to come out.'

'Fine,' Daphne said abruptly.

'Pardon?'

'I said fine. I'll go if you insist that I'm not capable of looking after my grandchildren by myself. I may as well.'

She knew she couldn't say that she wanted to stay in because she felt better at home because that would confirm Fiona's suspicion that her mother really was ill. If there's one thing worse than learning that your mother is right about something, it's a mother learning that her daughter is right. A smug child is a terrible curse.

And so she agreed to go. 'No thanks to you,' Fiona grumbled to Graham after her mother had gone upstairs to sulk.

Graham looked up from his paper. 'I'm on your side, you know that, but if you're being unreasonable I'll tell you. You've always said that your mum's problem is that your dad never told her when she was being unreasonable, so it became a habit. And then he left her because of it and it was too late for her to be able to change.'

Oh no, Fiona thought. He wants me to be reasonable. That's cast-iron proof that the excitement from our marriage has definitely gone. He's talking to me like an elderly man to an elderly woman. He'll start calling me 'dear' soon and bringing me a cardigan when it's chilly.

She was very proud of herself for having diagnosed the problem in her marriage before it reached crisis point. Now it was time to take action. I'm not going to end up like Millie and Tim, she resolved, needing a continental holiday to be able to loosen my inhibitions.

Spontaneity, that's what's missing. And the element of surprise. We need more surprises in our marriage. I need to show him that he doesn't know everything about me, that I still have the power to shock him. So Fiona started thinking about how, where and when she could shock her husband to make the greatest impact.

This was a shock that Tess didn't need. And it wasn't her husband draped across the ironing board in a thong.

'Four and a half thousand,' Tess said, repeating the figure a few different ways to see if it sounded any less daunting with a different voice. 'How can we owe another four and a half thousand on top of all the other debts that we can barely afford to repay?'

'It's not my fault,' Max said, hating himself for resorting to this now familiar mantra. 'I was given estimates for all the shop fittings but because they were sold at auction, there was never a guarantee that they'd fetch the full amount.'

'What are we going to do?' she asked herself.

Max assumed she was talking to him and was encouraged that she still trusted him to get them out of the mess of his making. 'The minicabbing is going really well. I can easily make over a hundred pounds a day and we won't have to worry about tax for a while because it's all cash in hand. Then there's your yoga . . .'

'Max, all of that put together won't pay off our debts and enable us to live here as well. Besides, we need that money quickly. And I wouldn't bank on much from my teaching. After buying the instruction book and video, then spending twenty-three pounds in Boots on muscle rubs, bath soaks and painkillers, I'm about in profit.'

She sank into the sofa in despair. Max rushed over to her. 'It'll be OK,' he kept saying.

'How?' Tess shouted. 'How can it be OK?' She jumped up and began pacing the floor, registering for the first time how few paces were available in their tiny living room. 'I'll have to get another job, in a shop or a pub or *anything*. I'll start looking tomorrow.'

Max shook his head. 'There's no point. We can't both be working all hours, not with Lara still needing us. And you'd never be able to earn enough quickly enough, not doing unskilled work.'

'Then what are we going to do? All the auctions have finished. We've sold everything we've got to sell. And the interest is going to go up every day.'

Max stopped himself from saying the obvious. He didn't know how she'd take it. But he looked at her sitting there on the verge of tears and he knew it was down to him to find solutions. This was a mess of his making, he would find a way out of it. She wouldn't like what he had to suggest but he couldn't think of anything else.

'We haven't sold everything,' he said quietly.

'What are you talking about?' Tess snapped. 'I hope you're not thinking I should sell my rings! Even if we were declared bankrupt, I'd be entitled to keep my rings, you assured me of that.'

'Of course I don't want you to sell your rings!'

Tess calmed down. Just about. Max was nervous about making his suggestion but, if he didn't, then Tess would think he had intended her to sell her rings after all.

'We do have other things to sell, if you think about it,' he said.

Tess glared at him. 'I've thought about nothing else.' She gestured around the spartanly decorated and furnished flat. 'Take a look.'

'Not here. But we've got a lot of stuff that we didn't bring.'

Tess didn't understand what he was referring to but he'd decided to let her work it out for herself. Then she got it.

'You mean all our things in storage? Everything?'

Max nodded. Tess stared at him in astonishment. 'We can't sell everything.'

'Why not?'

Tess sighed, frustrated at his stupidity. 'Because we'll need it when ...' And that's when she REALLY got it. 'Are you saying that we won't need it because we won't be going back?'

Max sat next to her and held her hands firmly. 'If you can think of another way, then we'll do it. But I just don't think there is any other solution.'

Tess was struggling to take this in. Everything they'd gone through had been tolerable because, deep down, they thought that it was only temporary. Even if it took a few years, she'd always assumed they'd go back to their old house.

Besides, just knowing that all their possessions were still theirs, still existing together somewhere, it was as if they hadn't completely left their past. That was a comfort to Tess and she assumed it was to Max. They hadn't discussed things like that. There were so many hard practical problems to solve, there'd been no time to discuss emotional implications.

'Everything?' Tess said weakly.

Max sighed. 'Don't you remember going through it all last week?'

God, it was only last week, they both thought. They felt years older. Max continued. 'Everything that really mattered to us we brought with us. If we were going to be able to live without the rest for a few years or even longer, then do we really need it at all?'

'It's nothing to do with need.' Tess spoke with unusual petulance. 'I just like knowing it's there.'

'And so do I,' Max said patiently. 'But we have no other choice. None.'

Tess tossed the idea around and around until she felt dizzy, sick and dizzy. She sighed deeply and looked around her. 'We won't be left with much to show for the past fifteen years, will we?'

Max smiled. 'Apart from Lara and a marriage that has survived the worst life can throw at it. That's not such a bad tally, is it?'

'I suppose not. Actually, I've thought of something else I can sell.'

Max held up a hand. 'You're not to sell anything from here. None of your jewellery, none of the presents I've bought you ...'

156

'I'm not thinking of those. Do you remember that shop, the Dress Exchange, a few doors down from Organique?'

Max looked blank. 'Why would I know a shop like that? If it didn't sell organic bananas that would compete with ours, I wasn't interested. What about it?'

'It's basically a posh second-hand shop. But unlike charity shops, the person getting rid of her clothes actually gets a percentage of the money when the goods are sold. These are expensive clothes, after all.'

'And they say philanthropy is dead,' Max observed wryly.

Tess ignored his sarcasm. 'The point is, I have a wardrobe full of things that are probably worth a lot of money. It's not as if I ever did much in them apart from shop and drink coffee.'

'But you can't sell your clothes. You have to wear something.'

'Yes, but I can buy new stuff, more practical things for what I'm doing now. I'll still be quids in, believe me, I know what people will pay for that stuff.'

Max shook his head. 'I won't let you do it. Those clothes are part of you.'

That's why I want to let them go, Tess thought. 'I've made up my mind,' she said firmly. 'But I'm doing it for selfish reasons, so don't worry about it.'

Max raised an eyebrow. 'I have to worry about something,' he joked.

We've only been here a few days, Tess thought, I suspect you'll have plenty to worry about as time goes on.


'And what would the beautiful lady like?'

Fiona, Tess and Millie all simpered dutifully until they realised that Carter was talking to Daphne. Then they giggled hysterically.

'Fiona, your mum's pulled!' Tess whispered across the table.

'Ssh!' Fiona hissed. 'She's smiling for the first time in ten years. Don't stop her.'

Daphne was doing her best not to show that she was flattered by Carter's attentions but nobody was fooled. Even under the protection of inch-thick 1950s foundation, a blush was rising to the surface.

'What would you recommend?' she asked, struggling with the enormous menu and not wanting to put her glasses on.

Carter stroked his chin and looked at Daphne appreciatively.

'You strike me as a lady with a sophisticated palate, so can I suggest the halibut with vegetables of the season?'

'That sounds lovely.'

'That'll probably be frozen peas and carrots,' Tim said to Graham.

Tess glared at him. 'You're wrong. Carter has a contract with a farmer in Kent. He brings in vegetables twice a week. If they're frozen, it'll be because there's been snow.'

Tim felt suitably rebuked. He didn't trust the prices in this place. Even at the hefty increase on bargain lunchtime prices, it was still worryingly cheap here. He tried to find something else to be angry at. Anything to distract him from the news that he was going to be the father of six children.

'Six children? Six children?'

Millie wondered if Tim was having some sort of psychiatric episode. He wasn't moving or blinking. He was just standing in the middle of the room saying over and over again: 'Six children?'

'I was as surprised as you,' Millie said, hoping that she was doing the right thing by talking to him. There might be some kind of rule for such mental displays, like the one about not waking a sleepwalker. She didn't want Tim to go berserk, not while the children were next door watching *The Simpsons*. The very idea screamed 'tabloid headline' at her. At least for the moment he was calm – in a psychotic kind of way.

'Six children?' Tim said again.

'Oh for God's sake, stop saying that!' Millie was no longer concerned for his state of mind, she was plain irritated. 'I'll have six children too and I think you'll find that I'll be the one with the staggering workload. You will still leave for the office each morning for nine or ten hours of child-free bliss.'

'Stop talking, I need to think.'

Millie punched him on the arm, not very playfully. 'Make the most of it, there won't be much time for thinking in six months time.'

I don't want them, Tim wanted to say. I don't want any of this. I want to disappear from here, travel round the world and come back when all the children are civilised. I want that family life where one child plays the piano in the evening and another sits embroidering a robin on a log and another translates Latin poetry enthusiastically and the last sits next to me, just being quiet, keeping me company, loving me. Is that too much to ask?

He wisely kept this question to himself, probably because he knew the answer. But however unhappy he'd been with his family of four children, a family with six was unthinkable.

'They won't fit in the car,' he said, all the oppositions flooding forth as the initial shock wore off. 'And we haven't got enough bedrooms. Or enough baby stuff. Or *any* baby stuff. We gave it all away after Nathan.'

'I kept some of it,' Millie said quietly.

Tim's head whipped round. 'You kept some? What for, when we'd decided that four was enough for any half-sane couple?'

'I just kept the best things to pass on to people we knew or even for our grandchildren. Lots of it had sentimental value. I couldn't just give it all to the charity shop.'

Tim was developing a twitch over his left eye. He was scrutinising Millie's face, looking for proof of her deception.

'This was planned, wasn't it?'

Millie wanted to slap him but she just shouted at him instead. 'No! If you remember, you were the one who got carried away, not me!'

Tim was taken aback by this accusation. He didn't remember and he didn't want to. He'd made up his mind that this was all Millie's fault and nothing was going to sway him from this conclusion.

The worst thing was that he could do nothing about it. He had no options. Even while he'd been enjoying the fantasy about running off with Alison and reliving their youth, he'd known it was just a fantasy. But he was still enjoying the tiny hope that it wouldn't be too many years before the children reached an age when they wouldn't miss him or need him so much.

Not that he seriously contemplated leaving them, although he could toy harmlessly with the possibility. But he couldn't leave six children. They'd need him for all eternity. Once their education had robbed him of every penny he'd ever earned, they'd start getting married or need deposits for houses which normal people would no longer be able to afford in the future.

He'd be working until he was 90 and even then he'd have to get a part-time job in a DIY superstore just to pay for birthday presents for his 700 grandchildren and great-grandchildren.

He'd seen the future and it was a pile of nappies reaching from here to the grave.

'Where are you going?' he'd asked Millie as she flounced towards the front door, as far as a nauseous woman carrying twins could flounce.

'I told you, I'm meeting an old friend.'

'What old friend?' he pressed, finding her evasiveness irritating.

'His name's Daniel,' she blurted out, recalling the name of the boy she had a crush on when she was six. Then she left.

Who the hell's Daniel? Tim had thought all evening.

'This is really great,' Graham said enthusiastically as he ploughed through the huge plateload of food. 'And it's not that far away from us. How come we'd never heard of it before?'

Weeks earlier, one of them would have made some clever comment about Crappy Valley, but now they all had to watch what they said. This was Tess and Max's neighbourhood, their home.

'Hi Tess!'

Tess jumped. She'd forgotten that she lived around here and that there was a strong possibility of bumping into someone she'd met during her short residence. She instantly regretted choosing this restaurant.

'Hi!' she said, recognising the woman from the yoga class. She didn't know how to get out of this situation. Everybody around the table was waiting for an introduction.

The woman saved her the embarrassment. 'Tess doesn't know my name. I'm Sandy.'

Polite murmurs of 'Hello, Sandy' were followed by a silence as everyone waited for Tess to explain their connection. There was no way out of this.

'Sandy's in my yoga class,' she announced.

They all nodded as if this made perfect sense. Of course it makes sense, Tess realised, they're not assuming I teach the class. Why would they? I've got away with it!

'She's a great teacher,' Sandy said.

I haven't got away with it.

Fiona and Millie looked to Tess for an explanation. Graham was too engrossed in his food. Tim seemed to be talking to his plate. Max appeared amused.

'I'll tell you about it later,' Tess said casually. When I've found a way of phrasing it so that I don't sound like a conwoman. She was given a temporary reprieve when Carter came along with the wine.

'I don't remember ordering the wine,' Max said.

Carter smiled. 'Compliments of your friend over there.' He pointed towards a window table where Rav was sitting with two immaculately dressed and perfectly behaved children. Rav raised a glass to Max who returned the gesture with a thumbs up. Max observed that Rav was not wearing one of his trademark sweaters tonight. Instead he sported an Asian tunic embroidered lavishly in gold and silver, decorated with swirly sequin patterns.

Graham was trying to read the label upside down while Carter poured the wine. He was frowning, obviously uncertain of what he was seeing.

'Yes, you are reading it correctly, it's from Bombay,' Max said knowledgeably.

Graham looked up. 'Where's Bombay?'

'In India, you fool,' Daphne said.

'Ah, brains as well as beauty,' Carter cooed. Daphne coughed in embarrassment.

'This must be another Bombay,' Graham said with exaggerated patience. 'They don't make wine in India.'

'Go tell that to my good friend Rav,' Max said.

Once their glasses were filled, they all lifted them to examine the colour. It was difficult to tell much, not because there was anything wrong with the light or the glasses but because none of them had ever found out what they were supposed to be looking for.

'Looks good,' Graham opined. This translated into: 'There are no bits floating in there and it's definitely red.' Once they'd agreed these crucial facts, they all took their first sip.

Nobody wanted to be the first to state an opinion. Max could feel Rav watching him anxiously and he felt that he had to take the initiative before any of his old friends said something to upset his new friend.

'Well I think this is very ... earthy.'

Graham took another sip. He could feel the enamel dissolving from his teeth and the top layer of his tongue peeling off. He sensed Max glaring at him and took the hint. He swallowed, hoping that he'd still be able to eat solid food once this stuff hit his intestines.

'Mmm,' he whispered. 'Gutsy. Full of ... guts.'

Tim downed the glass in one. 'Tastes fine to me.'

'Is something up with Tim?' Tess whispered to Fiona.

'I'll tell you later,' Fiona whispered back.

'Why is Millie doing that funny thing with her eyes?' Tess asked curiously.

Fiona looked over to Millie, who was frantically trying to communicate something to her. Then she remembered. She was supposed to be bringing up the subject of the holiday, testing the water to see if Tess would be offended by the other two couples going away without them.

Fiona wasn't good at discretion. She was very much a 'speak first, apologise later' person. But she knew that she had to do this. Millie was desperate for a holiday before the birth of the twins and she couldn't face going away with just Tim and the kids.

Fiona gave up on the idea of tact altogether. 'Have you thought about holidays this year?'

Tess laughed. 'We haven't even thought past next week! Gone are the days when we made plans. Although each day things are looking a little less hopeless than the day before.'

Tess was thinking about clearing out her wardrobe. But Fiona misinterpreted this as a possibility that they might still be able to go away together. She sat back, pleased to be able to offer Millie this crumb of hope later. She felt mean, but she and Graham had already agreed that they would rather not go away with Millie and Tim, not without the others. It wouldn't have felt right.

But even if the Provence trip was back on again, Fiona had Daphne to consider. There was no way she could manage the 12-hour car journey to France.

'Max!'

Everyone jumped as a voice grated across the table.

'Hello Archie! Come and meet my friends.' Max got up to greet his fellow club member warmly. He introduced everyone at the table. 'You didn't mention that you were going to be here?'

'I come here every evening. No point in cooking for myself and Carter does a special deal for me. Free meals in exchange for free minicabs. I also drive a van for him when he needs to pick up a load of stock.'

'You can't eat by yourself,' Max said. 'Come and join us.' He was deliberately ignoring Tess's cautionary eye flickers that he could feel transmitting messages in their marital eye-flickering SOS code.

'I couldn't intrude.'

'Nonsense, there's plenty of room for another chair.' Max pulled up another seat and placed it next to his own. Within seconds, Carter had brought him a plate of steak and kidney pie, potatoes and carrots.

'That's impressive service,' Max commented.

'I always have that on a Friday,' Archie said. 'And I always get here at eight forty-five. I can't be away from the office for too long. It's our busy time.'

'What do you do, Archie?' Graham asked politely.

'I'm a minicab controller. Max has just started working for me. He's already turning into my best driver. We've had no complaints about him in five days – that's practically a record in South London.'

Tim stared at Max. 'Since when have you been driving mini-cabs?'

'Archie just said: five days. Why don't you listen!' Daphne said, gracing Tim with her trademark 'they-think-I'm-stupid-because-I'm-old-but-at-least-I can-follow-a-conversation' pitying glare.

I wonder if Alison met people like Daphne on her travels, Tim wondered. Maybe they're revered in primitive cultures. There must be a reason why evolution has allowed them to survive, even proliferate. Perhaps she has some deep hidden purpose that we've yet to discover. I'd better not kill her in case anthropologists discover that her vitriol can cure cancer or something.

'Could somebody get me some more of this delicious wine, please?'

Everyone looked round to see who had uttered these fanciful words. They all considered themselves to be suave wits but this was a joke too surreal.

It was Daphne again.

'Mum, don't be sarcastic!' Fiona hissed.

Daphne stared at her. 'I'm not being sarcastic. I really would like some more of this wine. You drag me out to dinner even though I would have been perfectly happy to stay at home, and I ask – politely! – for some more wine, and I'm accused of being sarcastic. Now I know how teenagers feel when grown-ups treat them with continual injustice.'

'You mean, you truly think this wine is delicious?' Fiona said incredulously.

'Why would I say it if it wasn't? Sarcasm is a young person's game. When you get older, you realise that life is too short to try and be clever with your words all the time.'

That explains a lot, Graham thought, thinking of all the monumentally stupid and cruel things Daphne had said to Fiona in the past.

Max ordered another bottle from Carter. 'You have a very refined palate, if I may say so,' Carter observed to Daphne in admiration. 'Not everyone takes to the Bombay. It is something of an acquired taste.'

Daphne smiled sweetly and lowered her eyes. Actually, she agreed with the others that it tasted absolutely vile. But after the first glass she felt a tingling warmth spread through her body and, gradually, all her aches and pains simply melted away (probably along with the outer surfaces of her major organs). It was nothing less than a miracle.

'Perhaps you'd allow me to share this with you?' Archie offered. 'I don't normally drink in the evenings because I don't like to ask Carter to open a bottle just for one glass. But, if I could buy this and you'd do me the honour ...?'

Fiona watched her mother in astonishment. She'd brought her out so that she could assess how frail she was and the woman was attracting male attention like a geriatric page 3 girl. Everyone found themselves changing seats so that Archie could sit next to Daphne.

Graham got up to go to the gents and, as he passed Fiona, he whispered to her: 'I think we should come here every night. We could have her married off by Christmas.'

Fiona was amused, or at least she knew she was supposed to be amused. In fact she felt uncomfortable. Her mother was stepping out of her compartment, the one her daughter had constructed for her. She was supposed to stay there until Fiona had resolved all her lifelong differences with her. Only then could Fiona let her go.

\*

I'm not going to let him go, not this time, Alison thought. She sat by the back window of her cottage looking out onto her garden. Gabriel had set up some lighting around the flower beds before he left.

'I refuse to plant things,' he'd said, 'because that would be laying down roots. But we may as well appreciate the beauty of what is already here.'

They used to sit in the garden in the evenings, enjoying the silence. They talked endlessly of their travels, past and future. Sometimes they'd bring a globe out, spin it and stop it with their finger, then ask themselves if they should go to this or that place. There was never any stillness in their life, everything was moving forward.

'Gabriel,' Alison had asked one night. 'What will we do when we're old?'

He'd looked at her as if he didn't understand the question. 'That's a very Western concept,' he'd replied. 'You assume that things have to change after a certain age. It comes from your strange system of retiring when you're sixty or sixty-five. In other countries, you work until you die or until you're infirm.'

Alison shrugged. 'OK, so what if we get infirm before we die? What will we do then?'

Gabriel had stroked her hand pityingly. 'You and I will always be strong. I've seen you in the mountains and the desert. You are a fighter like me! That's why I love you.'

And that was the end of that subject as far as Gabriel was concerned. But Alison brooded on it all the time. Yes, she was strong, a fighter, but recently she'd been feeling tired. Not physically, but just tired of having to act as if she were the same person of 15 years earlier.

She'd read a lot of women's magazines since returning to Britain, catching up on the mass popular culture that she'd missed. It seemed to come down to one all-pervading message: women have to stay young until they're at least 60.

She was a woman of 38, she'd climbed Everest, achieved things, she'd earned the right to settle, to get fat, to be complacent. She wanted to act her age, her current age not the age she'd met Gabriel. She wanted to stop spending 20 minutes a day trying to minimise the visible ageing of her face with liberal applications of make-up. And she wanted a child.

The need for a child, and it was definitely a need rather than a desire, had been growing in her like a disease. It caused her real pain that nothing could alleviate it but a baby. Of course she'd broached the subject from all the different angles with Gabriel but he wouldn't budge on his position.

'We agreed right from the start,' he insisted. 'No children. I was very clear on that.'

'But it wouldn't have to change things,' Alison had begged. 'We could take the child with us. Think of all those kids we met when we were travelling, the fantastic childhoods they were having, experiencing the world at first hand. We could do that!'

But Gabriel was unmoved. 'It wouldn't be the same. We couldn't take a baby to a war zone and we always said that that would be our next move.'

As if to push her into making a final decision, Gabriel began making enquiries with Médecins Sans Frontières about positions for them both. The organisation was thrilled to have volunteers who were prepared to offer their services for unlimited periods of time in the most risky areas.

Alison went along with him for the interview, listened passively to all the stark warnings of the very real dangers involved, watched film footage of the recent work being done by doctors around the world and then knew, categorically, that she couldn't go.

'I'm too old,' she said.

Gabriel looked at her with scorn. 'Don't be so ridiculous. You're not old at all. There are doctors much older than you out there, you saw the film.'

'If I'm not too old now, then I certainly will be when I come back. You saw how exhausting the work is.'

Gabriel grabbed her in excitement. 'But that's the beauty of this,' he said eagerly. 'We don't have to come back. Ever. We can just keep moving. People only feel old when they stay in one place and see themselves in relation to everyone else around them, watching children become adults, watching old people die.'

But rather than convincing her to go, this was the observation that persuaded her to stay.

'I *want* to see myself in relation to others. I don't want to live in isolation for ever. People aren't meant to do that. Surely that's the one thing we've learned from visiting villages all over the world?

I want to watch people grow old. I want to feel *myself* grow old. I want to watch children grow up.'

Most of all I want to watch *my* children grow up.

It wasn't an amicable parting. Gabriel felt that Alison had married him under false pretences. He didn't think it was acceptable that she simply changed her mind.

So here I am, she thought. Creeping towards 40, alone and childless. It was natural to think of Tim and natural to contact him when it was so easy. She'd looked him up on the website and smiled at his predictably modest biography. But one fact jumped out at her. Four children! He had four children.

That could have been me, she'd thought bitterly. I could have married him and had four children. I could be with him in a house, with a garden containing flowers, trees even, that I'd planted. I could be as tired as I wanted because I'd have Tim to look after me. He was always good at that. And I could watch my children grow and I wouldn't have to do another thing in my life because they would be my lasting achievement.

She didn't actively plan to break up his marriage, steal him away from his wife and children. She wasn't a bad person. She was simply possessed with a need. And because, as Gabriel had observed, she'd spent her entire adult life in isolation from other people, having no long-term interaction with anyone apart from Gabriel, she'd never developed a faculty for social responsibility. Or unselfishness. She'd never considered consequences before and she wasn't thinking of the consequences now. She wanted two things only.

Tim. And a baby.


The bill arrived and was placed in front of Max. Before they could begin the customary squabble over who was paying, Tess had snatched it away.

'You must let us pay,' Graham said. 'No arguments!'

Max reddened at the offer. He was offended by the suggestion that he couldn't pay for this himself. Which, of course, he couldn't but that wasn't the point. He was equally worried that Tess had grabbed the bill. Surely she wasn't going to pay it all?

Tess was rummaging around in her handbag until she pulled out a handful of torn bits of newspaper. The others watched fascinated as she arranged them in front of her on the table.

'Right. Now we've got a "Buy one main course, get one free",
Max and I can have that one. Then "One free bottle of Bombay
wine for every four diners, not applicable with the main course
offer". You four can have that because that is a better saving than
the main course offer. However we *can* combine these with this
"Ten per cent off for a party of over six persons", so we'll share
this one. Then there's this one: "Two free desserts when two
people spend over ten pounds". Now I think Tim and Graham
probably spent over ten pounds because they had the steak, so if
you take that one ...'

They all watched her as if she were pulling out her eyeballs and
rolling them around the table. They were stunned by her maniacal
scrutiny of these coupons. Max was so mortified, he just wanted to
sweep them out of the way, pay for the whole bill himself and rush
Tess to a psychiatrist immediately.

But she hadn't yet finished. 'As this is our first time here in
the evening, we can ask for a loyalty card which will immediately give us another two and a half per cent off the total bill.
And Daphne is over sixty so she gets five per cent off her food
but not the wine. Oh look! Here's a good one. This one says:
'Diners seated before six-thirty p.m. pay lunchtime prices on
food ordered before seven." I know that doesn't apply but it's
worth remembering for next time. Now we ordered garlic
bread, but that was actually free if two people ordered from the
Italian section of the menu but not including the veal
escalope ...'

Before she could read out any more from her pile, which was
not diminishing, Graham calmly took the bill, slapped his
American Express card on it and took it over to Carter who was
standing by the till with a calculator.

After a few words, Graham came back. 'They don't take plastic
here,' he said tightly. 'Only cash.'

'Didn't I say that?' Tess said.

Her friends shook their heads, wanting to shove her coupons ...

Before they could complete the image, Carter had come over to
them. 'Shall I take those?' he said, smoothly picking up the crum-
pled heap of coupons and returning to his seat by the till.

They watched in awe as he tapped away at his calculator at a
freakish speed, writing figures on scraps of paper after each sum.
Eventually he came back and presented Tess with a handful of

individual bills, all covered in complicated maths. Each was headed by the name of a main course.

'Right,' Tess said cheerfully. 'Who had the peppered steak? Graham? Yours comes to eight pounds twenty-four. Lasagne?'

This took a further five minutes as Tess doled out the bills like school reports, with one ferocious argument about whether Tim had eaten any of the garlic bread.

They had all reverted to students, quibbling over every penny of the bill.

'The thing is,' Tim said firmly, 'I've got the garlic bread on my bill and I didn't have any of it. I ordered it for Millie so it should go on her bill.'

'It doesn't matter anyway,' Daphne said, 'because that was free with the two Italian main courses.' She tutted impatiently at his ignorance. It was all perfectly straightforward to her and jolly sensible too. Archie patted her hand in appreciation of her good sense. He was enjoying this. He would never complain about having to eat alone again, if this was what happened when you dined with friends.

As they all sat in silence holding their pieces of paper, Graham was the first to speak.

'Er, this is a bit embarrassing, but I don't have any cash on me.'

'Neither do I,' said Tim, followed by Fiona and Millie.

'I've only got enough for Tess and me,' Max said apologetically.

'Don't worry about it,' Carter said. 'I'll put it on the slate. You can pay me next time. Max is a member here. I trust him.'

Tim looked appalled. He turned to Graham. 'I've never had anything on a slate before. And now we'll have to come back! I don't think I could go through that coupon thing again.'

Graham had actually found it all quite entertaining. It had been different to their usual meals out, a complete distraction, and he hadn't thought about Christine all evening. Until now.

Rav watched them all from his table. Such nice people, he thought. It's good to see friends together like that. I don't have friends like that. Only family. And the men in the club. It's so kind of them to bring the other lady out with them. She is very beautiful but in terrible pain, I can see that. Her back, I think, and her legs too. My wine helped, though! I hope she will return soon. I would like to see her again, maybe speak to her next time, share a glass of wine with her.

He had seen the problem with the bill and taken Carter to one side. 'I will settle their bill. But don't tell them it was me, they'll only be embarrassed. Let them think it's on a slate so that they have to come back.'

Carter had agreed. Now Rav could look forward to seeing that beautiful lady again.

# 10

'I'm not comfortable about this,' Max said, fastening his tie unhappily. He hadn't worn a suit since going to the bank manager for the failed loan request.

'We've talked about this,' Tess replied. 'We're doing this for Lara. We agreed,'

'I know, but she's in the school now. They're not going to throw her out because we don't go to church. They don't do that, someone told me. Once you're in, you're in.'

Tess frowned at him. 'We told Miss Blowers that we would be going to church and I told John as well. It wouldn't be right to go back on that.'

'John? Since when do we know vicars by their first name? Since when do we know vicars at all?'

Tess sensibly ignored him. Lara was running about looking for her favourite hairband.

'Everyone's going to be there, Mum. It'll be great! And they have cakes afterwards!'

Max sighed and followed his wife and daughter out the door. *Normally I'd be having a lie-in on a Sunday morning. After six days of getting up early to work in the shop, this used to be my only chance to sleep late. Tess would bring me coffee and toast and the Sunday papers then she and Lara would do things quietly downstairs until lunchtime.*

*My first Sunday after a stressful week and I'm going to church. I haven't even* seen *the papers yet. Is nothing sacred?*

The church looked reassuringly traditional from the outside with its proper ancient brickwork, proper spire, proper stained-glass windows and noticeboards overflowing with ecclesiastical

171

forms that only the initiated could comprehend. Tess and Max were appropriately subdued as they entered through the massive oak doorway only to be stunned by the unconventional sight that greeted them.

They were overwhelmed by the crowd filling the church, not just the numbers but the volume. They weren't sitting in neat pews, heads bowed in prayer, but they were talking, shouting across to their friends.

'Are you sure this is the Church of England?' Max whispered. 'It's not very solemn. The Church of England is definitely supposed to be solemn. I bet they have tambourines here. I've heard about places like this.'

'Look Mum, there's Ruthie!' Lara waved at her new friend and then she was gone. She skipped over to join a group of children sitting at the front.

'She can't sit over there, she has to stay with us.' Max was sounding anxious.

'Why?' Tess asked.

'People will see us without a child and think we *want* to be here. They'll think we're church people.'

Tess patted his arm patronisingly. 'We should have brought placards to wear around our necks saying: PROUD TO BE UNHOLY SINNERS.'

'You can mock all you like, but I don't like churches,' Max said. 'And I particularly don't like churches like this. How are you supposed to know what to do with everyone wandering about? And there's no organ.'

Tess pulled him towards a couple of seats and gently encouraged him to sit down. He was now immersed in a major sulk. They both jumped when the sound of a keyboard filled the church, followed by some impressive rock drumming. Immediately, everybody stood and faced the front and began singing.

Max and Tess fumbled around for a hymn book until somebody turned to them to point out a large screen being lowered electronically from the ceiling. The lyrics were flashing up on the screen but they didn't help because the song was completely unfamiliar to them. They watched in astonishment as the congregation clapped and jigged along with the lively song. Tess found herself tapping her toes until Max glared at her.

The children were all at the front gathering round a huge box of musical instruments, tambourines, rattles, bells, all gaudy and loud.

'I told you there'd be tambourines!' Max hissed.

Tess was enjoying the sight of all the children enjoying themselves. In particular she loved watching Lara having fun. She nudged Max to encourage him to look at their daughter. She saw his face soften with pleasure that lasted until the end of the song.

Then John appeared. To Tess's relief, the vicar was not wearing a clown's suit, which was Max's other prediction. He looked, well, like a normal person. As vicars go, Max added to himself. His light brown hair was neatly but casually styled, which immediately filled Max with jealousy, and his face was boyish and smiley. He was probably in his mid-30s but he seemed untouched by the visible stresses that Max and his contemporaries all wore around their eyes. More cause for envy, Max thought, grumbling. He was pacified that at least the Incredible Vicar had some sense of decorum.

Tess and Max began to sit down, then the music started again. They jumped up, wondering if they were going to sing all morning. This time, the song seemed to involve everyone carrying out actions. Max watched in astonishment as grown men and women shook their arms up and down, spun about and made animal noises. To his dismay, Tess was joining in and apparently enjoying herself. The Incredible Vicar was actually leading the actions.

'They use tambourines in cults, you know,' he whispered to Tess.

Tess giggled at his observation, thinking that he was making a joke. This infuriated him even more.

Max wanted to walk out but he was pinned in by some late arrivals who'd sneaked in next to him and were now enthusiastically singing along.

Finally they sat down much to Max's great relief. Things calmed down although it was still too informal for Max's liking. Eventually, the children were led out to Sunday School, Lara waving to her parents happily as she left, arms linked with some other girls.

Once the children had left, John became more acceptably vicar-like, in the eyes of the traditionalists, a group to which Max had decided he belonged. He preached a sermon that Max and Tess found interesting, if a bit prescriptive, and even made them both laugh a few times.

After some liturgical bits that they found comforting with their old language, if meaningless, they sang a hymn that they both knew.

'This is more like it,' Max whispered as he joined in lustily with 'Thine Be the Glory'. The time passed quite quickly and they soon found themselves carried along with the crowd into the vestry where, as Lara had predicted, cakes were laid out along with tea and coffee.

'Can't we just go?' Max said, under his breath, hoping Tess would hear.

'We have to be seen first,' she whispered back. 'Otherwise there's no point. I think I've spotted Miss Blowers. I'll go and say hello to her, you speak to the vicar. Once our presence has been noted, then we can leave.'

She left Max standing alone with a cup of tea, a butterfly cake and absolutely no intention of speaking to any vicar, Incredible or otherwise.

'How did you manage to escape on a Sunday?' Alison asked.

'I haven't got long,' Tim said nervously. 'I told Millie that I needed to pop into the office and pick up some computer disks that I was supposed to be working on over the weekend. I can only get away with it for a couple of hours. I said it would take that long because public transport was so bad on a Sunday.'

'That's plenty of time,' Alison said, putting her arm through his casually and striding out across Battersea Park. 'I'll be able to drive you back to a couple of streets from your house. That'll give us a bit extra.'

Tim thrilled to have Alison on his arm but was still feeling sick from having lied, not just to Millie but to the children.

'But Daddy, you said you'd play Monopoly this morning!' Carly had cried.

'And you said you'd fix my bike!' Nathan accused.

'And we were going to make a robot,' Lucy said tearfully.

'And you promised you'd help with my Christopher Columbus project!' Ellie added.

Millie said nothing. If he was not moved by the disappointment of his children, if he could let them down so easily, then he would

174

certainly not be persuaded by her own complaints of promises being broken.

Sunday was a family day. It always had been, that was the rule. Whatever else was going on in their lives, they spent Sunday together. Occasionally they'd share it with close friends but that was really just like extending the concept of family. Tim had never, *never*, gone into work on a Sunday. As far as Millie knew, none of his colleagues did either. It was obvious to her that he was lying and she was scared to know exactly what he was doing.

She knew he was devastated by the news about the twins – she wasn't too happy about it herself – and she was hoping that he just needed some time to be by himself. Within a matter of months, what little time they now had for themselves would be taken from them. She couldn't even consider the possibility of anything else.

Except that when she wasn't thinking, an image kept popping into her mind. It was a picture of Tim and someone else. The woman was beautiful and serene and had a totally flat stomach. Tim was looking calm and relaxed. There were no children in the picture which, Millie suspected, was the reason. Millie had never seen pictures of Alison nor had Tim ever described her so she could only fear the worst.

It wasn't a difficult conclusion to reach. Tim had already been unhappy at home. A couple of weeks ago he has lunch with the girl he used to love, then he starts spending time away from home for reasons that can't possibly be true.

She now felt sick all day: in the morning from the pregnancy, the rest of the time from fear. But she was still too scared to confront him. So she bit her tongue, stopped herself from interrogating him, from nagging, and stepped up her ill-planned campaign to make him jealous of her imaginary ex-boyfriend.

As he'd been getting ready to go out, far too carefully, Millie observed, she casually walked into their bedroom to put away some ironing.

'In case I forget to mention it, I'll be out again tomorrow evening.'

Tim looked up in amazement. 'That's twice in less than a week,' he commented.

'Is it?'

'With, er, Daniel again?'

'Yes.' Millie left the room. Her minimalist answers were

driving Tim crazy, a strategy which would have impressed even a skilled devious manipulator like Alison. But Millie was only keeping things simple because she couldn't cope with a complicated imaginary affair, not while she had three hearts beating inside her.

Tim closed his mind to the worrying image of Millie watching him leave with an unfamiliar expression this morning. He'd thought it was suspicion. But maybe it was something else. He didn't know what was going on right now in her mind, in her life. He didn't have the time or the ability to work it out. But he did know she was suffering physically and, however sick she felt, he felt equally sick, hating himself for letting the family down. And for letting her down too, a feeling which surprised him.

'You're feeling guilty for letting your family down.'

Tim was startled. 'You always know what I'm thinking!'

Alison smiled to herself. She was grateful that Tim had married quite young without having much experience with women. It meant that he was still an innocent, easy to manipulate. Millie was a lucky woman, she thought, more fool her if she didn't realise this and didn't know how to hold onto him.

'I've always been able to see right through you,' she said softly. 'You know, you shouldn't feel guilty. You are entitled to some time to yourself. You work all week then you devote all your spare time to your family. Even Millie gets time to herself when the children are at school in the week.'

'That's absolutely true! I hadn't thought of that,' Tim said indignantly. 'She's always going on about how she barely has enough time to get everything done during the day but she's always got time for lunch or coffee with her friends.'

'So just think about this as being time for coffee with *your* friend.'

'That's right. Why shouldn't I have a friend? I should definitely make the most of my spare time while I can.'

'Why's that?' Alison assumed he was talking about a looming work commitment.

Tim looked away. He realised he hadn't told Alison that Millie was pregnant and he wasn't sure why. An instinct he didn't understand warned him that Alison wouldn't like this, but he had to tell her. He had to talk frankly about this to someone. And she was the only person available to him.

'Millie's pregnant,' he said. 'With twins.'

Alison felt her breathing stop abruptly. She'd often had patients claim that this happened to them and she always told them that they were imagining it. But now she knew that it was true. Her heart had stopped beating and her brain function was dragging to a halt.

This was not part of the plan. What had he written in his biography on the website? 'Four children under ten but the last one blissfully at school. Plans to begin civilised living again now underfoot!'

She would never have got in touch with him if she'd known another baby was on the way. And twins in particular. Not because she was too high-principled to steal a man from his pregnant wife but because it seemed an impossible challenge. She was no great seductress. Tim had been the only man ever to find her beautiful. Gabriel had always told her that he loved her for her spirit. She was hoping that her old unfinished history with Tim would be sufficient to draw him away during a lull in his life, post-babies and pre-marriage renewal. That's what the biography intimated.

But the Tim she remembered was far too honourable to walk out on his family with two more babies due. She continued walking with Tim in silence.

He enjoyed this silence, which was so blissful when compared to the normal bedlam of family walks in the park on a Sunday afternoon. One child would be up a tree, another would be trying to push him out, another would be kicking a ball at a frail old lady and the other would have disappeared from sight while Millie ran about screaming hysterically.

Alison enjoyed the silence because it allowed her to think.

'I know what you're thinking,' Tim said proudly.

Alison was alarmed until it occurred to her that he couldn't possibly know. He had never been that perceptive as a teenager and he didn't seem to have acquired the skill in the intervening years.

'What's that?'

'You're wondering what your life would have been like if you'd stayed with me instead of going off to Asia.'

Wrong! Alison smiled warmly. 'You're right. How did you guess?'

'Because I was thinking the same. Asking myself what we'd be doing at this very minute if you'd made a different choice then.'

'And what's your opinion?'

'We'd be somewhere that didn't appear on a map, just the two of us, maybe in a tent. We'd be watching amazing birds that had never been photographed flying overhead. There'd be a sunset with colours we'd never seen before. We wouldn't know what the date was, or the time. And we'd be holding hands, always holding hands.'

Wow, Alison thought. He's still 18, he never stopped being 18.

'So we'd still be together?' Alison asked lightly.

'Oh yes! We'd never have got bored of each other, not while we were travelling all the time.'

'And do you see four children in this picture?'

'Definitely not! You and I would never have needed children. We would have been happy with each other.'

They walked on, Tim glad to have shared this dream with Alison, hopeful that this temporary sense of contentment, however artificial, might sustain him in the years ahead. With his six children.

Alison was not content at all. She was being forced into a complete rethink. There was no way that Tim was going to leave his wife. And even if he did, Alison didn't believe she could bear to live with him. He was every bit as mawkish and sentimental as she remembered him.

She'd only ever been interested in him at school because she was going through a contrary phase. It had appealed to her sense of perversity to go after the least desirable boy in the sixth form. He played the saxophone, which was quite cool, but that was completely cancelled out by the Osmonds posters on his bedroom wall.

Admittedly, she did become fond of him. He was so devoted to her, it was quite flattering and she knew that she'd be going abroad after A-levels before the infatuation could begin to irritate her.

She wasn't sure why she'd asked him to go with her. Company, she presumed. She'd always anticipated dumping him once she met better travel companions. But then he turned her down, which shocked her. He'd said he would follow her to the ends of the earth but she couldn't actually get him to make it as far as Boulogne.

This rejection, her first ever and her last until Gabriel left her, motivated her to try harder to convince him, although he wouldn't be swayed. His resolve was the first genuinely attractive quality she'd seen in him. But it wasn't enough to make her want to stay. And now she'd seen how he turned out, she was relieved that she hadn't.

So she wouldn't have Tim. Even if she *could* have him, he made it plain that he wouldn't want any more children. But she still wanted a baby and there was just nobody else on the horizon. Think, think, think!

She came to the only conclusion. She'd have Tim's baby without telling him, reject him kindly and then he could go back to his wife and enormous family, restored by his little fling with the past, and spend the rest of his life happy that he'd finally put his past behind him.

Nobody would be hurt. It was perfect.

Don't let him come this way. Don't let him come this way. Please don't ... Too late.

'You must be Max Keane.' The vicar held out his hand. Max took it tentatively.

'I'm impressed! Max said. 'Is that a vicar-skill? Some kind of divinely attached, invisible name tag?' Why am I talking like such a pillock? he asked himself.

'Nothing so clever, I'm afraid. Your wife sent me over.'

Max looked over his shoulder at Tess, who was waving back mischievously. That's it, he thought, this is the last punishment I'm prepared to accept. I may have ruined her life but she didn't have to send for a vicar. The debt is now paid in full.

He was momentarily distracted by her appearance. He'd been so busy complaining about going to church that morning that he hadn't noticed she was wearing new clothes, very different to her usual style.

She'd almost completely emptied her wardrobe the morning before and taken the contents straight to the Dress Exchange. 'It could be a few weeks before they sell them, but I'm going to need some clothes in the meantime.'

'Not a problem,' Max said. 'It was a good day yesterday. Here you go.'

He pulled a wad of notes from his back pocket. Tess stared, first at the notes then at him.

'How much have you got there?' she asked in amazement.

'Two hundred and fifty pounds,' he said proudly. 'I worked over fourteen hours, did two airport runs in the night. Archie seems to be saving all the lucrative jobs for me at the moment. He's been really supportive to me since I joined his club.' And I told him the whole sad story of my failed business. And how I failed at trying to get us out of trouble without telling you. And how all I want is to prove to my wife that I can protect her. And how my wife isn't aware of half the problems that I'm trying to protect her from.

He couldn't believe how it had all spilled out. But he'd had no one to talk to since it happened. He was far too ashamed to talk to Graham or Tim about it. Their friendship had always seemed to be based on a foundation of shared lifestyles, successes and aspirations. He felt that they would be as underequipped to deal with failure as he was.

But Archie and the other men at the club were sympathetic *and* practical. Archie was going to increase his workload, providing Max maintained his reliability, and Carter had interrupted them at one point to say he'd like to chat to Max at some point about a couple of ideas.

It left him feeling hopeful, literally full of hope. And being able to give his wife money, money that he'd earned honourably, for her to splash out on clothes gave him as much pleasure as when he'd bought her that £5,000 eternity ring on the day Lara was born. On the other hand, he remembered that ring being a gift of love and gratitude whereas the predominant emotion he experienced when handing over the money just now was one of guilt.

'This is great,' Tess giggled. 'Lara! Do you want to come shopping?' She hadn't finished the sentence before Lara was there with her coat on. She had a sixth sense for that rare alignment of a mother, a full purse and the word "shopping".

'With real money?' Lara asked breathlessly.

Tess ached for her child, who had struggled as each new deprivation hit her. The thrilling novelty of moving had swiftly been replaced by an awareness that almost every meaningful activity in her life was being curtailed. Her gym course was being cancelled, the ballet lessons were out and she would not be handed £10 to spend on sparkly hair accessories just because there was an 'r' in the month.

Max could see why he hadn't immediately taken in the new Tess before church. She wasn't wearing a Lycra miniskirt or a sequinned boob tube. But she'd certainly moved away from the classic coordinates she'd favoured for so many years.

She was wearing a swirly black skirt and red cardigan that made her look faintly bohemian. And her hair was held back by two diamanté slides rather than her usual brown wooden hairband.

There was something untamed about her that reminded Max of someone. Then he worked out who it was. She reminded him of Tess when he first met her; Tess before years of heartache followed by the arrival of Lara followed by ten years of complacency that they assumed would carry them through to retirement.

I wonder if she knows she's dressing like her old self, he mused.

Max took another sip from his tea before remembering that the vicar was standing in front of him and had probably said some things of vital theological significance that Max had missed because he was admiring his wife.

He determined to be more responsive to make up for his rudeness. 'So are all churches like this nowadays?' he asked.

'Like what?' John replied. 'Popular? Lively? Fun? Thriving?'

Max was taken aback. 'No, I mean ... modern.'

John laughed. 'I presume you don't approve of all the new songs or the kids dancing around?'

'I just don't see what's wrong with proper churches with proper hymns and children sitting with their families. I think people like me are happier with the more traditional approach. It appeals to our sense of history.' He was quite proud of his articulacy.

'So you've usually gone to a church like that, have you?' John asked with amusement.

Max was regretting ever going down this road. 'No, but if I had been a churchgoer, then I would definitely have preferred something more along those lines.' He felt awkward, aware that he was being backed into a corner by the Incredible Vicar.

John nodded. 'That's what people who don't go to church always say.'

Max blushed.

John laughed and shook his head. 'I'm sorry, that was rude of me. I know you've been dragged here against your will and you were probably dreading being cornered by the vicar, it's a common nightmare.'

'No, no, of course not,' Max stammered. Help! Tess, rescue me! He wondered if it was appropriate under the circumstances to try out one of his new effective non-denominational prayers, this time asking to be released from this ordeal of confrontation with a Church of England vicar. But he wasn't sure where the Church of England's God stood on humour so he decided to give it a miss.

'I must be off now,' John said, shaking Max's hand once more.

Blimey, Max thought, I'm getting really good at this. I only have to think a thing for it to happen. You don't even have to say amen. I wish I'd known about this when my business was going down the tubes.

'Goodbye,' he said, more warmly now that the vicar was leaving.

'I'll probably see you at Carter's sometime,' John added.

'What do you mean?'

'Didn't Archie tell you? I'm one of the founder members of the men's club.'

Terrific, Max thought gloomily. Now all I need is for Daphne, the grim reaper herself, to be admitted and my joy there will be complete.


'I'm sorry, Mum, what did you say?' Fiona stared at her mother as if she'd said she was going to start voting for the Green Party.

'I said, Archie is coming to pick me up later to take me for a walk. Are you deaf or stupid?'

Daphne wanted her daughter to leave her alone so she could get ready. She'd timed her painkillers so she'd be comfortable for the hour or so she'd be out. Now she needed to experiment with a few clothes and a bit of make-up if she was going to look presentable.

'But you don't know him,' Fiona protested.

Daphne sighed with exaggerated patience. 'You met him yourself. He had dinner with us. Your friend's husband works for him. He's offered to take me for a walk around Battersea Park and a cup of tea in the café. We won't be out for long because he has to be back at work. If I'm not back by tonight, then you can assume I've been murdered and say "I told her so." Until then, can you please go away and let me get ready?'

Fiona walked downstairs in shock. 'Did you hear that?' she asked Graham.

'I think it's wonderful,' he said. 'Ever since your dad finally divorced her, I've said the best thing for her would be to marry again. It would get her off your back.' He nearly said 'our backs' and congratulated himself on the self-control.

182

'What are you saying? You think Mum should marry a minicab driver? Are you mad?'

'He's not a driver, he's the controller. He actually owns the company, he was telling me about it over dinner. That makes him a local businessman if that sits better with your sensibilities.' Graham kissed her affectionately before running upstairs to solve a violent dispute over the ownership of a sock.

Fiona irrationally blamed Tess for this. If she hadn't dragged them over to that place on Friday, then none of this would have happened. She picked up the phone and dialled her new number. The answerphone kicked in so Fiona hung up.

Where the hell could they be on a Sunday morning?

'Heather!' Tess spotted her friend leaving church and called her over. They hugged warmly.

'I didn't see you inside,' Tess said.

'I was running the crèche. I do it once a month. I'd recommend it as a great remedy for broodiness. They get about twenty babies in there and they seem to scream in harmony to the hymns!'

Tess smiled politely. She avoided babies as a general rule, finding they opened little grazes of achey pain inside her. She hadn't talked about this to Heather and didn't feel that this was a good time.

'What are you doing now?' Tess asked.

'We all go to lunch usually. Why don't you join us?'

Tess looked anxiously at Max. 'Er, no, we thought we'd have a family day. This is our first Sunday in the new flat.'

'Didn't I say? I'm going to be working for the rest of the day.' Max looked surprised that Tess hadn't realised this.

'No, you didn't tell me,' Tess said tightly. 'Are you planning to work seven days a week indefinitely?'

'If I have to, then I will. I got us into this situation and I'll get us out. Archie wants me to man the office while he pops out later. I'm being paid extra for that. Also Sundays are as good as nights, there's a twenty per cent surcharge on all fares.'

Tess felt uneasy. They seemed to be regressing here. This was like the early years of their marriage when they were both working at their careers while trying for a baby. There had never been any time just to be together and talk. Tess had secretly concluded that they had deliberately hidden themselves in work to avoid facing each other with their worries. If Lara hadn't come along they would almost certainly have split up.

Then Lara was at school full-time and they experienced another trough from which they clawed their way out by starting a business. Once more they buried themselves in work to avoid each other. For the years when Organique was open, Tess and Max probably talked about nothing except business and Lara.

Spotted the pattern yet, stupid? Tess said to herself. Because here they were again. In trouble in the first place because they didn't talk to each other and Max was trying to get them out of it by ... working so hard they never had the time to talk to each other. Great idea, Max.

'You may as well go to lunch with Heather,' Max said. 'I'll just pick something up at the club.'

Tess closed her eyes impatiently at the mention of the club. She'd thought it was quite sweet when Max first mentioned it. Now it just sounded ridiculous.

'Fine,' she said in a clipped voice. 'Do what you want.'

Max shrugged kissed Tess and left. It felt horribly like a Judas kiss.

Max sat in the minicab office wishing he knew how to handle this situation better, hoping he was doing the right thing. The problem was that he had lied to Tess. Quite a lot as well. He was as shocked as she had been when all those bills arrived last week. More so, probably, because he'd already intercepted and hidden a load more.

He'd messed up completely. He wasn't sure where he'd gone wrong, but somewhere in his calculations, he'd inverted figures or subtracted when he should have added. Tess had offered to go over all the paperwork, check everything but he'd refused, still humiliated by the business failure. He'd hoped that the shop fittings might fetch more than their estimate at auction. That would have helped a little. But the deficit was a disaster.

He didn't know how he was going to tell her that, the way things stood, unless they made a great deal of money, very quickly, they were going to be declared bankrupt. If that happened, the house would be repossessed and sold at a loss, along with all of their possessions in storage. That was why he was so anxious to sell as much as they could before it was all taken away from them.

If no miracle was forthcoming in the immediate future, they would find themselves in a situation from which even the Incredible Vicar couldn't rescue them.

Graham heard the beep on his mobile phone telling him that a message had come through. He had arranged for it to signal an alert every time he received an e-mail at work. It was useful for knowing that international communications had come through out of office hours and he could often then pick up and deal with the e-mails on his computer at home.

He sighed and checked his phone for the details. He wasn't expecting anything important but sometimes there were problems on foreign stock exchanges that he wouldn't otherwise know about until after the weekend.

But this was nothing to do with work. Christine had e-mailed him again. And he was shocked at the pleasure he felt.

'What's that?'

He jumped as Fiona came up behind him. He quickly cancelled the message on his phone. 'Nothing, just work. I wish you wouldn't creep up on me from behind like that.'

Fiona smarted at the rebuke. 'You used to like me creeping up on you from behind. Don't you remember?'

Graham was still struggling to bring his emotions under control. He'd been trying to avoid even thinking about Christine when he was at home. It felt like less of a betrayal if he kept every-thing to do with Christine separate from Fiona and his family. He'd done pretty well all his life by keeping all the conflicting elements of his world in separate boxes. Unlike Fiona who chucked her life on the table, swirled it around then presented it to everybody who walked by, screaming: 'See! Here it is! Everything about me! Love me or leave me!'

In Fiona's case, it was effective, because people mostly loved her; he certainly did. But he was scared that if he ever screamed: 'Here I am! Love me or leave me!' Fiona might leave. So he wasn't prepared to take the chance.

'Sorry,' he said, reaching for her hand which she pulled away.

'Forget it.' Fiona stormed off down to the kitchen where she made her mother a cup of tea with a tea bag, just to spite her.

Calming down, she realised that she couldn't leave it any longer to do something about Graham.

Tomorrow, she decided. Tomorrow I'll give him the surprise of his life.

Heather was looking pained at having to witness this exchange. 'Sorry I opened my big mouth.'

'Don't apologise,' Tess said. 'It wasn't your fault. Anyway, I'm not going to let today be ruined. Come on. Where are we going for lunch? No, let me guess. Carter's?'

'Good guess! Where are the kids?' They looked around to find Lara and Heather's two sons playing football with a chocolate chip muffin.

'Come on, kids!' Heather called. They caught up and started walking down to Carter's.

'There's going to be someone else joining us,' Heather said. 'I hope you don't mind.'

Tess looked at Heather. 'When you say someone, do you mean a man?'

Heather nodded awkwardly.

Tess shrieked. 'That's fantastic! Who is he? When did you meet him? What does he do?'

Heather groaned at the interrogation. 'Don't get too excited. It's early days yet. I've known him for ages but we've only been going out for a couple of months.'

'How come you didn't say anything?'

'I wanted to wait until I was more certain that he wasn't going to fall at the first fence. But I'm starting to get the feeling that this could be the one.'

'Oh that's wonderful! I'm really happy for you.'

'Talk of the devil,' Heather laughed, catching sight of a man coming round the corner towards them.

Tess followed her gaze, eager to catch her first glimpse of the man she hoped would make Heather happy. She frowned, narrowing her eyes to make sure. But there was no mistake. Heather's boyfriend, 'the one', was Jerry Newton, the teacher who had come to Tess's aid after her first school yoga class. Her first male friend. The one she'd been trying not to think about all week.

Without much success.

# 11

'So how long have you been seeing Jerry?' Tess asked, oh so casually.

'A couple of months,' Heather replied. 'I've known him for a couple of years since my kids have been at the school but it was only after I started helping out on the PTA that we became more friendly.'

They were walking down to the community centre for yoga. This time Tess was prepared. She'd drugged and anaesthetised herself in advance. Two ibuprofen slow-release capsules, an all-over spray of muscle relaxant, an hour's soak in a scalding bath the night before and a mental preparation straight out of *Rocky IV*.

'So what did you think of him?' Heather asked shyly.

'I thought he was nice.' Tess used sufficient coolness in her voice to hide the fact that she thought he was a lot more than nice.

In fact if she'd been asked before today what she thought of him, she would still have found the question difficult. The addition of Heather to the equation just took this to a whole new level of complication.

She was still undecided about him, or maybe confused. Certainly she liked his company and found it easy to be with him with none of the awkwardness of first encounters with strangers. But she couldn't hide the fact that she was attracted to him, the first real attraction she'd experienced for a man since she'd been married.

Of course she'd noticed other men and even acknowledged that, in another existence, she might well feel drawn towards them. But there had never been that spark that tipped her off-balance. Put simply, she didn't believe she was the type.

Even when her marriage had been struggling, she had never found herself truly tempted to cheat on her husband. On the contrary, she'd been put off men in general and had gone to her female friends for consolation and company,

This burgeoning friendship with a man was a novelty and a pleasant one. She'd enjoyed both the trip around the supermarket and the coffee afterwards. She'd enjoyed his gentle teasing and flirtation; they differentiated this situation from her friendships with women.

And she'd enjoyed talking to him, the way she'd once talked to Max when they were interested in what the other had to say. She'd been shocked to realise that the dwindling levels of communication with Max also indicated that they no longer respected each other. They'd stopped trying, caring, bothering a long time ago. And this contact with Jerry was reminding her of the vacuum in her life.

And, yes, she had wondered if maybe there was the potential for something more. Purely hypothetically, of course. It was just a bit of fun. It wasn't as if she would even consider having an affair, or even flirting inappropriately. No sir.

Well OK, maybe she would consider it, there was nothing wrong with that, she thought. And she'd read articles about how fantasising can positively benefit a marriage, particularly a marriage under pressure like this one.

But when she'd seen Heather with Jerry, it was as if a button had been pressed inside her, opening a trapdoor into a place she'd kept shut for years. Once she'd fallen down it, it was too late. If you've fallen through a trapdoor, you're stuck there until the end of the play. All you can do is listen to the action above you and curse yourself for standing on the wrong spot.

'Jerry, this is Tess, Tess, Jerry.'

'I'd say that I'd heard all about you, but actually Heather's been keeping you a secret,' Tess said, unsure how to play this, waiting to take Jerry's lead.

'Same here,' Jerry said.

So that's that, Tess thought. We're not going to mention that we've met, that he's rescued me twice, that we've spent time alone and that I, for one, have thought about it a lot.

With that decision made and endorsed, Tess and Jerry's relationship cranked up a notch, into the realm of, well, relationships.

Heather continued. 'You'll probably be bumping into each other at school. Actually, I'm surprised you haven't met already.'

Tess and Jerry exchanged tense glances. They realised that it had been totally unnecessary to lie but, now that they had, they were permanently sealed together in deceit.

Lunch was awkward. Heather seemed different in Jerry's company, lighter, less strident. Tess found herself experiencing the conflicting emotions of pleasure that her new friend had found happiness after a long difficult time on her own and envy that this happiness was with Jerry.

Too complicated, she concluded. Pull yourself together! You've met the man twice, he didn't pull a speck of dust from your eye then fall in love with you to the strains of Rachmaninov. There were no magical moments when you held your breath, no soul-searching conversations. He yanked you into a chair when you did your back in, he introduced you to cheap carrots in the supermarket then got you to buy him a doughnut. This was not *Brief Encounter*. It was the sort of contrived mismatch written into a soap opera to revive flagging ratings. If this were TV Land, it would end up in a bloodbath outside Carter's with Heather screaming over Tess and Jerry's bodies with a rusty steak knife. The image amused Tess.

'Why are you laughing?' Heather asked.

Tess hadn't realised that she was. Lara looked at her mother in distaste. 'Mum, do you mind if I go and sit with Ruthie? She's over there with her parents. We're going to be partners on the school trip to Switzerland next year!'

Before Tess could reply, Lara had gone. 'Switzerland?' she said weakly.

Heather nodded. 'It's a ski trip they can take in Year Six. Before you ask, there is a hardship fund for families who can't afford the cost.'

A hardship fund? Tess wanted to cry with the finality of the label. We are now officially charity cases, she thought. Max will go mad. But she couldn't be distracted by Max. They were united in their commitment to put Lara's happiness before their own pride or any of their own needs. He'd have to accept this, just as she was doing.

Thinking of Lara's happiness made her feel doubly uncomfortable sitting across the table from Jerry, considering possibilities that would be guaranteed to cause Lara profound unhappiness.

Tess was finding all this very very difficult. Jerry, on the other hand, didn't seem bothered. If anything, he found their deception (which Tess knew it was) amusing. He even appeared to be goading Tess.

'So Tess, what exactly do you do at the school?' he asked with a perfect expression of complete innocence.

'I teach yoga.' She felt the familiar redness start creeping towards the surface of her face again. I wish I didn't blush so easily, she thought. Heather's bound to notice and wonder what's wrong. What shall I do? 'Anyone fancy some wine?' she asked suddenly.

Heather looked surprised. 'I thought you said you didn't want a drink. That's why we didn't get a bottle. Red or white?'

'Red,' Tess said quickly. Brilliant idea! I'll drink a glass quickly then, when I blush, she'll put it down to the wine. I'm cleverer than I thought.

Sadly, Tess was not. On this matter, as in the decision to pretend that she was a yoga teacher, she was showing signs of being incredibly stupid. Because Tess had forgotten that she was not a good drinker, particularly when it came to drinking cheap wine very quickly. While she might be able to get away with blushing, she would now have an additional problem, the erosion of her inhibitions.

Within five minutes, Carter had brought them a bottle of Bombay Red (anyone's blood vessels would dilate frantically at the appearance of this, Tess surmised), she'd swallowed a glass and was tapping her toes cheerfully to Nana Mouskouri.

'Doesn't Carter have any other tapes?' Tess asked, her voice getting louder with each sip.

Heather looked amused. 'He loves Nana Mouskouri. He and his wife, Maria, used to dance to her records all the time. When Maria died, he couldn't bear to listen to the music any more. Then about six months ago, he decided that he'd mourned enough and he hasn't stopped playing his old records since. We're all hoping that this is just a phase that will pass.'

'I think it's sweet,' Jerry said. 'That kind of loyalty, till death do us part and beyond, is rare nowadays.'

Heather took Jerry's hand affectionately. 'Jerry is something of a rarity himself, Tess, a single man, never been married, waiting for the right woman to come along.'

Tess looked at him differently, knowing this. The way he'd flirted with her so easily had led her to believe that he was the opposite, a womaniser. The idea that his flirting was just that, nothing more meaningful, was a disappointment to her. As if I needed any more, she thought.

'Lucky Heather,' she said lightly. She'd meant it to be light, anyway, but it came out sounding bitter.

Heather stared at her. Tess panicked at her indiscretion, still surprised by the depth of her own jealousy. She pointed at the wine. 'Don't mind me, it's just the wine. And Max turning into a one-man moneymaking factory. I never see him any more. And things weren't that great when we were seeing each other.'

She clamped her lips together. When I start talking about my marriage I know I'm in trouble, she thought.

Now Heather was smiling. 'So that's the answer,' she said, cryptically.

'The answer to what?' Tess worried that she'd given something away.

Heather turned to Jerry. 'You and Tess have something in common,' she said. Jerry didn't flinch but Tess did. She decided to risk further indiscretions by drinking some Bombay Red.

'What's that?' Jerry asked.

'You both like to hide things from the rest of the world. *You* do it by laughing and joking all the time, trying to convince people you're so shallow, they won't bother trying to probe.'

Tess watched Jerry's smile slip a fraction. But then Heather turned to her. 'Whereas Tess hasn't formulated a cover act. She just thinks before she speaks, you can actually see her thinking sometimes, if the question she's just been asked could prove too revealing.'

Now it was Jerry's turn to watch Tess squirm. 'If you need some hints for a good cover act,' he said to her, 'I'm available for private tuition.'

Heather ignored the interruption. 'But I've just realised that Tess's self-control mechanism breaks down after a glass of wine. This is the first time we've ever drunk together so I've never noticed it before. I'll have to get you drunk one night, see what I can find out about you!'

191

Tess stopped drinking straightaway. I can still use it as an excuse for blushing for the rest of lunch. But I'll never be able to drink with Heather now, not until I've put Jerry back where he belongs, in the box marked Somebody Else's.

As Heather was unlocking the community centre doors the next day, she turned to Tess. 'I've been feeling guilty about yesterday. I made you stop drinking, didn't I?'

Tess shook her head. 'No, it wasn't you,' she lied. 'The wine was giving me a headache. I had been drinking too quickly. It was because I was annoyed at Max, that was all. But you're right, I do talk too much when I have a drink.'

Heather looked horrified. 'That wasn't what I said at all! I meant it in a positive way. I don't think it's healthy to keep things locked away. And that's supposed to be what friends are for, to let yourself go with them, tell them all the things you can't tell your husband or your mother!'

Sadly, Tess thought, with the single thing I've got locked away at this moment, you are one of the last people I can tell, or risk telling. Max was the other, which had added another layer of stress to the already difficult atmosphere building between them. One that was straining ever closer to breaking point.

Max had been particularly attentive towards her this morning, something that would have worried Tess if she hadn't been so preoccupied.

'Let me give you a massage,' he'd insisted. Tess had obediently turned onto her front so that he could loosen all her muscles. She lay in silence, gritting her teeth against his over-enthusiastic torture. If I can stand this, I can last 90 minutes of stretching beyond endurance to impress the women, and I can handle three classes of hyperactive children who can read the word VICTIM tattooed across my forehead.

'How did yesterday go?' Max asked. He hadn't got home until three a.m. Another wife might have wondered what he was getting up to all day and half the night. But when he'd finally crawled into bed, Tess had been stirred from sleep briefly by the lingering smell of his 15-hour shift.

The overwhelming stench of smoke told of hours in the minicab office and the synthetic scent of pine clinging to his hair testified to hours in the car, his head constantly banging the pine tree air freshener so essential in minicabs against the aroma of occasionally unwashed passengers.

He hoped she couldn't smell his fear. Every minute he'd been working, he'd kept a mental calculator constantly checking and adding to his running total. After a long, long day where he'd worked with almost no breaks, he'd realised that he hadn't earned enough to pay the interest accumulated on all their debts in just one day.

He'd never been in this situation before. Until now, he'd supported the family by working. Even if he didn't make a fortune, even when the shop had not been at its best, he'd made enough to pay the mortgage, pay for the best education for Lara and pay for the lifestyle that he thought Tess wanted, needed and expected. He now had to come to terms with the fact that he could work 24 hours a day and not be able to extricate them from the threat of bankruptcy. He felt sick with hopelessness.

Tess didn't notice. She was too engrossed in her own fear that Max might smell her treachery.

But I haven't actually done anything, she reassured herself, using the same skills she'd employed for so many years to cushion Max from unseen or non-existent threats. There's nothing in the marriage ceremony about forsaking doughnuts with other men, or not letting a man persuade you to abandon fabric conditioners.

That's all I've done. Everything else is just in my head and if I can keep it there (which I can apparently do very well as long as I don't drink Indian wine in company) then I'm not hurting Max.

No problem; or it wouldn't have been a problem if Heather hadn't told her that Jerry had proposed a week earlier.

'Don't tell him I'm here,' Fiona whispered to Graham's secretary. 'I want to surprise him.'

Annie, Graham's unimaginative but loyal assistant of five years, was alarmed at this unexpected turn of events. She knew Graham as well as she did her own husband. She knew he hated surprises; even more than that, she understood that he feared them. At the same time, she felt for Fiona.

Annie had noticed that Graham had been behaving strangely lately. Not in a way that anyone else would have called strange. He wasn't plucking his eyebrows or having botox injections, but he was closing his office door more frequently. She assumed that his problems were home-related since she knew everything about his work and that was going as smoothly as ever.

But Fiona's unannounced arrival at the office confirmed her suspicions. This was classic behaviour when a marriage was in trouble. It was usually a sign that the wife suspected the husband of cheating and was trying to catch him out when he was least expecting it.

She couldn't believe that Fiona would suspect that of Graham. Apart from anything else, Graham didn't have any opportunities to meet women. The company was notoriously sexist and women were seldom hired or promoted beyond the junior account executive level.

Annie did experience a momentary thrill when she wondered if Fiona might suspect something between Graham and herself, boss and secretary. But this passed quickly. Nobody who knew either of them would even countenance such a thing. Which made Annie very sad, a fact that no one would ever know during her lifetime.

There was only one other scenario that fitted, Annie concluded. She'd read a lot of romance books, a lot of magazines, to compensate for her unfulfilling marriage to the first man who asked her. When a wife starts 'wooing' her husband again, bringing new dimensions to the marriage, it usually means that she's the one who has been unfaithful and is horribly guilty.

Annie was bewildered by the possibility that anyone would feel the need to be unfaithful to Graham who represented, to Annie, the ideal man. Well, if that's the case, she thought resolutely, I will be there to pick up the pieces when that tramp of a wife lets him down.

'Hello? Annie?' Fiona was watching her.

Annie cleared her throat efficiently. 'Sorry. This is all very awkward. When he came in this morning, he closed his door and phoned through, asking me not to disturb him.'

Did he indeed? Fiona thought. Looks like I've got to this in the nick of time. 'That's OK,' she said. 'I'm sure he won't mind when he sees it's me.'

Graham sat in his office staring at the computer screen. He'd opened Christine's e-mail as soon as he arrived then read it ten, 20 times, checking each sentence for subtext, each word for double meaning. If he was going to reply to this, and he was, he had to be sure of where Christine was coming from. She'd hurt him once before, very badly, and although he wasn't going to allow her into a position where she could do that again, she still had the potential to unsettle him and he didn't want that either.

*Dear Graham,*

*I can't tell you how happy I was to get your message. Guess what, I'm going to ignore everything you implied about not wanting this to continue! I know you don't mean it. You think you do, but you don't.*

*You have questions, you must have. I deliberately haven't told you why I did everything I did. Maybe there are some things you'd rather not know and that's your right. But if you're feeling brave enough to hear some answers, I'm ready to provide them.*

*You wrote about the futility of going back, of wondering what our lives would be like. But I don't think it's an empty exercise. I think it can be helpful providing we do it realistically, not pretending that everything would be perfect when that would be unreasonable.*

*I just feel that, if we could go back 18 years to that day, clear up what happened to each of us, how it affected us both through the years, we could finally put it behind us. Once and for all. And don't say that you've already put it behind you. If that were the case, you would have had no hesitation in returning my first e-mail, you would have had nothing to fear.*

*I suppose the selfish reason for all this is that I also want your forgiveness. Now that's plain mean of me, isn't it, appealing to your honourable nature which I'll bet is as strong as it always was?*

*So come on, Graham, ask me what you need to know and then maybe you'll be able to forgive me. It's a great release, I know because I've had to do a lot of it myself recently!*

*Love*
*Chris*

He'd wasted nearly two hours of his morning playing around with clever words, constructing sentences that would wound her as pointedly as she had hurt him, as she still *was* hurting him. Then he tried a sincere version, one that he would obviously never send but that he hoped might provide him with a sense of release.

*Dear Christine*

he began in that one,

*I don't want to think about what our lives would be like because I spent years doing that and it was as painful as hell. I allowed you to know me in a way that nobody had ever known me and then you rejected me. Nothing personal, I think you wrote in that postcard. Well, how much more bloody personal does it get?*

*What if? If we'd stayed together, I would have been utterly happy, perfectly fulfilled, totally content. Maybe some people are able to shrug off losses like that, put it down to youthful over-expectations, first love, that sort of thing. Plenty more fish in the sea, all that stuff. But I wasn't like that. I'm still not.*

*You were the 'one', my 'one'. After you'd gone, I was perma-nently scarred, so much so that when Fiona met me, she was dealing with someone damaged. It couldn't be the same with her, you'd taken that part of me away with you.*

*So do I have any questions? Yes I do. I want to know why ...*

'Surprise!' Graham crashed his hand onto the keyboard in shock, frantically trying to shut down the screen. His brain was having real difficulty computing this combination of Fiona, his office and the word 'surprise' being shrieked at him all while he was taking himself on an agonising mental journey into his past, dredging up the murky silt, hoping to salvage a few unbroken treasures that lay protected deep down.

He couldn't face Fiona, not until he'd reassembled his own face into the one she recognised, the calm, reassuring one, the settled one, the reliable, unchanging one. It seemed like ages to him, but in fact it only took him a few seconds before he felt confident that he had returned to normal, at least to Fiona's idea of normal.

'Good God.' The words came out before he could stop them. But even if he'd had an hour to prepare a response, he doubted he would have been able to come up with anything more articulate.

Because his wife was standing in front of him with her Burberry raincoat stretched open to reveal her body dressed only in a very short nightshirt which had *Come And Get Me Tiger* embroidered across the front.

'It was the most humiliating moment of my life,' she said, sipping the scalding tea to try and stop herself from crying.

'Oh Fi!' Tess cried, rushing across the kitchen (the entire two-pace length of it) to comfort her friend. 'But what on earth possessed you? If I ever did that to Max, he'd be absolutely terrified. Apart from anything else, it's the unfamiliarity of it all. I'm not convinced that men – or women – necessarily want surprises. I don't. You can't blame Graham for not knowing how he was supposed to react.'

'Well, I wish you'd told me that before I made a fool of myself.' The unspoken accusation brought Tess up short.

'I'm so sorry I haven't been around this last week, Fi. I'm not going to make any more excuses, I could have made more of an effort. It's not as if we live miles away from each other. And I'm the one that messed up last Tuesday when we were supposed to be getting together. If it makes you feel any better, I'll take full responsibility for this.'

'Yeah, I'll tell Graham that when he comes home tonight and can't look me in the face. Tess, this tea is disgusting! It even makes that stuff you used to serve in Organique look good in comparison.'

'You get used to it after a while,' Tess assured her. Fiona took her word for it and carried on drinking. She'd hoped for something stronger but when Tess didn't offer her a glass of wine, she assumed that this was because of money problems and didn't push it.

In fact Tess was avoiding alcohol completely after realising that Heather's observation was accurate. She intended to keep full control of her tongue while her life was so stormy and since Heather's tea obviously worked for her, she'd stick to it herself.

Fiona was still hashing over the appalling experience. 'It's not as if I expected him to clear his desk with a masterful sweep of his arm, throw me across the leather inlay and ravish me. But I'd hoped he'd laugh!'

And Tess understood exactly what she meant. If she ever were to do anything as outrageous as Fiona's stunt, she'd fully expect Max to collapse in a heap. Because the laughter would be so much more intimate than any histrionic display of lust that normally accompanies such actions in bad films.

Graham had just been horrified. He'd sat there staring at her, wanting to jump up and pull the coat around her to cover her up but not even being able to do that.

'Say something,' Fiona had whispered nervously, wrapping the coat tightly around her as if she were freezing cold. Which, inside, she was.

What am I supposed to say? Graham thought. If I understood what this meant, I'd know the correct response. We've been married for 12 years; I'd assumed I knew all of her little ways, her moods. I know when to be quiet, when to make soothing noises, when she wants an argument. But this is something else altogether.

It must be something big so it's really important that I say the right thing. But what the hell is it all about?

'Fine, then don't say anything,' Fiona had said tightly, before turning and leaving the office, slamming the door behind her.

He wanted to go after her but that would mean involving the entire office in this debacle. No, he'd wait until he got home. By then he might have been able to make sense of it all, Fiona would have calmed down or transferred her frustration onto her mother and they could talk about it. Or not.

His hand brushed against the keyboard lighting up the screen once more. His words were still there, the ones he would never send to Christine. He had to get this out of his system now before any damage was done. He erased everything he'd written and started again.

The new version took two minutes.

*Dear Christine,*

*You're right, I do have questions. They are:*

*1) Why did you say you were going to marry me if you had doubts?*

*2) Why didn't you tell me before our wedding day that you couldn't go through with it?*

*3) Did you have our baby?*

*Graham*

*

198

'I wish you'd told me that you were worried about Graham,' Tess said. They'd eased back into their old slipper-fit rapport.

'What could you have done about it?' Fiona asked miserably.

'We could have had you round to dinner and I could have watched him, asked pointed questions, that sort of thing.'

'Maybe we could still do that?' Fiona suggested. 'Millie's next to useless, bless her. She's convinced that Tim is having an affair with an old girlfriend. And maybe he is. But I think it's all her panicking that made me start thinking along those lines.'

Tess snorted. 'Graham would never cheat on you.'

'Go on, say it, he's not the type.' Fiona jumped up and went to look out the window onto the tiny patch of garden. The desolation reminded her that Tess had problems of her own.

'Oh Tess, I'm so sorry! I come here practically blaming you for all this because you're not around and it's not actually your fault that you're not around.'

Her apology made Tess want to weep. Everything made Tess want to weep. The crunching pain coursing through her body made her want to lie down and die. After her less than over-whelming success during her first lesson, she was determined that she would win her students over this time.

She'd practised a few moves, found that she had fairly supple arms and discovered that she could bend them back quite a long way. Great, she'd thought, we'll do arm exercises for most of the lesson and I'll dazzle them with my virtuosity.

She had a cunning plan that she would warm up beforehand for an hour, stretching her arm muscles until they were as elongated as her unfit body allowed. But she wouldn't allow the class to prepare in the same way. Then when it came to the stretches, she would automatically exceed any of their attempts to copy her.

The plan would have been fine if the women were reasonably fit rather than as out of condition as she was. These were people who needed a lot of warming up to avoid serious injury. Most of them hadn't stretched much beyond the remote controls on their coffee tables since the week before.

After a cursory couple of arm flexes, Tess encouraged them to lean forward, lock their hands together and lift their arms back-wards over their heads. She demonstrated impressively and was gratified to see looks of admiration on their faces. They all then followed suit, accompanied by a chorus of clicks and groans and a mass collapse to the ground.

'Is everyone all right?' Tess cried out in alarm, coming out of her own stretch too quickly and hurting her own shoulders in the process. She rushed around the hall, checking each woman in turn. Fortunately, none of them seemed to have done any permanent damage. After some moaning and rubbing, they slowly rose to their feet.

Tess wanted to abandon the class but she needed the money she was due to be paid to give to Lara for a school trip tomorrow. She didn't want to ask Max for money, not when she could see he was so worried.

She reverted to her primary school strategy and encouraged them all onto the floor where she lulled them to sleep. She didn't manage to sleep herself this time; she was too terrified that she had compromised the safety of these women through her own negligence and would have to stop before someone got hurt.

'I wouldn't worry about it,' Heather had said, afterwards, 'it was their own fault.'

'How can it be?' Tess had asked. 'Surely safety is the teacher's responsibility?'

'They'd all decided that you were no better at this than they were, so they just threw themselves into that move, convinced that it must be basic if you were doing it so easily. Actually they were impressed. I think you've won them over.'

Great, Tess thought. So that's the way to do it, cause them pain and win their respect. It was another variation on the 'treat 'em mean, keep 'em keen' philosophy loved by teenage boys and unevolved men.

But even with the stretching preparation, Tess still paid the price for showing off later and her arms were shaking for the whole afternoon.

She told the whole story to Fiona, right from the moment when she'd first met Heather and lied to her about her teaching abilities.

'I think that's fantastic!' Fiona had exclaimed. 'I'd never have had the nerve to do that.'

'That's because you've got more sense than me.'

Fiona's mouth opened in shock. 'Now I know the world has truly gone crazy! So what are you going to do?'

'What do you mean?'

'Well, you can't carry on like this. Apart from the fact that you'll never live to see forty if you carry on punishing your body so hard, it doesn't sound as if you're making enough money for it to be worth your while.'

Tess looked sheepish. 'Actually, I was thinking of taking on more work, offering my services to other local schools and community centres. If I got enough contracts, I could make enough to cover our weekly living expenses.'

Fiona shook her head in astonishment. 'I think that's insane! There must be something else you can do, surely.'

'Think about it, Fi. What would you do if you were in my position?'

And when Fiona thought about it, she too was confronted with the unpleasant truth that she was qualified to do precisely nothing. Her practical response to this worrying fact was to stop thinking about it.

'So what's it like teaching children?' she asked.

This took Tess somewhere that she was trying to avoid. She knew she couldn't tell Fiona about Jerry, partly because she felt ridiculous for confessing what was little more than a crush but also because Fiona was feeling insecure in her own marriage and would not like to hear about problems in someone else's. She was clinging to the solidness of Tess and Max's marriage to reassure herself against the threats that Millie was facing.

'They're less knowledgeable so I can get away with a lot more. They are comparing me with their usual PE teacher rather than some elastic-limbed thin goddess, so their expectations are considerably lower. They're cheeky but then I'm used to that with Lara. No,' she summed up, 'all in all I can handle them.'

It's the teachers that cause all the problems.

'You'll have to tell me your secret,' the voice whispered. 'I could do with a sleeping hour every day in the classroom.'

Tess jumped. She hadn't heard Jerry come into the hall. 'This isn't your class as well, is it?' she asked. 'I thought you took Year Two?'

Jerry nodded. 'I've left my lot counting to a thousand with their eyes closed. I just wanted to pop in and say hello.'

Is that all? Tess thought. 'Hello,' she said crossly.

'You're angry about yesterday,' he observed. 'Sorry to land you in it like that. But you could have said something about having met me yourself.'

'I didn't know what to say. I was waiting to see what you did.'

Jerry shrugged. 'I was improvising. The truth is I was completely thrown by your being Heather's friend.'

'Friend is a bit strong,' Tess pointed out disloyally. 'We haven't known each other for long.' So if he wants to betray her for you, it's not as bad as if you were really close friends? suggested her conscience. Shut up, Tess said to her conscience, of course I don't mean that.

'I felt bad about it all last night,' Jerry said, the first serious sentence he'd uttered in their entire acquaintance. 'And I'm not even sure why I lied.'

'We didn't exactly lie,' Tess reassured him, knowing that this was the biggest lie of all.

Jerry raised an eyebrow. Tess felt the blush waking up for its now-regular journey up her neck towards her face. Buy that green concealer cream that covers redness, she told herself. Buy the industrial size if you're intending to carry on working at this school.

Tess glanced at her watch. It was almost time to stir the class. She didn't want all the teachers knowing that she made the children sleep during most of the session. It was only a temporary strategy until her body had become accustomed to all the activity and she wasn't in pain for 48 hours after every lesson.

Jerry spotted her anxiety. 'Do you want to meet up for lunch?'

No, Tess thought. 'Yes. Where?'

'Anywhere but Carter's.'

Tess remembered that her women's yoga group met there for lunch on Mondays. She'd said she wouldn't be able to join them now she was teaching at the school after their class.

'How about the café on the common?' Tess suggested. It was the one place nearby that she knew none of her friends would ever dream of frequenting. Too grubby, too greasy, too cheap. No one I know will see us there, she was thinking. Not that I'm hiding anything. It's just lunch with a friend, that's all. It will just be less complicated if we keep this to ourselves.

'By the way, I phoned earlier but you weren't in,' Fiona said as she left to pick up her children from school. 'And your mobile was switched off.'

202

'I was having lunch with a couple of the women from the yoga class,' Tess lied smoothly. And it was a lie of the first order, because at this lunch with Jerry, this prearranged lunch that they agreed not to tell anyone else about, they both realised that the casual acquaintance had taken a hesitant step towards something more significant.

It had been Tess who'd made the first move by asking Jerry about his proposal to Heather.

Graham got off the train two stations early so that he could walk slowly home and think. Also, he wanted to put off facing Fiona for a bit longer. After he'd sent his e-mail to Christine, an act he immediately regretted, he'd found himself unable to concentrate on his work.

Annie had tapped on his door at regular intervals, offering him tea, coffee, sandwiches, the benefit of her lifetime's reading of romantic novels that dealt with this precise marital dilemma. He became more irritated with her as the day went on and finally snapped at her.

I'll bring her flowers tomorrow as an apology, he said to himself. Maybe I should take them to Fiona as well. But I'm not sure what I'm supposed to be apologising for. As he walked along the road, he looked in all the shop windows, deciding that there was no point in labouring this subject any further. He'd spent the whole day at it and not made any progress.

He went past a new bar that had opened since the last time he'd been down this street. It had still not established itself and was not busy. He would never know why he peered through the windows but, looking in, he spotted a solitary drinker at a back table.

It was Millie.

Fiona flicked back the curtain for the hundredth time. He was late. He was never late, or hardly ever. She wanted to call him on his mobile but felt that, after this morning, she'd probably been pushy enough for one day, for one marriage even.

Daphne watched her daughter, aching for her, unable to comfort her because she knew Fiona would resent it. Damn the man! Daphne thought. Her own husband had been just like this. He'd started out so devoted to her, so steady and reliable. Everyone loved him, he was a mother's dream for a daughter. Then, after the children, he began to drift. He came home later and later, the excuses becoming more implausible until he stopped making excuses altogether. He left Daphne and the children for his girlfriend and never saw any of them again.

That was one of the reasons Daphne had never trusted Graham. Yes, he appeared to be a rock and no, she wouldn't have wanted Fiona to marry some fly-by-night good-for-nothing who was guaranteed to make her miserable. But someone like Graham was even more threatening. He could mislead Fiona into thinking she was secure for life then, when he did let her down, the fall would be so much more devastating.

And after what she'd seen yesterday, the prospect of yet another shattered marriage was at the front of Daphne's mind.

'So why did you never remarry?' Archie asked Daphne.

'That's a bit personal! You hardly know me and you ask me a question like that.'

'I'm sixty-three years old. Timing becomes more pressing at that age.'

Daphne was stunned. His insistence on dressing 15 years younger had proved effective. She'd never met a man over 50 who wore jeans.

Archie continued. 'If you don't do and say things when they come into your head, you might never get another chance.'

'I was saying that to my daughter the other day,' Daphne recalled. 'She didn't understand. She just thinks I'm rude.'

'My grown-up children think I'm a stroppy old sod. I couldn't care less.' Archie took Daphne's hand and linked it through his arm, patting it before they set off.

As he did this, Daphne experienced one of those rare, totally pain-free moments that gave her the resolve to continue living for a while longer. She hadn't held a man's arm for well over 20 years unless she counted all the male nurses who'd helped her up and down stairs in hospitals.

'I suppose I didn't think it would be fair on the children,' she said, answering his question five minutes later. 'They'd had a terrible time of it when our marriage was collapsing, all the rows and the tears. Then when their father left, they just seemed to need me so much. It would have been like their mother leaving them too if I'd found someone else. Besides, even if I had

204

married and they'd been happy about it, that could have gone wrong as well, then they'd have lost another father! I couldn't take that risk.'

Archie seemed to be thinking about this. 'It's funny but I think it was the same for me, although I never quite worked out the reasons. It just never seemed right.'

'Do you regret it?' Daphne asked him.

'All the time,' Archie said without hesitation. 'And you?'

'All the time,' she confessed with a smile.

After they'd walked for ten minutes, Archie could feel Daphne's grip on his arm become tighter.

'I could do with a cup of tea,' he said. 'I'm not as fit as you. How does that sound?'

Daphne wanted to hug him in relief. 'I never say no to a cup of tea.'

They turned along the path leading to the café. As they got nearer, Daphne caught sight of a couple talking intensely at a table in the window. They were holding hands and oblivious to anyone else.

Daphne tugged on Archie's hand suddenly. 'Wait. I think I've just seen someone I recognise.'

Archie followed her gaze to the café. 'Isn't that one of your daughter's friends?'

Daphne nodded. 'His name's Tim. He's got four children and another two on the way.'

Archie looked at the couple more closely. 'I don't remember that woman from Friday night though.'

'That's because she isn't his wife,' Daphne said finally.

Daphne had always been reassured by the apparent solidness of Fiona's friends' marriages. It gave her hope for Fiona and Graham. But all of a sudden, her hope was faltering. She was in unfamiliar territory. She didn't know what the rules were for discovering the infidelity of the friend of your grown-up child. Did you say something or keep quiet?

The answer, in Daphne's case, was determined by the fact that she didn't speak to her daughter about anything more meaningful than tea-brewing methods and the merits of acrylic jumpers (washable, practical) versus wool (tendency to shrink and bobble). Therefore she couldn't say anything. The subject was not on the prescribed list.

But it made her very nervous now that Graham was showing the classic early sign of straying – coming home late.

'Are you waiting for someone?'

Millie spilled her water. The last thing she'd expected was someone actually trying to chat her up. Don't make eye contact, she told herself firmly. Completely ignore him.

'Millie?'

Millie looked up in surprise. 'Graham? What are you doing here?'

Graham smiled. 'I was just walking past and I saw you in here by yourself. You're not expecting Fiona, are you?'

Millie shook her head. She hadn't anticipated meeting anyone she knew. Originally she was just going to walk around for a couple of hours, enjoying her own company before going home and acting mysteriously. But it had been too cold and Millie was too tired to walk for longer than 20 minutes. She'd stumbled on this place a couple of days earlier and decided that it would be perfect. Nobody she knew was likely to be passing and see her and it was quiet enough that she could sit here with a book.

Graham noticed the book and realised what she was doing. 'You've come here to read,?' he asked.

'You think that's silly.'

'Not at all. I do it every lunchtime.'

It was Millie's turn to look surprised. She didn't know Graham that well, despite all the holidays they'd spent together, despite the fact he'd seen her breastfeeding, despite the fact that they'd once sat up all night in Italy with sick children, changing bed linen and clothes, pacing up and down, soothing babies and toddlers.

She had no concept of him as a person outside of their circle of friends. She knew what his job was because he'd arranged a lot of their financial planning. But she couldn't imagine him reading a book or arguing with Fiona or having wild dreams.

'Do you really do it every day?' she asked, fascinated.

'Almost every day. I go to the library once a fortnight. That takes a lunch hour. Then I get through four books in two weeks.'

'I've hardly read a book in ten years,' Millie said. 'in fact, I'm finding it quite difficult to get back into the swing of it. I bet you think that's pathetic.'

'Not at all. Four kids take up a lot of time. I expect you're grateful to have any time at all to yourself. It must be hard to unwind.'

'You manage it,' Millie pointed out, slightly resentfully.

Graham could detect the beginning of one of the arguments Fiona periodically started with him. He deftly averted the crisis.

'So what does Tim think about these little outings?'

Now Millie was really alarmed. 'He doesn't know!' she blurted out. Graham said nothing. ''No, I mean obviously he knows I've gone out. But he doesn't know that I come here to read a book by myself.' She covered her face with her eyes, too tired and muddled to lie convincingly. 'I may as well tell you,' she sighed.

And she told Graham everything.

'You're the only person I've told,' she said after pouring out the complicated story. 'Not even Fiona knows and you mustn't tell her.'

Great. Another secret, Graham thought. But he was an honourable man who took promises seriously. And so he agreed.

He would keep their meeting tonight secret.

# 12

'What exactly is sequence dancing?' Tess asked.

Heather had arrived at the flat unannounced on Wednesday morning. Yesterday had been the first day they hadn't seen or spoken to each other since the day they'd met. Tess hoped that Heather wasn't reading anything into this.

'It's great!' Heather said with her customary enthusiasm. 'Everybody learns the same steps to the dances, that's the sequence, and then you can dance with anybody you like because you'll all be doing the same thing.'

'When you say "dances", what sort of dances are we talking about?' Tess hoped that she was wrong in her suspicions.

'Ballroom dancing, Latin-American, old-time, it's very varied.'

Tess was right in her suspicions. 'You mean like *Come Dancing* and all those ladies in dresses with the ten thousand sequins hand-sewn by their mums and the men in tails with shiny hair and shinier shoes?' She was giving Heather every opportunity to correct her misapprehensions.

But Heather was blissfully oblivious to Tess's horror. 'That's the one! Of course it's not like that any more. Young people are doing it now, if you can count people of our age as young.'

Tess was more offended that anyone who knew her even remotely would consider her suitable to take up ballroom dancing than worried about whether she could still call herself young. She was finding it difficult to come up with an excuse to get out of this without mocking Heather for her choice of hobby.

Heather wasn't giving up. 'I know what you're thinking. I was sceptical too the first time I heard about it. But the kids dragged me along.'

'Children do it too?' Tess asked, more interested now.

'Whole families go along. It's one of the few things we can all do together. You were saying only on Sunday that you and Max don't do anything together any more. Maybe you can persuade him to give it a try. It's just an hour a week and it would only cost five pounds for all three of you.'

Tess was now thinking about it more seriously. If she and Max didn't start doing something, anything, together then the rift between them would just continue to widen until it was finally uncrossable. After lunch with Jerry on Monday, she'd been forced to take a good objective look at her marriage.

'So if your marriage is so steady, what are you doing here with me?' Jerry had asked.

'Why are we suddenly talking about my marriage? I was asking about yours.'

'I'm not married yet,' Jerry replied. 'But you are. So I'll ask you again. Why are you having lunch with me? And don't give me all that about us just being friends and it all being innocent. We both know that you won't be telling Max and I won't be telling Heather.'

Tess felt hemmed in. She'd anticipated another chatty, flirty lunch, an hour that would make her tingle, keep her feeling alive for the rest of her day, give her a pocket of fantasy to which she could return when she was feeling low. She hadn't planned on anything heavy, anything with implications for her family and her future.

'I'll make you a deal,' she said. 'You tell me why you're marrying Heather and I'll tell you why I'm staying married to Max.'

She crossed her fingers, hoping that he'd renege on his side of the deal and they could return to the harmless banter of last week. But Jerry was not as cowardly as Tess.

'OK,' he agreed. 'I asked Heather to marry me because she's the first woman I've ever met that I completely trust; I admire her strength in bringing up her children alone, and doing it well; her values in putting their happiness before her own; she makes me laugh, she's decent and kind, she's a doer rather than a thinker and I respect that; and she wants more children and that's important to me.'

Tess closed her eyes as she heard yet another person make casual plans to have children as if it were as easy as placing an order from a catalogue. But she couldn't get into that. Not now.

'That's not the most romantic set of reasons I've ever heard,' she said. 'Where are all the declarations of love, the earth moving, that sort of thing?'

'Oh I love her,' Jerry then said bluntly. 'But then again, I've loved every woman I've ever gone out with, every single one of them. There's some kind of flaw in my make-up. Most people are apparently born with the receptor to love that one special someone who's plonked in front of them at a critical juncture and maybe the added bonus of one or even two spares in case of failure. But I've got an infinite number of receptors, rather like women being born with all the eggs they will ever have during their fertile lifetime.'

I wish he'd stop talking about fertility, Tess thought. 'So you think you fall in love with every woman you meet? Has it not occurred to you that you've never actually loved any of them, that the real thing hasn't happened for you yet and all these experiences are just the common-or-garden infatuation that everyone has in the early flush of a relationship?'

Jerry smiled. 'Yes, I've considered that. But it doesn't make a difference. If it feels real to me, then it is real. Perhaps that's all that's available to me. Like I said, it's a genetic flaw. So once I accepted that and stopped waiting for something more earth-shattering to come along, it allowed me to look for more sensible reasons to marry, to choose more rationally.'

Tess burst out laughing. 'I don't know why you didn't just go to one of those agencies. You list all the qualities that are essential for your compatibility and they match you with the ideal combination. It's like taking a swatch of material to a DIY shop and getting them to mix a perfect match of paint. If chemistry is irrelevant, the choice is easy!'

'I tried that,' Jerry said, surprising Tess again. 'I went to three different agencies and tried computer dating and even had a few goes at the Lonely Hearts columns. But the problem with all of those is that people either lie about themselves or they have no idea who they really are.'

'You mean unlike yourself, who is stuffed to overflowing with self-awareness?' Tess said teasingly.

'I know who I am,' he said. 'Don't you?'

Fortunately Tess had not had a glass of Bombay wine for over three days and was able to deflect that question with ease.

'So are you saying that you could more or less marry any woman and make it work?'

'Providing that we're compatible, yes.'

Tess was becoming reckless now, maybe because she had convinced herself that this was the last such conversation they would have. 'Then let me ask you a totally hypothetical question.'

Jerry didn't wait for the question. 'You're wondering if I would consider marrying you rather than Heather, if you weren't already married, even though we've only just met. And the answer is yes.'

Now Tess needed some Bombay Red.

'I am definitely, absolutely, categorically not going ballroom dancing,' Max said. He wanted to go to bed. He'd been working all night and only had six hours before he was due back on shift. Also he'd promised to pop into the club because Carter wanted to talk to him about something.

'That was my first reaction as well,' Tess said. 'I thought it was a completely wacky idea. But then Heather persuaded me that it was a really fun thing for us to do as a family. And it's cheap.'

'Good old Heather,' Max muttered, disliking the woman more with each passing day, still blaming her for Tess's transformation from someone he recognised to someone who was reinventing herself both inwardly and outwardly.

'Max, I want us to do this,' she said, more firmly. 'I think Lara needs to see us doing things together again. You can't keep up this intensity of work indefinitely. It'll make you ill. All I'm asking is for one hour a week.'

Max was about to make another objection when Tess interrupted. 'Let me make myself a little plainer since you're tired and not reading between the lines. I want us to do this *very much*. If you're not prepared to give up one hour of your week to do something as a family, I'll take that as a sign that you've given up on this marriage.'

Max stared at her. 'Where has this come from? I say I don't want to learn how to cha cha cha with a bunch of strangers and you start making veiled threats about divorce.'

Tess stayed silent, determined that she wasn't going to reassure him this time. In a way it wasn't his fault that he was so bemused.

Up until now, he'd believed that their only problems were financial. Only she knew that their troubles went far deeper. But since she was the only one in this marriage in possession of all the facts, she was having to fight on behalf of them both.

After Jerry's disturbing words, her determination to save her marriage was doubled. She couldn't be diverted along the dangerous track that Jerry represented. That way lay devastation for too many people. Only a fool would even consider such a path.

Max felt sick with exhaustion and pressure. 'Fine,' he said weakly. 'Whatever you want. But please don't expect me to enjoy myself just because you and your good friend Heather do.'

He turned away from her, went into the bedroom and shut the door, almost slamming it but just managing to hold himself back.

That was when it struck Tess. If Heather was going to be there, did that mean Jerry would be there too?

Fiona felt marginally better for having spoken to Tess on Monday. She'd been reassured that, although her actions in Graham's office did represent the behaviour of a madwoman, his stunned reaction did not mean anything. She'd tried to hang onto this assurance for the whole hour that she was waiting for him to arrive home and not to read any sinister motives into his lateness.

The evening had been strained, probably because the phone had rung every time Fiona had summoned up the courage to discuss the morning's fiasco with Graham. It was almost as if some malevolent being was watching Fiona, waiting for the most crucial moment to arise before prodding some unsuspecting soul into phoning her with yet further complications to add to her fraying world.

'Mum, it's for you,' Fiona had shouted the first time. She had just ordered Graham to stop reading the paper because they needed to talk. It had taken Daphne a couple of minutes to negotiate the stairs before reaching her increasingly impatient daughter holding the receiver.

Fiona had returned to the living room where Graham had obediently put down the newspaper so that his wife could interrogate him. 'What were you saying?' he asked, wanting to get this over with.

'Ssh!' Fiona hissed. 'I'm trying to listen.'

Graham watched with amusement as Fiona eavesdropped on

her mum's conversation, which consisted of far too many laughs, in Fiona's opinion. After she'd put the phone down, Fiona called her mum into the living room like a naughty girl.

'What was all that about?' she asked, her arms folded in the classic confrontational pose.

Daphne smiled. 'You sound like me twenty years ago when you'd just come off the phone to one of your boyfriends.'

'This is a bit different, Mum,' Fiona said crossly. 'I'm just taking an interest in what you're doing, making sure that you're all right.'

'Whereas I was just trying to spoil your fun?'

'Don't tell me if you don't want to.'

Daphne tutted. 'It's OK. I would have told you anyway, you didn't need to cross-examine me. There's nothing to hide. I'm going out tomorrow evening.'

'With Archie again? You only saw him yesterday!'

Graham coughed to swallow the chuckle that was threatening to emerge. He had been revising his opinion of Daphne since she'd been living here. He saw that a lot of the friction between them was instigated by Fiona. Not that he would ever say that to her. After her strip act in his office this morning, he was very cautious about upsetting her and triggering off another flamboyant display of . . . whatever feeling she was trying to convey. He was hoping that Come and get me, Tiger was meant to be figurative rather than literal.

'No it wasn't Archie,' Daphne said. 'That was Carter, the nice man who owned that restaurant. Well, I'll be off to bed now. Good night.'

'Can you believe that? That's two men in two days who've asked Mum out. What's going on here?'

'They obviously see more in your mum than we do. I suppose, if you think about it, she's quite attractive for her age.'

Fiona was horrified. 'Attractive? She's a wicked old woman, how can that be attractive?'

'Perhaps Archie and Carter haven't seen her wicked side.'

'Or perhaps she saves it all for me,' Fiona moaned. 'That would be more like it.'

She spent an hour sorting out all her confused thoughts on her mother having a better social life than her own before the memory of the morning's horror returned to her.

213

'Graham,' she began. 'About this morning . . .'

Again the phone rang. 'That'll probably be the postman for my "attractive" mum,' Fiona said irritably. But this time it was for her.

'Oh hi, Millie, how are you?' she asked dully, resenting this intrusion.

'Is everything all right?' Millie asked, sensing that her call was not welcome.

Fiona remembered Millie's problems, which were probably more challenging than her own right now. She softened her tone. 'Sorry. Bad day, that's all. What's up?'

Millie had really just called in a panic to make sure that Graham had grasped how essential it was that he didn't tell Fiona about her little play-acting. She was thoroughly embarrassed about her behaviour and, after her helpful chat with Graham, she'd decided to stop it. Had she known what Fiona had done this morning, she might have not felt so foolish but she was now regretting opening up so expansively to Graham. She'd hoped he might answer the phone but, as it was Fiona, she was just going to have to probe a little to find out if Graham had said anything. In her new position of not trusting her own husband, she found it hard to trust anybody.

'So how's Graham?' she asked clumsily. Fiona's antennae pricked up.

'Why are you asking that?'

'I was just being polite.' Millie cursed herself for not thinking this through before picking up the phone.

'No you weren't,' Fiona insisted. She closed the living-room door so that Graham couldn't hear their conversation. She needn't have worried; he had never taken any interest in her phone calls. They were always a blessed relief to him, offering him a peaceful respite from having to contribute to a conversation with Fiona himself.

Fiona lowered her voice. 'You never ask how Graham is, not unless he's been ill.'

Millie floundered for a way out of this corner. 'But I know you've been worried about him. And we haven't spoken since last week, so I was just wondering, you know . . .' She was fast losing the will to live, let alone the will to continue this particular ordeal.

Fiona relented. I'm being too sensitive, she thought. Millie's pregnant and she's terrified that Tim's having an affair. She probably just wanted reassurance that other people had problems too.

'Well, he's now behaving even more strangely,' she said, grateful to have someone she could open up to. 'He was an hour late home from work and that's not like him at all.' She wanted to be able to tell Millie what she'd done this morning but she couldn't. She felt too foolish. She was glad she'd told Tess though. Tess had understood.

'Well I've been thinking about Tim *and* Graham,' Millie said. 'I think this is all my fault for getting you thinking like this. I'm going to take your advice and just talk to Tim. I did think about what you said, you know, spicing up our marriage, but I think that could backfire and just make things more confusing.'

Thank you for telling me that now, Fiona thought. Perhaps next time you think I've made a stupid suggestion, you could let me know before I act on it.

'Well, I'm glad you're going to talk to Tim. I think that's the right thing to do,' she said, resolving to do exactly the same with Graham. Providing the phone didn't ring again.

'How was Millie?' Graham asked.

'Fine,' Fiona replied absently.

'What did she want?'

And that did it for Fiona. She might have been persuaded that Millie's enquiry about Graham was innocent. But his enquiry about Millie, involving no fewer than *two* questions, was unprecedented. He never asked how her friends were, mainly because he was terrified that she would answer. In great detail.

But these two insignificant questions of his put together added up to a big fat solid one. And Fiona could only think of one answer.

There's something going on between them. She was willing, desperate even, to be persuaded that this was ridiculous. But for that to happen, she needed to lay the accusation out in the open, expose it to denial. No, she thought, if I say something and I'm wrong, then I've ruined my friendship with Millie and as for Graham, well, he'll take my distrust as a betrayal.

Then it occurred to her that there was a more innocent possibility. She remembered a series of surreptitious phone calls with Tim when he was planning an anniversary surprise for Millie one year. As it turned out, Millie had never suspected a thing and had been stunned with the perfectly fitting ring Tim had given her.

Fiona sat back in exhausted relief to find a far more plausible explanation for her individual concerns. Her birthday was only a month away. And Graham wasn't famous for his imagination. It made perfect sense that he would involve one of her friends if he wanted to get her something unusual.

Besides, Millie is four months' pregnant, she reminded herself. This is not the time she would be considering embarking on affairs, if ever.

'Just arranging to meet up with Tess,' she answered vaguely. That seemed to satisfy him. 'Look Graham, I'm really sorry about ...'

And she was fully prepared to apologise unreservedly for her moment of madness this morning, kiss and make up and stop this crazy worrying.

But the phone rang again. 'I don't believe this!' she said in exasperation. Graham jumped up. 'Let me get this. Whoever it is, I'll tell them you're in the bath and your mother's social calendar is temporarily closed.'

He kissed her on the head as he passed.

'Hello?' Fiona listened for clues as to the caller. But all she could hear was a series of sighs and protests before Graham finally seemed to give in to whatever was being proposed.

'What have you bought?' she asked teasingly. He was always an easy sell, never able to slam the phone down on a pushy sales-woman.

'That was Tim,' he said quietly.

'What did he want?' The men in this circle never phoned each other. It wasn't their job.

'He wants me to go for a drink with him tonight. Apparently it's urgent.'

'I can't see you today,' Tess said apologetically. 'I'm teaching all day. And tomorrow I'm going into central London to take some yoga lessons. As a pupil, before you ask! I thought if I took an intensive course of advanced lessons, I could improve my standard quickly. I'm going to learn a few weird positions with impressive names to dazzle the sceptics.'

'I really need to see you,' Fiona repeated miserably.

'Has something happened?'

'It sounds stupid if I just say it, but if I could explain all the circumstances then I know you'd understand.'

Tess hated to let Fiona down when she'd more than proven herself as a friend. 'I'll tell you what. If you can get out tomorrow evening, you could come sequence dancing with us.'

Fiona then repeated all the things that Tess had said when Heather had first suggested it and all the things that Max had repeated when Tess suggested it. 'I know, I know, Fi. But if you can't come over then, we won't be able to get together until next week. Come on! It might be fun. And we're bound to get a chance to talk.'

Fiona reluctantly agreed. She had no choice. She couldn't talk to Millie, she couldn't talk to Graham. Of course there was always her mother.

Ha ha.

'We can give you a lift,' Daphne said.

'Who can give me a lift?'

'Carter and I. He's coming to collect me for the sequence dancing.'

Fiona gasped in horror. 'You're going as well?'

Daphne sighed. 'Didn't I just say that? So you'll have to sort out a babysitter if Graham is coming as well.'

'Of course Graham won't be coming! Don't be so stupid.' She was lashing out now because everything was slipping from its proper place.

'I was only asking,' Daphne said calmly.

Fiona made a joke of it later, mocking her mother for even suggesting she invite Graham.

'That sounds fun,' Graham said. 'Why don't we all go?'

Fiona looked at him carefully, to check he wasn't one of those pod-people who take over human bodies so convincingly that you think they're real people instead of warmongering aliens.

'Did you hear what I said?' Fiona repeated. 'Sequence dancing. Not a back-to-back showing of all the *Die Hard* films.'

'I used to go sequence dancing when I was a boy,' he said. 'The kids will really enjoy it.'

'You never told me.' Fiona wondered how many other things he hadn't told her.

'It never came up in conversation. And it was a bit

embarrassing. I was always aware that it was very uncool to go ballroom dancing with your family. It probably still is, that's why I haven't suggested it. But now that Tess has invited us, I think it's a really good idea. Let's give it a try.'

Fiona called Tess back and told her that they would all be coming along. 'That's great, Fi! Max will feel less left out if Graham is there as well. Hey, how about inviting Millie and Tim?'

Fiona didn't want to do that because she'd planned to talk about them to Tess. But she couldn't think of a good reason to refuse. Instead, she decided to make the invitation sound as unappealing as possible. Shouldn't be hard, she thought; Graham must be the only person under 60 in the Western world who would find the prospect of an hour's sequence dancing in a South London community centre a thrilling experience.

'That would be great!' Tim said enthusiastically when Fiona had put the suggestion to him. Millie was bathing the children at the time.

Has everyone gone mad? Fiona asked herself. 'So you're saying that you actually *want* to come dancing tomorrow. Ballroom dancing, I'm talking about, not lap dancing.'

Tim laughed, a little wildly, Fiona thought later. 'Well, I won't be able to come myself, of course,' he said. 'I've got a project on that I need to finish. But it would be good for Millie to get out.' Especially with people I know, rather than this Daniel person that she keeps sneaking off to see.

'We're taking the kids,' Fiona added.

'Even better!' Tim shouted. Fiona held the receiver away from her ear. He sounds as if he's been drinking. I don't care what Graham has promised him, I'm going to make him tell me what is going on, for Millie's sake.

'Who's on the phone, Tim?'

Fiona heard Millie coming into the kitchen, then some muffled bickering while Tim inexpertly held his hand over the mouthpiece. There was a scuffle over the handset and some tutting.

'Fiona? It's Millie. What's all this about?'

Fiona sighed and went through her low-key sales pitch once more.

'And Tim said we'd be coming?' Millie asked incredulously.

Fiona felt awkward. 'Actually, he said you'd be coming. He said he'd have to stay at home and do some work.'

Millie didn't say anything for a while. 'Then it looks like it'll just be me and the kids.'

Her sombre tone unnerved Fiona, who felt that she ought to be guessing at what was going on. I'm glad she's coming tomorrow night, she thought. Graham will see what a mess she's in because of Tim and maybe then he'll do something about it.

Good old Graham! Tim was thinking. He said he wouldn't help me and then he comes up with this brilliant idea and even gets Fiona to put it to Millie so she won't suspect anything! All I asked was for him to provide me with an alibi. I didn't expect him to find a way to get the whole family out for an evening so I'd have the house to myself for a couple of hours!

'No, I won't do it.' Graham had been calm but firm in his refusal.

'But you haven't listened to me,' Tim had argued. 'I'm not saying that we're going to do anything. But even if anything did happen, there's one thing you have to believe: I will never leave Millie and the kids – all six of them,' he added hoping for a crumb of sympathy.

He got none.

'That's very big of you,' Graham said sarcastically, 'but you can't possibly say that with any certainty. A week ago, you were talking about one lunch, then it was one picnic, now it's one evening for the two of you, somewhere private. What exactly are you planning to do that you can't do over lunch? Karaoke? Line dancing?'

'I just want to know what it's like to be a normal couple with her. Talk until we run out of things to say.'

Graham laughed. 'Run out of things to say? Your Alison might turn out to be like Fiona, in which case it could take twenty years. That's a lot of pork pies in the park.'

'So you won't cover for me?' Tim asked one last time. 'Even though we're supposed to be friends.'

'No. But because we're supposed to be friends, I won't say anything about this.'

'Thanks for nothing. You just don't understand what this means to me,' Tim said tightly before leaving. Unfortunately I do, Graham thought, that's why I'm not helping you.

Graham's mobile phone bleeped in the night. Fortunately Fiona didn't stir. He could scream 'HELP!' in her ear and she wouldn't even twitch. But if one of the kids so much as whimpered, she'd leap out of bed and yell at him for ignoring the children.

He checked his message bank to find the prompt he'd been waiting for. An e-mail was waiting for him. From Christine.

He went downstairs to the family room and switched on the computer. He decided to read the e-mail here rather than wait until he got to work in the morning. He had been finding it hard to concentrate at work recently and he felt it was time to draw a line under his personal concerns and not take them into the office.

There was something satisfying in reading this message late at night when there was no chance of being interrupted. It was like the late-night phone calls he and Christine had enjoyed when they were younger.

*Dear Graham*

*You returned my last message within hours. I'm impressed! Won't be long before I get you into an online conversation. Or is that too spontaneous for you? Sorry, that was unkind.*

*You had questions and I promised to answer them so here goes:*

*1) Why did I say I was going to marry you if I had doubts? I didn't have any doubts. You must have known this or you wouldn't have turned up on the day yourself!*

*2) Why didn't I tell you before our wedding day that I couldn't go through with it? Because I didn't know.*

*3) Did I have our baby? Yes.*

*Now I know you'll think I'm cheating by not going into any details. That's because they're too complicated to edit into the concise little sentences that I know you want to hear. Pick up the phone and call me. Please. Then I'll tell you everything.*

*Love*
*Chrissie.*
*XXXXXXX*

Cruel, cruel woman, he thought as he tried to control his breathing. One word to let me know I have a child, not even telling me if it's a boy or a girl. Those answers weren't answers at all. They were meant to tease me, to draw me in. Well, I won't be drawn. I won't.

He started typing fast, sending the final message without checking the text before his common sense told him that this was a bad idea.

*Dear Christine*

*What started off as a plea for resolution has turned into a nasty game. How could you do that to me? You've sent me six messages so far and in not one of them did you mention that you had the baby. Did you think it was unimportant?*

*If you ever cared anything for me, then please just tell me what happened. Please. I can't speak to you. Not yet. Please don't ask me.*

*Graham.*

Then he sat back and wondered what a 20-year-old child of his would look like.

# 13

Max cheered up when he saw Archie, Rav and some other of his new 'friends'. He left Tess to go and talk to them. Lara disappeared when she caught sight of her friend Ruthie.

'Here we are again,' the familiar voice said softly. This time Tess didn't need to turn to know that it was Jerry.

'Do you enjoy taking risks?' she asked. 'Heather's standing over there.'

Jerry shrugged. 'Unless you were planning to throw me on the floor and seduce me in front of her, using those oriental positions that yoga is said to improve, then I'm not sure what the risk is. Ah. There it comes! The blush!'

She swore under her breath. 'Not sure I heard that. Never mind, I'll ask the Incredible Vicar, he's right behind you.'

Tess held her breath until she spotted John pouring red wine into a massive punch bowl. 'Are vicars supposed to do that?' she asked, momentarily distracted from her discomfort.

'I'm not the most learned theologian but I've always thought that Christianity had the edge over other religions with its love of a good party. There are more references to wine in the New Testament than to woe, you know.'

Finally Tess smiled. 'So is that why you're here? For the punch? Or did Heather drag you here?'

Jerry looked amused. 'You make too many assumptions. I brought Heather, not the other way around. I love sequence dancing. Everybody does the same steps. Once you've learned them, you don't have anything more to prove. And it's comforting to know that you can go up to anybody in the world at a sequence dance session and just fall into step with them. It's an international language and much more sociable than learning Esperanto.'

'That's what I hate about musicals,' Tess said, 'having to suspend your disbelief and accept everyone knowing the words and the steps.'

'Well, this is like being in a real live musical. You'll see.'

'What about individuality?' Tess asked. 'If we're all doing exactly the same moves, where's the scope for free expression?'

'You can still use your body, or your eyes,' Jerry said. 'Watch this simple waltz step.'

He moved his feet in a basic one-two-three, two-two-three formation. 'Can you do that?'

'Of course I can,' Tess said indignantly. She copied the steps self-consciously. She needn't have been embarrassed because people were practising steps all around the hall.

'Right,' Jerry grabbed her suddenly into a dancer's hold. 'Now let's see what we can do with those basic steps.'

With exaggerated passion, he pulled her close to him, then led her backwards in the six steps, almost lifting her off her feet as he kept in tight contact with her throughout. Someone wolf-whistled from the back of the hall. Jerry took a theatrical bow before releasing her.

As he let her go, the exaggeration disappeared and his hand held on to hers for a few seconds.

At the exact moment that their fingers touched, her one and only brush with physical betrayal, Fiona walked in and saw them.

'It's not what you're thinking', Tess said anxiously.

'That's what bad screenwriters always make their characters say to communicate that this person is weak and thoughtless. I know you, Tess, don't forget. Forget the oh-so-casual brush of the fingers, I'm perfectly willing to accept that that was an accident. But I saw what was going on in your eyes.'

Tess didn't bother arguing any further. It was pointless. Jerry had gone back over to Heather once he'd felt the withering power of Fiona's icy stare.

'What are you playing at?' Fiona asked, while trying to keep an eye on her four children, who'd all disappeared. She spotted them out of the corner of her eye helping themselves to the fruit punch. Relieved that they were out of harm's way, she focused her attention on Tess.

'I promise you that nothing has happened and nothing is going to happen,' Tess whispered. 'I'm just unbalanced at the moment. This last month has been crazy. It would have been understandable if I'd become a serial killer or an agoraphobic shoplifter, but instead, I've chosen to buy doughnuts for a man who can make a packet of chicken thighs last two days.'

Fiona looked at her friend in horror. 'Have you been on that Indian wine again? You're not making any sense and that can be the only explanation.' She smiled, apparently having forgiven her friend's indiscretion. 'That stuff has powers that we mere mortals can never hope to understand.' She leant forward to whisper to Tess. 'Since my mother drank it last week, she's become irresistibly attractive to men.'

Tess giggled, something that she hadn't done since moving to Heaverbury. She was transported back to the day they'd met and reminded of a ten-year bond that she couldn't supplant so easily.

'Look!' Fiona pointed to Daphne, who was making a spectacular entrance limping through the doorway dressed in a cerise polyester creation that would have looked fabulous on a drag queen.

Before Tess could say something cruel about the woman to show solidarity with her friend, two men had rushed over to her as if she were a screen goddess arriving at a film premiere. Tess expected Daphne to pull out a cigarette so that the men could fight over who lit it. Before they could grab her arms, Tess saw Carter come through the door behind her and place his hand upon her arm possessively.

'How long's this been going on?' Tess asked with amusement.

'Well, the Indian chap is a new one on me. But the other two have been after her since last week apparently. I told you, it's got something to do with that wine. I haven't said anything yet, but I found a bottle in her bedroom.'

Tess giggled again. 'Is it making her more mellow?'

'I suppose it is,' Fiona grudgingly conceded.

'Then I'd buy her a case and stop complaining,' Tess suggested.

They watched in awe as Daphne was led like a princess towards a table in prime position on the edge of the dance floor. Fiona noticed that her children were being even more silly than usual.

'I hope that there aren't any E numbers in that punch,' she said.

Tess realised what had happened and was about to enlighten

Fiona as to the punch's ingredients but Heather and Jerry were approaching. She could feel Fiona tense up again. 'Don't say anything,' Tess hissed.

'Aren't you going to introduce us?' Heather said, having watched the interesting entrances from a distance.

'Of course!' Tess said. 'This is Fiona, my oldest friend. And Fiona, this is Heather, my newest!'

Fiona smiled politely at Heather then glared at Jerry. Tess spoke quickly. 'And this is Jerry, Heather's boyfriend.'

She watched Fiona compute this little snippet as her expression turned to one of disappointment with Tess.

'So who's the geriatric sex symbol?' Jerry asked.

Tess closed her eyes in silent supplication that he would keep his mouth shut for the rest of the evening.

'That's my mother,' Fiona said coldly.

Jerry smiled. 'Well if you're anything like her, then your husband will have to keep an eye on you when you're her age.'

Fiona smiled despite herself.

Before Jerry could say or do anything else, Millie arrived with the four children, looking harassed and tired. The children ran away in all directions as soon as they saw the large hall's freedom beckoning them. Tess resolved to give them all a large glass of the alcoholic punch and hope it rendered them unconscious for the rest of the evening.

She hugged Millie warmly, biting her lip to stop herself from telling her friend how terrible she looked. The woman's expecting twins and she already has four children. How is she supposed to look?

Millie pulled away from Tess briskly. 'Look Tess, I'm really sorry, but I've left something at home. Can you watch the kids while I pop home and get it?'

'But you've only just got here. What have you forgotten? I only live around the corner. Is it something I can get?'

'No!' Millie said impatiently. She checked herself when she saw the shocked reaction of her friends. 'Look, I'm sorry. It's, er, my other glasses. These ones give me a headache. I won't be long.'

With that, she'd gone.

Graham walked over with a tray of drinks. 'Where's Millie disappeared to in such a hurry?' he asked.

Tess shrugged. 'She said she had to dash home. She's left the kids with us.'

But while Tess's prime concern was for the children, Graham was thinking of Millie. He knew why she was going home and he knew what she was going to find. The only thing he didn't know was what he was supposed to do about it.

'Let's make two circles with beginners in the centre and experienced dancers around the outside. Now everybody on the outside, pick a partner from the inside.'

It took a while for everyone to be cajoled into their circles, particularly Max and Fiona who were the least keen people here. But eventually the floor was full and the inner circle could only stand and wait to be picked.

In less than a second, Jerry had dashed across the circle to grab Tess. She hoped Heather and Max hadn't noticed this demonstration of eagerness but there were too many other equally eager couplings going on.

Graham gallantly picked Fiona and Heather picked Max. There was a huddle around Daphne as Carter, Rav and Archie all argued over who had got to her first. Daphne decided that the fairest solution was to have the first dance with Carter, since he had invited her here.

Rav and Archie reluctantly agreed. They argued so bitterly that they missed out on the remaining female partners and had to partner each other.

'Well I'm being the man, because I'm the oldest,' Archie grumbled.

And so the dancing began.

This wasn't going as well as Tim had planned. He'd anticipated an evening in an empty house with Alison. He'd forgotten that this was more than a house. This was a family home, *his* family home. Every piece of furniture bore a history that Tim shared with Millie. All of the hundreds of photos covering the walls and shelves told of a shared life that far outranked the short year Tim had spent with Alison.

As soon as he'd decided to invite Alison here, he'd known that there was a possibility they might end up making love. Now he knew this to be an impossibility. As soon as Alison sat on a stick from Nathan's Kerplunk, the sexual tension of the evening was dead.

Never mind, he told himself. You'd said that you only wanted to talk to her. So talk!

'Can I get you a drink?' he said awkwardly.

'That would be great. What have you got?'

Tim opened the fridge. Ribena, Sunny Delight, organic milk, vitamin-enriched orange juice, Thomas the Tank Engine strawberry drink. No wine. Since Millie had been pregnant, the smell of wine had made her feel sick so she refused to have it in the house. Tim was allowed to drink it when they were out. It was just in the house that Millie made her objection.

'Orange juice will be fine,' Alison said, standing behind him, looking over his shoulder with curiosity. So this is what family fridges look like.

Tim poured her some juice, wanting to move her away from the kitchen. This felt like Millie's private space and he was uncomfortable bringing Alison into it. 'Let's go into my den,' he suggested.

Alison smiled.

'Oh God, I sound like a middle-aged pervert, don't I, luring the innocent maiden into his den? I call it my den but it's just the smallest of the spare rooms and it has a desk in it and ...'

Alison placed a finger on his lips to stop him babbling. 'I'd love to see your den,' she said.

When they got there, Tim realised that this wasn't a good idea either. There was only one chair and not even enough floor space for them both to sit. They stood for a while, Alison taking in the full glory of the computer, the desk, the chair.

'Where now?' she asked. 'Are you planning to march me around the whole house and never let me sit down?'

What next? Tim thought frantically. It had to be the living room again. That was the most public room and, therefore, the most innocent.

Alison sank into one of the comfy armchairs, first checking for plastic toys or squashed raisins.

'Will you excuse me?' Tim asked, before dashing to the bathroom and sinking onto the loo to try and calm himself down. What am I doing? What was I thinking of? Millie would be home with the kids in about an hour. He'd use this as an excuse to hurry

Alison out, maybe suggest they go to the wine bar for a nightcap before he saw her into a cab.

But when he returned to the living room, Alison had taken her jacket off; underneath she was just wearing a flimsy top. Is that a proper top, or is that underwear? he asked himself, knowing that he didn't have a clue and knowing that there was nobody he could ask this crucial question. But it didn't matter anyway.

Because he heard the key in the lock.

'On a scale of one to ten, just how much are you hating this?' Heather asked Max.

'Three hundred and eighty-four,' Max replied.

'I gather Tess dragged you along?'

'Didn't she tell you? I thought you women told each other everything?'

'Have I done something to annoy you or are you this offensive to everyone whose feet you tread on?'

Max relaxed. 'Sorry! Dancing's not really my thing. And no, you haven't done anything to annoy me. Sometimes I get angry that Tess can talk to her friends about anything but not to me.'

'Are you sure she doesn't try?'

Max tensed up again. Now the woman *was* annoying him. 'I'm sure. Or if she does try, she does it at the worst possible moments. When the football's on, or when I've been working for fifteen hours and am knackered, or when I'm reading the paper, or when I'm about to have a nap ...'

Heather added to his list. 'Or when there's a new moon, or when you've been sending out telepathic messages that you're not in the mood to talk?'

Heather was annoying him even more. Added to this, she was too tall. He didn't like tall women. Although she couldn't come close to his massive height, she was definitely encroaching on his airspace and that ruled out the possibility of talking over her head and avoiding all eye contact.

'So all men are rubbish at talking, we're all failures at maintaining relationships, everything is our fault, so what's new?'

'This is new, isn't it? Talking to one of your wife's friends?'

'I'd rather be talking to one of my own,' he said grumpily.

Heather stopped herself from crying out when his substantial left foot trod on her right one. She just hoped this dance wasn't going to be a long one.

Max was thinking the same thing. He held her more firmly, determined that he would lead even though he didn't have a clue about the steps. It's the first opportunity to control anything that I've had in weeks, he thought.

Carter held Daphne so gently, she wondered if he was afraid of hurting her.

'You're picking this up quickly,' he said, as she mastered each step after just one explanation.

'I've danced before. All of our generation have, haven't we?'

'I suppose so,' Carter agreed. 'But we weren't all necessarily good at it.'

'I can't remember the last time I went dancing,' Daphne said, to herself more than Carter.

'Does it hurt?'

Daphne looked up at him abruptly. 'Is it that obvious?'

Carter nodded. 'My wife had arthritis. I hated watching her suffer. But she couldn't bear all the strong pills. She wasn't going to spend all her life in bed asleep, that wasn't living, she used to say.'

'I'm the same,' Daphne admitted for the first time. 'It's a bit like childbirth. I know the modern way is to have all those drugs and injections, but if you haven't had a bit of pain, a whole bloody lot actually, I don't believe you can really appreciate the moment at the end when the pain stops and your baby is given to you.'

'I don't know about that,' Carter said. 'I think most men would happily have an epidural when they have a filling at the dentist. We don't do pain so well.'

Daphne laughed. 'Did you used to dance with your wife?'

'Yes, we used to dance here actually. We came to the very first social when they opened this community centre thirty years ago. Then we were here every Thursday night until the week she died. She didn't care how much it hurt, she danced every last dance. There was me and Maria, Archie and his Eileen and Rav and his Lila. It was a good life.'

Daphne envied the three men their happy marriages but clung to the hope this offered that happy marriages did exist. She was still agonising over whether she should say something about seeing that friend of Fiona's with another woman in Battersea

Park. But she put that out of her mind and concentrated on Carter and his happy memories. Maybe this could be Graham and Fiona's story after all. She watched them with concern.

'I can't remember the last time we danced together,' Fiona said to Graham.

'We always dance at weddings,' Graham argued.

Fiona disagreed. 'That's not dancing. That's either jigging on the spot to Abba or moving to a one-two rhythm around the floor in a clockwise direction with someone's auntie.'

'There's also the smoochie dance,' Graham said.

'Ah yes, the smoochie dance. We always do one of those. But this is different.'

'Different good or different bad?'

'Well at the moment, you're better at it than me, which I hate. But once I get the hang of it, I can see how I might start to enjoy it.'

'The best thing about it is you don't have to worry about the steps once you've learned them so you can concentrate on the person you're dancing with,' Graham said, as Fiona struggled to distinguish her left from her right foot.

Fiona smiled at Graham. 'I thought you would prefer the kind of dancing where you had to concentrate on the steps and not have to worry about talking to the other person.'

'I've got nothing against making conversation. But I'm just not very good at it. You're the one who said that I always put my foot in it and upset everybody.'

Yes I did, Fiona thought. That was clever of me. That's what comes of no foresight. If I'd known that I'd need him to talk to me properly one day, I'd willingly have put up with him alienating all my family and everybody we've ever met.

'That's why I don't hold with vasectomies,' she said, thinking out loud.

'Sorry?' Graham cried out in alarm.

Fiona jumped, unaware that she'd said anything. 'I was just thinking about vasectomies.' Actually I was thinking that I'd unwittingly enforced a verbal vasectomy on you all those years ago and now I'm living with the consequences.

'Why?' Graham said, more out of curiosity than alarm. With four children, the subject had been discussed more than once. While Graham had been willing to go ahead with the procedure (and after learning that Millie was pregnant again, he'd been nervous enough to start considering it seriously), Fiona hadn't mentioned it for years.

Fiona struggled to organise her treacherous thoughts into something more palatable. 'Just that none of us know what is going to happen and I don't think people should do anything that has irreversible consequences, just in case they change their mind.'

Graham looked worried. Fiona quickly reassured him.

'Ignore me,' she said, hoping he wouldn't take that as a permanent instruction. 'I was just thinking about what you said about not wanting to talk, in case you upset people. That was never supposed to include me. I want you to talk to me.'

'I do talk to you. We're talking now, aren't we?'

Not the way I'd like us to, Fiona thought, swearing as she kicked herself in the ankle.

'So are you going to avoid talking to me all evening?' Jerry asked.

'I can't dance and talk at the same time.' Tess felt grateful that she hadn't pretended to be a ballroom dancing teacher rather than a yoga teacher. There was not much potential for bluff here.

'I thought women claimed to be the supreme multi-taskers. I thought you were all able to cook a Jamie Oliver meal, read an improving book, hand-sew a fancy-dress costume and watch daytime television at the same time?'

'Will you shut up? I'll never get the hang of this.' Tess was watching Max occasionally. He and Heather seemed to be getting on well, she was relieved to see.

'Have you thought about what I said on Monday?' Jerry asked quietly.

Tess kept her eyes fixed firmly on her feet, which were proving to be as uncontrollable as her emotions.

'Of course I have,' she said irritably. 'But that was why you said it, wasn't it? To make me think about it? That's what you do, make these meaningless sweeping statements that wind people up. I don't believe for a minute that you meant it.'

Did you?

'You're not so bad at winding people up yourself,' he said. 'All that guff about real love. It got me thinking.'

Tess was only half-listening. He was obviously going to make one of his inflammatory declarations that would get her in a tizzy until she realised later that it was just a game to him.

231

'Did it?'

'And maybe you're right. Because I do have different feelings for you than I do for Heather. And the more I thought about it, the more I came to ask myself if that was because one was more real than the other.'

Tess shifted her focus from her feet to Jerry's face, looking for the crinkly eyes to tell her that he was joking. No crinkles.

'So what did you conclude?' she asked, keeping her tone light.

Now his eyes were crinkling. 'That maybe I could fall in love with you.'

Millie looked at them both calmly. 'Do you know, in a way it's a relief. I was beginning to think I was going mad, becoming paranoid. That's what Fiona kept telling me.'

Alison shrank into her armchair. Millie was blocking the exit so she couldn't sneak out, which was what she wanted to do. She was hoping that Millie wasn't going to go berserk and start smashing things. She'd watched scenes like this in films. The wronged wife smashes the wedding picture then uses a shard of glass from the frame to stab the mistress, then collapses to the floor hugging her child's teddy bear.

Or maybe she'd just stab Alison with the Kerplunk stick which was on the table inches from Millie's grasp. Either way, Alison was going for the invisible approach.

'All the signs were there,' Millie continued, watching Tim with a bitter expression. 'You even told me about going to meet her that first time.'

'That's because it was completely innocent,' Tim exclaimed. 'It still is. Nothing has happened, nothing at all.'

'So why is she sitting there in her underwear?'

So it wasn't just a rather insubstantial top, Tim thought. I'll know next time.

'This isn't my underwear. It's a very expensive top, actually,' Alison piped up indignantly. And I won't be wearing it again. The woman in the shop assured me that no one would mistake it for a vest.

Now Tim didn't know what to think. He'd ask, in future.

'Besides, he's telling the truth, nothing happened,' Alison added, not out of any loyalty to Tim but because she thought it improved her chances of getting out of this house unharmed.

232

'You can just sit there and say nothing,' Millie said, not looking at Alison.

'This wasn't planned or anything.' Tim blundered ahead, shooting himself in the foot, the leg and every other part of his body except his mouth where he could really have done with a silencing bullet. 'But when you said you were going out, it seemed obvious, rather than go out, to stay in. You weren't going to be here, so it wasn't as if you would be upset ...'

Alison closed her eyes. If I do have a child with this man, please let it inherit my brains and not his.

'So why did you bring her here at all, if it was all completely innocent? Why couldn't you have just gone to a restaurant and stared all googly-eyes at each other and sighed meaningfully while you explained that your wife didn't understand you? Or if you had something else in mind, why couldn't you have gone to some sordid hotel room that charges by the hour? That would have been far more appropriate.'

'I wanted Alison to see my house,' Tim said lamely.

I may have lived in the jungle, far away from civilisation, for years, Alison thought, but even I can tell that he's not saying the right things for this situation.

'Your house? *Your* house?' Millie picked up a family portrait.

Whoops, here we go! Alison thought, pulling her coat over her fleshy features.

Millie put it down again. 'Not *our* house? Your house.'

The clue here, Alison was telegraphing him, is in the repetition of the word 'house'. That is the sign that this is a bad subject and you should change it immediately.

'Of course it's our house,' Tim continued, warming to the theme. 'And I'm proud of it. That's why I wanted to show it to Alison. I mean, I've seen hers.'

Alison groaned.

Now Tim was getting the message but it didn't help. 'I haven't been in it, of course, we just drove past it to a picnic, a completely innocent picnic.'

'When was that?' Millie asked with terrifying evenness.

'Last week,' Tim replied, relieved that Millie seemed to have been calmed by his reassurances.

Millie nodded. She turned and walked through the door,

marching round the house, checking every room, playing particular attention to the bedrooms.

'We didn't go in any of the bedrooms,' Tim called, using the reassuring tone that had been so successful earlier. 'Only the kitchen. And the living room, of course. Oh, and my den. But we didn't spend too long in there. It's too small for two people, as you know.'

Alison was taking the opportunity to get her things together. 'I'll go now,' she whispered to Tim.

'How dare you whisper in my house, to my husband!' Millie screamed when she came back into the living room. 'You can take your things and get out!'

Alison did not need persuasion. She made straight for the front door, not looking back for an instant.

Tim watched her leave, almost grateful that she'd gone. Now he and Millie could sort out this misunderstanding.

'And what are you waiting for?' Millie shouted at him.

Tim looked confused. 'I thought we could talk now.'

Millie stared at him. 'We have talked. You've told me why you brought your old girlfriend here, the girlfriend you've been taking on secret picnics, the girlfriend who's shown you her house so you had to show her yours. There's nothing more to say. I'm going to pick up the children. When I get back I want you gone.'

'You're just overreacting because you're pregnant,' Tim said soothingly. 'You were like this with Nathan ...'

'GET OUT!' she screamed.

Finally, Tim understood that she meant it. He went upstairs to pack.

# 14

'I have to admit I enjoyed last night,' Max said. Apart from that first dance with your wretched friend Heather. He didn't mention that part, not when he needed Tess onside this morning.

'I told you it could be fun.' Tess hadn't taken much in after yet another of Jerry's bombshells. She'd avoided dancing with him for the rest of the evening, not prepared to go through another cryptic conversation that kept her awake all night.

'Although I thought Millie was acting a little strangely,' Max added. 'She turns up, dumps the kids, disappears, then turns up again at the end in a state, drags the kids away and disappears again, without even thanking us for looking after her children.'

'She didn't need to thank us,' Tess said guiltily. 'They were no bother.'

'You're right. That was strange too. Normally they're hyperactive hooligans. But last night they just sat slumped on the floor all evening.'

'They were probably tired.' Nothing at all to do with the large glasses of punch I gave them, thought Tess. She intended to phone Millie later, just to make sure everything was all right. She hadn't paid much attention to her last night, being more wrapped up in her own concerns.

'I think it's good that we've found something we can do together,' Max said. 'You were right about us needing to do more things like this. And I think we should talk more as well,' he added, remembering Heather's comments, irritating though they were.

Now Tess was suspicious. He hadn't been this conciliatory since those days before he announced that they were broke. He

235

simply wasn't good enough at prevarication to be able to get away with this.

'What are you trying to say?' she asked bluntly. When he raised his eyebrows, ready to protest his innocence, Tess raised a hand to stop him. 'Don't tell me I'm imagining it. I know you, and we've been through all this before. So just tell me what's on your mind.'

Max feigned a coughing fit to buy some time. She'd pre-empted his speech and now his timing was all gone.

'OK,' he said finally. 'I think we should sell everything now. You said that you were happy to go along with this and now is a good time to do it.'

Tess sat down. 'I said I was happy to think about it and consider going through with it when it became absolutely necessary. Are you saying that we need to release that money right now?'

'Sort of.'

Tess moaned in protest. 'Not more bills, surely? I thought we'd had the last of the big ones.'

Max sat beside her and put his arm round her. 'It's nothing like that, I promise you.'

'Then why do we have to do it right this minute?' This was a big decision and she didn't have much spare room for big decisions in her head, which was full of Jerry and his mind games.

'Do you remember what you said about us not looking back, about us planning a future together?'

Tess vaguely recalled one of the many motivational lectures that she'd delivered to Max in recent weeks.

'I think I said it was important that we keep focused on the future rather than bank on being able to go back to our old life. I was trying to be practical.'

Max was obviously pleased with her answer. 'I took what you said to heart. You were right. We need to move ahead. And we've both been treading water since we moved here, making as much cash as we could just to survive. But we can't carry on like that, can we?'

'I thought we'd agreed that we were going to do this until one or both of us got a better job?'

Max sat up proudly. 'Well, in a way, that's exactly what I've done.'

Tess didn't like the 'in a way' bit that qualified this apparent good news.

'Exactly what have you done?' she asked carefully.

'I've agreed to go into business with Carter, Archie and Rav.'

Alison was exhausted. Tim had kept her awake all night talking. After the trauma of the confrontation with Millie, she'd been looking forward to a hot bath, a mug of hot chocolate, a short wallow in self-pity and a long sleep.

'What do you think she'll do?' he had asked her over and over again.

'I don't know,' she'd answered, drawing on her dwindling stores of patience. 'You're the one who's been married to her for a hundred years. I'd never met the woman before last night.'

'Yes, but you're a woman. You must know how other women think.'

'But I've never been in her position.' And I haven't got six children to think of. I haven't even got one, she thought resentfully. I probably never will have if he insists on sleeping on the sofa.

'It wouldn't be right to sleep with you,' he'd said. 'I assured Millie that nothing had happened and I want to be able to repeat that until she forgives me and takes me back.'

'Are you saying that, when you invited me to your house last night, you weren't planning for something to happen?'

Tim had been hoping to avoid this question. 'I can't deny that I might have hoped that perhaps, possibly, we'd, well, you know.'

Alison cringed at his sudden attack of fastidiousness. 'Don't be so prim about this,' she said. 'You know perfectly well that you had every intention of making love to me in your house last night.'

Tim gestured to her to keep her voice down as if Millie might somehow hear them across two counties.

'But as soon as we were there together, I knew it wouldn't be right. Not in our family home.'

'So it wasn't the act that was wrong, just the location?'

'I suppose so.' Tim felt muddled by the argument.

'In that case, what's your objection to sleeping with me in my house?'

'Because now she knows about us, anything we do will definitely hurt her. When she didn't know, there was a chance we could get away with not causing her any pain.'

Alison shook her head with exhaustion and exasperation. 'Fine. But I'm going to bed. I have early surgery in the morning.'

Tim wasn't listening to her. 'Do you think she'll try and get back at me by finding someone else?'

'It's hardly likely she'll be able to pick someone up while she's pregnant with twins.'

Tim raised a finger in objection. 'But there's someone in the picture already. Somebody called Daniel.'

'Who's he?' Alison asked, vaguely curious.

'I don't know. Millie's been really mysterious about him. But she's been out with him a couple of times.'

This thought cheered Alison up slightly. 'Well, if she does decide to get back at you that way, there'll be no point in us holding back, will there?'

Tim considered this before shaking his head slowly. 'I have to think very carefully about everything I do from now on. I can't rush into anything. We'll need to talk this all through. The most important question I have to ask myself is whether my future lies with her or you.'

I don't need to talk anything through, Alison thought. I've asked the question and answered it. I've had you in my house for a few hours and you're already driving me crazy. Just give me a baby and go back to your deranged wife and your Kerplunk-obsessed kids! she wanted to scream.

Alison lay in bed, longing suddenly to be in a war zone with Gabriel, dodging bullets or maybe even taking one. Anything had to be better than this.

'I've thrown him out,' she said.

It took Fiona a few moments to assimilate this fact. 'Are you sure?'

Millie sighed. 'No, I'm not sure, maybe I hallucinated it, it's a normal symptom of pregnancy apparently. YES, I'M SURE!'

Fiona collected her thoughts cautiously. Watch what you say, she warned herself. 'I was just wondering how you could be sure that there was actually anything going on when you arrived. I mean, were they ...?'

'Were they spread-eagled across the futon? No. But he was in my house with her. Just the two of them. She was in her underwear and drinking Lucy's special orange juice and Tim was looking guilty.'

Fiona was surprised. 'I know that he was wrong to have her

there, even if they weren't doing anything, but I still think you have to talk to him.'

'That's what you said before, when you were insisting that I was imagining all this and it was just a mid-life crisis and I just needed to buy some saucy pants or something. Just talk to him, you said. Well, it's a bit late for that now.'

Fiona didn't press her. The wound was too raw for her to able to think rationally.

'What will you do now?' she asked.

Millie shrugged. 'Have a couple of babies. Bring all six kids up alone. The usual. Anyway, I just thought I'd let you know what was happening. I've got to go and throw up now.'

Fiona cursed Tim for his rotten treatment of Millie at a time like this. And she was angry for herself for not taking Millie's concerns more seriously. But how was she to know that this old girlfriend would turn into a real threat? If she'd known, she might have been able to do something, scared Tim into stopping it from going any further.

Then it came back to her. Tim's phone call to Graham earlier in the week and their little heart-to-heart that Graham refused to discuss.

Graham knew something about this, Fiona was convinced of it. If Graham knew about Tim and Alison and didn't do anything to stop things from getting this far, then it was going to be his responsibility to put it right.

Tess lay on the sofa screening her calls. They were all from Jerry, one after the other.

'I know you're there, Tess, please pick up the phone.'

'"Teachers in the night," he crooned, "doo bee doo bee doo".'

'Have you heard the one about the man who married the wrong woman?'

'I've just stolen your trick and sent my class to sleep, although in my case it wasn't planned. They were just bored to sleep by my explanation of gravity, so we've got ten minutes. I could embarrass you a whole lot more if you'd just pick up the phone and let me say some more dumb things.'

'Did you know that carrots were on special offer in Tesco? Fancy an illicit assignation by the fruit and veg later? My turn to pay for the doughnuts.'

'Hi Tess, it's just me . . .'

Tess jumped up and picked up the phone. 'Hi Fiona!'

'Screening your calls?' Fiona asked. 'Avoiding anyone in particular?'

'I was in the bathroom, actually.'

'Liar,' Fiona said smoothly. 'But it's not important now. I thought you'd want to know. Millie has thrown Tim out.'

Tess was stunned as Fiona told her the whole sordid story, right down to the woman sitting in the living room dressed only in some cheap underwear.

'Poor Millie,' Tess said. 'And those poor kids!'

'That's what happens when you mess around when you're married.'

'Fi. I know what you're getting at, but there's nothing to worry about. Nothing's happened and nothing's going to happen.'

'It didn't look like nothing to me. And I'm sure Tim was convinced that nothing would happen too. But things have a nasty habit of getting out of control and look where it's ended up. Do you want to do that to Lara?'

'I've just said, it won't come to that!'

Fiona backed off. She'd made her point; that was all she could do. 'What can we do for Millie?' she asked Tess. 'She's OK in the week with the kids at school but the weekend will be a bit grim.'

'Why don't we all get together on Sunday like we used to?' Tess suggested.

Fiona was dubious. 'It might feel strange for her without Tim.'

'Not if you all come over here. We've never done that before so it won't be so obvious that Tim is missing. We can go to Carter's. They do a great Sunday lunch.'

'I can't come up with a better idea,' Fiona said reluctantly. 'Shall we come over to you in the morning? Let the kids savour the full Crappy Valley experience?'

Tess ignored the friendly goad. 'We have to go to church in the morning. It's a condition of Lara's school.'

'God, I'm sorry, Tess,' Fiona said with genuine sympathy.

Tess laughed. 'It's not that bad actually. It's a bit different to the churches we went to when we were kids.'

'I didn't ever go to church. Too boring.'

'I can promise you that this church isn't boring.' Tess laughed. 'Why don't you all come? Make a full day of it?'

'We don't do church,' Fiona said sweetly. 'We're far too pagan.'

'What if I told you that the children go off to Sunday school for an hour?'

Fiona thought about an hour without her children on a Sunday and was converted in seconds. 'I could always have a nap while they're out,' she said. 'And Graham could bring a book to read under the pew. Maybe it wouldn't be so bad.'

'I think Millie would appreciate the peace,' Tess added.

Fiona agreed. 'Do they ever bar kids from Sunday school?' she asked, thinking of Millie's four juvenile delinquents.

'Not on the first day, I'm sure.' Tess laughed. 'So we're going to do this?'

'I suppose so. I'll call Millie and break the news to her. And, by the way, I haven't forgotten about you and that man. You might like to bear Millie in mind when you decide what you're going to do. Think about the carnage wreaked by a casual little fling.'

'What if it's more than a casual little fling? What if, purely hypothetically, of course, what if I loved him?'

'Maybe Tim loves this other woman,' Fiona said harshly. 'Do you think that gives him the right to ruin all these other lives?'

I'm not sure, was the answer that Tess was too ashamed to give to Fiona.


*Dear Graham*

*I didn't mean to make you angry. I truly wasn't playing games with you. It's just that this is so important, I really wanted to tell you in person. It's easier to clear up misunderstandings before they get out of hand.*

*But I should have given more thought to your feelings. I'm sorry.*

*We have a daughter. Her name is Eloise, after our favourite song, do you remember? She was born on 15 November 1983 at 17.33, weighing 8lbs 4oz. I could write a book about her life but I'll save all the details until we speak. She's at university now, down in Sussex, studying Philosophy. She's clever and beautiful.*

*She doesn't know about you. I got married to a man called David shortly before she was born and she grew up believing that David was her father.*

*But David died earlier this year and Eloise took it really badly. I don't know if I'm doing the right thing, but I think she needs to know that he was not her real father, that she still has you.*

*I know that, right now, you hate me for keeping our daughter from you for all these years. But I was thinking of her rather than you. And even now, she is all that matters. So I would ask you to try and put your bitterness towards me to one side, think about Eloise and ask yourself if you can find it in you to play a part in her life now.*

*This is a lot to take in so I'll wait patiently for you to get in touch with me.*

*Love*
*Chris.*

The phone rang. Graham picked it up without thinking.

'It's your wife,' Annie announced coldly.

'Hi Fi,' he said. He heard his voice but he wasn't aware of saying anything. He was somewhere else: in Sussex with his eldest daughter.

'Sorry, what did you just say?' he asked, yanked back to earth with a thud.

'Tim has left Millie,' Fiona repeated. 'And I think you know why.'

'How would I know anything?'

'Because he dragged you out for a drink on Monday, something he's never done before, and I don't believe it was to discuss the merits of the new BMW series.'

'I didn't know that he was going to do anything rash,' Graham said. 'I thought I'd talked him out of it.'

'Well, you didn't. Maybe if you'd told me, I might have been able to do something. But you didn't give anybody that chance and now it's too late.'

Graham felt sick. 'How's Millie taking it?'

'How do you think? I'm doing what I can my end but it's up to you to bring Tim to his senses.'

'What can I do? We're not best friends or anything.'

'You were on Monday apparently,' Fiona said acidly. 'I don't care how you do it. This is partly your fault, so you'd better find a

242

way to get him back to Millie before that poor woman has to have her twins alone.'

'Right.' Graham knew that this was not up for discussion.

'Oh, and by the way,' Fiona added, 'we're going to church on Sunday.'

Graham didn't understand that last cryptic comment so he ignored it, focusing instead on the one thing he did understand – that this was apparently all his fault. Reluctantly he switched off his e-mail screen while he turned his attention away from his own mistakes to someone else's.

'I was as surprised as you!' Max said at lunchtime. He'd come back to continue the discussion he'd started earlier. Tess had hoped that she'd imagined the whole thing. That she'd fallen asleep in between Jerry's endless phone calls and had a dreadful nightmare. But no, it was true and Max had returned to hammer his point home.

She sat on the sofa nursing a cup of tea which was almost up to Heather's strength. She could see why Heather liked this. The brew was so strong it was almost a drug, a cheap, legal drug that calmed for less than the price of a KitKat.

Max told her about the meeting in the club yesterday.

'I thought it was just going to be me and Carter, but Rav and Archie were there too. And John,' he added.

'Who's John?' Tess asked. The only John she knew was the Incredible Vicar and Max hadn't yet managed to pronounce his name without clenching his fists.

'John. The vicar. Apparently, this was partly his idea.'

Was it indeed? Tess thought. Since when have vicars had ideas? Why can't they stick to visiting the poor and encouraging old ladies to take up flower-arranging?

'Anyway,' Max continued. 'I'd told them all about Organique and the reasons it failed and, apparently, it was something they'd been talking about for ages.'

'What? Opening a business that's doomed to fail that would send them all into abject poverty?' I can see the appeal.'

'Are you going to take this seriously or not? Tess waved a hand that he interpreted as encouragement to continue.

'First of all,' Max went on with renewed enthusiasm, 'this is nothing like the Organique situation. Carter owns the freehold to

243

his restaurant outright as well as having planning permission to extend, which he's been meaning to do for years. So there would be hardly any overheads. He would add on a small shop area, just to sell the organic products that normal people want to buy, nothing extravagant or overpriced, and the restaurant would function as an organic café in the morning as well.'

Tess shook her head in astonishment. 'I don't understand you, Max. After all we've been through, all we're still going through, why on earth would you want to jump straight back into another business? How much further do you want to drag us down?'

Max looked back at her pleadingly. 'How can you not know?' he asked. 'How can you have spent so many years with me and still not understand me?'

Tess always worried when an argument shifted from the specific to the general. There was too much scope for broad recrimination. 'What don't I understand?' she asked defensively.

Max swallowed. 'All I want, all I've ever wanted, is to fulfil my potential, to achieve something. If I can't manage to make a go of a backstreet business, not a multinational corporation, note, then all my education was for nothing, all the work I've ever done has been for nothing, all my ambition was for nothing. I might just as well have joined the Civil Service like my father and buried myself in anonymous mediocrity.'

Then Tess understood. He needed to prove to his mum and dad that he'd come further than they had themselves. It was what most parents want for their children and the bare minimum that most children expect of themselves. He had to do this, she saw that, but she worried that his desperation was making him blind to the practicalities.

Max was just sitting there, waiting for Tess's reaction. She chose her words cautiously. 'So you've known these men for a few weeks, and they agree to finance a whole new business for us, a cast-iron certainty with absolutely no risk on our part?'

Max reddened slightly. 'It's not exactly no-risk. It was my experience that led to them coming up with the proposal and, you have to admit, it makes perfect sense, but obviously, we'd have to be making a contribution too.'

Here it comes, Tess thought. 'I thought so. So we have to put money into this venture?'

'Well, obviously we do, Tess. If we didn't, then it wouldn't be our business, I'd just be a shop assistant. Rav and Archie are putting up money as well. They're taking the biggest risk.'

'Well whoop-di-doop for them. The big difference between us and them is that they have money. We don't. In fact we have minus money if we take into account all our debts.'

'I know that, Tess, but I've been doing some sums.' He congratulated himself for never having told her what happened the last time he did sums. But this time he had checked his numbers a dozen times before accepting them.

'And?'

Max took this positively. She wasn't screaming at him. That mean she was prepared to listen.

'I've had our possessions valued, all the things in storage. I know I didn't tell you I was having it done but I didn't think you'd mind. It just helped me to know what assets we had before making any plans.'

'And?'

Tess's monosyllables were beginning to unnerve him.

'If we sell everything in storage, we'll have enough to pay off our debts' (apart from the ones you don't know about) 'and have enough to live on for another two months if we're very, very frugal. After that, we should be starting to make a decent profit.'

He didn't tell Tess that he'd already approached the creditors with the proposal. They were fairly impressed by the credentials of the other partners and thought it sounded a sensible scheme that could well generate enough to pay off the debts in time. Also they knew bankruptcy would guarantee that they would never see any more money, not now that all the assets had been sold off. There was still the house, of course, but the negative equity made it more sensible to leave it as a rental property. At least it would generate some income that way.

So far, it all sounded reasonable to Tess which convinced her, therefore, that this was not the end of the sums. She stared at him, unblinking.

'As I said,' Max went on nervously, 'that will clear up our past obligations but obviously, as I mentioned, we would need to make an investment into the business if we are going to have a future.'

'How much?' Tess asked bluntly.

'Four thousand pounds,' Max answered. 'It's not much if you think about it. The others are putting up much more. But I'll be putting in more time so they scaled my contribution down.'

Tess smiled. 'That's all right, then.'

'It is?' Max felt unsure of this turnaround.

'Of course. If we've sold everything we possess and we know that no bank will ever lend us any money, then that's that. We don't have four thousand pounds, we have no way of getting four thousand pounds, so we won't be investing four thousand pounds.'

'There is one way,' Max said softly.

Tess looked at him, unsure what he could be thinking of. Until she saw what he was looking at.

Her eternity ring.


Graham phoned Tim at the office.

'Can we meet for a quick lunch?' Graham asked without preamble.

Tim groaned. 'Who's sent you? Millie?'

'Fiona actually.'

'Well there's no point. This isn't anything to do with anyone except me and Millie.'

'And Alison,' Graham added.

They both waited for the other to say something. It was Tim who eventually broke the silence. 'If it's very quick, I'll meet you at twelve-thirty at the Bolingbroke Arms.'

Graham agreed although he'd been hoping that Tim would refuse point blank to see him. Now he was going to have to go through with this.

'So what are you going to do?' he asked Tim. There seemed no point in asking him why he'd done what he did. That was obvious. Graham understood only too well.

'I don't know. I want to talk to Millie, that's the most important thing. I mean, I've got Alison and she's been a great listener but I get the feeling that she could be finding this a bit difficult.'

Since Alison was sitting in her surgery thinking about breaking the rules and writing herself a prescription for Prozac, Tim was demonstrating his first accurate insight into the female psyche.

Graham had run out of questions after this first one. He'd hoped that the rest would just flow naturally as it seemed to for Fiona and her friends. But it wasn't flowing. Tim was just staring into space looking stressed and Graham was staring at his watch, looking for inspiration.

'I've been surprised at how much I missed the kids,' Tim said, grateful to be able to admit this to someone, sensing correctly that Alison wouldn't be sympathetic.

'Why are you so surprised?' Graham asked. 'I miss my kids when I have to work late in the office and they're in bed when I get home.'

'But we're talking about my kids, don't forget,' Tim reminded him. Graham thought of the four possessed creatures Tim shared a house with and conceded the point.

'Maybe all parents should have an enforced separation from their family when they start getting fed up with their home life. If I'd had the sort of job where I had to travel, maybe I'd appreciate them more.'

Graham took this as a hopeful sign. 'So it only took one night apart to learn that you really want to be with your family? No honeymoon period with Alison?'

Tim shook his head. 'I wish I knew what I wanted.'

Graham was exasperated. 'But you've just said you miss your family. So go back to them. Fight for them.'

'But I haven't got Alison out of my system yet and I feel I need to do that otherwise I'll just be going straight back into the same situation, resenting Millie for not being Alison.'

Only when he said it did he understand that this was at the heart of his disappointment with his life. 'I have to make up my mind who I want to be with,' he said determinedly. 'Alison or Millie.'

Graham laughed coldly. 'You haven't got a clue, have you?'

'What do you mean?'

'You're sitting here thinking that you have a choice between Alison and Millie.'

'I do,' Tim said. 'That's my whole problem.'

'Has it not occurred to you that you might end up losing both of them?'

Tim sat back in despair. Clearly it hadn't.


'That's a wonderful jumper, Rav,' Daphne said admiringly. The sweater had an elaborate picture of the Taj Mahal knitted across the front.

'Thank you,' Rav replied. 'My dear late wife knitted it for me. The strange thing was that, while she lived in England, she learned to knit to the most complicated patterns you could ever imagine, but she could never get the hang of English. She always said that she was happy for me to do all the talking and all the listening. She just wanted to do all the knitting. I've got a cupboard full of these. When I wear them, I feel she's still a part of our family.'

'That's lovely.' Daphne suddenly wanted to cry. She was prevented by the arrival of two lively youngsters.

'Daphne, I'd like you to meet my grandchildren, Meera and Geeta.' The two children stood up. 'Good afternoon, Mrs Guinn. How are you?'

Daphne was charmed by their shy manners.

'Run along and play. I'll call you when tea is ready.' Rav dispatched them with affectionate kisses.

'They are lovely children, Rav, a real credit to you.'

Rav dismissed the compliment. 'Their mother had done all the hard work. They were such good children already, even before their parents were killed.'

Rav poured Daphne a generous glass of his wine, which he noticed she drank gratefully. She must be in considerable pain today, he observed with genuine concern.

'It can't have been easy for you to take them on.' At your age, she added silently.

Rav waved his hands vaguely. 'What else could I do? If I hadn't taken them into my home, they would have had to go to India to be with my sister and these are English girls, they belong here.'

'How do you manage?' Daphne asked. She'd noticed that Rav was as stiff as she was and probably suffered as much in the cold weather as she did. She couldn't imagine how she'd cope with two children even if they were as well behaved as these two.

'You just do,' Rav said. 'How about you, living with four children?'

Daphne smiled sadly. 'It's not quite how I imagined. I thought I'd be able to help Fiona with them as well as enjoy seeing them grow up.'

'But actually you're finding them a bit much?'

Daphne nodded. 'It's all the noise. That house is never quiet except when they're at school. And they fight all the time. It's just like when my own children were little. I'd forgotten what it was like.'

'Still, it must be nice to live with your daughter,' Rav said wistfully.

That was even worse, Daphne thought, but knew that she could never admit that to a man who'd lost his only child.

As she enjoyed tea with Rav and his granddaughters, she couldn't help but imagine herself in this house, with this man and these children. What would it be like? she wondered. Am I capable of bringing up children who don't hate me? Is it worth having a go? Maybe seeing if I can do better a second time.

But she knew she had to resolve the gulf between herself and her own daughter before she even considered taking on somebody else's.


'What on earth are you doing here?'

Tess panicked as she stood there, closing the door of the Advanced Yoga Institute behind her, failing in her attempt to cover the sign which announced in big letters: BEGINNER'S YOGA, INTENSIVE COURSE.

'Heather! What a coincidence!'

'I was picking up some new exercise mats for the community centre. How about you?'

'Oh, you know, just keeping up,' Tess replied vaguely.

Heather read the sign with interest then looked at Tess. 'Fancy a spot of lunch?' she asked.

Tess was using all her faculties to control the pain; there were none left to handle lies. 'Oh Heather, I can't carry on lying to you! I was going to give you some story about how I was teaching there, but I can't keep this up any longer. Also, I need you to cut up my sandwich and place small pieces in my mouth because I've lost the use of my entire upper body.'

Heather began to laugh and started to feed Tess. 'Why are you laughing?' Tess asked miserably. 'It's not funny. I've deceived you! I'm not a yoga teacher and never have been. I'd never even taken a yoga class before that first time I was supposed to be teaching you.'

'That was obvious,' Heather said, wiping mayonnaise off Tess's chin.

249

'You mean you knew?'

Heather snorted. 'Of course I knew. You were hopeless. You didn't even have us doing a proper warm-up. And you got all the names of the positions wrong. And even for someone claiming to be a little out of condition, you were the most uncoordinated woman I'd ever seen. Not much better at sequence dancing either,' she added drily.

'This is the most embarrassing experience of my life,' Tess said.

'Actually I would dispute that. I think your attempts to dazzle us with your amazing arm movements were far more embarrassing.'

'I want to cover my eyes with shame, but I can't lift my hands that far.'

'Don't worry about it. If it makes you feel any better, I don't think anyone else noticed. Or if they did, I managed to cover for you.'

Tess lost her appetite and watched while Heather finished off both her own and Tess's lunch. 'Why didn't you say anything?' she asked.

'I told you that when I moved to Heaverbury, I was as broke as you.'

'I remember,' Tess said.

'Well, my husband was refusing to give me any money to try and force me to go back to him. At one stage I didn't even have enough to buy baby food.'

Tess was horrified. 'What did you do?'

'I'd just started going to church to get my eldest into the school, exactly like you're doing now. There was a notice up advertising for an experienced childcare professional to run the playgroup. So I applied to John.'

'Even though you weren't an experienced childcare professional?'

'But that wasn't the worst of it. John gave me the job even though I'd made feeble excuses for not having any of the certificates I was supposed to produce. I think he always knew I was lying.'

'But surely nobody got hurt,' Tess said. 'I could have been responsible for a class of women with broken arms!'

'One of my responsibilities was collecting the money from all the mums each day and passing it on to the church. I began stealing some of it, just the odd couple of pounds to buy food.'

Tess was appalled. Now it was Heather's turn to look ashamed.

'What happened?' Tess asked.

'John knew from the beginning. Contrary to my assumptions about vicars, he was very worldly wise and knew exactly how much money should be passing through the books each week.'

'What did he do?'

'Nothing. He waited for me to put the money back eventually, which of course I did. Then he took me to one side, asked if I was now on top of things and told me to ask him for money next time I was desperate.'

Tess was touched by this astonishing generosity. She vowed to be less cynical next time she was in church.

'So that's why I was only too happy to give a second chance to someone else, to pass the favour on.'

'I don't know how I can make it up though,' Tess said.

'You already are,' Heather said. 'You're taking classes at your own expense to improve your skills. Stick with it. Just keep the classes going. The women are happy enough; you're providing them with a service.'

Tess extended her little finger a painful inch to show her gratitude. 'I'm supposed to be taking your hand warmly. Do you know, I feel so much better now that it's out in the open. It's been awful having to pretend to you.'

'Tess, can I ask you something now that we're being honest with each other?'

'Please do,' Tess begged. 'Anything to take the spotlight off me!'

'Did you think Jerry was a bit off on Thursday?'

I want the spotlight back on me, Tess thought, I want a nice big juicy humiliating story that reflects badly on me and distracts Heather from this question. While Tess tried to formulate a tactful response, Heather went on.

'It wasn't just Thursday if I'm honest. He's been cooling for a couple of weeks. Maybe it was proposing that did it. You hear of men like that, don't you, they get all enthusiastic about marriage then get cold feet when the prospect becomes a reality.'

'Perhaps you're just imagining it,' Tess suggested, feeling sick with guilt, particularly in the light of Heather's huge kindness towards her.

'I don't think so. He was quite cold towards me during the dancing. Didn't you notice?'

How could I? Tess thought. I was too busy thinking about his declaration of love.

'It wouldn't be so bad if I wasn't more or less committed to him,' Heather continued.

Tess tried to sound light. 'I don't think you can be sued for breach of promise any more!'

Heather looked confused. 'What? Oh no, I don't mean that I have to marry him because I've said I would. No, it's more of a commitment than that. I think I'm pregnant.'


'I've thought about nothing else for the past twenty-four hours,' Tess said to Max that night.

Max swallowed, aware that she held his future, both of their futures in her hands. 'So what have you decided?'

'I'll agree to it all, selling everything we own, including my eternity ring, on one condition.'

'Which is?' Max asked.

'That we try for another baby.'

'We can't.' Max spoke without thinking. 'Think of what we went through all the other times. It nearly destroyed us, especially you.'

'I'm prepared to take that chance. You'll be so busy setting up your new business, it won't be so bad for you.'

Max was very uneasy. He didn't know where this was coming from but he could sense that Tess was determined. Also he had no choice. He'd planned the rest of his life on the understanding that Tess would support him in his decision to start up one more business, take one last risk with their every final penny.

She didn't know about the other debts, the ones he'd kept secret. But he had plans for that as well. He'd agreed with his new partners that a small percentage of his profits would be placed in a separate account. He'd use that to pay off his creditors. If it took the rest of his working life, then so be it. He almost relished the challenge. It was a form of penance, one he still felt he needed to pay.

'OK' he said quietly. 'I don't think it's a good idea, but if you're prepared to support me in the new business, then I'll support you through . . . this.'

They didn't kiss or hug or come together in any way that Max would have expected after an agreement that their lives were to be inextricably bound from this day on.

Tess handed over her eternity ring and the deal was done.

# 15

It was different this Sunday, Tess was thinking. There was less hostility from both Max and herself. And this time, they had all their friends with them. Apart from Tim.

Graham looked as horrified as Max had been the week before. 'You get used to it.' Max reassured him. 'Just do what everybody else does.'

'They don't do that thing where they all touch each other and go on about peace, do they?' Graham asked.

'I hope not,' Fiona whispered. 'I hate strangers touching me.'

'They didn't last week,' Max said.

Millie looked as if she was drugged. She sat reading all the bits of paper that were stuck into the backs of the seats. Two of her children were making paper planes and aiming them at the font. The other two were tearing up a muesli bar, chewing the morsels and then flicking them at the stone angels adorning the pillars.

The loud music shook them all. Tess and Max were less perturbed by it all this week. Max even joined in the songs, not with the actions of course, he was too inhibited, too tall, to draw attention to himself that way. But he joined in the singing and even attempted a few animal noises.

'Are you sure this is a proper church?' Graham whispered to Fiona. 'Everyone looks much too happy.'

He'd been looking forward to a gloomy sombre experience that would reflect his current mood. This was all wrong.

Daphne was watching the children with great pleasure. This was how she liked her grandchildren – having fun, in somebody else's house and a good 25 yards away from her. She thought she'd go crazy if she had to live with them for the rest of her life.

Millie stood and sat along with the rest of them but otherwise didn't join in. The only time she relaxed was when the children left for Sunday school. But they all relaxed then.

'No wonder people come to church if they take your kids away for an hour,' Graham whispered. 'You have to pay for this in other places.'

John stood at the front. 'We don't do this every week,' he announced, 'but there are a lot of new people here so this might be a good time to exchange the peace.'

'Here I go,' Graham declared.

'Ssh!' Fiona hissed. 'Stay where you are.'

He obeyed, wondering if she'd arranged this with the vicar to punish her husband for not physically carrying Tim back to Millie.

'If anyone touches me, I'll slap them,' Graham muttered, having checked with Max in advance that this was a perfectly natural response.

'Allow him his macho posturing,' Fiona advised Tess.

'Peace be with you,' a smiley woman said, holding out her hand.

'Righty-ho!' Graham said, shaking the hand vigorously before placing his hand back in his pocket and glaring at anyone else who approached him.

'I thought you were going to slap her?' Fiona reminded him.

'In my head, the woman is on the floor already.' Graham decided to be gloomy and sombre all by himself if this place was not going to offer him that luxury.

Tess watched in astonishment as Max shook hands cheerfully with everyone who came up to him.

'I thought you hated all this,' she said to him quietly.

Max glared at her. 'They're quite nice if you give them a chance.' He was hiding his embarrassment badly.

He caught John's eye and raised a thumb. John beamed and returned the gesture.

'You're the vicar's best friend all of a sudden,' Tess commented. 'I thought we didn't like vicars.'

'We're almost related now.'

'What is that supposed to mean?'

'Didn't I tell you? He's Carter's son.'

Tess sat back, absorbing this unexpected relationship, wondering at the implications. Max was smiling with too much enthusiasm for Tess's liking.

255

'Think about it,' Max continued cheerfully, 'now we're in business together, we'll all be like one big happy family!'

Fiona was watching Graham. He seemed to be staring at something.

'What are you looking at?' she whispered.

'I can't believe what I'm seeing,' he said.

Fiona tried to see what was so amazing. No streakers, no Cliff Richard, absolutely nothing out of the ordinary, as far as she could tell.

'Look,' Graham said, pointing at a couple seated near the front. 'That's Barry Downing, my managing director, with his wife.'

'And?' Fiona was clearly missing a vital point here.

'I can't believe it! He seems so normal. He even goes to the pub at lunchtime.'

Fiona feigned shock. 'You mean, he never pulls his tambourine out in board meetings or leads hymn sessions in the morning?'

Graham glared at her. 'I was just a bit surprised, that's all.'

Barry Downing spotted Graham and smiled warmly. Graham beamed back. He sat up a bit straighter and paid a bit more attention.

After an entertaining sermon, John faced the congregation.

'Let us pray,' he said.

I'm not going to pretend I believe in all this, Max prayed. But seeing as how I'm here, I may as well hedge my bets by giving it a go. And I've had a few successes with you, or someone, lately.

I don't know how many things you're allowed to ask for, so I'll lump everything together in one request, just to be on the safe side.

I just want the chance of redemption. There, a good solid biblical word! Hope that gets me a few brownie points.

I want to redeem myself with Tess. If this business can succeed and I don't need to make millions, just enough to appease my creditors and provide a decent living for my family, then we have a chance. You should be aware that one of my partners is a vicar's father and the vicar himself came up with the idea for this business. I don't want this to sway you in any way, but it should be worth something, don't you think?

And if you could throw in a baby for Tess, and for me as well, that would be even better.

I just know that if you could arrange that for us, then everything else will fall into place.

Oh, er, OK, amen.

Tess half-closed her eyes, the way she'd done in school assembly on the off-chance that a teacher might be watching and note her down as prefect material.

I am prepared to believe in you, she prayed, go the whole distance. I've got a straight deal for you. A baby for my soul. Let me have another child and I'll be yours forever. For eternity if that bit's really true. (Not convinced, personally, but willing to be persuaded. I quite like the concept.) I know you think I'm joking, doing the Faustian thing. But I need you to understand just how badly I want this baby.

It's all I care about. Well, apart from the obvious things like wanting to protect Lara from all harm, all disease, all boys until she marries a man of my choosing, all girls who tell her she has fat legs, all disappointment. That goes without saying, doesn't it? If not, then please add this to my list and leave it there as an ongoing prayer. Because actually, now I think of it, that's probably more important than the baby one.

And if it's possible to let me have a baby without years of suffering, that would be nice. Although at least trying for a baby is better than not trying. It's something to aim for rather than treading water, just hoping to survive.

I'd also be extremely grateful if you could stop all this stuff with Jerry. It's confusing me, muddling my thoughts. I've already offered you my soul, and it seems Max is selling everything else I own, so I haven't got much else to barter. Some nice shoes, a couple of Le Creuset casserole dishes, any use to you?

So there you have it. A baby, everlasting health and happiness for Lara, oh and of course for Max, too. And me. And Jerry to ... well, whatever. I haven't thought that through properly; I'll get back to you on that one. But if you could make a start on the rest of the list, I just know that everything else will fall into place.

Amen.

I've been coming here for a while now, Jerry began. I quite enjoy it. We've been chatting like this, on and off, since the start and I have to admit I've found it fairly comforting. But, then again, you'll have to admit that I'm not the most demanding of petitioners.

The occasional grey hair, the occasional red letter from the bank, the occasional period when the thought of a life alone fills me with dread, I might have been a bit pushy then. But the rest of the time, I've been quiet and, if you don't mind my boasting, not a bad person.

But I've got a biggie this time. I think I've deposited enough in the past that I'm now entitled to make a large withdrawal. So here goes.

It's a bit complicated so pay attention. I'm giving you a choice, thought that might double my chances of success.

I would like: either to fall in love with Heather, that real love that everybody talks about, the one that Tess insists is worth aiming for. Or, if that's too much to ask for, I would like for you at least to get rid of the feelings I have for Tess. I don't know what they mean, they feel a bit real to me, but that can't be right, not with her being married with a child and being Heather's friend.

So there you have it. If that was all rather muddled, feel free to ask questions. But try and avoid burning bushes in Heaverbury; it makes the police nervous.

I've heard that a little seed of faith can make a tree uproot itself and march into the sea. Seems a waste of a tree to me. But if you could see your way to granting one of my less cinematic prayers, I just know that everything else will fall into place.


I'm supposed to be a believer, Heather prayed. I tell everyone that but deep down I'm not convinced. You've got a good vicar working for you and I'm grateful for that, but my life's been short on miracles these last years.

I thought everything was looking up when Jerry came along. But I got complacent and apparently that's not allowed. So is this my punishment? Are you taking him away from me?

Well, I don't want him to go and I want to be pregnant. There! What do you think of that?

I haven't done a test; I wanted to have a chat with you first. And you've played tricks on me before, let me take tests that show positive, then made them negative a few days later. Mean of you, I think, but I'm sure you have your reasons.

Anyway, I'm going to give it until next Friday before I take the test. So any time this week will be fine. If you can give me this man and this baby, nothing else, I just know that everything else will fall into place.

This doesn't seem right, Daphne prayed. I was brought up to fall on my knees and beg for forgiveness. Nobody ever told me that you were allowed to ask for things (except when Mummy went to hospital to have a baby and never came home).

And it's all too happy here for me. It doesn't fit with my picture of you with the long hair and the beard and the fierce judging eyes. Do you really like all these children dancing around and these grown-ups clapping?

I suppose it might put you in a good mood. I feel more cheerful myself, I have to say. That vicar says we're supposed to ask for things for ourselves. So I may as well have a go. I've tried everything else: every pill on the market, copper bracelets, shouting at my children, Bombay Red (I can recommend that if you should ever find yourself with muscular problems yourself).

I want the pain to stop. Or if that's unreasonable, for it to be able to be controlled with minimal painkillers. I'm not that old and I don't fancy another 20 years or so like this.

If that's unacceptable, then can you at least make my daughter like me?

Whichever is the most feasible. They both seem impossible to me.

I only expect one of them. I just know that everything else will fall into place.

Amen.

Blimey, Fiona prayed, I haven't been in church since Dad died. I didn't behave very religiously then, but you probably know that.

I wasn't going to do this but everyone else seems to be having a go so I may as well. Anyway, Tess has got her eyes closed and I've got nothing to say to Graham, so you're the only one available.

So, how's things? I thought I liked a good conversation but you do it all day, millennium in, millennium out. I bet not many people ask after you, so I thought you might appreciate the enquiry. Don't you get sick of everyone whingeing? I do. I'll let you into a secret: I'm fed up with everyone else's problems. I know that sounds selfish but things were going fine until this year. I don't see why we can't all get back to that.

I know Tess and Max's café is gone now (maybe you decided to save the world from that vile herbal tea) and they've moved away, so that's done, but can't you make everyone start being nice to each other again?

Oh, is that a bit vague? Let me be more specific. I'd like Tim to go back to Millie, I'd like Tess and Max to get some money behind them, just enough for them not to worry and I'd like Graham to work out whatever is bothering him and come back to me.

Oh, one more thing. Is there any chance whatsoever that you might teach my mum how to like me?

If I have to pick just the one? I know this'll sound selfish, but I think I'd like the one about my mum. Then everything else will fall into place.

Erm, amen?

This is bloody stupid and I'm not falling for it. I'm not talking to you because I don't believe in you. If there's anything or anybody out there, then you can read my mind. This is not a prayer, do you hear me? Not a prayer.

I wonder what Eloise believes in. I can't remember where Christine stood on religion. One thing's for sure, if she finds out that her mother's been lying to her all her life, her faith in humanity will be shattered. I hope she can find something to replace that because I don't see her accepting me as her new hero.

Is there anything that could convince me that you exist? A miracle of some kind? I'm not going to go for a silly one. Not the 'I'll-believe-in-you-if-I-win-the-Lottery' one. Let me think. Ah, here's a challenging one.

Give me an easy decision. Make it obvious to me what I should do about Christine, about Eloise. Make me feel comfortable about whatever I decide.

Now that will be a miracle. Do that for me and we'll talk again. Because everything else will fall into place.

It's lovely and quiet here, Millie thought. I wonder what they're all thinking. I'm sure some of them are praying but I bet the rest are just drifting off like me. Wondering if they switched the oven on for the roast; thinking of clever, cruel things they should have said to clever, cruel people they've encountered this week; enjoying wicked fantasies about being married to someone else or not having kids; trying to remember if it's plain or patterned tops that make your bust look smaller; picking their fingernails to the quick.

Look at them all still at it. Haven't they all finished yet? They can't have that many problems. I know their lives aren't perfect but they've got it easy compared to me.

So Fiona's mother has moved in and she's a complete cow. They're all alive and well and living in a lovely house. Fiona has carnations flown in from the Channel Islands every week and has her eyelashes dyed every month. How traumatised can she be? So Tess and Max have had to move and are short of money. Well, they've only got one child, I repeat, ONE CHILD! If I had one child, I could live in a cardboard box and be perfectly content. And Max is still living with Tess, he hasn't run off with some tart he knew at school.

And Graham? God knows what the matter with him is. I don't care. He has no excuse. Fiona worships him and none of his kids have been sent home for stealing other children's PE kit or writing gynaecological words on the blackboard.

If I could ask for something, I'd ask for time to be turned back. There. OK? Satisfied? I'll go home and wait for that, shall I?

If they could just turn back time, I'd handle things differently. Then I know that everything else will fall into place.

But I'm only thinking. This is not a prayer.

Can I have a PlayStation 2? Lara pleaded in Sunday school, her eyes tightly closed. And some Skechers trainers and tickets to see Westlife and my own computer and rollerblades and my pocket money back to its old level and straighter hair and all wars to stop and Mum and Dad to smile and hold hands more?

Amen.

Where the hell are they all on a Sunday morning? Tim thought. They can't have gone out. Millie would never have been able to get them out this early, not by herself.

And Alison didn't even leave me a note. She just slammed the door when she left. I know she said she was on call but I thought she might wake me up.

I don't like being here by myself. In fact, I've come to realise that I don't like being anywhere by myself. I thought I was going mad at home, never having any time or space to myself, but it obviously suits me.

I don't miss the games though. That's the worst thing about having kids, the endless board games. It goes in phases. It was Cluedo for months. And no matter how hard you try to lose, to make the game over more quickly, they always know and play deliberately badly so you end up winning. In the longest way possible. And you have to keep on playing Cluedo until you lose one of the pieces, not the rope because you can replace that with a piece of string. The candlestick's the best one to lose. Then you move on to the other games. There are always other games.

In Scrabble, I always get the vowels and everyone knows that you can't win with just vowels; and Mouse Trap with that stupid contraption that never works properly and it takes hours before anyone catches a mouse; chess that I'm no good at and Carly beats me and I have to pretend that I'm letting her win; Hungry Hippos that Nathan's been playing for two years and you sit there bashing the hippo's tail, catching balls and it's so mindless and as for Monopoly, I *hate* Monopoly, it takes bloody hours and what's all that about the short version they suggest in the rules, you show me the child that is prepared to play the short version and I will adopt that child, and snap, you try and lose at snap without the small child guessing that you're losing on purpose, and ...

The phone rang. Tim came back to the grown-up world feeling disorientated. He answered, forgetting that Alison had told him not to.

'Millie's got your mobile number,' she'd insisted, 'anybody phoning here will be for me.'

'Hello?' he said.

'Hello?' a heavily accented voice said. 'Who's that?'

'Tim. Who's that?'

'What number is this?'

Tim read it out.

'Is Alison there?' the man asked.

'No I'm afraid she's out. Can I give her a message?'

'Can you tell her Gabriel called?'

'Of course.'

So that was Gabriel. He sounded like Julio Iglesias to Tim, and not very bright.

Tim sat by the window, thinking about what Graham had said, how he needed to decide what he wanted. Well, he'd worked that out exactly.

He wanted to go back to Millie and the children.

But he needed Alison. Millie would still be there in a few months.

I'll just get Alison out of my system then I'll go back to Millie. Other men do that. I know, I read the Sunday papers.

So I'll carry on like this just for a while longer. I know that everything else will fall into place.

I'll have his baby. Then I'll make him leave. I can put up with him for that long. Alison bought a bottle of wine on the way home, determined to get him drunk.

I just want a baby. That's all. Then everything else will fall into place.

*Dear Graham,*

*I know I said I wouldn't pressure you and that I'd wait for you to get in touch with me but there's been a development.*

*My mum has told Eloise about you. You must remember what an interfering old bag she was: well, she hasn't changed. Believe it or not, she was always on your side and never forgave me for not marrying you. She got used to David but she was always making snide comments about you in front of him. He was a good man and just took it from her, mainly to protect Eloise.*

*I told Mum I was going to get in touch with you and, of course, she was thrilled, had this crazy dream that you'd come back into our lives and be a family with us. I haven't told her that you have four children of your own. I didn't know how she'd react so I thought it best to let her carry on fantasising. It stopped her going on at me all the time.*

*I'd made her promise that she wouldn't say anything to Eloise until I'd cleared things with you. But apparently Eloise went to see her gran last week and was in a state about David. So Mum took it upon herself to tell her about you. Sorry. It*

*wasn't my fault. Needless to say, Eloise was completely hyster-*
*ical and won't talk to me. She blames me for keeping you from*
*her. She's right, of course, that's exactly what I've done.*

*She says she won't speak to me again if she doesn't see you*
*and hear your side of the story.*

*I'm really sorry about this, Graham. I'll wait to hear from*
*you. Don't take too long.*

*Love*
*Chrissie*
*XXXXX*

# 16

My side of the story? Graham thought. I don't know it myself. I wasn't even sure there was a story until last week. So what am I supposed to do now? Go and see this girl, this young woman, and tell her ... what? That I would have loved to have been her father but her mother didn't turn up on our wedding day and, no, I don't know why that was and that it's lovely to meet her but I can't do much for her because I have four children who have known me all their lives and are rather used to having me to themselves and ...

Graham switched his mind off. He'd been getting good at it as a matter of necessity. The dancing had helped enormously.

The first dance flowed seamlessly. They all knew the steps because it had been the first dance taught the previous week. Like old pros, they'd assembled into their circles and been happy to dance with whoever happened to be opposite them.

When it came to learning a new dance, and there was a lesson every week, they were advised to stick to their original partners.

But even dancing with Heather couldn't ruin Max's mood.

'You seem a bit more cheerful this week,' she said.

'Hasn't Tess told you our news?' Max asked. 'About us going into business again?'

Heather frowned. 'No. That's strange because I had lunch with her on Saturday and saw her in church and Carter's on Sunday and she didn't say a thing.'

Max looked pleased. 'Perhaps she wants to keep it between ourselves for now. She's thrilled. We both are.'

Heather looked over at Tess, who was dancing with Jerry. She didn't look thrilled.

'Tess,' Jerry began.

'Shut up,' Tess said. 'Don't talk to me. Let's just get this dance over with.'

'You've been avoiding me.'

'That's right, I have. So why don't you take the hint and leave me alone?'

'Because we haven't settled things between us.'

'Nothing to settle.'

'Well, I think there is.'

Tess stopped looking at her feet for a moment and looked up at Jerry. His eyes were very definitely not crinkly.

'I think I should tell you something. Two somethings actually. Max is going into business again and I'm supporting him. And we're trying for another baby. Is that simple enough for you to understand?'

Jerry didn't say anything else. He just concentrated on helping Tess not trip over her own feet in a tricky tango.

'Good God, Graham, have you seen Tess's hand?'

'Fiona, you have to pay attention, this is the fiddly part. If you don't turn at the right moment, you'll end up bumping into everybody else.'

'Her ring's gone, her eternity ring, you know the one.'

Graham glanced over at Tess without interest. 'Perhaps she's sent it away to be cleaned.'

Fiona tutted at him. 'This isn't a Jane Austen novel. Women don't send their jewellery to "little men in Bath" who clean them with weird unguents by candlelight. They swish them around in Fairy Liquid or get a free quick polish at the Ideal Home Exhibition once a year.'

'Then ask her, Fi. It'll be the first time you've actually had a reason to speak to her. Normally you would talk for hours about nothing.'

Fiona heard the impatience in his voice but didn't challenge him. She'd seen what had happened to Millie when she confronted Tim and it terrified her. She didn't think Graham was entertaining women in vests in the house when she was out. So whatever was bothering him, she was going to wait patiently for him to work through it in his own way. Then when he was fully hers again, she'd make his life hell for making her worry like this. The thought cheered her considerably.

Christine was a great dancer, Graham was thinking. We fitted perfectly, both learned at the same pace, understood each other. She still hasn't explained why she left me. Do I really want to know?

Heather didn't notice Tess's bare ring finger. She was too busy watching Jerry watching Tess who was avoiding watching Jerry. The dance was about to finish. Tess pulled away a few beats early. Jerry pulled her back. 'I need to talk to you. Just once more.'

'No,' Tess said flatly. 'Whatever it is I'm not interested. And please stop with all the ha-ha messages on my answering machine. Max could have picked one of them up. If you must play the music from *Riverdance* down the phone and make tap-dancing noises on the receiver, then do it to Heather. I think she could use a laugh right now.'

'This is the very last time, I promise. And then I'll never call again. Or talk to you. In fact if I pass you in the street, I'll pretend I don't know you. I'll cross the road. I'll close my eyes when I collect my kids from your coma class, sorry yoga class. I'll make up cruel limericks where you're the tagline. I'll ...'

'All right, you win,' Tess laughed, enjoying the sound after a few heavy days with Max. 'But this is the last time.'

'If you say so,' Jerry agreed.

'What were you and Tess talking about?' Heather asked nervously when he came over to her.

'She was telling me that she and Max are trying for a baby.'

Heather exhaled with relief. She was surprised that Tess would tell Jerry and not her but thought it might be out of some misguided concern because she knew that Heather was taking a pregnancy test the following morning. Perhaps she thinks I don't want to talk about the subject until I know for sure.

She was about to mention it but Tess had disappeared towards the door. She looked over to see Tess and Fiona greeting someone. It looked like the strange woman who'd come for a few minutes last week, left her untamed children to get drunk on alcoholic punch, then returned in a state to collect them an hour later.

But this was a different woman altogether.

'Millie, you look fantastic!'

'I can't get over it! What have you done to yourself?'

Fiona and Tess turned her round slowly, stunned at the transformation.

'I went to the hairdresser's this morning, had my highlights done for the first time in two years, then had a facial, manicure, pedicure and massage, then went shopping, bought some decent clothes that I'll be able to wear before and after the babies and, best of all, I had a nap.'

Tess clicked her fingers. 'I've just realised what is really different about you – no kids!'

'What have you done with them? Sold them into slavery?'

'Already tried that, but they were turned down,' Millie replied happily. 'No, Tim and his trollop picked them up from homework club and have taken them out for the whole evening.'

'And you don't mind?' Tess asked. She wouldn't like Lara going out with Max and some other woman trying to become a substitute mother.

'Are you kidding? This is bliss!' Then she walked out onto the dance floor where she joined John, who was the only available partner, in a complicated quickstep that she picked up in minutes – the benefits of an afternoon nap.

If they want to prepare doctors for working and living in a war zone, they don't need to send them on expensive Outward Bound survival courses; they could borrow Tim's four children for an evening. Alison intended to write to Médecins Sans Frontières to put this cost-effective suggestion to them.

This is the worst night of my life, she thought. Worse than that night with amoebic dysentery in Islamabad, worse than going to Brazil and meeting Gabriel's family who kept slapping me on the backside and giving me enormous fatty pork hocks for breakfast. Even worse than that night when we went to camp with the school and Tim made me sit up all night while he read Greek poetry to me. In Greek.

I'm in a bowling alley with four brats who should be heavily medicated and I'm not happy.

'Millie's always believed that it's important to let children develop freely, that we shouldn't stifle them or force them into a mould of our making.'

Tim was responding to a complaint from the management that Carly and Lucy kept pressing the buttons on other players' score panels, causing them to lose entire games.

After the first five minutes in the company of these monsters,

Alison believed in corporal punishment, boarding school and Ritalin. It's not their fault, she kept reminding herself. They just haven't been given boundaries. Alison had taken courses on child behaviour modification and knew all the theories.

She decided to introduce Carly and Lucy to the concept of boundaries, make her first impact on these children.

'This is our score panel,' she said, talking in a loud voice and enunciating like a bad actress. 'You can be in charge of it. You can take turns at pressing the buttons. All the other panels are out of bounds. You are not to touch them.' She remembered another useful principle. It's always important to explain to children why you're stopping them from doing something. 'If you touch them, it will spoil the other people's games. They will get cross and complain, then the evening will be spoiled for everyone, you included because you will be punished.'

There, she thought with satisfaction. I ended with a direct consequence that related to them. You can't expect them to care about other people, but they will not want to do anything that infringes on their own enjoyment.

Carly and Lucy ran from one end of the bowling hall to the other, pressing every reset button on every panel, then stood in front of Alison and smiled angelically.

'Can we go to McDonalds now?' they asked.


John stood at the front of the hall and tapped the microphone to attract the group's attention. 'It's party dance time!' he called out with a grin. The announcement was greeted by cheers of approval.

'What's a party dance?' Fiona asked Millie. Before Millie had the chance to formulate a sensible guess, everyone was on the floor, standing in lines.

John gave them all the thumbs up sign, which they returned happily. 'OK, now I'm sure you all know this one, but for those people who've never been to a party dance, let's go over the actions. Right, we stretch out our arms like this, that's the Y, curl your hands down to make an M, arms curved to one side for the C and hands together over your head for an A! Right then. Everybody up for the *YMCA*!'

Max watched John in astonishment. 'He *is* joking?' he said. 'He doesn't really expect us to get up and do this?'

'I haven't done this for years!' Graham exclaimed, before rushing up to the front of the dance floor.

Max called across to Fiona. 'Did you know he was like this when you married him? I've never seen this side of him before. It's very scary!'

'Just when you think you know someone they turn around and surprise you,' Fiona said bitterly.

'Come on, Dad!' Lara bounded up to Max and dragged him to his feet. 'Mum's doing it.'

Max saw Tess bobbing from side to side and joining in with the actions as if she'd done it a thousand times before. 'Now it's my turn to be surprised,' he muttered to himself.

He allowed Lara to pull him across to where Tess was dancing. 'Have you been going to party dances in secret while I've been slaving over a hot till every day?' he asked lightly. 'You've definitely done this before.'

Tess didn't look at him. 'Maybe you should have spent a little more time at home, then you'd know more about me and I'd know more about you.'

'Does everything you say have to be so cryptic?' he hissed, hoping that Lara wouldn't hear the beginnings of yet another argument. 'Can't you just say what you want to say?'

'You don't want to hear that.' Tess replied. 'Come on Millie!' she called, encouraging her friend onto the dance floor. Millie complied to the best of her ability but she was not enjoying the sensation of two babies jumping up and down inside her stomach.

'Come on, Fiona!' Graham shouted to Fiona. Fiona shook her head briefly. Graham wasn't going to accept this. He had become a Party Animal and Fiona was going to be his Dancing Queen. He jigged up to her, still making letters with his arms. 'Come on,' he repeated, 'I won't take no for an answer.'

'I'd rather not,' she said flatly. 'I'm going to the ladies'. With that, she got up and left.

Graham watched her leave, worried about her mood but putting it down to the presence of her mother. Then he heard the opening notes to 'Agadoo' and immediately forgot Fiona.

'There's a fight! Call the police!'

It was one of Fiona's children who raised the alarm. They'd never seen a fight before but they knew what you were supposed to shout. They'd watched *Grange Hill* and *Byker Grove* enough times.

Fiona sighed to Graham. 'Well, we knew this would happen one day. Whatever Tess says, this area has a reputation. I just hope it's not too serious.'

They joined the excited crowd outside the community centre. 'Where's Mum?' Fiona asked, worried that she hadn't seen Daphne since the first dance.

'I think she's over there,' Graham said, indicating the heart of the action.

Fiona jostled through the crowd, frantic to save her mother from the crackhead junkie dope dealers who were obviously trying to mug her for her pension.

The vicious assault by the crackhead junkie dope dealers turned out to be Carter, Archie and Rav scuffling pathetically around Daphne who was tutting loudly and telling them to stop playing silly buggers.

'He started it,' Rav said, shaking his fist at Archie.

''All I said was that I asked Daphne out first and that entitled me to certain courtesies such as the two of you asking me before you sneak around with the lady behind my back.'

'You didn't have to push me!' Carter said.

'I didn't push you,' Archie explained, 'You were standing there being all belligerent and I wanted to get past you. I gently manoeuvred you to one side when you refused to move. Then you pushed me.'

'You pushed me first!'

'And I saw you topping up her glass when she wasn't looking,' Rav shouted. 'That's not the behaviour of a gentleman.'

'It was for medicinal purposes,' Archie insisted. 'I could tell her arthritis was giving her some gyp. Tell him, Daphne!'

'I'll do no such thing,' Daphne said, thoroughly enjoying herself and having no intention of bringing the hostilities to a premature conclusion.

'You just wanted to get her tipsy,' Rav shouted. 'And when I was going to tell her what you'd done, you pulled my chair away from under me. Look! I've got a splinter in my finger now from where I grabbed onto the table when I fell.'

Daphne peered at the splinter. 'Come in with me where there's better light. I'll get that out for you.'

271

'I didn't pull his chair away,' Archie grumbled.

Daphne was walking more quickly now, feeling somewhat uncomfortable. She'd pulled the chair away herself so that she could sit on it. She hadn't expected Rav to fall back onto the non-existent chair in classic sitcom style.

Rav followed her back inside, smiling smugly at Carter and Archie as Daphne led him in.

John came outside just in time to stop Carter and Archie from continuing the dispute.

'Dad!' he hissed. 'You should be ashamed of yourself. Fighting in front of everyone.'

'I'd hardly call it fighting,' Carter protested. 'No blood was shed.'

'But Rav got a splinter and I'm getting a stress headache,' Archie argued.

'Get inside, the pair of you!' John ordered.

'Wait till I get her home!' Fiona growled to Graham still fuming at Daphne's role in the drama.

'Can't we take them home now?' Alison pleaded. 'We're running out of places to be thrown out of.'

'We can't go home until we know Millie's back. You know how she was about you being in our house before. The arrangement was that we take them home at nine and hand them over at the door.'

Alison looked at her watch. 'But that's another twenty-six minutes. What will we do with them until then?'

'Let's go to the playground on the common,' Tim suggested.

'It's far too dark for that,' Alison protested. I'm not even a mother and I know that's a stupid idea. And much as I'd love one or all of them to have a terrible accident that subdues them permanently, she thought, I don't fancy spending a night in A&E with hordes of screaming injured kids and their useless parents.

They ended up in Burger King (having been barred from ever returning to McDonald's and Kentucky Fried Chicken) where the kids were all promised £5 each if they sat still on their seats and ate an ice cream without throwing it at strangers, smearing it over the walls or Alison's clothes and definitely without singing that version of 'Jingle Bells' that attracted police attention in Streatham High Road.

'You're looking well,' Tim complained to Millie when at last they delivered the children home. 'What have you done to yourself?'

'Got myself a life, just like you,' Millie replied. 'Bye!'

She shut the door firmly on him and smiled to herself. She'd seen the dismay in his face. He'd expected her to be continuing her descent into despair, not washing, wearing her clothes inside out. He hadn't expected her to be looking better than she'd done for years.

'She's doing this for her boyfriend,' Tim said gloomily to Alison. 'She wasn't making any effort for me, but now she's got me out of the picture, she's putting on the full show for Daniel.' He spat the name out, hating the mysterious man even more since Millie had stopped mentioning him. He knew from his own secrecy about Alison that this was an ominous sign.

'What if she wants to marry him?' he moaned on the train. 'Then I'll be a stepfather. The kids will end up calling him "daddy". I'll get to see them every third weekend and have to traipse around zoos and parks with them and buy them expensive presents to make them like me more than him.' He suddenly clutched Alison's hand. 'Oh my God! What if he *is* their daddy, the twins, I mean?' Alison watched him performing some swift calculations. Tim almost collapsed in relief. 'No, they can't be, he's only come on the scene recently. And, besides, we'd sort of worked out when it happened. We'd been to the opera and Millie had ordered a double gin and tonic on an empty stomach and she was wearing this top that was cut really low like this ...'

'WILL YOU SHUT UP!'

Tim looked at Alison in astonishment. That was the sort of thing Millie might say, or rather shout. But she was his wife and that's what wives do. Alison was, well, whatever she was, and she was supposed to gaze adoringly at him and listen to his problems and make them all go away.

'Have you got a headache?' he asked, looking for an explanation for her outburst that he could understand.

'Yes,' Alison answered weakly. It was easier than telling him the truth. And it wasn't that much of a lie. Her head was aching. It was throbbing from all the conflicting thoughts exploding and banging into each other and preventing her from thinking clearly.

Some things were clear, however. She could not bear having

273

this man around her for much longer. With or without his wretched children, Tim drove her mad. Now she knew why she'd left him. Because he was like this as a teenager, wet and clingy and moany. And he hadn't changed.

But Alison wasn't a bad person, or at least she didn't believe so. I may have been planning to steal him from his wife, but that wouldn't have been possible if his marriage was in any shape. So it's not my fault. And I may be planning to trick him into giving me a baby. But since he won't know anything about it, that won't hurt anyone.

But the fact that he's been thrown out of his home, I have to take my share of responsibility for that. I went to his house knowing what he had in mind. I wore that ludicrous top to seduce him. So when his wife returned home unexpectedly, which she was fully entitled to do since she lived there, of course she thought the inevitable.

So how can I throw him out as well? I don't think I'm that cruel. In fact, Alison was grateful for the discovery. She'd wondered if maybe she was a hard person, especially after the savage fantasies she'd enjoyed while suffering for an evening with Tim's kids.

I'll put up with him for now, she decided. I have to. I'm not so sure about the baby now. Having seen what Tim's babies grow into, I'm wondering if I'd be better off getting a dog.

'You seemed to be enjoying yourself,' Max said happily.

'I'm glad you agreed we should keep going there,' Tess said cautiously. 'Lara loves us doing things as a family. But I don't think it's going to be enough.'

'Well, why don't you see what else is going on at the community centre? I won't be working evenings once the shop is up and running so we'll be able to do other things as well as the dancing.'

Max was tapping away at his calculator while he talked. He'd pulled out all his old suppliers' invoices and he was already working out profit margins.

'Can you stop doing that for a few minutes?' she asked.

Max carried on tapping. 'I want to get this finished for tomorrow. I'm meeting the partners at lunchtime.'

'Max. STOP IT.' She raised her voice as loudly as she could without waking Lara, who was sleeping just a paper-thin wall away.

Max put the calculator down.

'Will this take long?' he asked.

Tess inhaled, hoping there might be some spare patience in the atmosphere that she could absorb. 'Max, before we even start this new business, let's decide in advance that we won't make the same mistakes as we did last time.'

'But I've already said that we won't! There won't be the same overheads this time—'

'I'm not talking about the money,' Tess interrupted. 'I'm talking about us. I mean, look at you. You're already starting, spending every spare minute working at the books, planning, sourcing suppliers. Once the shop is open, you'll be staying late, testing new recipes, reorganising shelves. We'll end up the way we did before, never seeing each other, never talking.'

Max grabbed both her hands. 'That isn't going to happen! I promise. We'll go dancing every week and do something else as well if you like and we'll have to keep the church thing up now that we've got the business link with John and we'll be trying for a baby. That's loads of time together!'

He kissed her on the back of both hands then sank into the sofa and went back to his calculations.

As Tess watched him, all of his words flew out of her mind. That's all they were, she knew, just words. Because she knew, with absolute certainty, that their marriage would begin to end on the day their new business started.

Graham lay awake in bed, composing e-mails that he would never send. Maybe I could get hold of Eloise's e-mail address, he thought. But that wouldn't help. It would still be contact. I'd be starting something and would have to be prepared to follow it through. Forever. A child is not just for Christmas ...

He went downstairs and made himself some hot chocolate. I haven't done this for years, not since the kids were babies and I was kept up with them when they were ill. I wonder who sat up with Eloise when she was ill, Christine or David? Were they as patient with her as I was with my children, I mean my other children?

What do I do? What do I do? He tried an exercise that was often helpful with work-related problems. Stick to the facts and use those alone when drawing your final conclusion.

OK. The facts: I have a 20-year-old daughter. She knows that I am her father. She knows that I know that she is my daughter.

Two options: To make contact or not to make contact.

Option 1: If I make contact, I have to accept that this might have to continue for the rest of her life. It would be too cruel to offer myself to her, then withdraw immediately afterwards. Besides, what would she gain by talking to me once or even meeting me once?

Option 2: If I don't make contact, this girl will grow up in the knowledge that she has been personally rejected by her father. This will be her second loss, after the death of her father, or the third if you also count the loss of discovering that her father wasn't her father anyway.

But, but, but. With Eloise comes Christine. I can see what's happening to Tim and Millie. That started with a simple phone call and look where that's ended. I can't honestly say that I've got any more self-control than Tim. Dare I call her?

How can I not? And although it was 1.30 in the morning, he picked up the phone.

'So we're agreed that we can't continue like this?' Carter announced.

Rav and Archie nodded doubtfully. They were sitting in the area that was to be the organic shop while carpenters demolished the building around them,

'We've been friends for too many years,' Archie agreed.

'And we're about to be business partners,' Rav added. 'We can't allow this to come between us.'

'So what are we going to do about it?' Carter asked.

'That's easy,' Archie said.

Carter and Rav looked at him expectantly.

Archie cleared his throat. 'We all have ... intentions towards the lovely Daphne. Since we've proved that we're not very good at fighting, we have to find a more peaceful way of settling this.'

'Tossing a coin?' Rav suggested.

'Don't be stupid, a coin only has two sides and there are three of us,' Carter said irritably.

'Who's calling who stupid?' Rav pressed his hands on the table aggressively.

'Stop this!' Archie shouted.

Rav and Carter obeyed, glaring at each other and muttering under their breath.

'Thank you,' Archie said. 'No, we can't draw lots or anything like that. We're talking about a lady here, she's not a prize in a raffle. It's simple, really. We have to go to her and ask her to choose.'

'I shouldn't have come but I'm glad I did,' Tess said. They'd enjoyed a quick lunch in the café and were now strolling around the common.

'At what point do I have to start not bothering you and ignoring you?' Jerry asked.

Tess hit him on the shoulder. Jerry grabbed her hand and linked it through his arm. Tess left it there, unsure whether she liked the feeling.

It was an icy day and they had automatically huddled together for warmth.

'Should we be doing this?' Tess had asked nervously when Jerry suggested a walk.

'Of course we should. Only very foolish individuals would be out in this weather. The only people we're likely to bump into are park policemen, dog-walkers and other couples hoping not to be seen.'

They kept a slow pace, despite the freezing wind, as if they shared an unspoken commitment to prolong this final outing.

'Why did you marry Max?' Jerry asked suddenly. 'If you don't mind me saying so, you don't seem that compatible and you're definitely not that happy right now.'

Tess hadn't given this any thought for years. Even when she'd been considering divorce, she'd not been able to remember the exact feelings that inspired her to marry him.

'I think that a lot of it was down to us both being only children. It can be stifling, it was for us, and we both wanted to get away from home as quickly as possible and find company!'

'Isn't companionship what old people expect from marriage?' Jerry teased. 'Aren't young people supposed to aim for something more romantic?'

'Don't knock it. It worked for us. In a way, we were like you. We made sure we wanted the same things, shared the same values, felt the same way about each other. In the early years there was passion as well. It seemed like love to us.'

'So why hasn't it made you happy?'

'Because we didn't get the thing we wanted, the big family; our values began to diverge as we each dealt with our disappointment in different ways; and the feelings changed, they always do. As for the passion . . .' She shrugged.

'A modern tragedy,' Jerry said lightly. But he squeezed her hand and Tess accepted the comfort silently and gratefully.

'So what happens next?'

Tess walked a little more briskly. 'We carry on. That's what you do when you have a child. We'll be fine.'

'I could offer you better than fine.'

Tess ignored him.

'Don't you ever want to run away and explore, look for something better for yourself, take some really big risks?' he asked.

Tess looked surprised. 'Of course I do. There's a whole part of me that does that all the time. That's how I cope, holding a little piece of myself back, keeping it just for me. It's that part of me that does all my living while the rest of me gets on with daily existence. I thought everyone divided themselves up like that. Don't you?'

Jerry shook his head. 'I've committed a hundred per cent of myself to living. That's why I've waited all these years before marrying and settling down. I want to be totally certain.'

'No such thing,' Tess said flatly. 'So what happens next for you? With you and Heather, I mean.'

'I haven't decided,' Jerry admitted. 'I think we'll probably call it a day at some stage soon. I've thought a lot about what you said, waiting for the "proper love", whatever that is. It would be just my luck to get married and then the real thing comes along a week later!'

'So you wouldn't just up and leave your wife if that happened?'

Jerry stared at her. 'Of course I wouldn't. What sort of man do you think I am?'

'Then how do you expect *me* to react when you go on about having feelings for me? What's the point in even mentioning them if there's no chance of acting on them?'

Jerry shrugged. 'Because this is all new to me, so I just have to go with the flow and watch where it all ends up, say whatever comes into my mind and just see what response I get.'

Tess hated herself for continuing the subject but she reassured herself that this was the last time they'd talk about it, or indeed anything. 'Just so I've got it clear in my mind, have you made up your mind what you feel for me?' She hoped the question sounded flippant.

'Oh yes, I know that. It's definitely different to any feelings I've had before. This must be the "in love" thing you described.' He turned to her. 'So before I keep my promise never to darken your door again, I may as well say it: just in case I don't get the chance to say it again, to you or anyone else. I love you.'

And he kissed her for the first and last time.

I feel the same! she wanted to say. I love you! And, unlike you, I know what I'm talking about. I've had the real thing and a few phoney ones before that. And this is definitely real! But she couldn't.

Every sensation of love that Tess experienced would always have to be measured against her love for Lara and it would always fall short. Lara was her child, maybe the only one she would ever have. Tess believed with all her heart that every child had the right to a childhood where she felt absolutely secure that she was the most important element of her parents' lives. Sacrifice was a foregone conclusion if you took that approach.

Maybe if she hadn't had children, her resolve would have been weaker. Maybe, even, if she'd had more than one child, the intensity of maternal love and responsibility she felt would be diluted. Right now, she couldn't envisage any circumstances that would lead her to consider hurting Lara deliberately.

She was immediately appalled at her own discovery that a sense of loyalty towards Max didn't seem to be having any bearing on her choices. In fact, she was more bothered about Heather.

She wondered if Jerry hadn't been Heather's boyfriend, she might perhaps have chucked aside all her principles and embarked upon an affair with him, a secret temporary affair that would not touch Lara or Max. That might have worked, allowed Tess to get him out of her system, helped her through a rocky patch with her husband. But she couldn't do it to Heather. Not when she was pregnant.

*

279

Max felt his knees buckle. That's funny, he thought, I've often read about emotions having a physical impact but I never quite believed it. And yet my legs have gone shaky, I feel nauseous and even my heart is beating faster.

I've never even wondered how I might feel if I saw Tess with another man. I mean, it's not like Millie catching Tim with that woman in her underwear, but in a way this is worse.

Tess looks so soft with him. And vulnerable. And yielding. She was never like that with me. Even when she was having all the miscarriages, she never sank into me like that. She always held onto her emotions, hid them somewhere out of my reach, unavailable for me to comfort. But she seems to be letting herself go with that man. That's not fair.

And how far has it already gone? She's kissing him in public, who knows what they could be getting up to in private? After all, I'm never at home.

I'm never at home, he thought again. Why does that sound so familiar? Of course, it was the old accusation that Tess used to throw at him during the years of Organique, the opening salvo of countless rows. He'd always ignored her pleas.

It was then that he remembered her insistence that they talk last night. She'd been warning him about this and he'd ignored her again. Of course it would have been more helpful if she'd just said, 'Darling, buck your ideas up or I might need to go and kiss strange men. Or more.' She'd always been too subtle for him, too oblique.

But perhaps that's my fault too. I should have said to her: What the hell are you going on about, woman? Speak proper English. I'm a not very clever, insensitive man who doesn't read between lines. I thought all men were like that, you always say that they are. So before you take any rash action that could destroy our marriage, would you mind telling me what's on your mind in short clear sentences?

He was feeling restored as he sorted his jumbled thoughts into neat categories, filed under headings such as: 1) PERFECTLY NORMAL JEALOUSY 2) VIOLENT RAGE 3) WANTING TO PUNCH A TREE BUT NOT WANTING SUBSEQUENT BROKEN FINGERS 4) WANTING TO CRY BUT NOT BEING THE TYPE 5) WANTING TO HAVE AN AFFAIR WITH WIFE'S BEST FRIEND TO PAY HER BACK BUT DESPERATELY UNATTRACTED TO ALL SUCH FRIENDS, ESPECIALLY HEATHER.

Besides he had a meeting and now they were financially

committed to this business, he had to be sensible. So he would go to his meeting then he would go home to Tess and begin rebuilding his marriage.

'Hi Tess, Heather here. Just a quick call. Took the test and it was negative. Oh well, *c'est la vie* and all that. I hope you have better luck on the baby front than me. Bye for now.'

# 17

'Remind me again why we go to church every week now?' Graham asked.

'Because we've tried everything else and none of it works,' Fiona said flatly. 'Anyway, your boss goes and we've been invited to dinner with them next week. And if we didn't go, Millie wouldn't go. And the kids like it. And I quite like it. And nobody touches you any more, so stop complaining.' Graham had become skilled at hiding his hands as soon as anyone looked at him with a hint of enthusiasm or grace.

They were in Carter's for Sunday lunch. It was now a regular date and the families had settled into the new routine. Millie was still looking her new fabulous self.

'What's it like having a whole weekend without the children?' Fiona asked. 'You must miss them dreadfully.'

Millie laughed. 'Are you kidding? I admit I miss them in the evenings. I've always loved peeping into their bedrooms when they're asleep. All the mischief is gone from their faces and they're children to me again rather than trouble-bringing changelings. But the peace is so wonderful.'

She stroked her stomach which was swelling rapidly with two babies inside her.

'And you don't mind them staying in the same house as Tim and that woman?' Tess was amazed at Millie's acceptance of the situation.

'I'm enjoying every minute,' Millie gloated, 'imagining the kids wrecking all her priceless souvenirs from her globetrotting, rubbing pasta sauce into her white sofa, scratching her floors with their tile-destroying micro machines ...'

'Millie, you've become really sadistic!' Tess exclaimed with delight.

'And I'm thoroughly enjoying it. Last night I slept for ten hours. I didn't even have to wake up to go the loo. I feel fantastic. I was even thinking of phoning you up and asking if you wanted to go clubbing!'

'Don't say another word,' Fiona complained. 'I'm still imagining ten hours of sleep. Don't spoil my fantasy!'

'Have any of you thought about the weekend that John mentioned?' Tess announced suddenly.

Everyone became quiet. John had spoken of the community weekend in two weeks' time. It would be held in a holiday camp down in Bognor Regis and would only cost £50 per family. As soon as John had mentioned it Tess envisaged all of them going there together.

We could have a great time, she'd thought.

It's our idea of hell, everyone else had thought.

'Max thinks it's a great idea, don't you?' she said. Max smiled warmly. He'd made it his new philosophy to agree that all of Tess's ideas were great. If she ever wanted to pretend to be another teacher, say of welding or kick boxing, he intended to support her, join her classes *and* stick posters up all over the neighbourhood.

He'd decided not to confront her about what he'd seen. That could open up a sore that might never heal. Instead he was going to become the husband she wanted and win her back for good.

Graham cleared his throat. He'd been coerced into going to church, there was no way he'd be spending a weekend with all those people as well. 'The thing is, Tess, we're still considering Provence for the summer.'

Fiona glared at him. I told you not to mention that in front of Tess, was the message.

But Tess wasn't upset at all. 'I assumed that you would. Obviously we won't be able to join you this year, or for the next ten years probably! But since this is the only break we'll be able to take this year, I thought you might be able to do this as well as Provence. It's only fifty pounds, after all.'

'We want to go!' Fiona's kids were shouting. 'They've got fruit machines and go-karts and wrestling matches and push-your-dad-in-the-swimming-pool competitions and all-day burger bars and donkey derbies.'

Lara joined in. 'And the best thing of all is we get to sleep in caravans!'

The other children received this information with awe. 'Wow! We've never stayed in a caravan before.'

That's because we're not caravan people, Fiona thought. We stay in villas, gîtes, sometimes hotels or apartments, even in a Spanish castle once, but never caravans. I don't like the thought of the toilets. Fiona shuddered.

'I used to love staying in caravans when I was a child,' Graham said suddenly. 'We always went to the Isle of Wight to the same campsite. They were great holidays.'

'Then why do we always go abroad and spend five thousand pounds on luxury holiday homes?' Fiona asked acidly. 'Why don't we all go to the Isle of Wight and eat fish and chips in the rain?'

'Because you always said you hated that kind of holiday,' Graham said.

'So it's all my fault? You've hated all our family holidays, is that what you're saying?'

Millie could sense the atmosphere turning nasty and intervened swiftly. 'Well, before everyone gets carried away, I think I ought to mention that I've already booked a house in France for that weekend. I arranged it before all this business with Tim; it was supposed to be an opportunity to talk. I'd completely forgotten about it until now. I was hoping you'd all join me. I can't go by myself, not without Tim. As I say, it's all paid for.' She looked at Fiona and Graham for a reaction.

'That sounds great,' Fiona agreed tentatively. 'What do you think, Graham?'

Graham preferred the sound of Bognor. He'd already imagined the thrill of the caravan. But he remembered Fiona's antipathy to the party dance scenario earlier in the week. He knew she would hate a British holiday camp. 'I think we should go,' he said gently.

'Great!' Millie exclaimed. 'And you and Max must come too!' With Lara. It won't cost anything!'

'Except the ferry and all the petrol,' Tess pointed out sadly. 'I'm sorry, Millie, it's a lovely idea but we just can't do it. Besides, Lara is looking forward to going away with all her new friends.'

She hadn't asked Max for his opinion. There was an unspoken agreement between them, that she would take care of all domestic decisions and he would comply.

Carter came over to take their orders. He sensed the gloom that had descended on the group.

'Where's your beautiful mother today?' he asked Fiona.

'At home. She said she felt tired.'

Carter interpreted this to mean that Daphne was in a great deal of pain and couldn't even bring herself to get up. He hadn't had a chance to talk to her alone since he and his rivals had delivered their ultimatum and he thought of little else at the moment.

'Did I hear you correctly? Are you all coming on the community weekend?'

'Yes!' the children shouted.

'No,' Fiona said abruptly, ignoring the cries of protest from the children. 'We can't, we're going to France that weekend.'

'Will your mother be up for that long a journey?' Carter asked in concern.

Fiona smacked herself on the forehead. 'Damn! I'd forgotten all about Mum. She can't stay at home by herself. Well, that's that then.'

Carter thought about this problem. 'Of course, your mother could always come to Bognor with us, couldn't she?'

Fiona was floored by this suggestion. Her mother going away with her three suitors but without her daughter to guide her through the potential minefield. She didn't like the sound of that.

Alison watched the hands circling the clock with tortuous slowness. I thought I had suffered the worst experience of my life last week, four hours with Tim's children confined to South London fast food establishments. I thought it would be easier here with all the countryside. I thought they would run around the fields, skipping through hedges, releasing all the pent-up energy that was causing all their behavioural problems. I thought we'd toast crumpets around the fire and snuggle up together reading Beatrix Potter stories. Instead I have unwittingly unleashed Armageddon on this innocent corner of Kent. While they were releasing their pent-up energy, it was being converted on a continual basis into an invincible force for evil and destruction. Neighbouring farmers were threatening to call for Alison's eviction after the first day.

'The thing is, miss, if people let their dogs come on our land, worrying our animals like that, we'd be able to shoot them.'

Shoot the children! Alison longed to say. Please! I'll persuade their father not to press charges. I'll get him to adopt some placid little Chinese orphans as a replacement for them. Millie won't notice the difference. Not with two more on the way. They probably all blur into one when they're tearing around, wreaking havoc wherever they go.

'Don't any of these people have children of their own?' Tim said when Alison told him of the farmers' complaints.

'The thing is, Tim, they're trespassing, they're releasing chickens which could then be killed by foxes, they're disturbing cows' milk production. These farmers are businessmen and your children are disrupting their business.'

'The countryside belongs to the people, that's what I say.'

And that was when Alison knew that she hated him. She loathed and despised everything about him including, *especially*, his children, even the two that hadn't been born yet because they would inevitably be as awful as the other four.

Was he like this at school? she asked herself. Of course he was. He just hadn't had as much time to attach his weak, reactionary opinions to quite so many subjects. At that time, he'd seemed gentle, romantic and moderately original in his determination not to conform to current cool standards. Now she realised that he could never have been cool and his originality came from an inborn inability to see his social faults and realign them correctly to acceptable norms.

What he needs, Alison decided, is a whopping great bottle of Tipp-ex poured liberally over the excesses of his personality, just to bring him back in line with his contemporaries.

And when this weekend is over, I'm going to tell him so.


'Am I allowed to talk to you or is this harassment?'

Tess jumped. Jerry had followed her to the ladies'. 'This is practically stalking,' she pointed out. 'Follow me a few steps further into the loos and we'll be in adult film territory.'

'I'm up for it if you are.'

Tess smiled. 'We are not going into the ladies' together. We're being watched as it is.'

Jerry looked around to see Heather glancing over at him nervously. He smiled and waved. She looked away quickly.

'There. She's not looking any more.'

Tess giggled. 'Go away!'

Neither of them noticed Max, who was doing a good impression of a man with a stiff neck. He kept stretching up, twisting his head and rubbing the back of his neck as if trying to release the muscles. With each stretch he would take a good look at Tess standing there talking quietly with that man. It made him very, very scared.

'I'm leaving her,' Jerry said.

Tess stopped laughing. 'Not because of me, I hope.' Although, deep down, I hope it is because of me. I would like to be loved so powerfully that I can change lives like that .

'Of course because of you. But don't worry, I won't be standing under your bedroom window singing 'Our Love Will Go On' every night.'

'Good, because I hate that song. And any other song that's played at both weddings and funerals. There's something weird about songs that fit both occasions.'

'Robbie Williams' "Angels",' Jerry suggested.

' "Love is All Around Us", Wet Wet Wet,' Tess added.

'That song from *Robin Hood, Prince of Thieves* by the man with the hair,' Jerry offered.

'Definitely that one,' Tess agreed. God, this man feels right to me, she caught herself thinking. He fits me, he suits me, I can feel something letting go inside me, I'm wondering if it might be worth having a go at releasing the rest of me, the secret bits, seeing if all of me can be fulfilled by one person.

'I've decided not to give up,' Jerry said, as he looked to one side.

'On what?' Tess asked, knowing the answer but buying some time.

'I'm going to keep on at you, even though you'll keep telling me not to, because I think you want me to. I make you smile. And I think that, one day, you'll wake up and want to smile all the time. And that's when you'll come to me.'

Tess smiled. 'You could have a long wait.'

Jerry shook his head. 'I don't think so.'

They were in the Countryside Crafts Museum that Alison had been sure would entertain the children. having ascertained that there were no animals and no priceless displays of delicate china or fragile ancient artefacts. They had proceeded with confidence.

It had started slowly, largely because Alison had fed them the stodgiest lunch she could provide of roast beef, Yorkshire pudding, roast potatoes, pasta and rice.

'Shouldn't they be having vegetables?' Tim asked, concerned by the unbalanced combination.

'I'm a doctor, I know what to feed children,' she'd snapped. She'd stayed up late on the Internet researching foods guaranteed to make children sluggish. She had been tempted to just drug them, but she didn't want to be struck off the medical register for misconduct, not unless there was no other option.

But while this meal might have brought the average child to a complete standstill, it merely provided a temporary respite for these wonderkids. After a group trip to the toilets which they described in graphic detail, they were raring to go.

And off they went.

Carly stuck a twig in the loom where a sweet old lady was weaving llama hair. One of the wooden struts snapped, causing damage later estimated at £300.

Lucy was scratching swear words into some pottery that had just been thrown and was drying before going into the oven.

Ellie was unpicking a macramé curtain that had a £95 price tag attached and Nathan was standing in front of a woman with a pram, waving an axe and screaming 'Scooby-dooby-doo!'

Tim was paralysed and wanted Millie to be here, taking charge. Alison realised that it was down to her. She opened her mouth and screamed at them.

'Carly, Lucy, Ellie, Nathan! Get over here right now. Or do I have to come over to you and beat you black and blue?'

The words had come out before she'd had a chance to remember that she was in a public place and she was a local GP.

'Only joking!' she said weakly.

But the looks of distaste around her told her that she was in need of a new joke-writer. Well, sod you, she thought. I bet you've all yelled at your kids and said things you don't mean.

So her local reputation was finished but the thought of whacking those brats had given her a momentary thrill of pleasure.

All four children burst into tears, big wet noisy tears. Alison was horrified. Once more, everyone turned to stare at her. She rushed over to them. 'Ssh!' she whispered. 'If you stop crying, I'll give you five pounds each.'

'That's no way to teach children how to behave!' a passer-by commented.

'But he bribes them,' she shouted, pointing to Tim. 'He's their dad. I hardly know them. I don't even like them.'

The tears, which had stopped abruptly at the promise of £5, started up again. Even louder, wetter, noisier.

'Oh just shut up, the lot of you!' Alison screamed.

Tim sprang into action. 'Come on children, let's go.' He pushed past Alison and collected his children, guiding them towards the car park. As they passed Alison, each little angel graced her with a smile of supreme smugness.

She stopped herself from screaming again. She couldn't take any more condemnation from the misguided onlookers. She followed Tim and his brood to the car. They drove back to her cottage in silence. When they arrived, Tim sent the children to pack.

They responded with the first display of pure, attractive, child-like joy that Alison had ever witnessed.

'I've seen a side of you today that I didn't know you possessed,' Tim said slowly. 'I know you've never been a mother so you can't know much about children, but the way you shouted at them today was wicked.'

Alison didn't bother defending herself. She'd worked out that parents are completely deluded when it comes to their children. They see only the good things, although she would like to know exactly what good things Tim and Millie could see in their kids.

'I'm sorry you don't like my children,' Tim continued. 'But they are part of me, and a good part, I think. If you can't accept them and they can't accept you, then there's no future for us.'

Alison's mouth dropped open. He's dumping me? Again? I was going to throw him out but I let him stay out of the goodness of my heart until the day when I could dump him with a clear conscience and even up the score from 20 years ago.

How dare he? How dare ...? Before she could have the chance to deliver the speech of her life, Tim had gone to help his kids pack. 'Oh by the way,' he said coldly, turning round, 'I forgot to tell you. Your husband phoned last week.' Then he went back to his packing.

There was no point in yelling at him for not passing on the message, she thought. She wasn't going to waste another ounce of her energy on this man. She sat in her favourite armchair, lifting her arm briefly to scrape off a clot of congealed egg yolk. And she concentrated on her future without Tim, without his brats. With Gabriel, perhaps. With a baby, perhaps. But definitely with someone who lived a long way from here. And definitely someone with no children of his own.

'You're early,' Millie said, accusingly.

Tim looked at her as if he didn't recognise her. He *didn't* recognise her. With each day he'd been away, she'd changed further. And not just changing back into the girl he'd first known. She'd moved on and become someone totally new.

'Something's different about you,' he said.

'Contact lenses.'

'I thought you were finding them uncomfortable.'

Millie smiled. 'I'm getting used to them. Anyway, you haven't said why you're early.' Bet I can guess.

'Can I come in?' he pleaded. 'It's cold out here.'

Millie considered this then opened the door to let him pass.

'I've left her,' he announced.

Millie sat down and watched him, waiting for more. 'Is that it?'

Tim was confused. 'I've left her for good. And nothing ever happened. I told you it wouldn't and it didn't. I've stayed completely faithful to you.'

Millie applauded slowly. 'Is that what you want? Praise? Congratulations?'

Tim swallowed awkwardly. 'I just want you to take me back. I'll do anything. *Anything*. I made a terrible mistake. I missed you. I missed the children. I missed our life.'

'So the woman with the cheap vest – what about her?'

'She's leaving the country apparently.' I've driven her away once more, he thought. The unfinished business remains unfinished.

'And the reasons you left? What about them?' Millie was going to make him face everything. He almost wished he were back at the Countryside Craft Museum, the horror and pity of strangers being far preferable to this piercing dissection of his life.

'I was never going to leave you,' he began, raising a hand when

Millie was about to protest, 'but I did betray you and that led to you throwing me out, so I accept what you say. As for why I did it? I love my life but it's not perfect.'

'Really?' Millie observed drily. 'Mine is.'

'I know, I know, nobody's life is perfect. But you can't help wondering sometimes if perfection was an available option somewhere in your life and you missed it.'

'And you thought that you might have had a perfect life with Alison?' Millie asked.

'I know it sounds stupid . . .'

'We're agreed on something, at least.'

Time went on. 'But don't you sometimes like to fantasise that you have a parallel life running alongside your own, a better one?'

Millie closed her eyes. Of course I do, you idiot, but you'll never know how that fantasy plays out, that's my security blanket.

Tim was encouraged by Millie's silence. Or at least it was better than mockery. 'We were only teenagers. She was my first love, the only one before you.' He looked at Millie, her eyes were still closed. 'So I never had any experience of a relationship running its course, becoming stale until the fizz died out. I just assumed that it carried on ascending endlessly at the same rate it was climbing when Alison left.'

Millie understood. 'So then you got married and learned about relationships going stale and the fizz dying?'

Tim looked ashamed. 'I thought it was because there was something wrong with the marriage, that maybe if I'd followed Alison and stayed with her, I could have avoided that.'

'You sound as if you're still eighteen, Tim,' Millie said with disgust. 'Isn't it about time you grew up?'

Fiona couldn't ignore it any longer. She picked up the phone and dialled the number, careful to prefix it with 141 so she couldn't be traced back.

'Hello?' the woman's voice answered. 'Hello?' She sighed. 'If this is a pervert, I'm wearing a thick woolly jumper, dungarees and old slippers. If you find that exciting then I'm terribly sad for you . . .'

Fiona slammed the phone down. That didn't help her at all. She knew it was a private number and that a woman answered. That was enough to worry her.

The phone bill had arrived and she'd just been glancing through the breakdown to make sure the kids weren't phoning chatlines or entering hundreds of votes in *Pop Idol IV* or whatever number they were up to. It was the timing of the call that had leaped out. Nobody used the phone in the middle of the night, not even Fiona who knew that she spent an unhealthy proportion of her life phoning friends.

It had to have been Graham. Walburga had been at a friend's that night and Daphne and the children were unwakeable from the second they fell asleep until they were dragged lethargically from their beds in the morning.

So he'd phoned a woman at one o'clock in the morning. Even worse, he'd spoken to her for over an hour.

She needed to talk to someone about this, anyone but Graham; she was far too scared of what he might say. She started with Tess.

'She's out,' Max said curtly.

'Where?' Fiona asked. 'It's Sunday night.'

'Perhaps you'd like to tell her that yourself. Heather phoned and so Tess of course had to abandon her family to go to her. Even though the shop is opening tomorrow and I could do with some support.'

Fiona waited until he paused for breath then cut in quickly, made her excuses and hung up.

Blimey, they haven't even started this business and they're already in trouble. I thought this was going to solve everything.

Tess sat in Heather's flat, drinking tea, wanting a big glass of wine but not trusting herself.

'I'm so sorry,' she said helplessly.

Heather rubbed her face roughly. 'I knew it was coming, so I shouldn't be surprised. It was just too much on top of finding out that I wasn't pregnant.'

'Did he tell you why?' Tess asked, averting her eyes.

'The usual. Not sure of his feelings. Wouldn't be fair to make the commitment if he wasn't a hundred per cent sure that this was right for us both. Blah di blah.'

'Perhaps that was all there was to it,' Tess suggested hopefully.

Heather shook her head. 'I know him better than that. He's seeing someone else.'

Tess looked shocked. She felt guilty but was hoping that willpower alone would transform her feelings of guilt into a look of innocent surprise. 'I'm sure you're wrong! What makes you think that?'

Heather narrowed her mouth to show her distaste. 'I can tell. Anyone could tell. In fact I was wondering if he said anything to you.'

Now Tess *knew* she looked guilty. 'Why would he?'

'I just noticed him talking to you at Carter's. And I know you see him at school sometimes. And you're his dance partner.'

Put it like that, lining up the accusations one after the other, she couldn't believe that Heather hadn't worked out what was going on here. The fact that she hadn't made the connection stabbed Tess deeply. Heather trusted her so implicitly that she couldn't even pay lip service to the idea that her friend would betray her so cruelly.

She breathed in and out, counting steadily to slow her heart down, the way she'd been learning in her intensive yoga course. 'He hasn't said anything to me,' she said calmly.

Liar liar.

'What were you talking about this morning?' Heather asked. She looked interested to Tess rather than suspicious.

Tess rummaged around in her expanding storebox of lies, excuses and prevarications. 'He was asking if we were all going on the community weekend.'

'And are you?' Heather looked hopeful.

'Yes. Well, we're going and my friend's mother-in-law is coming too.' Heather looked confused. 'Don't ask,' Tess warned.

'Well I'm looking forward to it,' Heather said. 'I'll need a break by then. Mind you, it'll be a bit awkward with Jerry there.'

'Is he going as well?' Tess said without thinking. 'He didn't mention that.'

'Of course he is. He's the main organiser. He handles all the sleeping arrangements.'

'She's out,' Tim said.

'Tim! What are you doing there?' Fiona hadn't expected to hear his voice.

'I've moved back. Sort of.'

'What does that mean?' Fiona wanted to know, temporarily distracted from her own problem.

'I'm sleeping in the den, which I've got to turn into a mini-nursery. Only then will she consider letting me move back into our bedroom.'

Sounds like a good deal, Fiona thought. Save money on a decorator, keep Tim busy and out of trouble and punish him at the same time. Well done, Millie.

'So where is she?' Fiona asked.

'She's gone to a bar to read a book.'

Fiona was very confused. 'Is that code for something?'

Tim sighed. 'No, that's part of the deal, too. Once a week, she gets to go out by herself to sit in a bar and read a book.'

Fiona was even more bemused. 'Why would she want to do that?' Then she remembered Millie's children and understood perfectly.

'You could call her on her mobile, if you like. I'm not allowed to,' he said gloomily, 'but she didn't say anything about her friends.'

Fiona thought about Millie enjoying her weekly dose of peace for which she'd paid dearly and decided not to disturb her.

'By the way,' Tim added. 'You said something about a code. Millie tells me that we go to church now. Is that code for something nice?' He couldn't disguise the note of hope.

Fiona laughed. 'No code. We go to church. But don't worry, you'll enjoy it. They take your children away and amuse them for an hour while you get to sit with Millie in peace.'

I can live with that, Tim thought.

Who next? Fiona was becoming desperate. She was not an introspective person, she knew that. She needed other people, lots of contact, plenty of interaction. But this was Sunday and her two best friends were unavailable.

She heard the door close. Of course! 'Walburga!' she called.

The German au pair came into the kitchen nervously. 'It was not my fault. I told them they were not to touch. I will buy a new one tomorrow.'

Fiona stared at her. 'What are you talking about? I'm not going to tell you off.'

Walburga almost fainted with relief. And surprise, because this was usually why she was called in.

'Sit down,' Fiona said, patting the stool at the breakfast bar.

294

Walburga obeyed. Well, that's a first, Fiona thought cynically. The girl is normally pathologically incapable of following any simple instructions. And I thought the Germans were famous for their obedience.

'Would you like a cup of tea?' she asked.

Walburga looked terrified. She still hadn't recovered from Daphne's attack on her tea-making abilities. Not understanding how one warmed a teapot the English way was clearly as serious as dropping bombs on East London. More so perhaps.

'I'll make it,' Fiona reassured the girl. Good Lord. Is this worth it?

She presented Walburga with an acceptably weak cup of tea and then sat opposite her.

'You have lots of boyfriends, don't you?' she asked.

'Oh yes!' Walburga said, cheering up considerably. 'Many, many.'

'And I expect you'd like to get married one day?'

'Oh yes, one day. When I'm very old like you.'

I'll ignore that, Fiona decided. 'Mr Graham and I have been married for many years, I expect you can't imagine how that feels.'

Walburga sipped the tea. 'My parents are married for many years. My mother shouts at my father as you do to Mr Graham.'

Not exactly the rapport I was aiming for but better than nothing. Marginally. Fiona ploughed on painfully. 'How would your mother feel if your father, to whom she has been married for many, many years, started telephoning other women in the middle of the night.'

It was a long, complicated sentence and Walburga took a while to get to the end of it. Fiona sat back waiting for a half-intelligent response. Or even a stupid one. Anything will do. I'm desperate.

Fiona watched as Walburga's expression turned into one of abject horror.

'No, no, no!' she shouted.

Fiona jumped up. 'What is it? What's wrong?'

'It is not me! I am not a girl like that!'

'What isn't you? What are you talking about?'

'I am not telephoning Mr Graham in the night. I don't have enough money for mobile phone card. It cannot be me! I am a nice girl!'

'Oh no Walburga!' Fiona exclaimed. 'I didn't mean you! I wasn't accusing you! I know that you are a nice girl!'

Walburga wasn't listening. She was ranting away in German. When she calmed down, slightly, she turned on Fiona. 'You are not a nice person! You say bad things to me. I will tell the agency that you are cruel and unfair to me! Your husband is old and ugly! I have handsome English boyfriends. I do not want Mr Graham! I am going to the agency. I will find nice family with a nice mother. And I will insist that the mother has a nice mother too! '

Then she ran upstairs to pack.

Fiona rummaged around in the cupboard until she found Daphne's secret stash of Bombay Red. She poured herself a large glass. That went well, she thought.

About an hour later, Graham arrived home from the park with the children. 'Fi! There's a taxi outside.' Then he saw Walburga was dragging her suitcase downstairs.

'What's the matter?' he asked. 'Where are you going?'

'Do not talk to me!' the girl shouted. 'Your wife is a very bad person. I will tell the agency. They will not send nice girls here again.'

She inched past Graham, anxious not to make any physical contact with him. Then she left.

Graham walked into the kitchen, where he found Fiona halfway through a bottle of wine.

'What's going on? What have you done to upset Walburga?'

Fiona raised her hands in the air. 'I've no idea. I think she's unhinged. She's definitely not a proper German, not a bit compliant. Millie had a German au pair last year and she was nothing like Walburga.'

Graham sensed that it might be wise not to discuss this now. Or ever. He took the children upstairs to get them ready for the ritual night-time bath chaos.

Fiona swirled the wine around the glass. She couldn't get the phone call out of her head. Even the thought of being barred by the au pair agency (which was fairly devastating) couldn't shake her growing discomfort. I really *really* need to talk to someone.

But there wasn't anyone. Until she heard the door slam again.

'I'm back,' announced Daphne.

# 18

There were balloons tied to every pipe and fitting, pinned to every door and window frame.

WELCOME TO HEAVERBURY ORGANIQUE! the signs announced. It was 7.30 in the morning and the café was already full. Max had taken advice from his partners and kept the breakfast menu simple and short. Free-range eggs, sausages, bacon and mushrooms from local organic farmers, bread baked by a team of six women from Tess's yoga group. Two varieties of tea, two of coffee, three fruit juices. That was it.

Turnover was swift. Local and passing workers popped in for a quick cooked breakfast and were in and out within 25 minutes. There was even a queue at one point.

'This is amazing!' Max said to Tess, who was helping out with the serving. Lara had slept over at a friend's house so they'd both been able to get to the café before six a.m. to get things set up. 'It's much more streamlined than our last place. I wish I'd known that we didn't have to make everything so complicated for it to work.'

Tess brooded on those words all morning.

Carter, Rav and Archie were all on hand for the morning to share in the success. There was still some strain between them as they continued to wait for Daphne to tell them who she'd chosen, but they put their differences behind them for now.

'Is the shop ready?' Archie asked.

Max nodded. 'Shop' was something of an exaggeration. It was just a corner of the restaurant area divided off by crates of fruit and vegetables but it was a good selection.

'What you have to remember about Heaverbury,' Archie had explained, 'is that the residents aren't rich. They're not prepared to waste money on luxuries but they will spend a bit extra on quality. So yes to organic carrots, apples and potatoes but no to olives picked by Tuscan virgins.'

Max had used admirable self-restraint to stick to the basics and he was pleased with the results. Even Tess was impressed as the morning progressed and a steady flow of customers depleted the stocks quickly.

She found herself comparing this new venture to the old Organique with its impractical pretensions and complete disregard for profitability. She observed how every square centimetre of floor and counterspace was being efficiently utilised, displaying products that people actually wanted to buy. I think Max has finally got it right, she decided, smiling to herself, pleased for him despite the fact that he was neglecting his family to pursue his ambition.

Yet she wondered how he could allow anything to take precedence over his love and commitment for Lara, if not herself. To her eyes, this was the equivalent of an affair, a re-evaluation of priorities in which his own desires were rated as more important than the needs of his family.

The gulf between them widened further.

'Er, Rav?' Max asked. 'Is this Bombay wine really organic?' He'd just noticed that all the wine had been relabelled as Bombay Organic Rouge and was now occupying a large chunk of the limited floor space.

'Of course!' Rav exclaimed. 'If it says "organic" on the label, that means it's organic, doesn't it?'

'There's a bit more to that,' Max explained.

Rav made an impatient gesture with his arms. 'Well, if someone wants to go to Bombay, track down my family, find one of them that speaks English then ask them what they put on the grapes, then lovely jubbly as my little girls say! In the meanwhile, I decide if it's organic!'

That was good enough for Max.

Tess and Max worked well together and enjoyed lunch once the shop and café had closed for the morning.

'So how was Heather?' Max asked, trying very hard to sound as if he was interested, which he wasn't.

'She was feeling really down. She and Jerry have separated.'

Now Max *was* interested. 'Why?'

'Why do any couples split up?' Tess said vaguely, wanting to discourage this line of talk.

'Lots of reasons. Perhaps he was beating her. Perhaps she was beating him. Perhaps he wore socks in bed or tucked his vest into his pants. Perhaps there was somebody else ...'

Tess poured out some water. 'I don't know and neither does Heather. But it wasn't for any dramatic reasons. When are you going to pick up some more stock?'

It was a clumsy attempt to change the subject but Max let it pass. He knew that he wouldn't get any more out of her but he was even more worried than before. Still, the business was off to a brilliant start. If they could get on top of their money problems, he was sure that the marital hiccups would fade away.

It wasn't that he forgot everything that Tess had said about the necessity to keep working on their relationship, it was just he was sure he knew better.

I've been thinking too, he reminded himself. It was the money that caused all the trouble in the first place. She never kissed other men when we were living in Clapham and I was working much longer hours then. No, it's definitely the money. If I take care of that, then our marriage will take care of itself.

In a couple of weeks, when she sees how well we're doing and how good our future looks, she won't need to look elsewhere for reassurance or whatever it is she gets from that man. Then she'll come back to me.

'Hi Graham, it's me.'

'I asked you not to phone me at home. That's why I gave you my work number. This is just for emergencies.'

'I thought that, as you called so late last week, it was safe for me to do the same.'

Fiona and the children were in bed and Graham did tend to stay up later, to have some time to himself to read or listen to music. But he was terrified that this would be the one time his wife was woken by the phone.

He hated all the sneaking around. Once he had it clear in his own mind what he was going to do about Eloise, exactly what role he intended to play in her life, then he'd go to Fiona and explain what had been happening.

But there was one important issue to settle first. Before he could get onto that, Christine explained why she was phoning.

'I've spoken to Eloise and told her that you're prepared to meet her. She was crying when she heard the news. I can't tell you what that means to her.'

'Yes, but . . .'

'And here's the best thing. You mentioned that you were going to be in Provence the weekend after next, in Fayence, I think you said. Well, my parents have a small apartment in Castellane, only about twenty kilometres away. I'm going to take Eloise there. We could all meet up.'

'You're putting me on the spot,' Graham objected.

'What? I do hope you're not going to say that you've changed your mind.'

'No, nothing like that. I know I have obligations to Eloise but I have a condition to make.'

Christine said nothing, so Graham went on. 'I've given this more thought than you can imagine, believe me, and I've decided that I don't want to see you again. I can't, actually. Of course I'll see our daughter but I think it could be stirring up trouble for *us* to meet.'

'Do you hate me that much?' Christine asked quietly.

'I don't hate you at all.' Or maybe I do. 'But it took a long time to get my life back together after you left me. You damaged a part of me that never recovered.' He hesitated, not trusting himself to keep his voice level as emotions that had been weighted down and buried for many years floated to the surface.

'I'm sorry,' Christine said.

Graham closed his eyes. At last, he laughed to himself, she's finally apologised. He was so surprised by her words that he couldn't help what he said next. 'What I really want to know is why you married someone else so quickly after jilting me. I mean I can sort of understand how the thought of marrying was so terrifying in its finality that you ran away from it. But, in that case, why would you actually go through with it just months later? And with someone you didn't know as well as you knew me?'

He'd done it now, asked the question, taken the chance that the answer might be worse than the lifetime of uncertainty. The length of time Christine was taking to construct a response filled him with dread.

'I didn't want to marry you,' she said, finally and terribly. 'Or anybody else. Not at that time, on that particular afternoon. It was too much to take in, finding out I was pregnant the day before. All of a sudden, within twenty-four hours, the rest of my life was mapped out: one minute I'm a person in my own right, being loved for myself, preparing for a great adventure with you, the next I face a future of being married with a child. Bang, there go the next eighteen years.'

Graham watched his knuckles whiten as his clench tightened around the receiver.

'Then why didn't you just tell me that? Why did you have to run away? You must have known that I'd understand! We talked about everything, we understood each other. I would have waited, postponed the wedding until you were ready, done anything to make you happy.'

Christine's voice was breaking now. 'I know that. But you have to see it from my point of view. I was terrified. I felt as if I was going mad. And I was only twenty-one! I just thought if I ran away, pretended that none of it was happening, then it would all disappear.'

Graham exhaled in frustration at the stupidity of the girl he'd once adored for her keen intellect.

'I know, I know,' Christine said. 'You wouldn't believe how many times I've wished I could turn back the clock and do things differently.'

'But you didn't. You didn't even bother getting in touch with me when the baby was born, *my* baby. You just upped and married someone else.'

'I'd accepted the idea of a child by then. I'd had to. Once I knew that I was going to keep the baby, I felt different. And when David came along and was willing to take us both on, well then . . .'

Graham could almost hear her helpless shrug. He wanted to kill her at this very moment. 'Then why,' he said, 'WHY didn't you come back to me when you "felt different"? Did you think I might have changed my mind? That I might have rejected you and *our* baby? I don't understand. I just don't understand.'

He looked down at his hand, which was suddenly wet. You're crying, he commented to himself abstractly. After all those months of crying every day, I'd managed to control myself for years. And now I'm starting again.

'I can't explain it,' Christine said weakly, 'not properly because I don't really understand it myself. Something happened to me when I ran away from you. I suppose I detached myself, emotionally and mentally. It was a kind of breakdown, that's the only way I can describe it. I just got on with my new life and by the time I came to my senses and realised the enormity of what I'd done, I knew that it was too late to go back. What good would that have done? Eloise accepted David as her daddy.'

Once more, the silent shrug assailed Graham. He struggled with this muddled explanation that made sense in a perverse way. But he'd always believed that the truth would make him feel better. And, so far, it wasn't working. He took a deep breath. It was his turn now for self-defence.

'Thank you for telling me this,' he said abruptly. 'It might have been kinder for you to at least have said all this years ago but that's done now. It took me a long time but I found a way of moving on. So let me repeat myself. I'll see our daughter but I don't ever want to see you again. You might just "have another breakdown" and cause even more damage the second time around. And this time I have a family of my own to protect. Anyway, this is not up for negotiation. You said that this was about Eloise, so leave me to get to know her and stay away from me.'

'I'll get back to you.' Christine sounded shaky as she put the phone down.

Graham stared at the phone. Well, I did it. I made her tell me. I took it in and I stayed calm. And then I told her that I wouldn't let her hurt me again. But it was hard, so hard. She will never know how badly I want to see her, to tie her to a chair and refuse to let her go until she's told me every single thought that has passed through her mind from the moment she decided to leave me until the moment she contacted me 20 years later.

Fiona lay in bed waiting. She hadn't dropped off by the time the phone rang and had been startled by the sound. She couldn't pick the bedroom extension up, not without Graham knowing that she was listening. So she just had to imagine what he was saying and to whom.

But she managed to rein in her panic. She'd attained a shaky level of perspective that day. For the first time in her life, she was grateful to have been able to talk to her mother.

*

302

'If you're going to criticise Graham, then we can just stop this right now.'

'I didn't say anything,' Daphne was indignant.

'You did that look.'

'What look?'

'The one that you always gave me when I'd been on the phone to a boy you didn't like.'

Daphne sighed. 'Do you remember every tiny thing I ever said or did that annoyed, upset or hurt you?'

'Yes, I do,' Fiona said defiantly.

Daphne looked at her in wonder. 'I'm amazed there's any room left in your head for pleasant thoughts when you're so full of bitterness.'

Fiona scowled. 'I knew this was a bad idea.'

'Well it wasn't my idea. At least you can't blame me for that. You were sitting there drinking *my* wine, rubbing your head, then suddenly you plunge into this story about a phone number. I wasn't even going to ask why you were getting drunk, I didn't want to be accused of interfering.'

Fiona began pacing the kitchen edgily. 'It's not "a story about a phone number", it's something real. Graham did phone this woman in the middle of the night and he didn't tell me and I don't know why and I don't know what he's thinking any more which makes me wonder if I ever did, to which the answer is probably "no" and that frightens me!'

'Am I allowed to say something now?' Daphne asked with utmost caution as Fiona came up for oxygen.

'As long as you're not going to be hostile or negative or judge-mental.'

'Maybe you should send for that lovely vicar then.'

'Ha ha,' Fiona snorted then glared at her mother, which Daphne took as her cue to say something – obviously the wrong thing, she accepted with inevitability.

'Your father was not a good husband. He wasn't honest or particularly kind and he let me down all the time. But when he left, it wasn't a shock to me. I'd known for years that there were other women. I always knew when he was lying even though I defended him to anyone who called him a worthless piece of humanity.'

'If this is supposed to be making me feel better, it's not

working,' Fiona said. 'You know how much I hate it when you say those things about Dad.'

'Just for once in your selfish little life, will you accept that not everything in the world is about you!'

Fiona was taken aback. While her mother had always been a moaner and a nagger and a martyr of Olympic standards, she'd never been a shouter.

'I'm sorry,' Daphne said, not very graciously in Fiona's opinion, 'but we're not talking about *your* father, we're talking about *my* marriage.'

Fiona mumbled under her breath, never willing to let her mother think she held the upper hand in any argument.

'What I'm trying to say to you, and failing it seems, is that you know in your heart if Graham is a good or a bad husband. That doesn't mean you know all there is to know about him or that he won't have secrets, but you'll know if your marriage is good or bad. And I know you've made it your main guiding principle in life to disagree with anything I say, but I happen to think Graham is a good man, a good husband, a good father and you have a good marriage. So if at this time a few of his actions appear odd, then at least see them in the context of a long and happy marriage where you've had fewer of these worries than most women. There! I've said my piece, so shoot me down.'

God, Fiona thought. It galls me that she could be right. I'm not going to let her know that I'm grateful for this. I don't want to establish a precedent. The next thing I know, she'll expect me to top up her roots or go shopping for orthopaedic shoes with her or drink cocktails with rude names and umbrellas at lunchtime after fun shopping trips. She might even start sharing her gynaecological problems with me. She shuddered.

'Do you want to hear my problem?' Daphne said reluctantly.

No! Fiona wanted to scream. No more intimacy for today. Let's not make a habit of this, please!

'Is it anything to do with hysterectomies?'

'Of course it's not,' Daphne snapped.

'OK then.'

'It's about Carter, Archie and Rav.'

'No, no, no!' Fiona cried. 'Please! Anything but men problems! Mothers don't talk to their daughters about things like that. It's not ... proper. I know it's the sort of thing Joan Collins would do, but she has no sense of propriety. Ask me about indigestion remedies or squirrel-proof bird tables, that's what mothers and daughters ought to talk about.'

Daphne stared at her daughter. 'I wasn't going to talk about sex.'

Fiona stuck her fingers in her ears. 'La la la la la la. I CAN'T HEAR YOU. La la la la la la. Have you stopped talking about it yet?'

'Oh for goodness' sake, grow up, Fiona! My legs and my back hurt like hell and I feel I could cheerfully die. Now I want to ask you a simple question. Are you going to listen to me or not?'

Fiona swallowed uncomfortably and nodded. It was that or make more tea. There were no other options. It wasn't quite a fireside scene from *Little Women*, but Fiona and Daphne made a brave attempt at discussing the respective merits of Archie, Rav and Carter. They didn't giggle or bond but they managed to get through the conversation without bringing up past grievances, real or imaginary. That was a miracle in the history of mother/daughter relationships.

Fiona cleared her throat. 'I suppose we don't have to worry about what they look like.'

Daphne became indignant. 'Why not? Because we're too old for any of that? Because all I'll actually be looking for is the ability to push me around in a wheelchair and change my bedpan when I become totally dotty?'

Fiona sighed. 'That wasn't what I meant. I just thought you'd be less interested in the shallow things. Dad was a handsome man, after all, and look how that turned out.'

Daphne pressed her lips together. 'I happen to think these three men are all handsome as well. I mean, Carter is very distinguished, Rav is exotic and Archie is . . .'

'. . . a bit like a geriatric country and western singer?' Fiona suggested.

Daphne glared at her. 'They are all good men and you are judging them as being of little value because they are not young. Any woman would feel very fortunate to marry any of them. Look at how Rav cares for his grandchildren while running a shop. And Carter is such a kind man, the way he mourned his wife is testimony to the respect he feels for women.'

'And Archie?' Fiona asked, careful not to sound flippant.

305

Daphne smiled wistfully. 'Archie is just so alive, so unafraid to be what he wants to be.'

Fiona looked at her mother incredulously. 'Are you actually thinking of getting married?'

Daphne shrugged. 'I don't know, I might just shack up with one of them.'

Fiona slammed her wine glass on the table and prepared the 'outraged daughter' speech until she caught Daphne chuckling silently.

'You get that complete lack of sense of humour from your father,' Daphne said cheerfully.

And Fiona almost laughed. But this was her mother and it didn't do to encourage her.

'What do you mean, you're out with your mother?' Tess said. 'Are you taking her to the doctor? Or off to buy suppositories or something?'

'No,' Fiona whispered. 'We're going shopping.'

'What sort of shopping?' Tess wanted to know. 'Coffins? Shotguns? Rat poison?'

'Clothes shopping. I'll explain later. Bye.'

Tess wondered if she should call the police and report Daphne for kidnapping and brainwashing. Or maybe Fiona was having some kind of breakdown. She'd been very stressed lately and Max said she'd been anxious to talk to her yesterday.

She'd hoped to be able to speak to Fiona about Max. He'd gone from being the perfect doting husband, a role which lasted three days, to Businessman of the Year, spending his every minute working, talking about work or thinking about work.

If this is his way of telling me that our marriage is the second most important item on his list of priorities, then I've got the message. Fiona would understand without Tess having to explain all her fears. She'd been through this with Tess once before. Thank God for old friends, she thought, although if she's going to have a nervous breakdown, I wish she'd wait for a more stable period in my life. Only joking, she thought. Except I'm not.

She stood shivering at the bus stop with her shopping. I'll always read manifestos to see where politicians stand on public transport before I vote in the future, she told herself. Oh yes, and I'll always vote.

'Need a lift?' Heather pulled up and Tess jumped in happily.

'Thanks, I was freezing out there.'

'Are you in a hurry? Only I have to make a detour to drop off some papers with my ex-husband.'

'No problem,' Tess said. 'It'll give me a chance to thaw out.'

'And save on your central heating at home,' Heather pointed out.

Tess blushed because that was exactly what she'd been thinking. 'I can't believe how quickly I've got round to changing my whole way of thought. I used to leave the heating on all day and night in the winter.'

'And now you switch it off and put on extra cardies?'

Tess laughed but she was still not comfortable discussing her financial situation with anyone. It's only when you've got money that you're happy to talk about it, she now understood.

Heather's ex-husband lived in Kingston. It took about 20 minutes to get there. As they drove around the back streets, Tess could see the property values increasing dramatically. They eventually pulled into the drive of an imposing detached Edwardian house. Tess knew enough about current prices to estimate that this was probably worth over £500,000.

'Heather, I thought you said that your husband lost all your money.'

'He did,' Heather agreed, 'but then he made it all back and a shedload more.'

She got out and rang the doorbell. Tess watched a plain man with expensively styled hair and made-to-measure clothes take an envelope from Heather and exchange a few cold words before closing the door.

'Amicable divorce then?' Tess commented sarcastically.

'The worst. Although I don't know why he's complaining. He was so angry at me for refusing to go back to him that he was absolutely determined to make a success of his next business. And he did. It was the perfect revenge.'

'I don't mean to be cynical, but did you never think of going back to him once he was solvent again? You were resorting to stealing from the church, you were so desperate!'

'Of course I thought about it.'

'But you didn't want to go back on the stand you'd taken?' Tess asked.

Heather laughed. 'You have too high an opinion of me. I would have gone back to him like a shot but he'd found someone else by then.'

'God, I'm sorry, Heather.'

'Don't be.'

But as they drove back to Crappy Valley, Tess caught herself wondering why we ever take big decisions when we can't know the future. Isn't it better to just let yourself get carried along with the flow then, if it all goes wrong, you don't have to blame yourself and torment yourself with the what-ifs?


'We meet again!' Graham said in a bad French accent. 'Still alone?'

Millie put her book down, pleased to see him. 'Only you know about this place. I don't even tell Tim.'

'I always find myself glancing in when I pass.'

'So you're making it a regular thing to walk the last couple of miles home?' Millie asked, remembering how he'd come to discover her hideaway on that first occasion.

Graham smiled, flattered that she would have remembered. 'Yes and only you know that. So now we each know the other's secret!'

'Let's shake on it.' Millie offered her hand. Graham took her hand, sealing their pact. It felt good to them both.

'Shall I leave you to it?' Graham asked, not wanting to intrude.

'That's OK,' Millie said. 'To tell you the truth, sometimes I get a bit lonely here but I made such a big deal about insisting on my right to continue with this on a weekly basis that I feel obliged to keep it up.'

'Sometimes you wish you could just sit here and read with someone else?'

Millie leant forward. 'Yes! That's exactly how I feel.'

'Me too,' Graham agreed. 'I wish Fiona could just sit down in the evening with a book. I'd love her company, but she has to be moving around or talking or doing something every minute of the day. I find her exhausting. But don't tell her I said so!'

'I won't.' Millie laughed.

Graham looked at Millie appraisingly. 'It's funny how we never really know someone. We've spent so much time together but I never knew you were a reader.'

'That's about it for deep hidden secrets,' Millie said lightly. 'You can stop searching now. The rest is just what you see.'

'Fiona always compares you to a chameleon,' Graham told her. 'And now I see why. When you're with her, you're chatty and superficial. When you're with Tess, you're more introspective. And right now, you're the ideal reading companion, quiet, self-possessed, interesting.'

Millie looked embarrassed. 'I don't do it on purpose, it's a habit.'

'Where does it come from?'

'I was an only child, like Tess and Max, but I think they got a bit luckier with their parents. My mum and dad wanted a big family except I was all they got. But they didn't revise their original expectations, so they made me feel that I had to live the lives and fulfil the dreams of at least four children. I had to be sporty and funny and make Airfix submarines for Dad and be clever and play the piano and win mini beauty contests for my mum. In the end it came naturally. I could switch any part of me on or off at will. And I still can.'

'So when you're not switching bits of you on or off, who are you?' Graham asked.

Millie looked at him as if the question made no sense. 'I'm a mother, of course!'

Graham persisted. 'But what will you do when your kids have all grown up and left you?'

'I don't know,' Millie admitted. I might travel the world, she thought. Like Alison.

Daphne was enjoying the afternoon out. Archie had invited her to accompany him on a trip to one of his farm suppliers in Kent. He had bought her a hip flask and filled it with Bombay Organic Rouge for the journey.

'That's a lovely thoughtful present,' Daphne said gratefully.

'You'll need it,' Archie admitted. 'This truck doesn't have suspension to speak of and, once it's full up with fruit and veg, we'll be scraping along the road, feeling every tiny bump and pothole.'

Daphne had anticipated this and had taken an extra dose of painkillers. Fiona had talked her into it. 'It won't put you in a coma, Mum,' she'd insisted, 'but you'll be less likely to yell at the poor man every time he changes gear.'

'I'm not that bad,' Daphne had protested.

'Of course you are. Unless you're telling me that I'm the only one you yell at all the time?'

'Fiona!' warned Daphne.

'I know, I know. I'm not the centre of the universe.' Fiona mimicked her mother's voice wickedly.

'Well if you're going to be rude, I may as well be going.' She stormed out of the door. Well she wanted to storm out of the door. In fact, she limped to the door, making a grunting noise like a tennis player every time she put her right foot down.

During the journey, Daphne didn't bother hiding the regular swigs she was taking from the flask. 'That's what I like about being with people my own age,' she said, 'not having to hide my aches and pains because I know I'm not the only one whose body is letting her down.'

'I can relate to that. Do you want to hear about my polyps? Archie asked.

'Absolutely not,' Daphne said firmly. 'I refuse to spend one more second thinking or talking about ailments. And if you so much as tell me where your polyps are, then I will set my daughter on you with instructions that she is to give you her opinion on how old people should live their lives. If you're not screaming for forgiveness after five minutes of that, then your pain threshold is higher than mine.'

'You're lucky having your family around you,' Archie said after ten miles of companionable silence. 'Even though your daughter is a right pain in the backside, if you don't mind my saying so.'

'Feel free,' Daphne said. 'While we've got this truce going on, I quite miss annoying her. You can do it for me, if you like.'

'I miss having young Max in the minicab office with me. I know he was only there for a few weeks but I got used to having him around. He used to tell me all his problems.'

'It's good to be needed,' Daphne agreed. 'Anything to put off the day when we're the ones doing all the needing.'

And they drove the rest of the journey without feeling that they had to talk. There were too many things they each wanted to think about.


'What's all this?' Millie looked around the room in pleasant surprise. The entire ground floor of the house was filled with lit candles and Tim was standing in the hall wearing the jumper she'd bought him last Christmas that didn't fit and that he hated.

'I've made us dinner,' Tim said nervously.

Millie looked more closely and noticed all the vaguely familiar candles. 'Did you get these from the dresser drawer?' she asked.

'That was all right, wasn't it?' Tim prepared to be screamed at.

Millie nodded. 'Of course. Just as long as you know that the big ones cost thirty-five pounds each and the little ones are about a tenner. They were from Tess and Max's shop and being returned to the supplier. I was holding onto them until the owner came to pick them back up. If you've lit them all, you've just spent about five hundred pounds on candles.'

She smiled sweetly at him, pleased that she was unable to see the colour drain from his face in the candlelight.

'I don't care,' Tim said impulsively. 'You're worth it!'

Millie listened at the bottom of the stairs. 'It's very quiet up there. You haven't tied them to their beds and promised them twenty pounds if they don't scream, have you?'

Tim tutted. 'They've all gone to sleepovers.'

'Now that is impressive! How on earth did you find any parents, let alone four sets of them, prepared to take our children?' Millie was desperate to learn his trick because she'd never managed this herself.

Tim looked sheepish. 'I asked parents who didn't know our kids very well, parents of the really unpopular children that our lot wouldn't be seen dead with. They were so grateful their little Johnnies and Jennies had friends they'd agree to anything.'

Now it was Millie's turn to go pale. 'You did give them our phone number, didn't you? And the doctor's details? And you did tell them to put everything out of reach? EVERYTHING?'

'Calm down,' Tim said. He'd already made a mental note to himself to buy the four poor ignorant fathers a case of wine tomorrow.

He guided Millie into a chair and handed her a small glass of champagne. She was about to protest but Tim stopped her. 'You drank the occasional glass of champagne when you were pregnant with the others,' he reminded her.

Then he remembered how those babies had turned out and took the glass straight back. He poured her a mineral water and gave her that instead. He raised his glass. 'I'd like to make a toast: to an evening without children!'

Millie raised her glass and repeated the toast. 'So we're not going to talk about children at all?'

'Not at all.'

After nine minutes they'd run out of things to say.

'Do you want me to tell you about the church we go to now?' Millie offered.

Tim groaned.

'If you like,' Millie continued, 'I can teach you the foxtrot tonight because you'll need to know the steps before we go sequence dancing on Thursday. We go every Thursday, by the way.'

Tim grabbed a cushion from the sofa and pulled it over his ears.

'And did I tell you that, next week, we are going to Provence for a long weekend with Graham and Fiona and their kids?' Millie went on.

This at least made Tim smile. They sat in silence for a few minutes. 'All right. I give in!' Tim cried. 'We'll talk about the children!'

They spent a gloriously normal couple of hours discussing vaccinations, nits and baby names, making up for the last few fragmented weeks. Tim had drunk quite a lot of wine before he found the courage to ask Millie the question that had been bothering him.

'What about that Daniel chap?'

It took Millie a couple of minutes to work out who he was referring to. Then she remembered her imaginary old boyfriend. She'd planned to tell him she'd made the whole thing up until she saw that Tim was anxiously awaiting a reassuring reply.

She found an enigmatic smile from her repository of Expressions for Every Eventuality. 'You don't have to worry about him,' she said. 'He's in the past.'

# 19

Packing's much easier when you've reduced your possessions and the size of your home by three-quarters, Tess concluded. She was not finding this as unpleasant a task as usual, probably because she wa still enjoying the early thrills of experimenting with her new wardrobe.

I love having clothes that don't match, that aren't coordinated and that grate on the eye! she thought.

Millie had noticed the change before Fiona. 'You haven't had your old clothes repossessed as well, have you?' she'd asked.

'They've been arrested by the fashion police for crimes against individuality,' Tess intoned solemnly. She suddenly realised that Fiona was still devoted to her combat trousers and sports top combination. 'Not that there's anything wrong with dressing in one style all the time' she added.

Fiona raised her eyebrows. 'You don't need to apologise to me,' she said. 'I like the way I dress, I like having the decisions made for me and looking like everyone else. I think it's individuality that's the crime! How's a woman supposed to cope with changing fashions without making mistakes? It's much easier to find a top that doesn't cut into your armpits and buy twenty of them in different colours.'

Millie tutted. 'Now you're just being contrary.'

That's when Tess and Fiona noticed that Millie, too, was looking different. Pregnant, of course, but she was not wearing the compulsory leggings and fleece top that made the pregnant woman look acceptably tidy. She was wearing a long Indian dress with jingly bells around the hem that highlighted her bump and made her look dangerous, as if she might grab your hand, thrust a bunch of lucky heather into it and tell you that you'll live happily ever after if you give her a pound.

'You've gone all ethnic!' Fiona observed. 'Buy yourself a crystal ball and you could get a job on Brighton pier telling fortunes.'

'I just felt like a change,' Millie said quietly. 'Like Tess.' She didn't need to say any more. Fiona and Tess had watched her reinvent herself after Tim's departure with the Lady in the Cheap Vest.

'Do you think she's trying to look like Alison?' Fiona had asked Tess.

Tess hadn't thought so. Having gone through the act of deliberately transforming herself, she knew that the motives were less subtle. 'I think she just wants to look different to before.' Maybe that would lead to her feeling different and, who knows, maybe eventually she could be different. That was Tess's unexpressed hope.

Tess had bought a few more things for the weekend away, just some cheap separates that could get ruined in the 'It's a Family Knockout' competition of Saturday afternoon.

'It sounds grim,' Max had complained. 'I'd rather stay here and reorganise the shelves in the shop. I think I could make room for another couple of display cases if I move the fruit crates to the till area.'

Tess closed her ears whenever he started talking about the business. She didn't want to know. Max was hammering away at their marriage with each word and she didn't want to be forced to witness the actual destruction.

'Besides,' Max continued, 'I'm worried about leaving the place unattended. Carter's going to Bognor, I presume? Then there'll be nobody around to keep an eye on things.'

Tess sighed. 'Yes, he is going, but I don't think you need to be too concerned about burglars or vandals. All the local criminals are coming with us. That's what a community weekend means, the whole community goes.'

'Wonderful,' Max said miserably. 'So we'd better make sure we keep our caravan locked all the time.'

'No need,' Tess pointed out. 'We don't have anything worth stealing any more.' She held up her bare finger where the white band of skin left by her eternity ring told a sad story.

'I'm going to the shop,' Max said abruptly and left to pack.

314

Tess still hadn't got used to the flat and found herself opening all the drawers and cupboards before she could remember where anything was. That's how she came upon the bills, all the bills that Max had been hiding from her.

'I am capable of packing for myself,' Daphne grumbled, thoroughly relieved that her daughter was doing this for her.

'Yes, but it's going to be cold down at the coast and I want to make sure that you have enough warm clothes. I may not be able to keep an eye on you in Bognor, but at least I can make sure you're well prepared.'

'Who's the mother here?' Daphne asked in astonishment.

Fiona looked at her mum. 'Since you've become the pin-up girl of every OAP in Heaverbury, I've noticed that you've been dressing flamboyantly rather than practically.'

'Can you be sectioned under the Mental Health Act for that?'

Fiona sighed patiently. 'I'm just saying that you need layers, thermals, lots of woollies. You're the one who's always complaining about the cold.'

'I never complain,' Daphne retorted.

'You don't have to say anything, I can tell by the way your face goes pinched that you're in pain.'

Fiona felt that she had begun to know her mother at last or rather she'd begun to try and get to know her, she realised with shame. They were never going to be best buddies but they might be able to live alongside each other without arguing daily about who'd ruined whose life first.

Daphne enjoyed this implicit understanding of both her condition and maybe even the reasons why she'd been less than chirpy in recent years.

'Did I tell you that Tim and Millie were back together?' Fiona asked. 'He's coming to Provence with Millie. Isn't that great?'

'I think that's wonderful news,' Daphne agreed. 'I felt sick at the thought of that poor Millie bringing up six children by herself. I know what that's like and I wouldn't wish it on anyone.'

Daphne watched Fiona folding her mother's least attractive thick tights and polyester trousers, the ones with the strip of material that went under the foot and itched all day. She held her tongue. There are shops in Bognor. I'll go and buy some new clothes when I get there.

'I think it was just a moment of madness,' Fiona said. 'She was an old girlfriend and she didn't have any kids apparently. That probably means she was gorgeous, unlined, unstressed and with a flat stomach. I can see the temptation from a man's point of view.'

'I though she was rather plain,' Daphne mused.

Fiona stopped mid-folding and stared at her mum. 'How would you know?'

Daphne clamped her lips together, cursing herself for taking the tablets that had loosened her tongue. But she could sense that her daughter was not going to let her get away with this. She took a breath and confessed. 'I saw your friend Tim with her in Battersea Park that Sunday I went out with Archie.'

'And you didn't think to tell me about it?' Fiona asked tightly.

'I thought it best not to get involved! You'd have told me I was interfering.'

Fiona gasped. 'That's because you're always interfering! But in things that don't concern you, like my choice of husband or the way I bring my children up or even the way I make bloody tea! But the first time you can actually do something constructive, you keep your mouth shut!'

'What good would it have done?' Daphne pleaded. 'It all worked out for the best in the end.'

'No it didn't ! Millie will never be able to trust him completely again. Just because they ended up back together doesn't make it all right. If you'd said something to me, I could have talked to Tim, threatened him, made him see sense. I might have been able to make him finish it before Millie ever found out. Now their marriage will never be the same again.'

'Perhaps it will be better,' Daphne suggested hopefully.

Fiona stared at her mother. 'So you were pleased when Dad had all those affairs, were you? It made your marriage better? And do you think the same about Graham? Do you think it might be good for our marriage if he sees other women? Perhaps you know about that as well! Maybe you've caught Graham with a woman in a cheap vest and decided it would be best not to interfere!'

'Now you're getting hysterical.' Daphne kept her voice level to try and calm Fiona down.

'I'm entitled to!' Fiona shook her head slowly. 'You're incredible. You sat there the other day pouring your heart out to me about how your life was basically shattered by Dad's behaviour and that was supposed to justify why you made it your mission to shatter ours. But then you sit back and let it happen to my friend because you don't want to interfere?'

She tried to slow down her breathing. She had an awful feeling that she was going to burst into tears.

Then Daphne said an unwise thing. Mothers do. 'Fiona, I think you're upset about yourself, not Millie, and I think this has made you worry about your own marriage.'

Fiona turned on Daphne, hating her viciously for being right. 'Is that what you think? Well, I think you're a wicked, evil old woman and I'd like you to move out. Go and live with one of your perfect sons and their perfect wives. Go and ruin all their lives and their friends' as well.'

She ran out of the room before her mother saw her cry.

Tess added them all up. £37,000. We owe thirty-seven thousand pounds. And that's after we've sold everything we own including my precious ring, and paid off the debts that I *did* know about.

What can he be thinking of? How could he possibly have hoped to hide this from me indefinitely? And what else is he concealing?

The one remaining stone underpinning their marriage crumbled into dust as Tess returned the bills to their (not very good) hiding place. She tried to work out what hurt most of all, whether it was the sheer scale of the debt which would imprison them for the rest of their lives, or the fact that he deceived her.

No question, deceit is always the most effective weapon if you want to kill trust.

She laughed to herself unpleasantly. Lucky I'm not like that then, isn't it? It's a good thing I'm so honest! Apart from lying my way into two jobs which could well constitute obtaining money by deception. Oh, and sympathising with a good friend while I'm the one responsible for her relationship ending. Oh, and pretending to Max that I want to make our marriage work while I'm seriously considering running off into the sunset with somebody else. Apart from that, I'm a saint and in a solid virtuous position to condemn Max from above.

Yeah right.

But at least I know I'm wrong and I'm prepared to do something about it. From this moment on, I am going to start telling the truth. About everything.

'So did I pass?' Alison sat in front of the doctor, bored and impatient. She wanted this medical over so she could start making plans to join Gabriel. The whole business with Tim was beginning to feel like a distant nightmare. She occasionally woke up sweating, imagining four children mauling her, smearing ketchup over her best white sheets, calling her Mummy.

The doctor looked over her file. 'We took a blood test on Tuesday,' he began.

Alison froze. Don't say I'm going to be rejected because they found Night Nurse in my system. I'm going to the cocaine capital of the world, let's hope they're not that picky.

The doctor suddenly gave her a beaming smile, albeit a puzzled one.

'When you applied for a war zone posting, did you know that you were pregnant?'

'Before I start this class, I have to make an announcement. I'm going to be giving up my teaching after today.'

All the women groaned, and not in delight, Tess was surprised to hear.

'I know that this is short notice and, no, I'm not pregnant, unlike my predecessor!'

Everyone laughed. Tess carried on. 'As you all know, my husband has set up a local business, some of you are even involved in it, and I've decided to help him on a permanent basis.'

OK, this wasn't particularly honest. She had no intention of working in that place with Max, but it was the excuse that sounded the most plausible. At least it would extricate her from this job which she was feeling increasingly guilty in continuing. A person can't just suddenly become truthful overnight, she had come to realise, it had to be done in stages.

She felt like weeping as the women watched her with disappointed faces. If only they knew how undeserving of that disappointment I am.

'Anyway, as this is my last lesson, I thought we'd have a bit of fun.'

She opened her gym bag, pulled out a mini hi-fi and switched it on. As the *Greatest Hits of the 1970s* blared out, the whole class jumped to their feet and began dancing to The Partridge Family.

I should have done this from the start, Tess thought 90 minutes later as the class collapsed in exhaustion on the floor. More fun, more relaxing, more invigorating and a million times more honest!

As she left the community centre, having refused to accept her last pay packet from Heather, she ticked a box on her mental list. One down, two to go.

'I can't be pregnant,' Alison protested. 'I haven't done anything.'

The doctor raised his eyebrows. 'You *are* a doctor, aren't you?'

Alison scowled at him. 'Of course I am. And I'm not stupid. I'm just telling you that I don't see how I can be pregnant when I haven't seen my husband for over six weeks.' I know Tim must be incredibly fertile from the way he seems to get his wife pregnant apparently by just going to Ikea with her occasionally. But I really don't see how I could be carrying his baby when we haven't even been in the same room without three layers of clothes on. And if anyone ever calls that top a cheap vest again ...

'Are you sure you're a doctor?' the now-irritating man repeated. 'Because I would have thought you could work out for yourself that you are eight weeks pregnant.'

So it's Gabriel's baby, Alison thought with amusement. I was already pregnant when I went through all that drama with Tim. All that for nothing.

Oh well, no harm done.

'What are you doing here? Has something happened?' Graham panicked at seeing Tim in his office. The last time he'd had an unannounced visitor, it was Fiona, half-naked under her mac. He noticed nervously that Tim's coat was buttoned up.

Surely not, Graham thought in alarm. Fiona wouldn't put him up to this as some kind of joke, would she?

Tim began to undo his mac. Oh my God, Graham thought. This can't be happening to me!

Tim pulled out a bottle of whisky and placed it on the desk.

'What's that for?' Graham asked in relief.

Tim looked uncomfortable. 'Closure, I think they call it. It's to thank you for the part you played in it and to ask you if, er, you could not mention anything about it to Millie. Ever. Although she says she wants to know all the details, I don't think she means it.' Tim had become a sensitive man. It was a miracle.

'As far as I'm concerned, it's over,' Graham said. 'And I never had any intention of mentioning that it was me who first gave you the idea of logging onto that website. I regret even opening my mouth. I can't believe that any good came of it.'

He meant to add a question mark to that last sentence, to probe Tim, find out whether anything good did come from his trip back into the past. But it wasn't necessary. Tim was only too happy to talk about his experience for one last time.

'I can't say that it was a disaster from start to finish because in the beginning it was wonderful.'

Graham remembered Tim's elation in those first days. It had tempted him to take the same chance with Christine. But now he'd seen the outcome, he was less confident.

'So when did it turn sour?' he asked.

'For me, it was when Millie found out. It was only then that I realised how much damage I was doing to the whole family. I started looking at Alison differently then, as someone with the capacity to wreck my present life rather than someone who could restore the past.'

'So, any regrets?'

'Loads.' Tim sounded sad. 'I never learned for myself whether my life would have been any better with Alison and I think that's what I wanted to find out.'

'Sounds like a complete waste of time,' Graham observed.

'Not really. Millie and I are stronger than ever.' Then he looked bashful. 'Can I confess something to you, something that you must forget as soon as I've said it?'

'If you must,' Graham agreed doubtfully.

'I regret not sleeping with her after all this time. I think that might have made a difference to me.'

'A good one or a bad one?'

Tim shrugged. 'Just a difference. Isn't that what we all want?'

'You can't shout at me this time. I'm phoning you at work, just like you told me to.'

Graham felt his hand tighten around the receiver. He didn't

320

want to talk to Christine right now. He was still disturbed by Tim's visit.

'Can this wait?' he asked.

'No,' Christine said bluntly. 'You're travelling to France tonight, aren't you? So we need to make arrangements.'

'I thought we'd agreed that I'd call Eloise tomorrow, when I got there, and sort something out.'

'There's been a change of plan.'

Graham sighed. How did I guess?

Christine continued. 'I told Eloise that you didn't want me there and she became really upset.'

Feeling cynical, Graham wondered how much of this was down to Christine herself. He waited for her to explain the change of plan.

'Anyway, she will only agree to see you if I can be there too. She wants us both there, to see her parents, her *real* parents, together.'

Graham started rubbing his temples, waiting for solutions to pop up in his head. Nothing popped.

Christine hadn't finished. 'I'm guessing she has this crazy idea that she has a chance of having her family back again, that once we're all in the same place, you'll think about coming back to me. Then she's back to being a girl with two parents once more.'

'Except she's not a girl,' Graham argued. 'She's a twenty-year-old woman. She can't be that naive as to think I'm going to leave my family and come and live with you after all these years, just so that when she comes home for occasional visits there's a man there to fix her bike or carry her suitcases?'

'I told you, she was devastated when David died. She's not thinking straight. You can understand that, can't you?'

I can, but I don't want to, he thought. 'Then I don't think it will help to delude her into thinking that anything like that is going to happen. She'll feel even worse when I turn around and go back to my wife and four other children.'

Christine's voice became cold. 'I'm just telling you how things stand. I'll be in France with her this weekend. If you want to see her, I will be there too. Otherwise don't come. But this is your only chance. Eloise has said that if you let her down this weekend, then she never wants to hear from you again.'

*

321

'This is rather short notice,' Miss Blowers said sternly.

'I'm so sorry,' Tess apologised, feeling as if she'd been sent to see the head for pulling her skirt up in assembly. 'This has all happened rather suddenly. Of course I'll finish this week's lessons. And I'm sure you'll be able to find a new teacher. I can put a notice up for you in the yoga school where I . . . teach.' OK, another little departure from the commitment to truth. One step at a time.

Miss Blowers raised a hand. 'No, no that won't be necessary. Actually, this might all be for the best. I was revising the provision of yoga in school after a number of complaints from parents.'

Tess's cheeks burned and she inhaled sharply. 'What have they been saying?'

The headmistress was quick to reassure Tess. 'Nothing bad, don't worry. By all accounts the children have loved your classes.'

Tess started breathing again.

Miss Blowers continued. 'And the teachers have been thrilled with the results. They all say that the children are much more relaxed and teachable after your lessons and vandalism seems to take a notable dip in the hours following your class.'

Wow, I was even better at this than I imagined, Tess thought.

'Unfortunately parents have complained that, on the days that their children do yoga, they have disturbed nights. The children become hyperactive in the evening and refuse to go to bed. Then once they are finally persuaded into bed, they refuse to go to sleep. I can't think why that might be.'

Probably because they've had a lovely nap during the day, Tess answered silently.

Miss Blowers clasped her hands together. 'Anyway, it's been a valuable learning experience for us all and I wish you well in the future.'

She shook Tess's hand before leading her to the door.

Before Tess's final classes began, she dashed to the newsagent to buy piles of sweets, anything with E-numbers, the more sugar and colourings the better. She intended her last lessons to be fun and to guarantee that the kids didn't fall asleep during the day.

As for the state the little dears would be in when they got home, bouncing from the ceiling after all the additives she would be stuffing down them, well, serves the parents right for complaining.

This honesty stuff is more fun than I thought. But the next is going to be the hardest. And no fun at all.

Fiona was searching Graham's desk and his chest of drawers and all of his pockets. She hated herself all the while but couldn't stop. She went through the laundry basket checking his shirts for suspicious stains or smells. She fished out his last mobile phone bill and called every number that she didn't recognise.

In the course of her first call, she ended up spending half an hour speaking to a Glaswegian client who'd just got divorced and had been sorting out his investments with Graham. He wanted to tell her why his wife had left him and didn't care whether she wanted to listen or not. Fiona understood about every twelfth word, that was when he wasn't crying. After reassuring him that his wife was a tramp and he deserved better, she hung up. Wisely, after that, she put the phone down after each person replied, just guessing about the nature of the relationship each stranger shared with her husband.

She found nothing that tied in to the two mysterious calls to and from the woman in Sussex (the dialling code told her the location) and she felt grubby. Everything that her mum had said about what a good man Graham was had become meaningless. She didn't trust Daphne any more. She didn't trust Graham any more. And she couldn't live like this, not knowing.

She was going to have to confront him.

'Australia?' Daphne sat on the stained Formica-topped chair, trying to compose herself. 'Australia?'

Archie nodded slowly. 'I've been thinking about it for some time. Years, I suppose, ever since both my kids decided to take their families out there to settle.'

'I know you said you miss them,' Daphne recalled.

'It was talking to you in the van the other day that really brought it home to me. I thought about you living with your daughter, watching your grandchildren growing up, and I envied you.'

'It's not as wonderful as it sounds,' Daphne said weakly.

Archie patted her hand. 'You're just saying that to try and make me feel better. Actually before you moved here, I'd already begun making enquiries about emigrating.'

'What stopped you?'

Archie gave her the flirtatious smile she'd learned to love. 'You of course, you gorgeous old thing! That's why I decided to invest in Max's organic venture. I was making plans to wind down my minicab business, put my money somewhere it could work for me and start spending some time on myself. Maybe with you.'

Daphne brightened up at this. 'So if I'm such a gorgeous old thing, you're going to move to the other side of the world to be as far away from me as possible?'

Archie shook his head sadly. 'There's more to it than that. My eldest son, well his wife has left him, run off with some other chap, left the kids, said they'd be in the way.'

Daphne was horrified. 'Oh Archie, I'm so sorry.'

'He works all hours on his business. He doesn't know what to do with the children.'

'So you feel you have to move over there and help him out.'

Archie nodded. 'I look at Rav and all that he's doing for his granddaughters. That's the right thing to do. It's what parents *have* to do, isn't it, put their kids first right up until the end?'

Take me with you! Daphne wanted to shout. My family don't need me! I could come and help you. And the weather would work wonders on my arthritis. Ask me! Please ask me!

Archie stroked Daphne's lined fingers tenderly. 'Anyway, that leaves the way clear for Rav and Carter. It will be a lucky man that wins your heart.'

But you've already won it! That's what I came over to tell you.

Archie rubbed his hands together to help him look cheerful when he felt unutterably sad. 'So to what do I owe the honour of this visit?' he asked.

Daphne coughed. 'Oh er, I was just wondering if you had room to offer me a lift for the trip to Bognor. Fiona's car is going to be a bit cramped. Carter will be going with John and Rav will have the girls so I thought you might be able to help. But I suppose you won't be coming now. I expect you've got a lot to do.'

So I wasn't even your first choice for a lift? Archie thought sadly after she'd gone. I knew she wouldn't choose me. I was right not to ask her if she'd come to Australia with me even though I thought of nothing else for days. It was a stupid idea anyway.

'Why are the kids running around pretending to be dive

bombers?' Jerry asked as he tried to bring his class under some semblance of control.

'I've given them lots of sweets, played them loud music and stirred them up into a crazed frenzy,' Tess explained calmly.

'I presume that it would be a foolish man who asked why you would do that during a yoga lesson?'

'It would be foolish but I'll tell you anyway. It's my last lesson.' She explained that she was giving up all her teaching commitments.

Jerry couldn't hide his concern that he wouldn't be bumping into her so often in the future. 'Is it to avoid me?' he asked nervously.

Tess smiled at him. 'Typical man, thinks everything has to be about him! No, I just want to try something different, I feel I need to make some changes in my life.'

'Any changes in particular?' Jerry asked, examining the back of his hand with extreme interest.

'Yes,' Tess said seriously. 'I'm considering switching to non-biological detergent and dyeing my hair pink.'

Jerry slapped her arm affectionately. Tess liked how it felt. 'Those are obviously the big things. Any others?'

'Just the one. After the weekend, I'm leaving Max.'

# 20

'She'll be wearing yellow knickers when she comes,' the children sang lustily.

'We don't say "knickers", we say "pants",' Fiona shouted automatically.

That did it. 'Pants, pants, panty-pants, knickers and pants ...' The kids were in agreement, this song was much better.

'I'd forgotten how much I hated long car journeys,' Fiona moaned.

'It's only twelve hours,' Graham pointed out. 'It took almost twenty-four to get to Tuscany last year, with all the stops.'

'Yes but we'd drugged them, so it didn't seem as long.' Fiona had been ecstatic to discover a medicine that was supposed to prevent travel sickness but was actually given to kids by grateful parents everywhere to dope them into submission.

'You could have given them some before we left today.'

Fiona stared at him. 'I'm saving that for when we come off the ferry and have the longest part of the journey ahead of us. I can't drug them twice. What kind of mother do you think I am?'

I know the answer to that one, Graham thought, it is to remain absolutely silent.

Millie and Tim listened to *Madam Butterfly*, impervious to the bedlam from the back of the car. The advantage to having the four worst-behaved children in the Western world was that their tolerance thresholds were considerably higher than those of average parents. Providing that noone was being unstrapped from their child seat and hurled from the window while the car was doing 100 along the motorway, Tim and Millie could switch off happily.

\*

Max and Tess drove in complete silence. Lara was listening to a tape about a goblin who decapitates girls with curly hair.

Max considered asking Tess if she thought that this was appropriate listening for a sensitive child but her stiff back made it plain that she wasn't open to conversation.

'Is everything all right?' he'd asked when he got home.

'Why shouldn't it be?' she'd snapped.

She's answering questions with questions, he noted. Bad sign. He wisely kept his distance, allowing her to finish the packing alone. She took a very small pleasure from packing the underpants that cut off the circulation to his legs and the socks that played different Rodgers and Hammerstein tunes whenever he moved his feet.

I suppose I ought to be kind to him this weekend when I'm about to ruin his life but I don't feel like it. Whenever she felt shaky about what she was going to do she thought about that pile of bills and she thought about Jerry.

'This is going to be a great weekend!' Lara cried out as they saw the first sign for Bognor Regis. 'Isn't it?'

Tess turned the tape up.

Fiona and Millie were keeping in touch with each other at two-hourly intervals. Their tempers were becoming audibly more frayed as the evening went on.

'How are your lot?' Millie asked wearily.

Fiona sighed. 'Either throwing up, threatening to throw up or eating so many of the sweets my mum gave them that they're guaranteed to throw up in the next few hours. How about yours?'

Millie held the receiver in the direction of her own out-of-control offspring who were all screaming in perfect four-part harmony. 'No severed fingers or swallowed tongues so far. We're doing fine.'

Fiona closed her eyes at the prospect of a weekend in the presence of this destructive force. It didn't bode well for her attempts to talk seriously to Graham. But nothing was going to stop her from bringing all the secrets out in the open.

'I've never stayed in a holiday camp,' Tess murmured as they drove through the brightly coloured gates. It was a foreign country, a self-contained republic cut off from the world outside.

The brochure had informed them that there would be no need to leave the campsite for any reason; everything a person could ever require was inside the boundaries. Not everything, Tess thought sadly as she glanced at Max, who would be helpless when she announced her intention to leave him.

Tess looked around the caravan, taking in every aspect of this place where her marriage would be ending. Lara had loved it of course. It was about the size of the Wendy house that they'd had in the garden of their old home. But whereas Lara saw a fun-sized playhouse, Tess saw four thin walls, enclosing a claustrophobically small, sparsely furnished living area. It would be impossible to speak privately in here.

She slammed the door open and dragged Lara out for a walk around the campsite, desperate for air or inspiration, anything. She left Max to unload the car.

The grounds were surprisingly large and crammed to overflowing with caravans. Dozens of signs pointed in all directions, indicating swimming pools, crazy golf courses, ballrooms, amusement arcades, places where you could find activity and company any minute of the day or night. Everywhere was the noise of cheerful holidaymakers and Tess felt some of her despair lift slightly, only slightly, to be surrounded by so much joy.

She walked past a play area and Lara spotted some of her friends from school and church. She rushed to join them in delight. 'This is the best holiday ever!' she called out. Tess found herself melting at the sight of her daughter so perfectly happy. Not spending money, not asking for things that she couldn't have, not anxiously looking for danger signs in her parents' marriage, just playing joyfully with her friends.

Over the last 24 hours, she'd felt her mind frothing over with resentment and bitterness, all centred generally around Max who had not only betrayed her dreadfully but who was ultimately responsible for the state of affairs which left them unable to afford to go to Provence with their old friends.

But as she watched Lara playing under a grey Sussex sky, she knew there was nowhere else that she would rather be.

'I feel terrible, thinking about poor Tess and Max stuck in Bognor all weekend. Do you think this is how it's going to be for them forever, never able to afford anything better than appalling holiday camps in grotty England.'

Graham raised his eyebrows. 'Most of my happiest childhood memories are of summer weeks in holiday camps. We didn't go every year because we couldn't afford it, but when we did ...! They were the best fun. I used to be up at six o'clock every morning reading the kids' programme for the day, planning where I would have to be at every hour. I'd join in everything, treasure hunts, fancy dress contests, talent shows, insect hunts. I once won a spelling contest.'

Now it was Fiona's turn to raise an eyebrow. 'You sound as if you'd rather be there than here.'

Graham smiled sadly. 'This is lovely too, in a different way. I would just love our children to have the sort of holiday that I used to enjoy, maybe just once.'

Fiona looked at him affectionately, realising that he very rarely asked for anything from their marriage. She liked being able to please him. 'We'll go next year,' she said.

Graham beamed. 'Really?' He hugged Fiona. 'Thanks!'

Fiona collapsed on the bed, suddenly exhausted from the journey. 'Why didn't we fly?' she asked Graham moodily. 'It was crazy to drive all this way just for a long weekend.'

Graham sat on the bed next to her and stroked her hair. 'We can stop off somewhere on the way home, without Tim and Millie, have a couple of days as a family. I cleared it with the office.'

Fiona tried to look pleased but she was more worried than ever. Graham didn't like surprises, either giving or receiving them, it was something she'd appreciated after her little fiasco in his office.

They weren't permitted the luxury of a nap, not with four children trying to remove the swimming pool cover. They dragged themselves downstairs where they found the kids' excitement contagious.

'This house has got a thousand bedrooms!' they were shouting, 'and a hundred toilets and one of those bottom toilets that Gran says are common.'

The stunning house was certainly spacious, with six bedrooms set on a square balcony that looked over a massive open-plan living area. They were surrounded by gardens where unfamiliar flowers blossomed and towered, releasing heavy comforting scents. And if they closed their ears to the noise of their children, they could hear ... nothing. They stood there for a few seconds, just absorbing the peace, waiting for it to reach their inner selves.

But Fiona's peace was interrupted by the nagging reminder of the conversation that she would have to have with her husband. While Graham looked out over the breathtaking Provence panorama and imagined a tormented young woman on every gently peaking hilltop.

Max and Tess were still not talking and now Max was getting seriously worried. 'Are you going to be like this all weekend?' he whispered. 'It was your idea to come, don't forget.'

Tess didn't reply. She just looked at him with an expression that began as accusing and ended up as sad.

Now he was scared.

Daphne found herself sitting in between Carter and Rav. They'd thoughtfully brought along a supply of Bombay Organic Rouge, as Rav insisted it be referred to, and were topping Daphne's glass up under the table when no waiters were passing.

'What's Archie going to do about his investment in the business?' Rav asked anxiously.

'He's leaving it there,' Carter replied. 'He said he didn't believe in burning bridges.'

Daphne thought about this.

Jerry was going from table to table, checking that everyone was happy with their accommodation. Max watched him carefully, plotting his route around the large room. I bet he'll avoid Heather who is sitting over there trying not to look miserable and I bet he'll end up at our table.

He was right. Jerry jumped in front of him, stealing Max's trademark Mine Host pose and extending his arms in dramatic greeting.

'Hi-de-hi!' he cried.

'Ho-de-ho!' Lara cried back excitedly.

Traitor, Max thought miserably.

'How is your caravan?' Jerry asked, avoiding any eye contact with Tess, Max noticed.

'It's fine,' Max said curtly. 'What about you? Where are you staying?'

Jerry went through the motions of checking his plan before

answering. 'It looks as if I'm right next door to you,' he said. 'Howdy, neighbour!'

Max wanted to punch him but Lara was sitting at the table. Also he'd never punched anybody in his life and was worried that he'd just end up hurting his hand. So he glared at him instead.

Jerry withdrew his hand awkwardly. 'Er, right, well I'll be seeing you after dinner for the welcome party dance.'

'Yes!' Lara shouted, punching the air, 'a party dance!'

As Jerry turned and made his way to the exit, Max got up quietly and followed him.

He tapped Jerry on the shoulder, or rather jabbed him.

'What can I do for you?' Jerry asked uncomfortably.

'I know all about you and Tess,' Max said. 'Everything.'

Jerry considered this for a moment. 'Well, if you know everything, then you'll know that there's nothing to know.' He tried to walk past but Max was blocking his way.

'OK, so I don't know everything, but I've seen you kiss her and now she's not talking to me and she's looking at me with sad eyes so I can guess the rest.' His voice was beginning to shake now.

Jerry felt sorry for Max. It was an easy emotion when he believed that he'd won the prize that the other man thought was in the bag. 'You'll have to talk to Tess about all this,' he said gently. 'But I will tell you that this has got nothing to do with me. I wish it had, I won't lie to you, but this is about you and her.'

'Do you love her?' Max asked Jerry suddenly.

Jerry toyed with the question before answering. It still wasn't straightforward to him. 'Yes, I think so. Why, do you?'

Max's head flew back at the question. 'What's that supposed to mean? Of course I do. Shall I tell you how much I love her? Enough to spend the rest of my life working every minute to protect her and give her the life she deserves. And shall I tell you something else? I love her enough to forgive her for all the truly wicked things she's said to me over the years when I tried to comfort her as she lost one baby after another. I love her enough to forgive her for not loving *me* enough. And I love her enough to forgive her for loving you. Now you compare that to your couple of foxtrots and tangos, your sordid little kiss on Wandsworth Common and, what else, a grope in the school cleaning cupboard? Compare that, and then tell me that you deserve her more than I do!'

331

He pushed past Jerry, needing fresh air. As he ran away, Jerry called after him. 'It's not about what we deserve, it's about what she wants.'

Millie opened the car door and her four kids ran out and promptly ran off in four different directions. She and Tim stood admiring the house, each having complete faith that no harm would come to any of the children.

'This was a good idea,' Tim said, placing his arms affectionately round her swollen stomach. 'I think we needed a change.'

Millie allowed his hands to rest on her bump but didn't cover his hands with her own. Not yet. 'Maybe we both needed to change a few other things in our life,' she said. 'Maybe we had to go through all that to get to this point. But as long as the good things stay as they were and the others don't get any worse, I'll think we've done OK.'

Tim smiled in agreement but really he'd wanted a whole lot more than doing OK. That was why he had behaved so rashly. He'd assumed Millie felt the same too. The challenge was going to be to live together while they clearly had such different standards by which they measured the quality of their lives.

Daphne watched Rav gamely joining in the dances with his granddaughters. She envied him and she didn't envy him at the same time.

'A penny for them?' Carter said as he sat slowly down beside her.

Daphne gestured towards Rav. 'He's amazing,' she said. 'He's father and grandfather to those girls. I don't know how he does it. I'm exhausted after a game of Pictionary with my grandchildren.'

'He does what he has to do,' Carter said simply. 'I'm sure you could do the same if you had to.'

Daphne shook her head. 'I couldn't. I'm too old. Everything hurts too much. I wish I could, I want to be able to but I can't.'

Carter understood what she was saying. 'Have you told him?'

'Not yet. I don't want to spoil his weekend. I'll leave it for now.'

Carter didn't ask his next question.

'Welcome to *It's A Family Knockout*!' John shouted. Everyone cheered, except Max, who just stared at Jerry.

'Let's have the ladies on this side and gentlemen over here!'

'Go on, Daddy!' Lara shouted. 'Mummy's playing!' Max dragged himself over to the left-hand side of the huge inflatable fortress, watching Tess across the netting. She looked as if she was enjoying herself with Heather.

'Are you wishing you were in Provence right now?' Heather asked wryly.

Tess thought about this as she shivered in the cold. 'I have to confess that I did look up at the clouds this morning and realised for the first time that we would no longer be able to run away to the sun whenever we wanted to escape. We used to do that a lot.' She drifted away into old memories and new uncertainties.

Heather looked at her new friend perceptively. 'There are other ways of running away,' she observed, 'that don't cost a penny.'

Tess decided to ignore the undertones of Heather's observation. 'Maybe, but anyway now that we're here I love it. Lara is ecstatic, she's surrounded by children her own age, out all day getting wet, running wild.' She shrugged happily. 'We're converted. Lara has begged for us to come back next year. She now tells us that France was dead boring!'

'So, something good has come out of all your troubles?' Heather suggested.

Tess wasn't sure she was ready to go that far. 'I will say that I've learned that change does not always have to be bad. I think we're all afraid of change, I know I was, but I hope that I'll embrace it in future, maybe even positively introduce it into my life.'

Max watched them talking about something serious. Well lucky old Tess and Heather to have a friend in each other, he thought. My only friend here is Tess and she's withdrawn from me. I don't know why and I'm scared to find out.

Eventually they were all in their places.

'Now ladies,' John shouted. 'I want you to throw these wet sponges at the men as hard as you can. They will try and catch them and squeeze the water into these measuring cylinders at the back. OK, three–two–one – go!'

Tess and Heather aimed every sponge with vicious precision at Max and Jerry who gave up trying to catch them and just tried to protect themselves from being soaked through. It was, after all, March and extremely cold.

After a while, Max was consoling himself from being attacked by picking up the sponges and throwing them at Jerry, imagining them to be heat-seeking missiles that would tear through his flesh and cause him to die slowly in agony.

'I don't think we're allowed to do that,' another man pointed out cheerfully.

Max responded by throwing a particularly sodden sponge in his face before returning to his preferred target.

'Don't you wish you were joining in?' Rav asked Daphne who'd been given the job of measuring the water. He was out of breath after throwing himself into the game with gusto.

'No,' Daphne said flatly.

Rav was taken aback. 'You're having a bad day. You need some of my wine, then we'll maybe see you in the grannies' talent contest later on?'

'I'm going to have a rest this afternoon, Rav. This is too strenuous for me.'

Rav's face dropped. 'The girls will be disappointed. They've been talking about you all week. They were going to cheer you on. Since they haven't got a granny of their own, they've adopted you.'

Daphne touched his hands very gently. 'They've still got their grandad to cheer on in the grandads' darts match. And the memory of their real granny. The three of you are lucky to have each other.'

Rav heard the emphasis on the word 'three'. It was very final, with no potential to develop into a 'four'. He grabbed her hand and kissed it recklessly. 'You have a lot of living to do yet, Daphne. Don't give up for the sake of a few aches and pains.'

'I don't intend to,' Daphne said, glancing at Carter.

Tim had been unilaterally elected in charge of the children for the first afternoon. His standing with Millie, as well as his friends, was still tenuous enough that he accepted his fate with calm resignation. He proceeded to amuse them by sitting at the edge of the swimming pool and throwing a ball into the water for the kids to chase. Over and over again. For three hours.

Fiona and Graham had gone for a long walk, to get as far away from their children and their friends as they could.

They held hands loosely and Graham helped Fiona over every

difficult rocky outcrop with an endlessly patient concern that touched her.

'Isn't this beautiful?' he said when they sat down to rest in an isolated spot with views that mesmerised them both. 'Better than Bognor,' he added cheekily, worried that he'd upset Fiona by hinting that he'd rather be there than here.

Fiona felt her breathing speed up. I'm going to say it now, she thought, I can feel it. 'It would be beautiful,' Fiona said carefully, 'except that everything I see and feel is tainted by the misery you're putting me through.' She wished she could take the words back as soon she'd spoken them, that she could just be satisfied enjoying this time together and then returning home to a life where everything was as it had always been, unconfronted, unchanged, undamaged.

The beauty of the moment disappeared in an instant for Graham. He sat down next to Fiona. 'You think I'm going to ask you how I'm making you miserable?'

'Aren't you?' Fiona asked resentfully, still angry with herself for bringing this up.

'No', Graham said. 'I know what I've done.'

Stop, stop! Fiona wanted to shout. Don't tell me! I've changed my mind. I'll pretend I was never worried about those phone calls and you can never make any more and we'll get back to how we were. I don't want to know any more!

Unfortunately Graham wasn't reading her mind. He was as bad at that as he was at talking tactfully to a dinner table of strangers.

'First of all, you have absolutely nothing to worry about and I haven't done anything to betray you. I never would. Unlike Tim, I'm not tempted by women in cheap vests, nor am I unhappy with my life with you. You know that, don't you?'

Fiona slumped. He's taking too long to get to the 'but'. The rule is: the longer it takes, the worse the 'but' is.

And he still hadn't got there.

'And anything I did, which, as I say, I didn't actually do ...'

'OH, FOR GOD'S SAKE, WHO IS SHE?'

Graham was thrown by Fiona's outburst. He'd been building up to the 'but' and now his timing was shot.

'Who is she?' Fiona asked, more calmly this time.

'Did I ever tell you that I was engaged to a girl called Christine?'

Fiona gaped at him. 'No! And I think I would have remembered if you had.'

Graham kept his head firmly down. 'Well anyway, I was only twenty-one and she didn't turn up on the day we were supposed to get married.'

Fiona sat back, trying to absorb this massive event in her husband's life that explained so much about him and that he had chosen to keep from her.

'And now she wants to get get back together with you, is that it? What exactly does she want?' Her voice was shaking.

Graham froze. Fiona wasn't supposed to ask this question until he'd worked out the answer. That was why he was taking so long to get to the 'but'. He had a parallel narrative going on his head trying to decide what he was going to do about Eloise. And about Christine.

When the answer came to him, it was with a clarity so pure, so inescapable, that Graham accepted it with relief and without argument.

'Nothing,' he said. 'She just wanted to get in touch, find out what I'd done with my life. We exchanged e-mails, I spoke to her a couple of times, I confess I was tempted to meet her again to ask her some of the questions that I'd never had answered. But in the end, I decided that nothing she had to say could do anything to make my life better. So I won't be contacting her again.'

I'm so sorry, Eloise, he whispered to himself. If there's a God, then please take this message to her. You're asking too much. I can't see your mother again. It would open doors in too many other people's lives, doors that they'd relied on me to keep firmly shut. You'll hate me, of course, and if that helps you to deal with the rejection then I can't blame you for it.

But don't waste too much energy hating me. I've tried that and it doesn't work. There's a great relief in forgiveness, I experienced it the day I forgave your mother.

I know you've imagined a life where you join my other family or maybe I get back together with your mother. Neither of these is going to happen. Of course I can't stop you looking for me yourself. And if you do, I will not reject you. But I would ask you to think carefully before you do that.

You have a mother and by all accounts you had a wonderful father. That makes you very lucky. Don't undermine the reality of that by chasing a fantasy. Grieve for your father, because he was your 'real' father in the true sense of the word, then mend the relationship with your mother.

I've seen how much damage a mother and daughter can inflict on each other and I don't wish that for you.

When I get home, I will write all this down for you. You'll misinterpret it at first as the action of a coward but one day I hope you'll understand that I could never have offered you what you needed. I would always have disappointed you.

The worst lesson a young person can learn is that they are not the only consideration in their parents' lives. And my life is more complicated than most with a wife and four other children. And you'll hate me for saying so but I have to consider them in all this. It's hopelessly inadequate but, believe me, I've agonised over the situation and this is truly the best I can do. Maybe that will give you some idea of what kind of father I could be to you at this stage in your life.

Do I have to add an 'amen'?

'Graham?' Fiona was looking at him strangely. 'Are you OK?'

He took her face and held it firmly in his hands. 'Yep. Absolutely OK. How about you? Are you fine?'

'Just about,' she replied uncertainly.

So we're both fine, Graham thought as they walked back to the gîte, arms round each other for support. That's good enough for me.

Daphne watched all the families getting cheerfully drenched in the chaotic game.

'It's always nice to see people happy,' she said contentedly to Carter. 'I do hope that Fiona and Graham are laughing like this in France.'

'You're entitled to be happy too,' Carter said sternly.

'I will be.' She reached out her hand to him to pull her to her feet. After she'd made it up, she kept hold of his hand.

'I'm off to my caravan for a nap, but perhaps you'd like to take me into town this afternoon. I feel like buying some new clothes.'

Carter knew what she was saying and squeezed her hand in gratitude.

'I'd love to.'

And Daphne knew what Carter was saying too.

*

Saturday night was sequence dancing night and everyone made an effort to dress up. Daphne attracted the most attention in a lime green creation with a sequinned bodice that wouldn't have looked out of place at a cross-dressers' convention.

Her smile was even brighter than her outfit. Carter had persuaded her to phone Fiona in Provence. He'd lent her his mobile phone, even dialled the number for her. Daphne held the handset away from her ear, worried that her hair might go frizzy under the onslaught of all the radiation she'd read about.

'Mum! What's the matter? Is it your back? Have you seen a doctor? Do you want me to come home? I can catch a flight in a couple of hours and be there in . . .'

'I'M FINE,' Daphne shouted impatiently. 'Carter made me phone you. I was just wondering if you're having a nice time.'

Fiona pondered all the possible hidden meanings behind this deceptively simple question, before concluding that there was no hidden meaning. It was one of her new resolutions, not to ferret around for complication when simplicity was available.

She was thrilled that her mother had phoned. She'd been feeling guilty about the things she'd said to Daphne the previous day. She was also feeling mellow after resolving her differences with Graham. Maybe they weren't fully resolved but she'd decided to believe that they were. She still suspected that he had not given her the whole story but he'd told her enough.

Maybe my mum was right, she grudgingly conceded. Graham is a good man, a good husband and a good father. I should just accept that and not make him out to be any more complex than that.

'We're having a great time, Mum!' she said, almost with warmth. 'What about you? Are you dressed warmly?'

Daphne described her dress with devilish pleasure.

Fiona gasped. 'But you'll catch your death!'

Daphne laughed tolerantly. 'I bought it to celebrate my engagement,' she announced. 'I can't do that in thermals and a twinset, can I?'

Fiona closed her eyes nervously. 'Who to?' she whispered. 'Which one are you marrying?'

'She's marrying me,' Carter said, suddenly grabbing the phone. 'And I promise to look after her, to keep her safe and to make her happy.'

Fiona inhaled deeply to stop herself from crying, although she couldn't tell whether she was tearful with happiness or sadness. There were altogether too many emotions curdling inside her to rationalise them. 'Congratulations.'

Carter handed the phone back to Daphne.

'Thank you,' Daphne said as Fiona repeated her congratulations.

'But if you think I'm going to be a bridesmaid and wear a huge turquoise tea cosy . . .' Fiona continued.

Carter was pointing to his watch. The dancing was about to start. Daphne said goodbye to Fiona and handed the phone back to the kind man who was holding his arm out to her.

Together, they entered the ballroom.

'Is everything all right?' Graham sounded anxious.

'Mum's marrying Carter,' Fiona replied calmly.

Graham waited for a cue to signpost the correct response. But there were no sighs or tears or tuts.

'Are you pleased for her?'

Fiona smiled. 'I am. She repeated it more firmly. 'Carter appears to be a good man and that is all we can wish for anyone we truly love.'

She looked at her husband and saw him as the good man that her mother had always insisted he was. She grabbed his hands suddenly and kissed his palms. Graham was moved desperately by the gesture. He pulled her close and she just leant into his body, closing her eyes and letting him support her.

They stood like that, in perfect silence, until the sun had finally set.

Tess found herself sitting next to Carter as they settled themselves at a table near the band.

'You must be thrilled,' Tess said. 'I'm really happy for you both.'

'I consider myself very lucky,' Carter agreed.

'Luck has nothing to do with it. Obviously the best man won!'

Carter looked at her calmly. 'Actually he didn't. I was second choice. She wanted to marry Archie but he's leaving the country and it seems he didn't think to ask her to go with him.'

Tess became serious. 'And you don't mind?'

339

Carter smiled. 'Why should I? It's only the final decision that counts, not how it was made.'

'But won't you always feel second-best?' she asked, not realising how cruel she sounded.

Carter wasn't offended. 'That's how young people think, always analysing their feelings, churning over every tiny twist and turn of fate. When you get to my age, you stop doing that. You know what is right, for you and the other person, and you just do it. And you stick to it.'

'What if something more right comes along?' Tess asked, looking at Max, thinking of Jerry.

'You have to ask yourself if it's really right or just different. Usually it's just different. And you don't hurt people for novelty value.'

Jerry held her carefully, sensing Max's stare and Tess's tension. They'd done this dance several times by now and were able to let their feet carry them round while they concentrated on each other. The opposite to the first time, Tess thought wryly.

'Does this feel right to you?' she asked Jerry without preamble.

'You're not kicking me as often as you did,' Jerry conceded.

'That's not what I meant.'

Jerry knew that. He had a bad feeling about this opening question. And the absence of a smile. And the distance between their two bodies. 'It feels completely right to me,' he said with conviction.

'It doesn't to me,' she said after a while. 'It feels good, exciting, intimate, maybe the most powerful emotion I've ever known, maybe my one and only experience of true love. But it doesn't feel right.'

Jerry pulled her a little closer. 'You're wrong about that and I think you know it. I think this feels as right to you as it does to me.'

Tess considered this, believing and rejecting the words simultaneously. She recalled Carter urging her to discern between what was right and what was different. She had never understood that discernment was an essentially practical faculty. Once she brought it into use, a previously impossible decision suddenly became straightforward.

Heather was watching them with a disinterested expression.

340

She was dancing with John and seemed to be enjoying herself. No! Tess thought. Surely not the Incredible Vicar! Could it be? It was a combination she would never have predicted but seemed, well, right.

Jerry watched her watching Heather. 'Do you know that you always watch other people?' he commented.

Tess looked back at him. 'That's because I'm affecting their lives. I have responsibilities to them, and so do you.'

She looked over at Max, who was partnering Lara. She was standing with her feet on top of his so that he was effectively carrying her.

'Look at us Mum!'

Tess blinked to stop herself from crying. 'I'm looking, sweetie!' She looked back at Jerry. 'That's why this isn't right,' she said quietly. And if it isn't right, she told herself insistently, then what I feel for Jerry is no more than the thrill of the new, the different. And if I tell myself that often enough, I may actually believe it.

'So you're going to stay with him for your daughter's sake?' he asked bitterly.

Tess looked at him for the last time. 'I'm going to stay with him because it's right.'

Tim was stumbling. 'It's all right for you,' he complained to Millie. 'You've been doing it for longer than me.'

'Whose fault is that?' she hissed back.

He remembered where he was during those first lessons and kept quiet.

Millie had set up the CD player on the terrace and was playing a romantic waltz that she'd first heard when Tim was out on that disastrous evening with Alison and the four children. She liked knowing that this memory belonged to a part of her life where he was not present. It was like a secret, an innocent secret.

'I don't really see the point of this,' he said after his fifth collision.

Millie looked up at him, briefly abandoning her feet to the onslaught of Tim's. 'The point is that we both do the same steps, we both move in the same direction and we both know where we stand.'

'Isn't that boring?'

'No, it's comforting.'

Tim decided to take her word for it and settle for comfort. It was better than anything else he'd come across. He immediately concentrated hard on keeping in step with his wife. Millie noticed his efforts and finally allowed herself to relax into his supporting arms.

It was time to change partners. Tess went and rescued Max from Lara.

She didn't say goodbye to Jerry and she didn't look back.

'Oh Mum!' Lara complained as Tess broke in.

'Mummy wants to dance with Daddy too,' she said.

Lara pretended to be cross but Tess could see she was secretly pleased that her parents were still together in a way she recognised.

Max was reluctant to hold Tess. He had a sickening premonition that she was going to tell him she was leaving him. If I avoid her for long enough, he reasoned, then all her hostility will pass and she'll forget why she stopped loving me. She might even start loving me again, just out of habit.

'I've decided I'm going to go back to work,' she said. 'I'll start looking next week. I think we need the money.' She wasn't going to mention the hidden bills, finally understanding that Max needed to deal with it himself, just as she'd had to sort out her own mistakes herself.

Max was surprised. This wasn't what he'd expected to hear. 'Is that what you want?' he asked carefully. Is that *all* you want, he wanted to ask.

Tess nodded. 'Yes. it will be difficult but I think we can manage. You'll have to fit your working hours in with me so that Lara always has someone at home when she gets home from school.'

Max only heard certain words. He heard 'when' and 'will'. He'd expected to hear 'if', 'can't' and 'won't'.

He opened his mouth to ask her why. There were a lot of whys begging for attention. But he spotted the way she looked at him and changed his mind. Suddenly the whys didn't matter.

Hey, Tess told herself, you know you were always wondering how you'd know if you'd grown up. Well, I think you just did.

I don't know where I went wrong, Jerry said to himself as he watched Tess dance with her husband. She's doing the same steps she learned with me, but it looks different when they do it even though they're stumbling over each other and he doesn't know how to lead. I wonder if that's what she means by 'right'.

He watched everyone else dancing. He didn't have a partner now. Not that this was a problem: he could ask anyone. That was the joy of sequence dancing, always knowing that the steps remained the same, even when the partners changed.

All he had to do was ask someone. But not today.


Alison settled back in her seat, watching the countryside shrink below her. She rested her hand on her stomach, stroking it, imagining the beginnings of a swelling.

Gabriel would be meeting her at the other end. She hadn't told him about the baby but he was thrilled about her decision to join him. And I know he'll be thrilled about the baby, she told herself.

And even if he's not, well, I will still have the child that I wanted and needed and the child will be wanted and needed by me.

If there's anything else in the world that matters more, I certainly haven't found it.


Christine watched the plane flying overhead. I wonder where it's going, she asked herself. I wonder if someone is escaping on it as I did twenty years ago. If she is, and it always seems to be the woman who needs to escape, I hope she's thought it through more clearly that I did.

Graham was not coming, she'd finally accepted. And yes, she was surprised, because he'd always been so decent, so proper that she'd been convinced he would do the right thing. Surely he would come to his daughter. She'd been banking on it.

It's my fault. There, I've admitted it. She sat down, resting her head in her hands. I can blame it on breakdowns or impulsive decisions or bad judgement but, by any reckoning, this is all my fault.

The brutal truth is that I wanted Graham back for myself. For Eloise as well, of course, but first and foremost for me. I treated it like a game, I played my hand badly and I lost. But the person who's suffered most is Eloise and now I have to convince her that her father is not to blame.

As the plane faded from view, she watched her daughter standing by the other window, trying to make sense of the world, suddenly looking exactly like her father.

I hadn't seen the resemblance before, Christine thought, but he's been with me all these years in his daughter. No wonder I didn't miss him as much as I think he missed me. He was here all the time.

And whatever man, whatever person, he grew into, the best part of him will always be in Eloise. In that way, I never left him.

I wish I'd told him that.